SUPERVOLCANO
ALL FALL DOWN

SUPERVOLCANO
ALL FALL DOWN

HARRY TURTLEDOVE

A ROC BOOK

ROC
Published by New American Library,
a division of Penguin Group (USA) Inc.,
375 Hudson Street, New York, New York 10014, USA
Penguin Group (Canada), 90 Eglinton Avenue East, Suite 700, Toronto,
Ontario M4P 2Y3, Canada (a division of Pearson Penguin Canada Inc.)
Penguin Books Ltd., 80 Strand, London WC2R 0RL, England
Penguin Ireland, 25 St. Stephen's Green, Dublin 2,
Ireland (a division of Penguin Books Ltd.)
Penguin Group (Australia), 250 Camberwell Road, Camberwell,
Victoria 3124, Australia (a division of Pearson Australia Group Pty. Ltd.)
Penguin Books India Pvt. Ltd., 11 Community Centre,
Panchsheel Park, New Delhi - 110 017, India
Penguin Group (NZ), 67 Apollo Drive, Rosedale, Auckland 0632,
New Zealand (a division of Pearson New Zealand Ltd.)
Penguin Books (South Africa) (Pty.) Ltd., 24 Sturdee Avenue,
Rosebank, Johannesburg 2196, South Africa

Penguin Books Ltd., Registered Offices:
80 Strand, London WC2R 0RL, England

First published by Roc, an imprint of New American Library,
a division of Penguin Group (USA) Inc.

 REGISTERED TRADEMARK—MARCA REGISTRADA

ISBN 978-0-451-46481-1

Set in Sabon LT
Designed by Elke Sigal

Printed in the United States of America

SUPERVOLCANO
ALL FALL DOWN

I

Colin Ferguson called upstairs to his wife: "You ready?"

"Just about—not even a minute," Kelly answered.

"We need to get going," he muttered discontentedly. He was punctual to a fault. A police lieutenant had to be. In his younger days, the Navy'd rammed being on time down his throat. To be fair, he hadn't needed much ramming. He'd never been the kind of person who always ran fifteen minutes or half an hour behind schedule—unlike one poor sailor a pissed-off CPO finally tagged *the late Seaman Kurowski*.

And, to be fair, neither was Kelly. As quickly as she'd promised, she joined him by the front door. Patting at her honey-blond hair, she asked, "Do I look okay?"

"I'm the wrong guy for that question, babe," he said. "You know you always look good to me."

"You!" She shook her head, but she was smiling. Colin meant every word of it. He was happy the way only a man in his early fifties still pretty newly wed to a damned fine-looking woman in her late thirties can be: happier than he figured he had any business being, in other words. After Louise walked out the door on him, after she and the lawyers got through with him, he'd never dreamt he could be this happy this way again.

One never knows, do one? he thought. Which, like his earlier woolgathering, was beside the point. "Let's head on out," he said.

Kelly nodded. "Sounds good."

Out they went. Colin locked the dead bolt. There'd been a break-in the next block over last week. You didn't want to make things easy for burglars. They might get you anyway, but why help 'em along?

"Brr!" Kelly said, and buttoned her denim jacket. It didn't exactly go with Colin's blue wool suit and maroon tie, but she did what she liked while he dressed the way he did more from force of habit than for any other reason. San Atanasio was a South Bay town. The nearby Pacific and the good old sea breeze had always moderated its climate. It didn't get as cold or as hot as downtown L.A., to say nothing of the San Fernando Valley (as far as Colin was concerned, the best thing you could say about the Valley).

But this was June. It was supposed to be mild, if not hot. The sun wasn't supposed to shine palely from a sky more nearly gray than blue. This past winter—if winter *was* past—the L.A. basin had got its first all-over snowfall in more than sixty years . . . and then, a month later, its second.

"You and your supervolcano," Colin said. If he and Kelly had been in an interrogation room, it would have done duty for an accusation.

"I was just studying it. I didn't make it go off. And if the copter that got me out of Yellowstone had taken off fifteen minutes later, chances are I wouldn't be here for you to complain to," she replied in at least medium dudgeon.

"Well, I'm glad you are," he admitted. Nothing much was left of Yellowstone. For that matter, nothing much was left of Wyoming, or of big chunks of Montana and Idaho. Most of the Rocky

Mountain West and the Great Plains was pretty much screwed, too. When the supervolcano erupted—for the first time in close to seven hundred thousand years—he'd heard the roar and felt the quake here in San Atanasio, eight hundred and some odd miles away. Volcanic ash and dust had rained down here, too, but not the way they had closer to the eruption site.

As he and Kelly walked over to his silver Taurus, Wes Jones waved from across the street. Wes—an aerospace engineer, now retired—and his wife had been neighbors for more than twenty years. Colin waved back. Pointing to the Taurus, Wes called, "You got gas?"

"Darn right," Colin said solemnly. "That kimchi I ate last night'd do it to anybody."

Wes laughed more than the joke deserved. "Ah, you're nutso," he said—his word for anything out of the ordinary. After hearing it for so many years, Colin found himself using it, too. Wes went on, "Say congratulations to Marshall from Ida and me. We'll have a little something for him when he gets back to town."

"Thanks. Will do." Colin didn't bother telling Wes that his younger son was less than thrilled about finally graduating from UC Santa Barbara, and about the idea of coming back home to live. Marshall, in fact, had often seemed to try his best *not* to graduate. But accumulated time and units caught up with him at last. Like it or not—and he didn't—he'd have to face the real world.

Colin used his key-ring control to open the car doors. He sat down behind the wheel. Kelly slid in on the passenger side. When he started the engine, the fuel gauge shot all the way up to the capital F. Kelly pointed to the gauge. "A year ago, we would have taken that for granted."

"Uh-huh." Colin nodded. Less crude was coming up out of the ground in the USA because of the supervolcano. The spasmodic nuclear war between Iran and Israel hadn't done production any favors, either. Quite a bit less oil was getting refined into gasoline. And what did get refined had a devil of a time reaching L.A. Put it all together, and a full tank was something of a coup.

North on La Merced, the little street he lived on. The left onto Braxton Bragg Boulevard was easy: not much traffic these days. West on Braxton Bragg toward the ocean—and, more toward the point, toward the 405. Most of the gas stations flew red flags to show they were out of fuel. Cars queued up at the few that were open. The date was an odd number. So was the last digit of Colin's license plate. If he had to, he could gas up today. He hoped he wouldn't have to. North on the 405, past LAX, past UCLA, through the Sepulveda Pass, to the 101. West on the 101, even if the sign said north.

About 125 miles from San Atanasio to Santa Barbara. Two hours—likely less, with the freeways. Once they got out of the Valley and into Ventura County, the 101 came down close to the Pacific. It was a pretty drive, a hell of a lot prettier than if Marshall had chosen UC Riverside. Riverside was, or had been, as hot as the Valley. It was also where the sea breeze blew the smog from the L.A. basin.

"The hills are so green," Kelly marveled. "It's June. Everything is supposed to be brown by now." She'd grown up in Torrance, not far from San Atanasio, though she'd gone to grad school up at Berkeley. She knew how things in Southern California worked, or had worked.

"Everything *was* supposed to be brown by now." Colin remembered years when everything was brown and bare by April Fool's Day. He remembered the horrendous brush fires that often followed in such years, too. No one hereabouts remembered a year where it snowed twice during the winter. There'd never been a year like that, not till the Yellowstone supervolcano blew. And things were just warming up—or rather, cooling down.

"Yeah, yeah. Los Angeles is the new Seattle." Kelly quoted the new conventional wisdom.

"Sure it is." Colin snorted. "And fifty is the new thirty. And the check is in the mail." *Fifty is the new thirty* was part of the Baby Boom's fanatical effort to deny the obvious: like it or not, the Boomers *were* getting older. Fifty might or might not be so bad. Thirty it wasn't. Colin had seen both, and he knew the difference. As far as he was concerned, anybody who didn't was a goddamn fool.

Something with one hell of a wingspan floated over the freeway. Hawk? Eagle? Vulture? He didn't get a good enough look to tell. He had to keep most of his attention on the asphalt ahead and the morons all around.

They were nearing Santa Barbara when Kelly suddenly said, "It's cool with Marshall that I'm coming to his graduation and his mother isn't?"

That kind of thing was and always would be a second wife's worry. It probably got more acute when the second wife was closer in age to her husband's children than she was to him. But Colin's answer came quick and certain: "As far as I know, he's fine with it."

"Yes, but how far do you know?" Kelly persisted. "Marshall . . . doesn't leave a lot of clues about what's going on inside his head."

"If anything is, with all the weed he smokes," Colin said disgustedly. Here he was, a cop, and both his boys got wasted every chance they could. Rob, the older one, used his engineering degree to play bass in a band called Squirt Frog and the Evolving Tadpoles. They'd been stuck in the middle of Maine since winter came down. And winter there didn't want to let up. If L.A. was—or was alleged to be—the new Seattle, Maine could double as the new Baffin Island.

Vanessa, who fit in between Rob and Marshall, didn't do a

lot of dope. Or if she did, it sure didn't mellow her out. Colin wondered when, or if, she'd escape from that refugee camp somewhere near the Oklahoma-Arkansas border: just past the eastern edge of the ashfall from the supervolcano. She'd got out of Denver alive, which most people who'd lived there hadn't, so he was inclined to count his blessings. Here most of a year after the eruption, nobody knew how many people it had killed, not to the nearest hundred thousand. Well up into seven figures, that was for sure.

Kelly clicked her tongue between her teeth. "He's plenty smart," she said. "And he knows what he thinks—he just doesn't want to tell the rest of the world."

"It could be, for most things," Colin allowed. "But I'm as sure as I need to be that he doesn't want to see Louise right now, not when she's going to present him with a little half-brother or half-sister pretty soon."

He also wasn't exactly thrilled that his ex was pregnant again. For that matter, neither was Louise. Everything with the aerobics instructor for whom she'd left Colin had been all lovey-dovey—till Teo found out he'd knocked her up. Then, when she didn't want to get rid of the baby right away, he'd dropped her like a live grenade.

"Why *is* she having it?" Kelly asked hesitantly.

Colin had known Louise for upwards of thirty years now. He shrugged anyway. "You tell me and you win the prize," he said. "My best guess is because dear sweet Teo told her to lose it and then bailed. So she won't do anything he would've wanted her to. But that's only a WAG." He didn't like to cuss where women could hear him do it. The acronym didn't seem to count, though.

"Wouldn't be reason enough for me," Kelly said. "When I have a baby, it'll be because I want to, not because somebody I can't even stand any more doesn't want me to."

"I feel the same way." Having said that, Colin realized his

wife wasn't speaking hypothetically. *When I have a baby,* she'd said, not *If I have a baby.* When she had a baby, Colin figured he would be very much involved in the process. He wondered whether he was ready to be a dad again at his age. Fifty the new thirty? If only, with a newborn screaming in the house! He glanced over at Kelly. "When you do decide to, you'll let me know first?"

"Oh, I suppose." She sounded as much like him as a contralto was ever likely to. She sure sounded as dry as he ever did, which wasn't easy. Had she had that tone before they started hanging out together? Colin was inclined to doubt it. But couples rubbed off on each other all kinds of ways they never would have expected before they hooked up.

Colin drove past the campus exit, and past the ones for Isla Vista beyond it. Most UCSB students lived in Isla Vista, just west of the university. It was a rowdy place, with bars everywhere and such quaint tribal rituals as couch-burnings to celebrate the end of spring quarter. It was full of college kids, in other words.

Marshall's apartment was in Ellwood, farther west still. The part of Goleta called Ellwood housed plenty of students, too, but it wasn't just kids and their amusements. A lot of the students who did live there were in grad school, which made them a little older and—with luck—a little more sensible. All things considered, Ellwood was more staid than Isla Vista. That was one of the reasons Colin had chosen that particular apartment building. Marshall needed more temptations the way he needed an extra set of ears.

Off the 101. South—toward the ocean here—to Hollister. Right on Hollister to the street excitingly called Entrance Road. Left at the light there. After making its entrance, the road divided, so that on a map it resembled a tuning fork. Marshall's building, which looked an awful lot like apartments of 1970s vintage in San Atanasio, lay halfway down the right-hand tine.

Fewer buildings up here had underground garages than they did down there. That meant more people had to park on the street, so finding a space was always an adventure. Colin parallel-parked his way into one half a block down from his son's place.

Kelly softly clapped her hands. "Very neat."

"No big deal," Colin said. He'd had to parallel-park, yeah, but he hadn't really had to squeeze. "Trying to find somewhere to put the car within a mile of your place in Berkeley, *that* was combat parking."

"You did it, though," she said.

"Yeah, well, I had incentives." He let his right hand drop to her denim-covered thigh.

"Incentives." Kelly swatted the hand away. "Is that what they call it these days?"

"I dunno. All I know is, it's what I just called it." Colin opened the car door. "Come on. Let's go round up the graduate. I haven't been waiting for this forever—but it sure feels that way."

The air was cool and moist. Morning air in Santa Barbara was apt to be cool and moist the year around. Still and all, this was cooler and moister than Colin would have looked for before the supervolcano erupted. A soft breeze blew mist—not quite fog, but close—in off the ocean. It carried with it the camphory smell of the eucalyptus grove in back of the beach.

Marshall's apartment was on the second floor. The living-room window faced west, which gave him a terrific view of the gorgeously gaudy sunsets that had become the norm since the eruption filled the air all over the world with what people with high foreheads who wore lab coats called particulate matter. In plain English, that meant finely ground crud.

From what Kelly said, the Yellowstone supervolcano had belched out over six hundred cubic miles of rock—say, a hundred times as much as Krakatoa, which wasn't east of Java. There'd been a couple of years of spectacular sunsets in the 1880s. They'd probably last longer yet this time around.

How long they would last wasn't the first thing in Colin's mind as he knocked on the door. He wondered if his son had ever used one of those over-the-top sunsets as background music, so to speak, to help get himself laid. If Marshall hadn't, he'd missed one hell of a chance.

He opened the door now. He had on slacks, a dress shirt, and a tie: not his usual choice in clothes, but you were supposed to spiff yourself up under your robes. He was an inch taller than Colin's five-eleven, a good deal slimmer, and also sharper-featured. Of Colin's three kids, the one who most resembled him was Vanessa. Somehow, though, on her it looked good.

"Hey, Dad. Hi, Kelly." Marshall shook hands with Colin and hugged his new stepmother. Then he moved aside. "C'mon in."

The apartment was imperfectly neat. A sweater lay across one arm of the sofa. The kitchen table was all over papers. (Kelly worked the same way, which made Colin a little more willing to cut his youngest some slack.) Colin would have bet dishes filled the sink, though he didn't go check it out. A stretch in the service might have worked wonders for Marshall. It wasn't the first time that had crossed Colin's mind.

His son grabbed one of those papers and held it up. "Here—check this out," he said.

Colin tilted his head back to look through the bottom half of his bifocals. Kelly just leaned forward; that indignity of age hadn't caught up with her yet. The sheet Marshall was showing off looked like a printout of some e-mail.

It said something called *Storytastic* was buying a piece called "Sunset Beach" and would be sending a check for $286.65, which was five cents a word. The story would be going up on their Web site as soon as Marshall made a couple of what sounded like tiny changes.

This time, Kelly hugged him. "Awesome!" she said. "That's twice now!"

"Pretty amazing, huh?" Marshall said.

"It is." Colin wasn't kidding. Marshall had sold another short story near the end of the year before. Anybody, Colin figured, could do it once. Well, maybe not anybody, but lots of people. Doing it more than once probably took both talent and stubbornness: a good combination. He said, "This isn't as much per word as you got for the first one, is it?"

"Colin!" Kelly sent him a reproachful look.

"You would remember that, wouldn't you?" Marshall said. Colin only shrugged; remembering details was part of his job. His son continued. "I sent this one to *New Fictions*, too, but they turned me down. So I tried some other places, and it stuck here. A nickel a word's not bad."

"Okay. Congratulations, believe me." Colin set a hand on Marshall's shoulder. The kid hadn't let getting rejected keep him from sending his story out again: more than once, by the sound of it. Stubbornness, sure as hell. And Marshall was bound to be right about the pay rate. Colin had stayed friends with Bryce Miller, Vanessa's old boyfriend, even after she dumped him. Bryce was a published poet, and had yet to be paid in anything more than copies.

Of course, Bryce's poems were modeled after Greek pastorals from the third century B.C. That was one way to use the Ph.D. he'd just earned, but not one likely to make Hollywood start banging on his door and seducing him with armored trucks full of cash.

"What's 'Sunset Beach' about?" Colin asked. It had to have more to do with here and now than the stuff Bryce turned out.

Sure enough, Marshall answered, "A guy who's just graduating from college and trying to figure out what to do with himself when he's got like zero chance of landing any kind of real job."

"Sounds cheerful," Colin said. Marshall's first sale—which still hadn't seen print, though he'd gone over the galleys by now—had been about a college student caught in the middle of his parents' divorce. If he could write about his own life and get paid for it . . . well, that was a real job, if he could do it often enough. Not the smallest if in the world, not even close.

Still, other prospects *were* bleak. Nothing like getting the country's midsection trashed to shoot the economy right behind the ear. The stock market had fallen and couldn't get up. The crash wasn't so spectacular as 1929, but things sure didn't look good. And, with the weather going to hell in a refrigerated hand-basket, heaven only knew when, or if, things would ever straighten out.

"Enough of this doom and gloom," Kelly declared. "Marshall, you're getting your bachelor's. Today, we celebrate. We can worry about all the rest of the crap some other time."

"Okay." Marshall raised an eyebrow at Colin. Colin knew what his son wasn't saying: something like *What's an old cynic like you doing with an optimist?* He'd asked himself the same question. Right this minute, he was being happier than he had been in he couldn't remember how long. If that wasn't a good enough answer, he had no idea what would be.

He looked at his watch (that he checked it instead of his phone was another sign he was getting up there). "Ceremony starts at half past ten, right? We better get it in gear. Grab your robe and your fancy hat, kiddo."

"It's a mortarboard," Kelly said.

"Fancy hat," Colin repeated. "I thought the board they used for moving mortar was a hod."

Marshall topped him: "Hod-de-ha-ha!"

"You've both hod it if you keep that up," Kelly said. Groaning companionably, they went down to Marshall's Toyota in the little apartment lot. It was smaller than the Taurus, but Marshall had a guaranteed parking space when they got back. Either car would have to pay to park on campus. The University of California didn't give anything away for nothing, not these days it didn't.

Marshall drove. He knew the car and the town better than Colin did. His cell phone stayed in his pocket. He also knew better than to talk on it or text where his old man could catch him. Colin hoped like hell he knew better than to do that stuff even when nobody was watching. Texting behind the wheel was asking—begging, really—to wrap your car around the nearest tree or light pole.

Kids in gowns and mortarboards fled from the parking structure toward the soccer and track stadium, along with parents and siblings and friends. Every so often, there'd be a squeal. Somebody would throw her- or himself into somebody else's arms. Maybe the tears that flowed were tears of joy. Colin suspected they were more likely to be tears of fear. He kept his trap shut. Better to stay quiet and be thought cynical than to speak up and remove all doubt.

He and Kelly went up into the stands, which were no more comfortable than they had to be. Marshall took his place among the other graduates from the creative-writing program. He'd changed majors more than once in his erratic academic career, not least to stretch his time here as far as he could. Still and all, two sold stories argued that he hadn't ended up in the worst of all possible places.

In due course, the UCSB chancellor came to the mike. Her academic regalia was a hell of a lot more impressive than the cheap polyester crap the undergrads rented. Colin tried to decide whether that made her look imposing or like a pompous jerk. Again, he said nothing about his conclusions.

After some pious blather of her own, the chancellor introduced the main commencement speaker: the Vice President of the

United States. *He* definitely looked like a jerk in his cap and gown. People said he'd restored the Vice Presidency to its proper insignificance after the excesses at the start of the century. Colin hadn't voted for him, but he sure agreed with those people.

"We are on the way back." The Vice President's foggy baritone boomed out of the sound system by the podium. "We *are* on the way back." As plenty of comics had noticed, he believed in saying things twice, and in repeating himself. "The United States has taken a heavy blow, the heaviest blow in our history, but we *will* pick ourselves up and get back on our feet."

Beside Colin, Kelly made a small but discontented noise. One of the many reasons he loved her was that she knew bullshit when somebody slung it.

"Natural catastrophes, no matter how large and violent, cannot keep this great country on its knees for long." The Vice President waved out to the kids in the folding chairs on the soccer pitch. "You are our hope. We know you can overcome whatever Mother Nature throws at us. We know you can, and we know you will."

Kelly made another discontented noise, this one not so small. Colin touched her hand. She rolled her eyes. She knew what the supervolcano had done and was doing. Colin often wondered whether anyone back in Washington really did. When he was feeling charitable, he figured the disaster was too damn big for anyone to cope with. When he wasn't . . .

One of the new graduates yelled, "Do you know where I can get a job, maybe?" He wasn't electronically amplified. The whole stadium heard him anyhow.

The Vice President looked confused. No enormous surprise: get him off-script and he'd stick a foot in his face. Once upon a time, he'd thought about running for President himself. Then his campaign struck the iceberg of his gaffes, and sank faster than the *Titanic*.

"I'm sure something will turn up for you," he said now, and tried to get back to his speech.

That seemed safe enough. It shouldn't have been another gaffe. It shouldn't have been, but.... "What? Where? When? How?" the graduates shouted, and variations on all those themes. They knew their prospects were rotten. How blind was the Vice President, if he didn't?

"Ladies and gentlemen, please!" The chancellor came to the microphone to try to quiet them down. "Let's give our speaker the chance to finish his address."

They booed her, and they booed the Vice President. A couple of them made paper airplanes out of program pages and flung them toward the podium, but that was as far as it went. Back when Colin was a kid, rioting UCSB students had wrecked Isla Vista and burned down the Bank of America there. These kids had better reason to rise up than their elders could have imagined. So it seemed to Colin, at any rate. But they subsided after some more jeers and catcalls. In due course, the Vice President did finish, and sat down. He got a lot of applause when he did, along with more derisive hoots.

He said something to the dean or vice chancellor next to him. They both chuckled. Why not? They didn't need to worry about where their next paycheck would come from. The kids, on the other hand . . .

Colin noticed something odd when the chancellor finished the ceremony by formally awarding the degrees. She announced each group separately: the A.B.s from the College of Letters and Sciences, the B.S.s from the College of Letters and Sciences, and so on. Each group in turn whooped and cheered and hollered as it turned its mortarboard tassels from left to right to show it was now full of graduates (to say nothing of those B.S.s).

Each group in turn . . . till the chancellor awarded the Ph.D.s. The newly minted holders of doctorates turned their tassels silently and without any fuss. "Same thing happened when Rob graduated here a few years back," Colin told Kelly in a low voice. "Isn't that funny?"

"It doesn't surprise me one bit. When I finally get my diss done, I'll be too tired to feel like making a fuss even if I do go to the ceremony," Kelly said. Right now she was teaching geology at Cal State Dominguez Hills, not far from San Atanasio. The slot was probably a wedding present from her chairman up at Berkeley, and a very welcome one. She kept working on the dissertation in her copious spare time.

"Huh," Colin said thoughtfully. "Hadn't looked at it like that. Sure makes more sense than any of my guesses."

"Trust me," Kelly said. Most of the time, few phrases set off more alarm bells in Colin's head than that one. He nodded now.

Along with the rest of the graduates' relatives, he and Kelly went down onto the pitch to meet up with their hero of the moment and to immortalize that moment in ones and zeros. Marshall duly pantomimed turning his tassel. He started to do it again, but paused in midturn to hug a pretty Asian girl. "Sorry about that," he said as he went back to posing. "She was in my writing class this past quarter."

"Don't worry about it," Colin answered. "If I'd come up here by myself, I would've wanted to hug her, too."

Kelly poked him in the ribs. "You want to tell me some more about that, mister?" she said in a mock-fierce growl.

"Didn't say I would've done it. I said I would've wanted to," Colin explained. "I'm married, but I'm not blind."

"Hmm. Let's see how much deeper you can dig yourself in here," Kelly said. "What you're telling me is, it's all a question of impulse control. You can have the impulse, but as long as you don't do anything about it, you're golden."

After some thought, Colin cautiously nodded. "Yeah, that's pretty much what I'm saying. An awful lot of policework is catching the jerks who go ahead and do the first thing that pops into their heads. If they'd stop for five seconds to wonder what happened next, half the cops in the country'd be out of work. But they don't. Chances are, they can't."

Marshall made vague waving motions. "Listen, guys, I gotta go give the gown back and get my receipt for it. See you in a few." He headed off towards an exit already crowded with new graduates. Eyeing that crowd, Colin suspected returning the gown would take more than a few. Waiting till tomorrow, though, would bring on a fee. The University of California system missed few tricks when it came to revenue enhancement.

The UC system did let you keep your mortarboard and tassel. Colin prayed such untrammeled generosity wouldn't bankrupt it.

In due course, Marshall made it back. He was usually the most even-tempered of Colin's children, even when he wasn't stoned. Now, though, he looked and sounded irked. "Boy, that was fun," he muttered darkly.

"I bet," Colin said.

"Sure looks like they could've organized it better," Kelly said. A beat later, she corrected herself: "Sure looks like they could've organized it."

"There you go!" Marshall said. He turned to his father and spoke in serious tones: "You should keep this one."

"That'd be nice." Colin could hardly have sounded dryer. All the same, he was most sincere. He wasn't sure how he'd survived one divorce. If he had to try to survive two . . . He shivered as if a goose had just walked over his grave. An awful lot of cops' marriages failed. That was one reason why eating your gun was an occupational hazard of the trade.

"I think so, too," Kelly said pointedly, and took his hand. Colin didn't need to worry about things falling apart right this minute, so he didn't.

"Where do we go now?" Marshall asked. He'd got done with

college at long, long last. Too much to hope for to expect him to have any real notion of what came next.

"Well, I got us reservations for the China Pavilion, but they aren't till six," Colin answered. "We have some time to kill first."

"You did? How?" Marshall, cool Marshall, actually seemed impressed. The China Pavilion was downtown Santa Barbara's best Chinese restaurant, and the race wasn't even close. The place was always jammed.

"I'll tell you how—I did it three months ago, as soon as I was sure you really would get your sheepskin," Colin replied. Marshall just gaped. Advance planning was almost as alien to him as it was to a drive-by shooter with a head full of crack.

To use up the afternoon, they went to the Santa Barbara Zoo. It wasn't the kind of place that would drive the San Diego Zoo or even the one in Los Angeles out of business any time soon. It was small and funky: one of FDR's swarm of WPA projects. Nobody nowadays would built a zoo like this, but nobody in the 1930s had worried about that. Animals prowled or dozed in concrete enclosures. Peanut shells littered the walkways (the signs at the concession stands warning about peanut allergy were relatively new, though). You weren't supposed to toss the monkeys peanuts, but people did anyhow. Colin thought it was terrific.

When they got to the China Pavilion just before six, it was as crowded as usual. More crowded than usual, in fact: along with prosperous locals (almost a redundancy if you weren't going to school here—prices knocked the China Pavilion out of most starving students' price range), the restaurant was full of parents celebrating with their kids.

Sure enough, though, the receptionist ran a perfectly manicured finger down her list and nodded. "Yes, your table is waiting, Mr. Ferguson. Please come this way." She grabbed menus and led Colin, Kelly, and Marshall to a table by the window. "Is this all right?"

"Couldn't be better," Colin said.

"Someone will be along to take your drink orders soon." The receptionist swayed back to her station.

Colin asked for Laphroaig over ice. Kelly and Marshall both chose Tsingtaos. If you were going to drink beer with Chinese food, why not Chinese beer? And the brewery in Tsingtao dated from the days before the First World War, when the Germans ran the town. Say what you wanted about Germans, but they knew how to make beer.

Marshall eyed the menu with astonished respect. "Boy, this place is even more expensive than I remembered," he said, and looked a question at his father.

"Don't worry about it. It's not like you graduate every day," Colin said. For quite a while there, it hadn't been as if Marshall graduated *any* day. Now Colin wouldn't have to worry about tuition or rent or utilities at the apartment. He'd got to like the Armenian couple who owned the building (and several others in Ellwood), which didn't mean he'd be sorry to quit writing them checks every month.

A waiter—a Hispanic guy, like most people in his line of work in Southern California—brought the drinks. "You folks ready to order dinner yet?"

"I think so," Colin answered. Courses revolved around crab and duck. Marshall grinned in anticipation. His old man hadn't been kidding about ignoring the cost for a night. After the waiter hustled off to the kitchen, Colin said, "This is why God made plastic."

His son and his new wife snorted on almost identical notes. "Aliens must have grabbed hold of your brain, Dad," Marshall said. "That can't be you talking."

Colin was the kind who paid off his credit card balance in full every month. Except for his mortgage, he owed nobody in the world a dime—and he'd lived in his house long enough that he wasn't far from waving bye-bye to the mortgage, too. Even when he was going through his divorce, he'd paid the lawyers on time. It hadn't been easy, but he'd done it.

Like a bear bedeviled by mosquitoes, he shook his big, square head. He didn't want to remember the divorce now, not while he was out having a good time with Kelly. But he couldn't very well forget it, not when he saw Louise's face every time he looked at Marshall. How much of life was rolling with the difference between what you wanted and what you got? A hell of a big chunk, for sure.

Then the food came. He couldn't imagine a better, or a more delicious, amnesia inducer. No, he couldn't afford to do this every day, or even very often. All the more reason to enjoy it when he could.

He'd reached blissfully overloaded nirvana when Kelly touched his hand. "Look outside," she said softly. "It's raining."

It never rained in June in Southern California. Sure as hell, though, the sidewalk and the street out there glistened with water. Cars went by with their wipers and lights on. He couldn't forget about his divorce. The supervolcano insisted on being remembered, too.

II

In the Year Without a Summer, back two centuries ago now, it had snowed in Maine in June. As a matter of fact, it had snowed in June as far south as Pennsylvania. Rob Ferguson knew more about the Year Without a Summer than he'd ever wanted to find out. The eruption of Mount Tambora, down in what had been the Dutch East Indies and was now Indonesia, touched it off. Mount Tambora had been one hellacious boom—two and a half times as big as Krakatoa, a lifetime later, though without such a good press agent.

And that hellacious boom was maybe—maybe—five percent the size of the Yellowstone supervolcano eruption. Guilford, Maine, had a park that ran along by the banks of the Piscataquis River. Rob stood in the park on the Fourth of July and watched snow drift down from a sky the color of a flock of dirty sheep.

"Boy, this is fun," Justin Nachman said, his breath smoking at every word.

"Now that you mention it," Rob answered, "no."

"We could bail out," Justin said, not for the first time. He played lead guitar and did most of the singing for Squirt Frog and the Evolving Tadpoles: he would have been Squirt Frog, had they reckoned things that way. He was short and kind of chunky. He'd worn a perm he described as a Yiddish Afro till the band got stranded in Guilford not long after the eruption. He hadn't kept it up since, but his hair was still plenty curly.

"We could, yeah." Rob's words showed agreement; his tone didn't. For a long time, getting into and out of Guilford had been as near impossible as made no difference. Rob had never seen, never dreamt of, so much snow in his life. He was from L.A., so that didn't prove much. All the guys in the band were Californians; they'd come together at UCSB. But people who'd lived in Guilford their whole lives said the same thing.

Basically, Maine north and west of I-95 had been left to its own devices by a country that had bigger catastrophes to worry about than too goddamn much snow way the hell off in its far northeastern corner. Food, fuel oil, and gasoline stopped coming in. The power went out—not all at once, but now here, now there, till eventually nobody had any. The nineteenth century came back in a big way.

And the locals made it through better than Rob would have believed. They cut down a lot of second-growth pines. They shot a lot of moose and white-tailed deer and ducks and geese. Rob had shot a moose himself, with a rifle borrowed from Dick Barber, the proprietor of the Trebor Mansion Inn, the B & B where the band was staying.

Barber was a longtime Navy man who had a pretty fair arsenal. And Rob, a cop's kid, knew what to do with guns. Except for occasional target practice with his father, he'd never used what he knew till this winter. Eating something you'd killed yourself, he discovered, made both the hunt and the following meals feel special, almost sanctified.

This time around, Justin didn't want to let it alone: "It's not as bad as it was. We can get to Bangor. The airport's open. We can go anywhere we want."

He had a point . . . of sorts. It didn't snow all the time any more—only some of the time. When it wasn't snowing, it got warm enough so the stuff that had already fallen started melting. It had climbed all the way up into the sixties once or twice in June.

Roads emerged from under snowdrifts. Here and there, food and fuel started coming in, though it wasn't as if the rest of the country had a whole lot to spare. It seemed to matter less than anyone would have dreamt possible before northern and central Maine got stranded.

"Sure. We can," Rob said, again with that mismatch between tone and voice. "I bet we blow up the band if we do, though."

Justin had expressive features. Right now what they expressed was annoyance verging on disgust. "Biff will come along if the rest of us decide to go back to civilization," he said.

"Don't bet anything you can't afford to lose," Rob said. Biff Thorvald played rhythm guitar. He was also the guy in the band who trolled hardest for girls. They all did some of it. What the hell was the point of playing in a band if it wasn't to help you get laid? But Biff took it further than Justin or Rob or Charlie Storer, the drummer. The phrase *hard-on with legs* hadn't been coined with him in mind, but it might as well have been.

Justin still looked annoyed. "He's not *that* serious about Sarah or Cindy or whatever her name is."

"Bullshit he's not," Rob retorted. Cindy—he thought that was her name—was a waitress at Caleb's Kitchen, on Water Street. If Rob turned his head, and if the snow eased up a little, he could see the diner from where he stood. It was tolerable for breakfast, but hadn't been much for lunch or dinner till they put moose stew and venisonburgers on the menu. Whatever her name was, Biff was all head over heels for her, and she was just as crazy about him.

"Oh, man!" Justin waved in frustration at the trees on the far bank of the Piscataquis. The ones that weren't pines were mostly bare-branched. All the late frosts and snowfalls had screwed their leaf-growing to the wall. Rob wondered if they'd die. This was a town park, so nobody'd chopped them down over the winter. But if they were nothing but firewood waiting to happen . . . Justin went on, "This is Nowhere with a capital N."

"Uh-huh." Rob admitted what he couldn't very well deny. But he also said, "I kinda like it, y'know?"

The look Justin gave him had *Et tu, Brute?* written all over it. "You've got to be kidding me," he said.

"Nope." Rob shook his head. "Right after we got stranded, I would've kissed a pig for a plane ticket to, well, anywhere. But it grows on me, honest to God it does."

"Like a wart." Justin was not a happy camper.

"Look, dude, if you just gotta go, then you gotta go, and that's all there is to it," Rob said. "We'll be sorry and we'll miss you and all that good shit, but we won't hate you or anything. The band's not worth squat if the only reason you're in it is you think you have to stay in it. If you leave, well, hell, we had a better run than most outfits do. We even made a living at it for a while."

"Up from obscurity," Justin muttered.

"Most outfits never make it that far," Rob said. "They don't call 'em garage bands by accident. The drummer's loud and crappy and annoys the neighbors, and the guys say fuck it and get on with their lives. Coming as far as we have, we beat the odds."

"We got all the way up to cult band," Justin said.

He didn't mean it in any good way, but Rob nodded even so.

"We sure did, and it paid the bills. What's wrong with that? I mean, would you rather play gigs or sit in a cubicle next to Dilbert and stare at a monitor all day?"

Justin flinched. He might have been stuck in a lab, not a cubicle—he was an escaped biologist. But one of the reasons you got into a band was so you wouldn't get trapped in a nine-to-five. Of course, you could get trapped in a band, too. "Up from obscurity," he repeated. "And then down to obscurity again."

That was how it went. It wasn't so exact as calculating where a missile that went up on this course at that angle with the other velocity would come down, but it came close. Nobody'd ever heard of you. Then people did hear about you, and you were as hot as you ever got. Then they started forgetting about you and looking for something new. But if enough people got to like you while you were It, you could still make a living on the afterglow.

Like really powerful missiles, a few bands went into orbit and never did come back to earth. Squirt Frog and the Evolving Tadpoles never would have been one of those; it was too quirky, and probably too smart for its own good. As long as everybody in the band accepted that, they could have fun anyhow.

Justin sighed now. "I know what it is. That Farrell guy's got a mojo on you."

"Oh, give me a break!" Rob said. "Everything around here would have gone to hell if he hadn't pitched in." Jim Farrell was a retired history prof; Dick Barber had helped run his failed campaign for Congress in the last election. The successful Democrat stayed in Washington. He showed no interest in sharing his constituents' frigid fate. Farrell was still here, and better adapted to the new reality than most younger people. He also had a bugle-like baritone that made people—people on this side of I-95, anyhow—take notice of him.

"He's, uh, kind of out there." By the way Justin said it, he was giving Farrell the benefit of the doubt.

Rob only laughed. "And we're not?"

"Not *that* way." A big, wet snowflake landed on the end of Justin's nose. His eyes crossed, trying to focus on it. Then it melted, and they uncrossed again. He let out another sigh. "I guess I'm not going anywhere—for now."

"Okay," Rob said. If Justin waited much longer, winter would clamp down hard on Guilford once more—and on big stretches of the rest of the country, too. Snow in L.A. twice in one season? How crazy was that?

Crazy as a supervolcano eruption. You never thought it could happen. Then it did, and you had to live with the aftermath . . . if you could.

Vanessa Ferguson checked the time on her cell phone. A quarter past three. She let out a sigh full of theatrical disgust. Part of that was because she had to meet Micah at four. The other part was because, although Camp Constitution had been up and running for almost a year, only little gadgets like cell phones had power here. And sometimes you stood in line for a couple of hours before you got to use the charging station, too.

She didn't know how many refugee centers there were, set up just past the edges of the ashfall from the supervolcano. She did know they stretched from Iowa to Louisiana on this side of the eruption, and from Washington State down into California in the west. They all had patriotic-sounding names: Camp Constitution, Camp Independence, Camp Federalist, Camp Liberation, and on and on. Some FEMA flunky back in D.C. probably got a bonus for every fancy moniker he thought up.

She didn't think anybody knew how many people remained stuck in these miserable camps. As with deaths from the eruption, she didn't think anybody could guess to the nearest hundred thousand. Till she ended up here, she'd never imagined there was this much tent canvas in the whole U.S. of A. And if she never saw another MRE for the rest of her life . . . it would mean they were finally running out of them, and then all the refugees would *really* be in trouble.

The roof over her head right now was olive-drab canvas. She sprawled on a bunk—next to the top in a stack of five. She had a two-inch-thick foam-rubber pad over the plywood bottom of the bunk. In Camp Constitution, that was luxury.

And this was a pretty quiet tent. That was luxury, too. The three little brats in the first tent where she'd washed up . . . They couldn't watch TV. They couldn't play video games. They couldn't get on Facebook. So they drove everybody nuts instead. Vanessa'd wanted to rip their little heads off. She didn't suffer fools or pests gladly. But what you wanted to do and what you could get away with were two different critters, dammit.

Micah had got her out of there. Of course, everything came with a price. Pretty soon, she'd deliver another payment. Not long after she'd come to this tent, she'd figured she didn't need to deliver any more. That only proved she'd been naive. Once you let somebody know what bugged you, you left yourself vulnerable to him.

Who would have dreamt Micah could find kids even more horrible than the ones she'd left behind? Well, he did it, damn him. These were boys, not girls, which only made them wilder. And there were four of them, not three. Their mother had long since given up trying to keep them under control. They had no father in evidence.

Just to make matters worse, they were African-American. If Vanessa complained about them through regular channels, she'd look like a racist.

So, irregularly, she went back to Micah. He raised an eyebrow. He looked surprised. "Is that so?" he said, and he sounded surprised, too, damn him. He was *such* a dweeb. "How unfortunate for you. I was not aware of the situation." Another government agency called that kind of thing plausible deniability. Vanessa called it horseshit. She was learning.

"What can you do about it?" she asked him.

"I'm not sure," he said. "If they were properly transferred into that residence area, I may not be able to do much at all." Only a bureaucrat who didn't have to live in one would call a surplus gynormous Army tent a residence area. And only someone who knew damn well he could take care of things if he decided to would deny it that way.

She'd paid off before, to get away from her first tent. That made picking it up again easier, but left her more disgusted with herself than ever. If Micah had been greedier . . . But he wasn't, not with any one person. Vanessa was as sure as made no difference that he had plenty of others coming around.

That African-American mother and her four monsters vanished from the tent as abruptly as they'd appeared in it. Everybody else breathed a sigh of relief. Vanessa breathed a sigh of resignation. Micah had delivered. Now she would have to deliver, too. She kept delivering, every couple of weeks, the way she would have kept up her auto-insurance payments out in the real world.

"Everything worked out for the best," Micah told her one afternoon. "I was able to gain the Washington family access to a relocatable unit."

Relocatable unit was more bureaucratese, this time for *trailer*. FEMA trailers had had an evil reputation since Katrina. The ones at Camp Constitution looked as if they'd been working hard at least since the hurricane hit New Orleans. They were the refugee camp's equivalent of Beverly Hills anyway. Only large families got to stay in them.

"Yippee skip," Vanessa had said, in lieu of *Hot shit!* She would rather have seen all four of the little gangbangers in cells.

Now she checked the time once more. Three thirty. The minutes just flew by when you were having so much fun. *Yeah, right,* she thought. She climbed down from her bunk: carefully, so as not to bother the people in the bunks below hers. They were as bored and miserable as she was. What else were places like Camp Constitution but breeding grounds for boredom and misery? She understood where Palestinian terrorists came from much better than she ever could have before the supervolcano erupted.

Camp Constitution lay somewhere between Muskogee, Oklahoma, and Fort Smith, Arkansas. It should have been up in the nineties, with humidity to match. But the sun shone pale from a sky drained of blue the way a vampire's victim was drained of pink. It might have been seventy. Then again, it might not.

The breeze came out of the west. Vanessa slipped on a surgical mask. All kinds of volcanic ash and dust remained in the air, especially when the wind blew from that quarter. Coughing was one of the characteristic sounds of the camp. You didn't hear it as much now as you had when the miserable place first opened, though. Most of the people who'd had lung troubles when they got here were already dead.

That breeze also brought the reek of row upon row of outhouses. There were showers—cold showers. There were spigots where you could fill bottles and jugs and whatever else you happened to have with potable water. And that was about the extent of the running water in these parts. A sewage system there was not.

People in ugly, ill-fitting clothes tramped the camp's dusty, unpaved avenues. Vanessa knew she was one of them, knew it and hated it. Like everybody else here, she'd arrived with only what she had on her back. Everything else came from donations. She'd never seen—she'd never worn—so much polyester in so many garish colors in her life.

A real building, the only one in the camp, housed the FEMA functionaries who ran the place. *They* had electricity and plumbing and high-speed Internet access and all the other benefits of Western civilization. They were workers, after all, not refugees. They were there to help—if they happened to feel like it.

A long line of people snaked out the front door and down the street. Every one of them wanted something. Some would get it: the deserving, the persistent, or, sometimes, just the attractive.

Vanessa's mouth twisted. On her, her father's strong, blunt features looked good. She sometimes—these days, more and more often—wished they didn't. But all you could do was play the cards you had. She'd used her looks to her advantage before. Like most nice-looking people, she'd sometimes done it without even noticing. In a way, she was still doing it. In a way . . .

There was another door around the back. No line at this one. Just a sign next to it, with big red letters: FEMA STAFF ONLY. A guard wearing a Fritz hat and body armor and carrying an M16 stood there to back up the sign. Vanessa nodded to him; she'd been here before. "I have an appointment with Mr. Husak," she said.

"Let me check." He spoke into a telephone mounted beside the door. Hanging up, he nodded. "Go on in, then."

Before she passed through the metal detector, she took a .38 revolver out of her purse and handed it to the guard. He accepted it without surprise; plenty of people in Camp Constitution packed heat. There were also metal detectors at the front door. There hadn't been, till what the camp administration kept calling an unfortunate incident (three dead, seven wounded—yeah, that was unfortunate, all right) prompted their urgent installation.

She and the rest of the junk in her handbag passed muster. So she got to go inside. Everything in the building was, or should have been, achingly normal. Fluorescent tubes glowed behind frosted-glass panels set into the ceiling. Cheap, battleship-gray industrial carpet lay underfoot. Keyboards clicked. Before the supervolcano blew up, she'd worked in a place in Denver not too different from this. If you were stuck under canvas with nothing to look forward to but another MRE, it was a lost world.

A clock on the corridor wall said it was four straight up. Vanessa knocked on the second door past that clock. Micah Husak opened it. His smile showed a broken front tooth. "You're right on time," he said.

"Wonderful." Vanessa was compulsively punctual. When she kept these appointments, she wished she weren't. "Let's get it over with, okay?"

The smile slipped. He wanted her to like him for the favors he'd done her. And he had done them, too. She wouldn't have come here if he hadn't. But wanting her to like him . . . Hey, people in hell wanted mint juleps to drink. That didn't mean they'd get them.

"Well," he said. He closed the door and clicked the locking button in the center of the knob. Then he sat down in the swivel chair behind the generic office desk. He undid his belt, unzipped his slacks, and slid them down around his ankles. He hiked up his blue cotton dress shirt.

Vanessa got down on her knees in front of him. She took him in her hand and then, muttering, took him in her mouth. She sucked hard. She wanted to get it over with as fast as she could. A few minutes every couple of weeks, in exchange for living better than she would have otherwise . . . A simple enough bargain, she'd thought so when she made it. Payback was a bitch, though, as it often was.

He opened his pale, hairy knees a little wider, trying to stretch it out. But he wanted to come, too. Just before he did, Vanessa pulled her head away so the nasty stuff landed on his belly and in his pubic hair.

She wiped her chin off on her sleeve. Micah Husak pulled a couple of Kleenexes out of a box on the desk and tidied himself up. "I wish you'd let me finish in your mouth," he said peevishly.

"Forget it," she answered as she got to her feet. "I don't do that for anybody." *Not even for men I do like*, she thought, but coming right out with that wouldn't have been smart, even if it was true. She thought the idea totally gross. She'd got a bad-tasting, slimy surprise the first time she sucked a guy off, and she'd vowed then and there she'd never let it happen again. She hadn't, either.

"Well," Micah said once more. But a guy who'd just been blown wasn't in the mood to do a lot of complaining. He wasn't the first with whom Vanessa had seen that. As he set his clothes to rights, he went on, "I'll see you in two weeks, then."

"Yeah," Vanessa said tightly. She was sure one of the reasons he didn't insist more with her was that he had his other side girls. If he wanted to come in somebody's mouth, no doubt he could.

Camp Constitution was a humongous place. And it was only one of too many, all depressingly alike. How much petty corruption like his went on in them? Lots and lots. She was all too sure of that. Enough so people on the outside didn't get up in arms when some of it surfaced. Up in arms? Hell, most of the time they didn't even notice. It wasn't as if they didn't have troubles of their own.

She couldn't even slam the door behind her when she walked out of the little office. It had a compressed-air cylinder attachment at the top that thwarted tantrums. She left the administration building by way of the FEMA STAFF ONLY door. "Have a good one," the guard said as he handed the pistol back to her.

"Here? Fat chance!" she answered. He only chuckled. Did he know what went on with the women who had appointments with Micah Husak? If he didn't know, could he guess? Vanessa wouldn't have been surprised.

A new thought occurred to her as she trudged grimly back toward her tent. Was Micah the only one there who collected favors for favors? Or did half, or more than half, the FEMA guys get what they wanted when they wanted it? That wouldn't have surprised her one bit, either. There were bound to be too many chances, too many temptations, to resist.

A cat ambling down the lane glanced back over its shoulder at her and picked the amble up to a trot. It was mostly white, with a couple of black spots. It had a fat bottom and a small head. When it paused for a moment to wash a foot, it looked like a bowling pin with ears.

Loneliness stabbed through Vanessa. "Kitty, kitty, kitty!" she called. They'd made her turn her cat loose when she got to the refugee center in Garden City, Kansas. The high school there had no room for pets. She kept hoping someone else had realized how wonderful Pickles was and taken him in, but she knew he was bound to be dead. So were most of the people who'd lived in Garden City. An awful lot a volcanic ash had come down there: not as much as in Denver, but an awful lot all the same.

She called the fat-assed white cat again. Its ears twitched toward her, but it decided that foot was clean enough and trotted on.

"Stupid thing," Vanessa muttered. More likely, though, it already had a human—or, like Micah Husak, more than one—on its string. Even if it didn't, cats had a fine old time at Camp Constitution. Swarms of people in one none-too-sanitary place meant corresponding swarms of mice and rats.

You could have pets here. Some people had brought in big, mean dogs. Those mostly didn't last long. They either had sad accidents or they started starving and had to be released outside the camp or put down. There were no kibble distributions here. You fed pets from your own rations. A cat? No problem. A Rottweiler? That was a different story.

A little dog might be okay. Cats could like you pretty well, but they were also in the deal for what they could get out of it. Dogs loved you whether you deserved it or not. That kind of slavish devotion had always grated on Vanessa. The longer she had anything to do with Micah Husak, though, the less attractive feline expediency looked.

"A puppy?" she said, and nodded to herself. "A puppy." They wouldn't be hard to find. And something that wouldn't care for her just on account of what she did for it seemed especially wonderful right after she'd visited the administration building.

Louise Ferguson glanced at the clock on the wall across from her desk. She stood up. She'd forgotten how much effort that took when you were pregnant out to here. The bowling ball in your belly messed up your balance, too, just at the time when falling would be most disastrous.

She stuck her head into Mr. Nobashi's inner office. Her boss was on the phone, yelling in Japanese mixed with occasional English swearwords. The ramen company's corporate headquarters were in Hiroshima. The San Atanasio building was only a colonial outpost.

Mr. Nobashi raised a questioning eyebrow. "Please excuse me," Louise said, "but I have a doctor's appointment at eleven o'clock." She patted her bulging belly to show what kind of appointment it was.

"Oh, Jesus Christ!" Her boss covered the phone's mouthpiece with the palm of one hand. "Okay. You go. I see you after lunch, yes?" His English was telegraphic and heavily accented, but Louise rarely had trouble figuring out what he meant.

"Thank you. Yes," Louise answered. The baby kicked or stretched or did whatever the hell he did. People talked about the miracle of life. What that amounted to for a woman was, stuff was going on inside you, but it wasn't stuff you were doing. It was wonderful, sure. But this was the fourth time Louise had gone through it, and it still weirded her out.

She walked out to the parking lot. The ramen works' American center had been on Braxton Bragg Boulevard since the 1970s. The neighborhood was a lot rougher now than it had been back in the day. A fence of stout steel palings topped by razor wire surrounded the lot. Despite the fence, an armed guard stayed on duty 24/7.

The Hispanic guy out there now nodded to Louise and touched an index finger to the brim of his dark blue Smokey the Bear hat in what was almost but not quite a salute. He remained watchful and alert. He'd probably done a tour or two in Iraq or Afghanistan. How much easier was this? He didn't have to worry about IEDs in San Atanasio, anyhow.

He kept an eye on her till she'd left the lot. She didn't know where the ramen company hired its guards, but they were all solid.

She flicked on her headlights. The morning fog had thinned, but it was still there. The lights wouldn't do anything to help her see. They'd help other people see her, though, which also counted. The South Bay could get some real pea-soupers, but at this time of year? She shook her head. Not before the supervolcano erupted. Not a chance.

Her OB-GYN's office was only about ten minutes away. The doc she'd gone to when Rob, Vanessa, and Marshall were born had long since retired. Dr. Travis Suzuki was one of the new breed: younger than she was, brusque, and efficient. He thought she was nutso for having the baby. He didn't come right out and say so, but she also didn't need a magnifying glass to read between the lines.

When she walked into the waiting room, two other pregnant women were sitting there. They were both in their twenties. The blonde chewed gum while she listened to her iPod. The Asian gal was leafing through a copy of *People*. They both gaped at her stomach as if they couldn't believe their eyes. They probably couldn't. She was about as old as the two of them put together.

She grabbed the first magazine in the rack and sat down to look at it. It was *Vegetarian Times*, hardly something she would have chosen if she'd been paying attention. Teo had talked about not eating meat any more—an aerobics instructor feared fat even more than he feared the IRS. But he'd never done more than talk. He needed protein to stay strong. And, just as much to the point, meat tasted so good.

Well, she didn't need to worry about Teo any more. Except, of course, for the small detail he'd given her to remember him by, the detail that was getting bigger by the day and would pop pretty soon. *Yeah, except for that,* she thought.

One of the other women got called into an examination room, then the second. A Hispanic gal came in. She was older than both of those two—in her thirties somewhere. She still gave Louise a look that said *You gotta be jiving me.*

Louise stared stonily back. *In your ear, lady.* The Hispanic woman looked away first. She sat down and started texting on her BlackBerry.

The door to the back part of the office opened. "You can come in now, Ms. Ferguson," the receptionist said.

"Happy day." Louise levered herself out of the chair with one arm. She wasn't sorry to put *Vegetarian Times* back in the rack. It was a sad little magazine, skinny and printed on crappy paper. Who would have thought the supervolcano could screw up something like that? It did, though, along with so much else.

A nurse took charge of Louise. "Why don't we climb on the scales?" she said.

"We? You're getting on with me?" Louise said. The nurse (her name was Terri—Louise felt proud of herself for remembering) laughed. It wasn't that funny, but then, neither was Terri's assumption that, because she was having a baby, she was also turning back into one.

She got on the scale. She weighed . . . what she weighed. She wondered how much would come off after the kid finally emerged. She wondered if any would. One more thing to worry about. It wasn't even close to the top of her list—and, when she couldn't worry too much about her weight, that was one honking list.

Terri led her into an examination room and took her temperature and her blood pressure. The nurse wrote in the chart. "What are they?" Louise asked.

"Both normal," Terri answered after a moment's pause. *The nerve of some people, wanting to know their own numbers!* Louise had seen that attitude before in other nurses. Terri went on, "Dr. Suzuki will see you in a few minutes." Out she went.

There was a magazine rack in the examination room, too, but the only magazine in it was a *Car and Driver* from before the eruption. Louise was more interested in it than in jumping out the window into the parking lot, but not much more. She left it in the rack. She wouldn't die of boredom before the doctor came in.

And in he swept, Terri in his wake to keep the proprieties proped or whatever. He reminded her of Mr. Sulu from *Star Trek*. His weapons of choice, though, were rubber gloves, not photon torpedoes. "How are you feeling today?" he asked briskly.

"Like the Goodyear Blimp. How else am I gonna feel?" she retorted. He laughed. She added, "And I do wish he'd come out and get it over with. I'm sick of lugging him around."

Dr. Suzuki nodded. How many times had he heard variations on that theme? Probably from every woman close to her due date. He glanced into the chart. "Your numbers have been good all along. Your BP is low. You've never had protein in your urine or anything like that. It should be a normal delivery. We will be extra careful, though. I don't mean to offend you, but at your age we can't take anything for granted."

"I'm not offended. I know how old I am. I'd better," Louise said.

"Er—yes." Dr. Suzuki didn't seem to know what to make of that. *Was I so dry before I married Colin, or did it rub off from him?* Louise wondered. Chances were it had rubbed off. She still thought of anything peculiar as nutso because of Wes Jones. And he was just the guy who'd lived across the street, not somebody who'd fathered her three children.

Three out of four now, she thought.

Dr. Suzuki tried again: "If anything seems even a little out of the ordinary, call me or go to the hospital right away. Don't waste time and don't take chances. Do you understand?"

"I can't very well not understand that, can I?" Louise returned sharply.

He rolled his eyes. "Ms. Ferguson, you'd be amazed."

And that was bound to be true. If anybody learned never to underestimate the power of human stupidity, someone who'd been married to a cop for a long time sure would. The armed robber who'd left his driver's license on the counter of the liquor store he'd knocked over but who seemed surprised anyway when he got busted . . . The gal who'd stabbed her husband in the neck over a six-pack of Big Red chewing gum . . . Oh, the list went on and on.

"Well, I hope I'm not dumb that way, anyhow," Louise said.

"Okay, fair enough." Dr. Suzuki nodded. "I'll see you again in two weeks or when your contractions start, whichever comes first."

Louise made the appointment with the receptionist. Whether she'd keep it, as the OB-GYN had said, was more up to Junior than to her. The doctor's office was in a better part of town than the ramen works. It didn't have, or need, a fortified parking lot. Louise sighed. She remembered the days when no business in San Atanasio did.

Which proved . . . what, exactly? That the world changed whether she liked it or not? That she wasn't so young as she had been once upon a time? All of the above? The baby kicked inside her as she got into her car. "Stop that," she told him, not that he listened. She wasn't too old to get pregnant. She'd thought she was, but nooooo. Life was full of surprises, wasn't it? Uh-huh. You betcha.

When she walked into the ramen place, Patty asked her, "How you doing?" In the old days, Patty would have been a man with a green eyeshade. What she couldn't do with and to numbers couldn't be done.

"Except for this"—Louise patted her front bumper—"I'm fine."

"Yeah. Except." Patty would have to fill Louise's slot, too, when Louise had the baby. It wasn't that she couldn't. She could do the job better than Louise could; she'd taught it to Louise. But she couldn't stand Mr. Nobashi—he drove her nutso.

As soon as Louise got back to her desk, he yelled for a Coke and a danish. He ran on them. Why he didn't have diabetes, Louise couldn't imagine. Not from lack of effort, that was for sure. Fetching the stuff for himself would have been beneath a Japanese boss' dignity. Having a massively pregnant woman do it for him wasn't.

All things considered, Patty had a point.

Once she'd supplied Mr. Nobashi with his early-afternoon sugar and caffeine, Louise went back to figuring inventories and sales trends. It wasn't what you'd call exciting. Well, if she wanted excitement, all she had to do was wait till Junior came out. He'd take care of that for her. Oh, wouldn't he just!

III

The door to Marshall Ferguson's room had a strip of yellow police tape running diagonally across it. CRIME SCENE—DO NOT CROSS was printed on it in big black block letters. Like any newly returned college graduate living in a house with his father and his father's new wife, he was sensitive about his privacy.

Unlike some, he realized they were sensitive about theirs, too. And they didn't pry. He could even smoke dope in there if he didn't make it too obvious he was getting wasted. For somebody whose dad was a cop, that was a small, or maybe not such a small, miracle.

About the only thing his father required of him was that he sit in front of his computer for a couple of hours every day, working on whatever he was working on. "Look," Colin Ferguson said, "I know turning into a writer doesn't happen overnight. But it doesn't happen if you don't work at it, either. So you'll work."

Marshall resented that, but not as much as he might have. He was old enough to have got past the teenage thing of being sure anything his old man said was bullshit just because his old man said it. But he did bristle when his dad suggested—no, ordained was the better word—that he pay a third of whatever he made as rent.

"What happens if I get a fat book contract?" he asked. Two sold stories, and he had big ambitions—or dreams, anyhow.

"Then we dicker," Dad said at once, which tossed a bucket of water on Marshall's sparking temper. His father went on, "Look, I'm not trying to screw you. I'm just trying to remind you that you've got some obligations. You're allegedly a grown-up, after all."

"Thanks for that *allegedly*. I appreciate it," Marshall said.

"Figured you would." Dad didn't even blink. Trying to top him at sarcasm was a losing game. He eyed Marshall. "Other thing is, if I get sick of nothing coming in after a while, you'll start looking for a job or you'll find yourself somewhere else to stay."

"How long is a while? Who gets to decide?"

"I decide how long it is." Colin Ferguson answered both questions at once. He even explained why: "After all, I'm the guy paying the mortgage."

What am I supposed to say to that? Marshall wondered. He almost asked if Kelly was paying rent. Fortunately, he had the sense not to. For one thing, she was married to Dad. For another, she had a paying job at Dominguez Hills. So all Marshall did say, after that brief pause for thought, was, "Okay."

His father had inhaled. Dad was braced for an argument, all right, and ready to blow Marshall out of the water. Now he exhaled again: he'd got dressed up, and he didn't have any place to go. He sent Marshall a crooked grin. "You are growing up, aren't you?"

Marshall was convinced he'd been grown up for years now. Whenever he tried to say as much, his old man gave him the horse laugh. Since they'd come through this exchange without the fireworks that might have soured things between them, he let it go without offering Dad such a juicy target. "Whatever," he said, and left it right there. The less you came out with, the less you'd regret later on.

Then his father caught him by surprise: "I bet I know where you'll be able to make some money, anyhow. Not enough to live on, but some."

"Oh, yeah? Where?" Marshall wondered what kind of hare-brained scheme was dancing through Dad's beady little mind.

Only it turned out not to be so harebrained after all. "Taking care of your half-brother, that's where," Colin Ferguson answered. "Your mother will be looking for somebody to do that, I'm sure, once she runs through however much maternity leave they give her."

"Huh," Marshall said thoughtfully. Whatever he might have been looking for, that wasn't it. "I'm . . . not sure I want to do that. I . . . don't know how much I want to have to do with Mom these days. And taking care of, of *that* kid?" He didn't even want to say Teo's name. Teo, after all, had stolen Mom away from Dad and screwed up the family. That was how he'd seen it at the time, anyhow. Little by little, he'd come to realize things weren't so simple (which was another part of growing up). The first approximation still ruled his gut, though.

His father sighed. "Well, it's your call. If you don't want to, I sure won't try and make you. But it's not like I'd mind or anything. I . . . wish your mother the best in spite of everything. I don't want her back. Too much water over the dam for that. But I do wish her the best. And she'll need the help. Better if she gets it from somebody she knows, somebody she can trust, and not somebody she hires off a supermarket bulletin board or from Craigslist or somewhere."

"I'll think about it." Marshall hadn't expected to say even that much.

"Thanks. You do that." Dad gave him another one of those lopsided grins. "Five gets you ten taking care of a baby gives you something new to write about, too."

"Hot shit!" If Marshall sounded distinctly unenthusiastic, it was only because he was. He didn't let Dad beat him to the punch line, either: "That's what I'd be writing about, too, isn't it?"

"Hot shit and cold shit and piss and spit-up and all kinds of gross stuff," his father agreed. "But there'd be other stuff, too. Getting to know your half-brother, and him getting to know you, when you're old enough to be his father."

"I guess." Marshall didn't want to think of it in those terms. If he was old enough to be his mother's son's father . . . Somewhere, a goose was walking on old Oedipus' grave. The idea creeped him out bigtime.

Maybe that showed on his face, because his father said, "I'll let it go. You don't have to make up your mind right away. One thing you should do, though, if you're even halfway thinking about it, is poke around online and see what kind of money child-care providers or whatever they call 'em make. If you do decide to take it on, you'll want to get what you deserve."

"Makes sense," Marshall said. To his relief, Dad did leave him alone then. He chewed on it for a while, chewed on it without deciding one way or the other. He had Mom's number on his phone, of course. He could count on the fingers of one hand how often he'd used it since his folks broke up. Odds were she wouldn't even recognize his number if he did call her again.

The baby might be stillborn. It might be kidnapped by Gypsies—or even by Roma, if you wanted to be PC about baby thieves. All sorts of things might happen to keep him from needing to make up his mind. He might even sell some more stories. If he sold enough, he wouldn't need to worry about playing nanny to his mother's bastard.

Writers find inspiration and incentive wherever they can. Any excuse for sitting down in front of a keyboard and monitor instead of doing something—anything—else is a good one. Marshall was still very new to the game, but he'd already figured that out. And, for the next several days, he wrote a hell of a lot more than usual.

Bryce Miller had a fancy new Ph.D. in classics from UCLA, with all the rights and privileges appertaining to the doctorate of philosophy. Chief among those privileges, it seemed, was the privilege to starve.

He'd saved money from his TAships and research assistantships. His only real vice was books. As vices went, it was a cheap one. His old car was paid for. His apartment wasn't expensive. So he starved slowly, an inch at a time, instead of in a hurry.

He scoured the online *Chronicle of Higher Education*, Craigslist, monster.com, anything that might possibly land him an academic job. He sent out zillions of résumés, by e-mail and snailmail both. Nobody wanted anything to do with a new-minted classicist, even one who could also teach ancient history.

He wasn't fussy. He was desperate. If he ran out of money before he landed something, he'd have to move back in with his mother. Boomerang kids were a phenomenon of his generation before the supervolcano blew. There were more of them now, with the economy still on its back with its feet in the air and X's where its eyes ought to be. The idea humiliated him all the same. He *wasn't* a little boy any more, dammit, no matter how much his mother wanted to keep him one.

He sent his c.v. to every Catholic school in Los Angeles and Orange Counties. If anybody needed a Latin teacher, a Catholic school was likeliest to. Most of them didn't answer his queries. The ones that did either already had a Latin teacher they liked or didn't want any.

And so his alarm went off before six one morning. He had to

get out of bed to turn it off: a sensible precaution for anyone who slept as soundly as he did. He hopped in the shower, gulped bread and jam and coffee for breakfast, and drove downtown to the offices of the Department of Water and Power.

They had, or so their online ad said, an opening for a grant writer. The requirements were a bachelor's degree and three years of writing experience. He'd published his first poem almost exactly three years earlier. Fortunately, they didn't ask how much he'd made from his writing. Even if you put a cash value on the copies the journals paid in, his total earnings would barely touch three figures.

But they didn't. He'd got through that round of vetting. And here he was, at the DWP, taking a test along with several dozen other worried-looking people. The men and women ranged from his age up to their early sixties. Maybe a civil-service job wasn't exactly what they had in mind, either. It beat the hell out of no job at all, though.

They took the test in what looked like the lunchroom, though the food-serving part was closed off. Everyone had a stock of number-two pencils. It might have been the SAT all over again.

In came a plump woman in a burgundy polyester pantsuit his mother would have loved—he couldn't think of anything worse to say about it. She carried a fat manila envelope. "I'm Stella Garcia," she said. "I will be administering this assessment instrument. Before we begin, I want everyone to put their cell phone on the table in front of you, upside down and in the off position."

There were more ways to cheat on exams now than there had been back in the day, even if you did call them assessment instruments. Had anyone brought more than one phone? Would it help? Bryce hadn't. He wasn't hardened enough to this game. Besides, he had only one.

Mrs. Garcia—her ring flashed under the fluorescents—passed

out the exams facedown. "Do not turn them over and begin until I tell you to do so," she said. "You will have two hours precisely to complete them." She checked her own cell phone for the time, even though there was a clock on the wall behind her. "Begin!" It was eight on the dot, or near enough.

Bryce put his name, address, and e-mail on the front page of the booklet, then dug in. It *was* like the SAT English test: grammar, analogies, taking the meaning from passages. Only the passages were mind-numbing bureaucratese, not the fairly straightforward stuff on the SAT.

He didn't care. He aced standardized tests. He always had. And he could read bureaucratese, even if he didn't write it well. He filled in bubble after bubble.

One poor shlub strolled into the lunchroom at half past eight. Mrs. Garcia gave him a booklet and made him put his cell where she could see it. Bryce didn't figure him for serious competition.

But what about the woman who handed in her test at five to nine? Was she brilliant or hopeless? She walked out of the room before Bryce could make up his mind.

He finished about nine twenty. He was the sixth, or maybe seventh, to turn in the exam. Another guy handed his in a moment later. They walked out together. "What did you think?" the other guy asked once the door closed behind them. He was forty-five or so, heavyset, and needed a shave. He hadn't showered before he came in, either.

It had been easier than Bryce expected. He didn't want to say that, so he shrugged and answered, "Who knows? How about you?"

"I did the best I could," the older man said, which also might mean anything. He went on, "Hope I land the job. I'm gettin' awful sick of pork and beans, know what I mean?"

"Oh, man, do I ever!" Bryce said. "Not much out there these days."

"Not much? There's fuckin' nothin'," the other guy said. "Good luck to you, Jack—but not too much, no offense."

"Yeah, well, back atcha," Bryce replied. They swapped wry grins.

It was raining when Bryce went to his car. The only rain L.A. was supposed to get in later summer was the occasional thunder-shower when the monsoon slopped over the mountains from the desert to the east. This wasn't like that. It was chilly. Clouds blanketed the sky. It felt like December or February.

He turned on his wipers and his lights. He made sure he remembered to turn the lights off again when he got back to his apartment building. Calling AAA to come out and give you a jump was a pain in the ass.

Waiting in his mailbox were a couple of bills and a letter from a no-account university in Florida. It was a form rejection. He didn't even remember applying for a job there, but that proved nothing much. He'd sent out a hell of a lot of résumés, all right.

He carried the depressing snailmail up to his place. If he wanted to apply to some school in Minnesota or the Upper Peninsula in Michigan, he might have a decent chance of landing something. But he wouldn't have wanted to live in Minnesota or Michigan even before the supervolcano went boom. These days . . . Los Angeles was getting what would have been unseasonable rain. Minnesota and Michigan were getting what would have been out-of-season snow, though not all of what they'd got this past winter had ever melted. If you were into sled dogs, they weren't bad places to go. Otherwise? He shook his head. Next to those places, even moving back in with his mom looked, well, not so bad.

When he called Susan, he got her voice mail. He thumped his forehead with the heel of his hand. Classes at UCLA had already started. That didn't matter so much to him, not any more, but it did to her. She was finishing her diss on the eleventh-century Holy Roman Empire. And she had a TAship, so she was probably ramming *The Epic of Gilgamesh* down the undergrads' throats right this minute.

At the tone, he said, "Well, I took the DWP test. I guess I did okay. Call when you get a chance. Love you. 'Bye."

As he stuck the phone back in his pocket, he shook his head again, this time in slow wonder. Had they really been going together for three years? Longer than that now. He'd had a few random dates after Vanessa dumped him, but nothing that was going anywhere—till he met Susan Ruppelt. They'd just clicked.

One of these days, he'd ask her to marry him. He had no doubt she'd say yes. But he wanted to be able to support her before he did. Fathers-in-law with jobs—hers was a mechanical engineer—tended to look down their noses at unemployed sons-in-law.

She called back about four that afternoon. "Hi, hon," she said. "So it went all right?"

"It didn't seem that hard. Not as bad as the SAT," Bryce answered.

"How many other people were taking it?" she asked.

"Bunches. Fifty, maybe seventy-five. It was in this big lunchroom thing." Bryce sighed. Every job that got advertised drew swarms of people. He did his best to stay hopeful: "They've got to pick somebody. Maybe it'll be me."

"I hope it is." Susan paused. "I guess I hope it is. I mean, you worked so hard, doing what you wanted to do. Seems a shame if you don't get to use it."

"Welcome to the real world," Bryce said. "That's pretty much what my chairperson told me when I turned in the thesis. Hey, it was fun while it lasted."

"Yeah." Every day brought Susan closer to banging her head against the same wall. She tried to look on the bright side: "Like you said, somebody's going to get that job. You know how things are at the universities. When somebody retires or dies, half the time they just close the damn position. More than half."

"Tell me about it!" Bryce said bitterly. How many times had some classics department's chair or, more often, boss secretary signed a letter saying their slot wouldn't be filled after all? More than he cared to remember—he knew that.

"Well . . . Something good will happen. People got through the Great Depression. We'll get through this." Susan had a sunny temperament. She sometimes needed it, too, to put up with Bryce's spells of gloom.

"We didn't have the whole planet screwing us to the wall then, though," he said now. "It was just bank failures and stuff."

"They wouldn't have called it *just*," she said.

"That's 'cause they hadn't seen this," he returned. But she kept trying to cheer him up, and he let her think she had. Making her worry less about him actually did make him feel—some—better. It was convoluted, but it was there.

Two days later, he got an e-mail from the DWP asking if he could come back for an interview and more testing on the following Monday. He wrote back that he could. He'd made them think twice about him, anyhow. He'd already sent his confirmation before he wondered how much he honest to God wanted a real-world job.

More than he wanted to live with his mother ever again. That pretty much settled that.

"Yes, this was a large eruption, even by supervolcano standards— nearly six hundred cubic miles," Kelly Ferguson told her class at Cal State Dominguez Hills. "This was just about the size of the first Yellowstone eruption, more than two million years ago, and almost as big as the Mount Toba blast in Indonesia seventy-five thousand years ago." She paused. "Anybody remember how 'many times the Yellowstone supervolcano blew between that first big boom and this last one?"

Anybody remember? was a prof's shorthand for *How many of you did your reading?* A couple of tentative hands went up. Kelly pointed at one of them. The owner of the hand, a big, broad brown guy she guessed was a Samoan, said, "Uh, two?"

He didn't sound very sure, but he was right. She beamed at him. "Good!" she said.

He looked relieved. If she remembered how he'd done on the last quiz, he had reason to look that way. The State University was California's second tier, behind the University of California. Students here came in two kinds: the ones who couldn't get into the UC system, and the ones who couldn't afford it. Some of the latter bunch were as good as anybody who did get into the University of California. The others . . . mostly weren't. Kelly'd done enough TAing to know the kind of work UC students did. Too many of these kids couldn't come close to that standard.

Well, you did what you could with what you had. She went on, "Both those other eruptions were still enormous. Even the smaller one ejected about sixty-four cubic miles of rock and dust and ash. That's four times the size of the blast from Mount Tambora, back two hundred years ago, and Mount Tambora's the volcano that gave the United States and Europe what they called the Year Without a Summer." She glared out at them. "And anybody who mixes up Mount Tambora and Mount Toba is in big trouble, you hear? Mount Tambora is still there. One of these days, it'll go off again. What used to be Mount Toba is *Lake* Toba now—the volcano blew itself to hell and gone. One of these days, *it'll* go off again, too, but I pretty much promise *we* won't have to worry about it. We've got enough other things to worry about."

The kids laughed nervously, for all the world as if she were kidding. They scribbled notes. Some of them just recorded what she said, so they could listen to it again before the test. She'd always thought putting the material into her own words helped make it hers. She still did, but she'd come to see not everybody worked the same way. Recording sure was easier than taking notes.

"Okay," she said. "The smallest Yellowstone eruption was four times the size of the one from Mount Tambora—and Mount Tambora was pretty big for an ordinary volcano. How much bigger than that 'little' supervolcano eruption was this last one?"

She waited. She'd told them how many cubic miles of ejecta the Yellowstone supervolcano'd belched this last time. Now they had to remember that or find it in their notes and make the calculation. Calculators and cell phones came out. Doing math in your head wasn't quite so obsolete as writing in cuneiform, but it came close.

A girl in the front row indignantly hit what had to be the CLEAR ERROR button. Either she'd made a mistake or she didn't believe the answer she'd got. A skinny black guy tentatively raised his hand. Kelly nodded to him. "Nine times?" By the way he said it, he had trouble believing it, too.

But Kelly nodded again. "That's right," she said. The girl in the front row looked disgusted, so she must have thought a right answer was wrong. Well, it was pretty unbelievable, all right. "If you spread the ash and dust and rock evenly all over California, it would be about twenty feet deep."

The ones who wrote wrote that down. Of course, the ejecta weren't spread evenly. Lava and pyroclastic flows—the really dense stuff—stayed relatively close to the supervolcano caldera. But *relatively* was a relative term. Jackson, Wyoming, lay maybe sixty miles south of what had been the southern edge of Yellowstone National Park. Today, it was as one with Pompeii and Herculaneum. One of these centuries, it would probably astonish archaeologists.

There was a hell of a funny book, one whose author she couldn't remember, called *Motel of the Mysteries*. It was all about the stupid conclusions excavators with no cultural context would jump to when they dug up a twentieth-century motel. It also made you wonder how much of what you thought you knew about ancient Egypt was nothing but bullshit. Well, Jackson—and a good many other towns—would give future diggers their chance at dumbness.

A girl who could have been anything and probably was an L.A. mutt—a little bit of everything—raised her hand. "Question?" Kelly asked.

"Uh-huh," the girl said. "Somebody told me you were, like, *in* Yellowstone when the supervolcano went off. Is that right?"

"Um, no," Kelly answered. "If I'd been there then, I wouldn't be here now. Trust me on that one." The class laughed nervously. She decided she needed to say more: "I was part of a team of geologists doing research in the park while the supervolcano was ramping up. A couple of helicopters flew us out when things started looking really scary. We'd just landed in Butte, Montana, about two hundred miles away, when it blew. I was on the runway—I mean, we'd *just* landed. The earthquake knocked me over, and then the wind—the blast wave, if you want to think of it like that—blew out most of the windows in the terminal, blew me down the strip, and knocked my copter over on its side."

"From two hundred miles away?" the girl said. "Wow!"

"Wow," Kelly agreed. "Yeah, from two hundred miles away. It's—what?—eight hundred miles from Yellowstone to L.A., and you guys heard the blast here, right?" She knew Colin had. Hell, they'd heard it across the whole country. They'd heard it in Western Europe.

"We felt the quake, too," the girl replied. "We felt it before we heard the boom."

Kelly nodded. "You would have. Earthquake waves travel faster than sound."

"I thought the world ended," the skinny black kid said. "Way things're at right now, maybe I wasn't so far wrong, either. Snow in L.A.? If that ain't the end of the world, what is it? Anybody know for sure how long the cold weather's gonna last?"

Regretfully, Kelly shook her head. "Anywhere from a few years to a few hundred years. No one can tell you any closer than that. We've never had a supervolcano go off before when we were equipped to study it."

The big Samoan guy raised his hand. When Kelly pointed to him, he asked, "While you were in that helicopter just before the big eruption, were you, like, y'know, scared?"

"No shit!" Kelly blurted.

The undergrads burst into startled laughter. They didn't expect that kind of language from a prof, even one who wasn't all ancient and dusty. But what else could you say when somebody sent you a really silly question? Maybe they'd decide she was a human being after all. It might be too much to hope for, but maybe.

"You've got to remember, the hot spot under the supervolcano has been active a lot longer than it's been under Yellowstone—under what used to be Yellowstone." Kelly had loved the park, loved hiking in it, loved the geological formations without a match anywhere in the world. All gone now. The ecosystem would be tens—more likely hundreds—of thousands of years healing. "It started up under northeastern Oregon seventeen or eighteen million years ago. As the North American tectonic plate slid along on top of it, it erupted every so often across Idaho till it got to where it is now. The Snake River Valley follows the path of the eruptions pretty well."

A few of the kids looked impressed. Kelly knew damn well she was. A single geological feature active across so much time . . . The hot spot that created the Hawaiian chain had been around even longer. So had the collision between India and Asia that pushed up the Himalayas. Not a whole lot of things like that.

"There are a couple of museums in Nebraska full of beautifully preserved rhinoceros bones from eleven or twelve million years ago. The animals died around a water hole and got buried by the ash from one of the blasts when the hot spot was under Idaho." Kelly'd known about Ashfall Historical Park for a long time. You heard of it when you studied the Yellowstone supervolcano. Funny, though, that Bryce Miller'd seen bones from that excavation when he was in Lincoln. Funny also that Kelly, as Colin's new wife, should get to be friends with his daughter's ex-live-in. Rocks weren't the only things that laid down strata. So did relationships.

It was ten till twelve. She let the class go, warning them they'd get another quiz Friday. They gave the predictable groans as they trooped out.

She hoped she'd find an open gas station before she got home. If she didn't, she'd have to see how the bus lines worked before she left tomorrow. She'd have to see how long getting here by bus took, too. L.A. buses sucked—a technical term. But you did what you had to do . . . if you could do anything at all.

There'd been a boom in apartment buildings in San Atanasio—hell, in the whole South Bay—in the 1970s. Colin Ferguson, who'd lived there a long time, remembered when they were still pretty new. The two-story courtyards with the pools and the rec rooms and the underground parking garages had had an almost Jetsons kind of cool.

Well, platform soles and leisure suits weren't what they had been when you could wear them without irony. Neither were those apartment buildings. They got old. They got shabby. They got run-down. Young people on the way up stopped living in them till they could afford to buy a house.

Some of the folks who'd moved in a long time ago got old along with their apartments. Poorer people moved into other units. These days, the papers (when there were papers—the supervolcano'd almost finished the job the Net had started) always called San Atanasio a working-class community. That was the polite way to put it, anyhow.

This particular building had a bronze plaque out front that said MARSEILLE GARDENS. The stucco was faded and cracked and chipped. It needed a new paint job. The newest paint on it was a patch where someone had halfheartedly covered up graffiti. That must have been a while ago; fresh spray squiggles writhed across the cover-up.

The entrance and exit to the parking garage both reminded Colin of tank traps. There was a security door to get into the lobby and another one up the flight of stairs from the lobby to the courtyard.

Colin sighed as he got out of the unmarked cop car that was a privilege of his rank. "Another gorgeous spot," he said.

"Oh, hell, yes, man." Sergeant Gabe Sanchez scratched at his salt-and-pepper mustache. He kept it as bushy as regs allowed, and then a little more besides. Officious superiors got on his ass about it. Colin couldn't have cared less. Gabe made a hell of a good cop. Next to that, what was some face fuzz? Jack diddly, that's what.

A black-and-white had got there ahead of them. The red, yellow, and blue lights in the roof bar flashed one after another. In the glassed-off lobby, a uniformed cop was talking to a tiny, gray-haired woman who broke off every once in a while to cover her face with her hands. Seeing Colin and Sanchez, the cop waved. Colin nodded back.

Gabe Sanchez sighed. "Gotta do it," he said.

"I'll go in. You take a minute," Colin told him. Gabe sent back a grateful look. He lit a cigarette as Colin climbed the stairs to the lobby. San Atanasio was as aggressively smokefree as any other SoCal city. There would have been stereophonic hell to pay had the sergeant lit up inside the car. He smoked now in quick, fierce puffs. Colin knew he'd come along as soon as he got his fix.

When Colin walked into the lobby, the cop wearing navy blue said, "Lieutenant, this is Mrs. Nagumo—Kiyoko Nagumo. She's the one who called 911. Her sister is in apartment, uh"—he glanced at the notes he'd been taking— "apartment 71."

"Thanks, Pete." Colin turned to Mrs. Nagumo and showed his badge. "I'm Lieutenant Ferguson, Mrs. Nagumo. Your sister's name is Eiko Ryan?" There were still some Japanese in San Atanasio. There'd been more before a lot of them headed south to Torrance and Palos Verdes as blacks and Mexicans moved in. Quite a few had intermarried with whites. Some of the resulting names were a lot more amusing than this one.

Mrs. Nagumo said, "That's right. We were supposed to have lunch today. I called her. She didn't answer. I came over to see if she was okay. She's lived here ten years now, since her husband passed away."

"I see." Colin wondered how many times he'd heard stories like this. The Ryans had probably had a little tract house somewhere not far from here. After he died, even a little house might have seemed too big. Or the memories there might have hurt too much. But if Eiko Ryan wanted to stay independent, a place like this would have seemed pretty good. "What happened when you got here, ma'am?"

By the way Pete shifted from foot to foot, he'd already asked her that. Well, tough. "I buzzed. She didn't let me in. I rang for the manager. He knows me. He let me go in. I knocked on her door. Still nothing. I went back to the manager and asked him to open the apartment. I was afraid maybe she'd fallen or something." She was of an age—and her sister would be, too—where a fall was liable to mean a broken hip.

When she didn't go on, Colin gently prodded her: "What happened then, Mrs. Nagumo? Oh—and when was the last time you did talk with your sister?"

"It was last Friday. When we set up lunch. This is Wednesday, so—five days ago. Mr. Svanda, he complained, but he always complains. He did what I wanted him to do." Chances were, most people did. Mrs. Nagumo couldn't have been taller than four feet nine, but she had immense dignity. Her grief was all the more stark on account of it. "He opened the door . . . and we found her. In the bedroom. I called 911 then." A tear ran down her wrinkled cheek.

"Did you or Mr., uh, Svanda touch anything inside the apartment?" Colin asked. He wondered why he bothered. If this was another South Bay Strangler case, the bastard never left prints. He'd been raping and murdering little old ladies all through this part of L.A. County for years now, and nobody'd laid a glove on him.

"Nothing much, anyway," Kiyoko Nagumo said. "We watch TV. We know about fingerprints—oh, yes."

"Okay." Colin fought a sigh. Everybody watched TV—and everybody thought the cops always caught the bad guy right before the closing commercials. Real life, unfortunately, could be a lot messier and less conclusive. And real-life cops took the heat when it was.

"I've got a pretty good statement from her, Lieutenant," Pete said as Gabe Sanchez came up the stairs to join them. "If you want to have a look at the crime scene before the forensics guys and the coroner get here—"

"Yeah, I'll do that," Colin said resignedly. Mrs. Nagumo

started crying again. Hearing about the coroner must have reminded her her sister was dead.

The door up into the courtyard was open. People milled around there, the way they always did after something bad happened. A grizzled fellow limped up to Colin and Gabe. Like anyone with an ounce of sense, he knew cops when he saw them.

"I'm Oscar Svanda," he said. "My wife Glinda and me, we manage this building. I let Mrs. Ryan's sister into her place, and then we seen the poor lady's body." He crossed himself. He looked green around the gills, and well he might. Civilians rarely saw things like that, and rarely knew how lucky they were not to.

"Gabe, why don't you take Mr. Svanda's statement?" Colin said. "I do want to have a look at the apartment."

"Okay. I'll catch up with you." Gabe pulled a notebook from an inside pocket of his blue blazer. "You want to spell your last name for me so I make sure I have it right, Mr. Svanda . . . ?"

The other uniformed officer from the black-and-white stood at the door to apartment 71. She looked a trifle green herself. "Your first Strangler case, Heather?" Colin asked, understanding that all too well.

She managed a nod. " 'Fraid so, Lieutenant."

"Well, welcome to the club. Now you see why we hate the son of a gun so much," Colin said grimly. Heather nodded again, this time with more conviction.

He walked inside. The furniture was that furnished-apartment blend of tacky and functional. The Naugahyde covering on the dinette chairs had orange flowers; the couch and chair were upholstered in industrial-strength fabric with a really horrible red, white, and black plaid. But everything was scrupulously clean and neat.

A faint but unmistakable odor led him into the bedroom.

Eiko Ryan had been there two or three days, all right. Her long flannel nightgown was hiked up to her waist. Alive, she might have been an inch or two taller than her sister—which would have done her a hell of a lot of good trying to fight off the bastard who'd killed her.

Colin clasped his hands behind his back to make sure he didn't touch anything. It wouldn't matter, but he did it anyway. Habit was strong in him, and got stronger as he got older.

He heard some kind of commotion outside. He feared he knew what kind, too. Sure as hell, Heather called, "The reporters are here, Lieutenant."

"Oh, joy," Colin said, and went out to meet the press.

IV

Louise Ferguson felt as if she'd gone fifteen rounds with Mike Tyson, and he'd thrown nothing but body punches the whole time. They called it labor for a reason. She'd found that out when she'd had her first three kids. But she'd been in her early twenties then. Now she was old enough to be a granny. She felt every year of it, too, and about twenty more besides.

She lay on the bed, flicking the TV remote. Her roommate wasn't there—they were running some kind of test on her. She was a Korean gal who didn't speak a whole lot of English. When she was there, she kept stealing glances at Louise, as if to say *What the hell were you doing?* But the answer to that was only too obvious, wasn't it?

James Henry Ferguson—seven pounds, nine ounces; twenty-one and a half inches—wasn't there, either. They'd asked if she wanted him with her 24/7 or if he should stay in the nursery when she wasn't feeding him. She'd had Rob with her all the time. Despite her own exhaustion, she'd started at his every twitch and sneeze and wiggle. And she'd learned her lesson.

Vanessa and Marshall had stayed in the nursery. James Henry could damn well do the same thing.

Here was the local news. Living with Colin for so many years had given her a jaundiced view of it: blow-dried male robots and beauty-contest third runner-ups struggling to read from tele-prompters. The newsies didn't seem a whole lot smarter once she'd walked out on Colin, either.

But the headline behind this toothy blonde in a clinging red sweater was SOUTH BAY STRANGLER STRIKES AGAIN! Louise decided not to change the channel again. Colin had started chasing the Strangler while they were still married. He still hadn't caught him. Neither had any of the other South Bay police departments.

"Found dead in her San Atanasio apartment was Eiko Ryan, age seventy-nine," the newswoman said. "DNA analysis has not been completed, but the M.O. seems consistent with the notorious South Bay Strangler. Our Jerry Michaelson was on the scene."

Their Jerry Michaelson thrust a mike in Colin Ferguson's face. "What can you say about this latest Strangler atrocity, Lieutenant?" he asked excitedly.

"I don't want to say much of anything till the lab team and the coroner do their job," Colin answered.

"But it is a Strangler case, isn't it?" Michaelson persisted.

"Right now it looks like one. And that's about as much as I can tell you," Colin said.

Their Jerry Michaelson wasn't about to let him off so easily. "When will you catch this monster who's been terrorizing South Bay senior women for so long?"

"Believe me, there's nothing I'd like better." Colin's impatience was starting to show. He'd always had a short fuse with reporters. "If you've got any good ideas, I'd love to hear 'em."

Michaelson started to splutter. The news cut back to the studio. The blonde in the tight sweater deplored the cops' failure to apprehend anybody. She had a little trouble with *apprehend*, but managed almost well enough.

Then a Filipina nurse walked in, and Louise stopped worrying about the news. "How you feeling?" the young woman asked.

"Run over by a truck," Louise answered honestly.

The nurse's eyes widened. She laughed. "Oh, I bet you do," she said. "Having a baby not easy for anybody, harder when you get a little older." That was a polite way to put it. The nurse grabbed a gadget on a pole, stuck Louise's finger in a clip, and wrapped a cuff around her arm. The cuff inflated painfully tight, then relaxed. The nurse wrote in the chart.

"Well?" Louise always wanted to know what was what.

"Blood pressure good. Blood oxygen normal." The nurse stuck something in Louise's ear, then wrote again. "Temperature normal, too. You okay." *Except you're crazy.* She didn't come out with it, but it was written all over her face.

"Oh, boy." Louise fought a yawn. Then she didn't fight it any more. She'd earned the right to be worn out, by God! And she knew she'd better sleep while she had any chance at all. The baby sure wouldn't let her once she got home. She wanted a shower, too; she was all over greasy sweat. But she lacked the energy right now. Tomorrow would do.

"Epesiotomy hurt?" the nurse asked.

"It's starting to," Louise admitted. They'd given her a local down there while they sewed her up. It was wearing off now. One more delight of childbirth she'd managed to forget. If women remembered all the lovely details, they would never have more than one kid, and the human race would have vanished a long time ago.

"Father come see baby?" the nurse inquired.

"I doubt it." Louise's voice was colder than supervolcano winter in Greenland. If Teo had wanted anything to do with his oops of an offspring . . . If he'd wanted anything to do with the kid, a lot of things now would be different. But he damn well hadn't, and they damn well weren't. "I don't expect any visitors."

"No?" The Filipina girl's eyebrows rose. "Too bad. You have pretty baby."

Those things were relative. Newborn babies weren't the cute, laughing things they became in a few months. James Henry was very pink, he had next to no hair, and he looked like a Conehead because he'd got kind of squashed coming out. That he would look that way, at least, Louise had recalled.

Shaking her head, the nurse went away. The news was doing the weather report. It would be chilly and rainy. It was either chilly and rainy or just plain chilly most of the time. And L.A. had it way better than most of the country.

Dinner came. It was unexciting hospital food, a redundancy if ever there was one. Louise didn't care. In the classic phrase, she could have eaten a horse and chased the driver.

An attendant wheeled in the Korean lady in the other bed. She'd just got her tray when her husband showed up. They pulled the curtain and chattered in their own language, with occasional English words thrown in. It reminded Louise of Mr. Nobashi talking to Hiroshima, though neither side of this couple was in the habit of yelling, "Oh, Jesus Christ!"

Then Colin walked in.

Louise knew she looked like hell. She felt like hell, too. And she wasn't only sore and beat. All her hormones were working on emergency overdrive. It wasn't the ideal moment for a visit from an ex-husband, in other words.

"Come to gloat, did you?" she snapped.

His face never showed much. That was a useful attribute for a cop, but it had always irked her. His mouth did tighten a little; she'd managed to piss him off. "Well, I can always leave if you want me to," he said. "I heard you'd had the baby, and I wanted to see how you were doing."

"I'm trampled, that's how," Louise replied.

"I remember," he said. "But you're okay, and the kid is, too?" He waited for her to nod, then did the same himself. "Good. That's the only thing that really matters."

"Does Kelly know you're here?" Louise asked, a touch of acid in her voice.

"Uh-huh." Colin nodded again. "She gets that I wasn't rolled up in bubble wrap before we ran into each other. There's still stuff in my life from days gone by."

"Like the Strangler," Louise said.

His mouth didn't just tighten this time. It twisted. "Yeah. Like him."

"I'm sorry," Louise said. The rational part of her, what there was of it right this minute, knew she'd hit too hard. He'd done more for her after she got knocked up by the other man than an ex had to, more than most exes would have. The checks he'd sent really had helped her out.

"One of these days, I will catch him. I'll see they stick a needle in his arm, too," Colin said.

"I hope you do." Louise meant that.

"Marshall says maybe he'll come tomorrow." Colin shifted gears. "He was working on something now, typing away pretty fast."

"Okay." If Marshall wanted thing one to do with her, that would be an improvement. If he could be persuaded to help take care of the baby when she had to go back to work . . . She had hopes. "Will he really make a writer?"

"Believe it or not, I think stranger things have happened. Who woulda thunk it?" Colin awkwardly dipped his head. "Listen, I better get home. I did want to check on you, though. Take care of yourself, Louise." He lumbered out of the room.

Now, when she most wanted to sleep, Louise found she couldn't. The Korean couple on the other side of the curtain didn't bother her. They wouldn't have bothered her if they were speaking English. Memory had more weight. She was still wide awake when the Filipina nurse brought in James Henry. Louise set the baby on her breast. He rooted, then settled down and started to nurse.

Rank, they said (whoever the hell *they* were), had its privileges. Vanessa Ferguson thought blowing the FEMA dweeb was odds-on the rankest thing she'd ever done, but that also had its privileges. Every once in a while, for instance, Micah Husak let her use his computer. In Camp Constitution, with next to no electricity, that was more precious than rubies.

Or it would have been, had it done her any good. Before she moved to Denver, she'd banked with Wells Fargo. Had she kept her money there, she could have got at it here. She could have got the hell out of here, in fact. Even Fort Smith looked like heaven next to this.

But she'd gone native. She'd put her money into the Rocky Mountains Savings Bank. It paid higher interest. You could deal with human beings who actually seemed to care about what you wanted. It was local.

Yes, it was local. And there, as Hamlet said, was the rub. Wells Fargo had servers all over the country—all over the world, as far as Vanessa knew. The Rocky Mountains Savings Bank had servers in, well, Denver. Whoever'd set up their data system hadn't anticipated a supervolcano eruption burying the place in several feet of ash and dust.

And so, whenever Vanessa accessed their Web site, all she got was a '90s GIF of a couple of sawhorses and some yellow-and-black tape, with the all-caps legend UNDER CONSTRUCTION below it.

"Shit!" she snarled when she saw it yet again. By all the signs, that site would stay under construction till the day after doomsday. Her bank account was as one with Nineveh and Tyre ... and Denver.

Micah had himself wiped off and his trousers (as opposed to his cock) up again. He looked over her shoulder. "How unfortunate for you," he said.

She glared at him. "Yeah, you really think so, don't you? If I had the money to bail, you think I'd stick around here to get your rocks off?" She did what he wanted. She didn't have to waste time being polite about it.

Neither did he. "There are others," he answered, shrugging. And there were bound to be. Men wanted the pleasure women could give them. Some women would always give that pleasure in exchange for what they could get from the men they did it for. If that made them want to break every mirror they owned afterwards, hey, it was a rough old world.

There was a word for women who gave in exchange for what they could get. No cash changed hands in these transactions. Vanessa knew the word stuck to her all the same.

"You must have relatives you could get a loan from," Micah said.

She'd chewed on that before. Her father probably would front her the money to get back to California, or at least out of the camp. She'd had too much pride to ask him. She'd made her own way since she dropped out of college to try the real world instead. Asking him for anything would seem like failure.

So what exactly do you call sucking this guy's joint in exchange for a better tent and a chance to use the Net once in a while? she asked herself. But this was—or she'd always figured this was—temporary. Once she got the hell out of here, she could always pretend Micah Husak had never been born. Taking money from her old man was different. She wouldn't forget it. Neither would he.

"I don't want to do that," she said after a short pause.

"Evidently not." His smile showed off that half-missing front tooth. "Well, I can't say I'm sorry you don't."

It was a peculiar kind of smile, but she needed only a moment to recognize it. He didn't just get off on having her go down on him. Anybody could do that. He got off on having her go down on him even though—or rather, especially because—she hated it. She was acquainted with those complicated pleasures, too. They turned out to be less enjoyable when you were on the wrong end.

"I think I'd better go," she said, her voice thick with not-quite-suppressed fury. It was a good thing for the dweeb that they made you check your firearms before you walked into the FEMA building. Otherwise, he would have been lying on the floor with that nasty smile still on his face and with the back of his head blown out.

"Er—yes," he said. If her rage didn't give him pause, he was even dumber than she thought—and that was saying something. But he had, or figured he had, the whip hand, because he added, "I'll see you again before too long."

Vanessa grunted and got out of there as fast as she could. Doing what she wanted to do would make her happy now, but she'd be sorry for a long time later. No, she wouldn't be sorry. Nothing that happened to Micah Husak could make her sorry. But she didn't want to spend umpty-ump years in jail, either.

No? What do you call this place? Even jail food might be better than MREs. She tried not to think like that as she stormed down the corridor to the back door. Thinking like that *would* leave the dweeb dead and bleeding.

The big black guy who stood guard there studied her thoughtfully. "You sure I ought to give you back your piece right now?" he asked, doubt all over his voice and on his face. "Maybe everybody'd do better if you came back for it later."

"I'm okay," Vanessa said. And so she was, as long as she

didn't think about looking at Micah Husak's blind snake from eye-crossingly close range. Trying *not* to think about something, of course, was as impossible as usual. Grinding her teeth, she made herself go on, "I won't plug the son of a bitch no matter how much he deserves it."

"Huh." The guard seemed no happier. He explained why: "You don't want to go hurting yourself, neither. We got too much of that around here."

He had his reasons for worrying. The number of people at Camp Constitution and all the rest of the refugee centers near the edge of the ashfall line who took the long road out was a national shame and disgrace—or it was when the rest of the United States wasn't full of its own screams of anguish. The camps didn't—couldn't—even got noticed a lot of the time.

All the same, suicide wasn't on Vanessa's radar, not the way turning the dweeb into a colander was. "You don't need to worry about *that*," she assured the black man. "I wouldn't give him the satisfaction." She gave him other kinds of satisfaction: not just getting his rocks off but making her blow him when she would rather have blown him away.

"Well, okay," the guard said slowly. Even more slowly, he turned around, took her .38 out of its slot, and handed it back to her. "Don't you do anything silly, now, you hear?" He had a deep, buttery-rich voice, as if he ought to be singing gospel music instead of standing here in a polyester uniform and a Stetson.

"I won't," Vanessa answered reluctantly, because she really did feel as if saying that to him was like making a promise. It wasn't as if she'd never broken a promise or told a lie, but even so . . .

"Better not," he said. "That'd be a waste, you know?"

"What difference does any one person make?" Vanessa didn't try to hide her bitterness. "The whole country's been wasted. Hell, the whole *world's* been wasted." As soon as she saw the cloud of ash and dust from Yellowstone boiling toward Denver, she'd known nothing would stay the same any more. But she'd had no idea—no one had had any idea—*how* different from Before After would be.

"Jesus loves us any which way," the guard said. "You accept Him as your personal Savior, hon?"

Vanessa got out of there in a hurry without answering. She didn't want to talk about religion with him, or with anybody else. If he had one he was happy with, terrific. Groovy, even. But if he wanted to go around inflicting his beliefs on other people, that wasn't so terrific.

Of course, he might have tried inflicting himself on her, too, the way the damn dweeb had. That would probably come next. Well, she still had the revolver. And the way things looked, it was a damn good thing she did.

"Ooh-*wahh*!" James Henry Ferguson owned a voice like an air-raid siren.

"Shut up, you little bastard," Marshall Ferguson said. His mother—and James Henry's—wasn't there to disapprove of his literal accuracy. It wasn't feeding time at the zoo yet—pretty soon, but not quite yet. Marshall went into the bedroom to find out why his tiny half-brother had ants in his pants.

Only it wouldn't be ants. It would be something a lot more disgusting than ants. What babies could do to breast milk and formula . . . Guys made gross-out jokes all the way from second grade through high school. Dealing with genuine, no-shit shit, though, was something the guys making those jokes mostly didn't know thing one about.

Marshall stuck a finger in there. He pulled it out slimy and yellow-brown. This wouldn't be the first diaper he'd changed on his half-brother. His stomach still lurched as if the plane of his life had hit an air pocket every time he did it, though.

James Henry wiggled aimlessly while Marshall got him out of the soiled Huggy and cleaned crap off his bottom. Eventually, Mom said, he'd be able to fight back when he got changed. He hadn't figured that out yet, though. *Something else I get to look forward to,* Marshall thought gloomily.

What he did look forward to was getting paid. He was still writing. He hadn't sold anything since he graduated, though. His father wasn't on his case about it. Dad didn't need to be. Marshall was on his own case.

Before he could even close the new diaper's tapes, his half-brother peed in it. Marshall kept a piece of cloth over his middle. He'd got it in the face once, but only once. He learned fast, if not quite fast enough.

"Well, piss," Marshall muttered. Piss it was, all right. He rolled up the new diaper and chucked it into the plastic pail after the other one. The sack inside was filling fast. The reek of stale urine got him in the nose again. Baby poop didn't stink as much as what grown-ups produced.

One more diaper went onto James Henry's bottom. The kid didn't ruin this one before Marshall could get it all the way on to him. A good thing, too, as far as Marshall was concerned. There was talk the authorities would stop letting disposable diapers come into L.A. They took up room that could go to food and fuel instead.

Marshall eyed the baby. "What do I do then?" he asked, not altogether rhetorically. Oh, he knew the answer: cloth diapers and safety pins, right out of *Ozzie and Harriet* and *The Lucy Show*. But how were you supposed to fasten those without sticking the kid who was wearing them? If the disposables stopped coming, he'd damn well find out.

He picked up James Henry. The baby had a lot of coal-black hair. He was swarthier than Marshall or Vanessa or Rob— swarthier than Mom, too. Anybody would think his father was Mexican or something.

Changing him changed the note on which he cried, but didn't shut him up. Marshall pulled out his phone. Yeah, now it was feeding time at the zoo, all right. He carried James Henry into the kitchen. Mom had expressed—that was the word she used for it—enough breast milk to keep the little bugger from starving before she got home.

Marshall heated it in the microwave, waited till it cooled down some, and poured it from measuring cup to bottle. James Henry ate, but he wasn't enthusiastic about it. Marshal didn't figure *he* would have been, either. Given a choice between a rubber nipple and the real thing, he would have taken the McCoy every time.

But his half-brother didn't have the choice, not with Mom back at work. He didn't refuse his bottle; he just didn't like it as well as a tit. After he finished, Marshall got a hell of a burp out of him. If James Henry had known the alphabet, he could have made it at least to R. A guy who'd chugged a couple of cans of Coors would have been proud of this one.

After chow, the baby showed signs of sacking out again. Marshall stuck his finger inside the diaper. James Henry was dry. "Yesss!" Marshall said. Changing him again might have perked him up. This way . . .

Settling in a rocking chair, Marshall went forward and back for a while. His half-brother's eyes sagged shut. He rocked for a few minutes longer to make sure the kid was good and out. Then he rose and carried James Henry back to the crib.

Down the baby went, on his back. Marshall and his older brother and sister had gone into their cribs on their stomachs. That was what the experts back then had said you should do. Now they said this. By the time James Henry was raising his own kids, they might change their minds again.

Getting him into the crib was always the tricky part. If he woke up and started to scream . . .

SUPERVOLCANO: ALL FALL DOWN | 71

But he didn't. Marshall breathed a sigh of relief. Now he had his own life back till James Henry woke up again. The first thing he did was make himself a sandwich. He thought *Blondie* was one of the lamest comics in the paper, a relic from the days when Hearsts and Pulitzers and other dinosaurs roamed the earth. No matter what he thought, the monster he concocted out of leftovers, lunch meat, cheese, lettuce, tomatoes, jalapeños, and anything else in the fridge that looked interesting would have turned Dagwood Bumstead green with envy.

He attacked his creation like an anaconda engulfing a half-grown tapir. For a few anxious seconds, he wondered if his first bite would go down. It did, and he used a little more restraint with the ones that followed.

After the sandwich disappeared, he wondered if he should fix another one. He contented himself with potato chips, and washed them down with about a liter of Coke. He'd talked Mom into getting some of the real stuff for him. She might worry about her weight, but he stayed skinny without effort.

Once he stopped feeling peckish, he fired up his laptop and started noodling on a story. He didn't know how much he could do before his half-brother woke up again, but anything was better than nothing. He'd already saved in the middle of a sentence more than once.

When he started trying to write stories, he'd counted on red-hot inspiration to sweep him along to the end. Inspiration was great. You needed it to get ideas to begin with. It could sweep you along—for a while. But you had to keep going even after it ran out. Otherwise, you wouldn't finish very much.

And you had to polish what did come out of the mill. It wasn't just about art. It was about craft, too. They talked less about craft in creative-writing classes than they should have. It was like cooking, except you had to figure out all the recipes for yourself.

He worked till he got tired of staring at the words on the monitor. Then he worked another twenty minutes on top of that so the Colin Ferguson he carried inside his head couldn't growl *Quitter!* at him. His actual flesh-and-blood father was a good deal more easygoing than the virtual one who ordered him around. Maybe his construct was tougher than the genuine article. Maybe Dad had been harder on him when he was younger. Or maybe marrying Kelly had mellowed his father out. Who the hell knew?

Whatever the answer was, Marshall would have worked longer yet if James Henry hadn't started crying again. Marshall checked him. He was wet but not poopy. Into the pail went the Huggy. Marshall got the new one on him and closed up before he could ruin it.

After that, Marshall went back to the rocker and held him for a while. His half-brother wasn't smiling yet. He just stared up at Marshall. He looked confused, the way he did a lot of the time. Who could blame him, either? Babies didn't have to figure out anything so comparatively simple as how to be a writer. They needed to work out how they were supposed to turn into human beings. Even if there were manuals explaining it all, they couldn't have read them.

"If you start squawking again, I'm gonna feed you early," Marshall said. Mom would get bent out of shape at him for screwing up James Henry's schedule. Marshall didn't care. A wailing baby drove him battier than fingers on a chalkboard. If Mom didn't like it, she could damn well hire somebody else.

But James Henry didn't squawk. He kept looking at Marshall. Nobody'd ever thought Marshall was that interesting before. The baby made little squeaky noises.

Marshall didn't even notice the door open. There stood Mom, looking tired but smiling. "Aww," she said.

That broke the spell. James Henry might be able to charm

Marshall. His mother didn't stand a chance. "He hasn't had dinner yet," Marshall said, all business now. "He'll probably want it pretty soon, though. He did okay with lunch. I changed him whenever he needed it."

"Thank you," Mom said. "Do you want to stay for dinner? I've got enough ground round to make us both hamburgers."

"That's okay. I'll see you tomorrow morning." Marshall got out of there as soon as he politely could, or else a little sooner. He'd take Mom's money and help her out of a tight spot. Past that, though, he didn't want anything to do with her.

The sun was setting in the usual Technicolor splendor when he walked out to his car. The wet-dust smell of rain filled the air, as it did so often these days. He was getting used to both the gorgeous sunsets and sunrises and the crappy weather. Eventually, he supposed, he'd forget things had ever been any other way. So would everyone else his age. And people like James Henry wouldn't even know things had changed.

Louise Ferguson didn't mind too much when James Henry woke up once in the night. She could even deal with twice. She was tired enough, going back to sleep was no big deal.

But three or four times . . . That wore you down. That had worn her down even when she was half her current age. She remembered. And it was more than doubly tough now that she'd reached her present state of decrepitude. Caffeine helped, but only so much. She didn't know what she would have done if coffee hadn't started tasting good to her again. Cocaine and crank were uppers, too, but she'd stayed married to Colin too long to look at anything illegal.

When the baby left her really exhausted, she thought that was a goddamn shame.

Mr. Nobashi gave her a fishy stare when she sat down at her desk in Ramen Central. "You good, Mrs. Ferguson?" he asked.

What he did to her last name was a caution. It sounded like *Fugu-san*, as if she were an honorable puffer fish.

"*Ichi-ban*, Mr. Nobashi," she answered. He giggled, so her Japanese was probably even lousier than his English. Well, too bad. She was also lying through her teeth—she was a long way from being A number one.

Ichi-ban or not, she could do the job. Riding herd on noodles and flavoring packets was a hell of a lot easier than taking care of a baby, as a matter of fact. She hadn't exactly missed it while she was having the kid, but she didn't mind coming back to it.

She also didn't mind when Mr. Nobashi started yelling for coffee and sweet rolls, just as if she'd never left. If he was dead set on jitters and Type 2 diabetes, she'd lend a helping hand.

Patty came by and asked, "Everything okay?" in her harsh Midwestern tones.

"Could be worse," Louise answered.

"I bet," the other woman said. "So, who's taking care of Junior now that you're back here?"

"One of my sons. He needs money, and I need a babysitter. It works out."

Patty nodded. "That's handy, anyways. You prolly don't gotta pay him as much as you would if you hired somebody from an agency or somewheres, either."

"I wish!" Louise exclaimed. "It's cash on the barrelhead with Marshall."

"Sharper than a serpent's tooth is an ungrateful child, the Good Book says," Patty clucked. "It knows what it's talking about, too. It mostly does."

"I guess," Louise said uncomfortably. She'd ditched her family's stern Presbyterian faith a long time ago. Despite endless New Age experiments, though, she'd never found anything that really filled the gap. Her kids seemed to get along fine with Nothing, but she couldn't. She wanted Answers, dammit. As the old TV show said, the truth was out there.

Somewhere. She was sure of it. Where was a different question, and one of the Answers she hadn't found. Yet.

To her relief, Patty didn't push it. Louise couldn't stand people who liked their religion so much they tried to sell you on it, too. There she agreed with her ex, and with her children. She couldn't think of many other places where they were all in accord.

What had felt strangest about coming back was how normal it seemed. She knew the inventories she needed to ride herd on. She hadn't seen the latest and greatest numbers since she went on maternity leave, but they were in ranges and patterns she found familiar.

The more it changes, the more it stays the same. There was a reason clichés got endlessly repeated. They were the ramen of thought: quick, easy, and filling, but without much real nourishment.

She remembered how to ride herd on Mr. Nobashi, too. He'd changed even less than the inventories. He still spent a lot of the time on the phone, spewing impassioned Japanese laced with English profanity. Louise presumed he was talking to the home office in Hiroshima, but for all she could prove he might have been getting bets down with his bookie. She knew a few Japanese words and phrases—anybody who'd lived in San Atanasio for a while picked them up, the same way Southern Californians generally had fragments of Spanish even if their folks came from Denmark—but she didn't speak the language.

Mr. Nobashi was just hanging up when she brought him coffee a few minutes before quitting time. "Thank you," he said, which, along with his bad language, proved he was getting Americanized. A boss in Japan, from everything Louise had heard, would take getting waited on for granted.

"You're welcome," Louise said to encourage him.

He gulped sugary caffeine and smacked his thin lips. "I talk with Hiroshima," he said. "Very bad weather, Hiroshima. Cold like nobody remember."

"Here, too," Louise agreed. "Snow!" Like any good Angeleno, she said it as if it were a word for people in other, less lucky, parts of the world. And so it had been, till the supervolcano went off. "Not just snow, either. Rain all year long! It's ridiculous!"

"Snow in Hiroshima, too," Mr. Nobashi said. "Snow now. Crops in Japan very bad this year."

"Crops everywhere are bad this year," Louise said. In most of the American Midwest, there were no crops. Dust and ash buried much of what had been the world's breadbasket. Even where it didn't, the horrible weather the supervolcano had caused screwed up crops and shortened growing seasons.

"*Hai,*" Mr. Nobashi said. "Not much wheat—and cost so much! Oh, Jesus Christ! Company have trouble afford."

It sounded as if the price of ramen would go up. The price of everything had gone up as if inflated with helium. College students would particularly mourn this bump, though.

Mr. Nobashi eyed the clock on his wall. "You go home," he told Louise, even if it was early. "You got to be tired."

"Thank you, Mr. Nobashi!" She bailed out before he had the chance to change his mind.

Marshall was changing James Henry's diaper when Louise walked into the condo. "Good job," she said, to encourage him. "You're doing super with him. No diaper rash or anything."

"Yeah, well, when he's wet or stinky I deal with it," he answered, and she could hear the shrug in his voice. He washed his hands, grabbed his laptop, and headed for the door. "See you in the morning."

"Marshall—" Louise began. He paused, but his face didn't open. She swallowed a sigh. "Never mind. I'll see you tomorrow."

Out he went, not quite slamming the door behind him. No, he hadn't forgiven her for leaving Colin. Odds were he never would. She'd tried to explain how stifled she'd felt while she was married to his father. She'd tried, and heard herself failing. He didn't understand, or want to.

Louise sighed. Yes, she'd lost the children, and she couldn't do a damn thing about it. She'd hoped Vanessa would get it, but Vanessa's own troubles were the only ones that were real to her. James Henry made a baby noise, halfway between a gurgle and a burp. Louise picked him up and cuddled him. He couldn't even smile yet, but she didn't care. He'd love her no matter what.

For a while, anyhow.

V

"I've got a job for you, Colin," Mike Pitcavage said. He didn't look like a police chief. He looked like a national news anchor, or maybe a Senator who was thinking about running for President. He was tall and fit and tan, with a full head of iron-gray hair. He wore custom-made Italian suits, not the off-the-rack stuff most cops—Colin included—put on every day.

Colin didn't even particularly resent him for winning the chief's job, though he'd put in for it himself. Pitcavage could make nice, a talent Colin knew he lacked. You could get by as a lieutenant if people saw what you really thought of them. When you had to deal with the mayor and the city council all the damn time, that didn't fly any more.

"What's up?" he asked, looking across the desk at Pitcavage.

The desk was about the size of an aircraft-carrier flight deck. It was almost entirely bare. The only things on it were two framed photographs, one of Pitcavage's wife, the other of his son. Caroline was a nice gal. She wasn't a trophy wife or anything; they'd been married a long time. Colin's opinion of Darren Pitcavage was rather lower. If he weren't a prominent cop's kid . . .

But he was, so the drunk-driving charge quietly got reduced to speeding. That fight in the bar? People said the other guy threw the first punch. There'd been something that had to do with vandalism, too, but that also didn't stick. Darren was even better-looking than his old man, but his eyes didn't seem to want to meet the camera.

Mike Pitcavage opened a desk drawer, took out a piece of paper, and slid it across the desk at Colin. "We've got a big oil tanker coming into San Pedro next week," he said. "The crude will go to the refineries in El Segundo. All the impacted departments will participate in security arrangements. I want you to take leadership in San Atanasio."

Before Colin said anything, he took a long look at the paper. Then he clicked his tongue between his teeth. "So this oil is for South Bay police departments? How'd we manage that?"

"We managed, with some help from the politicians. Trust me—you don't want to know the gory details," Pitcavage answered.

Colin believed him. The world seemed to get dog-eat-doggier every day. With more and more people grabbing for less and less, where was the surprise in that? "San Pedro's part of Los Angeles. I don't see the LAPD mentioned here anywhere."

"No, and you won't, either." The San Atanasio police chief looked sly.

"Huh," Colin said. A narrow strip of territory—part of it ran just east of San Atanasio—connected San Pedro to the rest of L.A. The port helped make Los Angeles a great city; it had for more than a hundred years. "So, are we going to have to protect this crude from the L.A. cops, then?"

"They aren't supposed to know about the tanker," Pitcavage said.

"And then you wake up!" Colin exclaimed. The chief looked blank. Colin put it in words of one syllable: "What are the odds of that?"

"We've made the necessary arrangements," Pitcavage insisted. How many bureaucrats had been persuaded to look the other way and keep their mouths shut? How much had it cost?

"If LAPD does find out, we're liable to have a war on our hands." Colin meant it literally. The *To protect and to serve* boys were as hard up for gasoline as anybody else. If they found out this big shipment was coming into their port, under their noses, and all earmarked for other people, there'd be stereophonic hell to pay.

"Well, that's one of the reasons I want you in charge of our part of the security," Chief Pitcavage answered. "You've got the military experience we need."

To Colin's way of thinking, a hitch in the Navy didn't exactly equate him to General Patton (although one might work wonders for Darren Pitcavage). He could see that saying so would do him less than no good, though. Swallowing a sigh, he asked, "This takes priority over . . . ?"

"Everything," Pitcavage said flatly.

"Including the Strangler case?"

"Everything includes everything," the chief said. "If we don't get our hands on this gas, pretty soon we'll we chasing the damn Strangler on skateboards and scooters."

It wasn't *that* bad. Colin knew it, and Pitcavage had to know it, too. Civilians could still buy—some—gas. But the price went up every day. The supervolcano had wrecked refineries and pipelines. The spasmodic nuclear war in the Middle East had knocked production over the head. If the South Bay towns had to pay anything close to retail for the fuel their cops used, they wouldn't be able to do much else. Thus—Colin supposed—this skulduggery.

"Well, I'll do it," he said: the only possible reply. "And I'll make damn sure I've got Gabe Sanchez right beside me."

"However you want it." Something in Pitcavage's voice told

Colin he'd just lost points with the chief. Gabe was too . . . too unpolished, that was the polite word, to stand high on Mike Pitcavage's gold-star list. Gabe didn't worry about it; he loved his *capo di tutti capi*, too. Colin didn't worry about it, either. If Pitcavage needed him so bad, he'd have to live with Gabe. And he evidently did.

Something else occurred to Colin: "Whatever we've bought the SWAT team in the way of heavy weapons, I want that, too."

The chief frowned, plainly trying to remember. "I know we've got some military rifles that'll fire full auto. We may have a real machine gun. If we do, nobody's taken it out of storage except maybe to clean it for a hell of a long time."

Colin nodded; he also couldn't remember the San Atanasio PD hauling out a machine gun. God, the paperwork that would have taken! But, as the man said, the times, they were a-changin'. No, they'd a-changed.

"Let me have the Door-Knocker, too," he said. "I'll lead the parade with it."

"There you go!" He actually made Pitcavage grin. "You got it." The Door-Knocker was a Ford Explorer armored against small-arms fire, with a ram sticking out from the front of the hood and with vision slits and firing slits for the cops inside. A do-it-yourself armored car, in other words. It was ugly as sin, but terrific for smashing down barricaded entryways to crack houses, meth labs, and lots of other places where the bad guys really didn't want company.

"Okay," Colin said, anything but sure if it was. "Let me get my people together, and I'll see what kind of toys we have in the playroom. When does this tanker get in?"

"Next Tuesday," the chief answered. "Our convoy of trucks will exit the 110 at Braxton Bragg Boulevard. You'll meet them at the exit ramp and escort them west through the city before handing off to the Hawthorne PD."

"Right." Colin had to hope it would be. His opinion of the neighboring department was not high. Hawthorne was full of gangbangers, and its cops were chronically underfunded. "I'm worrying about the LAPD, but they'll have to make sure the Crips don't hijack our crude."

"Lord knows the Crips get into all kinds of shit, but I don't think they have a rogue refinery." Pitcavage grinned to show he'd made a joke.

He thought he had, anyhow. The Crips wouldn't have to turn the crude into gas and motor oil to get value for it. All they'd have to do was steal it and threaten to light a match. How big a ransom could they squeeze out of people if they did that? Big. Big, big, big. Colin could see as much. Could Mike Pitcavage? It didn't seem so. He might be able to make nice, but he had all the imagination of a cherrystone clam.

Well, when he wore a uniform instead of Giorgio Armani, he had the row of stars on either side of his collar. He knew where to find a guy with imagination, and knew how to give him orders. Which he'd gone and done.

"I'll get on it," Colin said.

The first thing he did, of course, was tell Gabe Sanchez. The sergeant pursed his lips and blew out through them. It might have been a whistle without sound or an exhalation without a cigarette. "We've got the fix in good, huh?" he said when Colin finished.

"Sure sounds that way." After a meditative moment, Colin added, "We'd damn well better."

"Boy, you can sing that in church!" Gabe agreed. "The LAPD doesn't know thing one about it, huh?"

"Not Thing One, and not Thing Two, either." How many times had Colin read his kids *The Cat in the Hat*? A zillion, at least. "That's what the heap big boss says, anyway."

"Could get interesting if he's wrong," Sanchez observed.

"That also crossed my mind, as a matter of fact. I have the feeling it crossed Mike's mind, too. Which is why we meet the tanker trucks loaded for bear."

"Yeah!" Gabe sounded enthusiastic. He might have rough edges, but he didn't know how to back up. "Wonder what an LAPD squad car'd look like after it ran into the Door-Knocker." By the way he said it, he couldn't wait to find out.

"Mm, the idea is for the Door-Knocker to run into stuff, not the other way around," Colin reminded him.

"Details, details." Gabe waved that aside. "Can't wait to see the L.A. cops' faces when they find out we've got the goods and they don't."

"If everything works right, they won't find out," Colin said. Gabe shrugged, as if to note that everything never worked right.

Tuesday dawned chilly and rainy, as too many days in San Atanasio had since the eruption. If this was what Seattle had been like before the supervolcano went off, all the Californicators who'd moved to the Northwest got what they deserved. Only now SoCal was getting it, too.

Rain or no rain, Colin and his armed party took their stations on the Braxton Bragg Boulevard overpass to the Harbor Freeway, waiting for the precious petroleum convoy to come up from the south. Gabe Sanchez stood by the rail, the hood to his plastic poncho shielding his face well enough to let him smoke. Colin had his own share of bad habits and then some. He didn't know how he'd missed tobacco, but he had.

Watching Gabe crush one cigarette under his shoe and then light another, he wondered what would have happened if people had discovered the filthy weed about 1950 instead of way the hell back when. He didn't need to wonder long. He was convinced governments all over the world would have outlawed it as a dangerous, addictive drug. And, no doubt, bad guys would be growing it on secret farms right this minute and making stacks of illegal cash off it. There'd be books and earnest, concerned TV movies and obscene hip-hop records glorifying the cigar dealer. . . .

He shook his head. Gabe saw the motion. "What's up?" he asked, breathing out smoke.

"Nothing." Colin's speculation left him faintly embarrassed. Gabe would only guffaw. "Just woolgathering."

Before Gabe could come up with any more blush-worthy questions, a uniformed cop called, "Won't be long now. They're moving past the Goodyear Blimp's mooring mast. Five, ten minutes."

"Gotcha, Jimmy," Colin said. "Tell 'em we're ready and waiting as soon as they get off the freeway." He walked over to another black-and-white and asked the man inside, "Anything interesting going on on the LAPD frequencies?" Monitoring the enemy was always a good idea when you were at war.

The San Atanasio policeman wore headphones to help him monitor the radio without interference from the freeway's unending whoosh and roar. Colin had to repeat his question, louder the second time. Then the fellow answered, "Everything seems pretty quiet. Maybe the fix really is in."

"Here's hoping." Colin still had trouble believing it. He turned east, toward the offramp the fuel trucks would use. A couple of minutes later, a Torrance police car—part of the advance guard, no doubt—pulled off. The cops inside waved when they saw the waiting San Atanasio police officers. Colin waved back.

"Uh-oh!" exclaimed the cop monitoring LAPD radio traffic. "Cars on the way to Braxton Bragg Boulevard and the 110."

Which was where they were. And the entrance to the southbound freeway was west of the one coming up from San Pedro. They could block the tanker trucks if they got here soon enough. The freeway ran through the L.A. strip, too—the LAPD had all the jurisdiction here it needed.

Here came the first precious tanker. And here, sirens screaming and light bars blazing, came three LAPD police cars. Sure as
hell, they positioned themselves to block the westbound lanes of
Braxton Bragg Boulevard. Uniformed men with riot guns piled
out of them.

"Get out of the way!" Colin yelled.

"Like hell we will!" an LAPD man yelled back, hefting his
shotgun.

"Sonny, we will fucking bury you if you don't get out of the
way *right now*," Colin assured him, waving toward the Door-
Knocker. As if on cue, the machine gun they'd found in storage
and mounted on it swung to cover the LAPD man, who wasn't
wearing a helmet. His bulletproof vest might stop a rifle-caliber
round, but *might* wasn't something you really wanted to test.

"You wouldn't dare." The Los Angeles cop's voice wobbled;
he wasn't altogether convinced they wouldn't.

Colin was convinced he would. A police force couldn't function without fuel—Mike Pitcavage was dead right about that.
Horses and bikes and shoe leather didn't cut it, not in L.A.
County, they didn't. "This is our oil. We'll do whatever we need
to do to keep it," he answered. The fuel trucks were piling up on
the offramp. The LAPD guys would already be screaming for
their SWAT team and other reinforcements. "Get out of the way.
Last warning! We'll clear you out if you don't."

About then, the LAPD officer noticed that the San Atanasio
cops were toting M16s, not shotguns. Colin waved to the Door-
Knocker again. It rumbled forward with intent to squash.

"You people are fucking insane!" the L.A. cop bleated.

"Yeah? And so?" Colin answered.

The LAPD guy called him something that would have made a
CPO with twenty-five years in the Navy blanch. With far less
time in the service, Colin only laughed. On came the Door-
Knocker, inexorable as fate. Still swearing a very blue streak, the

LAPD cop dove back into his squad car and got it out of the way just before the Door-Knocker did the job for him.

As the other LAPD black-and-whites also opened a lane so the fuel trucks could go west, young man, Colin posted armed San Atanasio officers on the southbound offramp from the 110 to Braxton Bragg Boulevard. "Make 'em run over you if they want to get past you," he told his troops—that was how he thought of them. "And if they look like they want to run over you, shoot first. Got it?"

"Got it!" the San Atanasio cops roared in testosterone-fueled unison. Colin hadn't taken any female officers on this particular run. He wanted the headstrong craziness that could only come with a pair of balls.

It was maybe half a mile, maybe a little less, from the freeway to New Hampshire Avenue, where the L.A. strip ended and San Atanasio's jurisdiction actually began. One by one, the fuel trucks followed the Door-Knocker through the gap. San Atanasio cop cars went through, too. They looked a lot like LAPD cars, but the guys inside them were grinning. The Los Angeles policemen ran the gamut from glum to homicidal.

San Atanasio police cars looked a lot like L.A.'s *now*. Old-timers had told Colin about a '70s experiment that, for some reason, didn't last. The city painted its cars a color it called lime yellow—a bureaucrat's weaseling name for chartreuse. And it slapped POLICE on their sides in enormous diffraction-grating letters.

He'd seen photos, too. But he'd believed the old-timers even without them. Some shit was just too weird to make up. And a decade responsible for Grand Funk Railroad *would* have to answer for lime-yellow cop cars with rainbow letters as well.

After the last tanker truck rumbled off the freeway and through the LAPD's would-be roadblock, Colin turned to Gabe Sanchez and said, "Piece of cake."

Gabe scratched his thick, bushy mustache. "L.A. cops'll call it a piece of something else," he said with unusual delicacy.

"Too bad," Colin answered. "C'mon. Let's go. I want to be leading the parade again when we hand off to the Hawthorne guys."

They got into their unmarked Ford. Colin waved sweetly to the guys from the LAPD as they went by. At least three Los Angeles policemen flipped him off in reply. He smiled even wider—he gave them a shit-eating grin, if the truth be known—and went right on waving. As long as they didn't open fire on him, everything was jake.

Gabe drove with a splendid disregard for what little traffic there was. "Who's gonna write me a ticket, huh?" he demanded.

"Not me, dude," Colin said.

At the border between San Atanasio and Hawthorne, one of the latter town's finest asked him, "You get any trouble from LAPD?" By the way one eyebrow quirked, he already knew the answer. Well, he would. Every LAPD radio frequency would have been sulfurous. And the Hawthorne cops would have monitored the scanners just so they could stay informed, of course. Yeah, of course.

Colin shrugged and jerked a thumb at the Door-Knocker. "They didn't want to see whether we really would have shot them up and knocked them out of the way."

The guy from Hawthorne studied him. "I think they worked out the answer on their own."

"Maybe." Colin shrugged again. "The trucks are your babies now. Take good care of 'em. Tell the El Segundo guys the same thing when you make the handoff."

"Will do," the Hawthorne officer promised. Like Colin, he wore a suit not too new and not too stylish. If you became a cop to get rich and look cool, you were more than a few boulders short of a rock pile.

Or maybe you were Mike Pitcavage. Colin reported back to the elegant chief of the San Atanasio PD after the Hawthorne cops took charge of the fuel trucks. On the other side of his flight-deck desk, Pitcavage nodded. "Yeah, that pretty much matches the complaint I got from LAPD," he said, and then stood up and stuck out his hand. "Good job, Colin."

He was manicured, too. Colin noted as much as he shook with the chief. Just as you'd expect, Pitcavage had a smooth, firm grip. "Sometimes us small-town boys can surprise the city slickers," Colin said, putting on a cornpone drawl.

"There you go. They want to draw you and quarter you and put your pieces at the city gates to warn off anybody else who gets ideas like that," Pitcavage said.

"What did you tell 'em?" Colin wondered if he'd get thrown to the wolves, a sacrifice to the great god Petroleum.

But Pitcavage answered, "I said, if they wanted to try it, they'd have to do me first."

"Thanks." Colin sounded less dry than usual. Yes, he'd wondered whether Pitcavage would grab the chance to hang him out to dry. He'd been a rival for the leather swivel chair the chief sat in now. He didn't want it any more, but Pitcavage didn't know that, and probably wouldn't believe it if he found out. Ambitious himself, he'd always figure everybody else was, too. But here he'd done everything a subordinate could want from his CO. After a momentary pause, Colin asked, "What did they say when you told 'em that?"

"They told me to fuck myself in the ass. They said they'd drive spikes through a telephone pole, and I could use that." Pitcavage grinned. "They were righteously pissed off."

"I guess," Colin agreed. "If they're that up in arms, are they really so low on gas themselves? They're L.A., for crying out loud. They always get what they want."

"Not this time. This time they get hind tit. They aren't used to it, and they don't like it for beans." Pitcavage stuck out his hand again. As Colin took it, the chief went on, "I won't forget the number you did on them, either. Way to go."

That was dismissal. Even Colin, who didn't always notice hints, got this one and took it. Leaving the chief's inner sanctum, he liked Pitcavage better than he had for years. If Mike had a prick for a son, it could happen to anybody. Colin knew that only too well. Rob and Marshall weren't perfect. Neither was Vanessa.

And neither am I, Colin thought. *And neither is anybody else.*

Kelly looked up bemusedly at the ceiling of the Benson Hotel's lobby. It was a pretty fancy place, all dark, mellow wood. And she had to look a long way up at the molded and gilded plaster on the ceiling. The Benson dated from 1912, when splendor, by God, was splendor. Across the street stood the colonnaded magnificence of the First National Bank building, which might almost have come to Portland from the acropolis of Athens.

She shivered, not because she mourned the glory that was Greece and the grandeur that was Rome but because she was bloody cold. They'd scheduled the American geologists' conclave for December in northern Oregon before the supervolcano erupted. It must have seemed a good idea at the time. Now . . .

People kept saying Los Angeles was the new Seattle. Kelly didn't think that was true, but people kept saying it no matter what she thought. Going with it for the sake of argument, that made Portland the new . . . well, what?

Seattle lay about 1,100 miles north of L.A. What was 1,100 miles north of Portland? *The end of the world* was the first thing that occurred to Kelly, but she'd actually checked on a map before she came up here. On that same crappy scale of analogies, Portland was the new Skagway, Alaska.

And it felt like it. Snow swirled through the air and drifted on the sidewalks. Heat was in short supply. By law, the only places where you could set your thermostat higher than fifty were schools and hospitals. She wore the same clothes she would have taken to Yellowstone in winter, and she was glad to have them. Ice was forming on the Willamette and even on the broad, swift-flowing Columbia.

When the assembled geologists weren't giving papers or listening to them, they did the same thing as every other group of conventioneers ever hatched: they headed for the bar. It was just off the lobby, to the right of the glass-and-bronze revolving door that let you in.

Booze didn't really warm you up, but it made you feel as if it did, which was often good enough. And Oregon was microbrew heaven. Even the new, abbreviated growing season around here seemed to be enough to let barley mature. Behind the bar stood a rack of Oregon reds and whites from before the eruption. When those were gone, they'd be gone for good. Oregon wasn't wine country any more, and wouldn't be for nobody knew how many years to come.

And booze lubricated social gatherings. Kelly was halfway down a hoppy IPA when a friend of hers walked in. She waved. Daniel Olson nodded back. He picked his way through the chattering crowd. They hugged. They'd both been plucked from Yellowstone by helicopters just ahead of the supervolcano eruption. Along with two other rescued geologists, Kelly had crashed in his apartment in Missoula till Colin finagled a way out for her.

Daniel ordered himself a pale ale, too, and clinked bottles with her. "Did I hear you got married?" he said. She spread the fingers on her left hand to show off the ring. He nodded. "Sweet. And a job, too? At—what is it? Dominguez State?"

"Cal State Dominguez, yeah," Kelly agreed. People said *San Francisco State* and *Long Beach State*, but *Cal State Northridge* and *Cal State Dominguez* or *Cal State Dominguez Hills*. Why they did that, she had no idea, but they did. She asked, "How's Missoula these days? Do I want to know?"

"Well, it's still there and still kind of in business, which is more than you can say for most of Montana," Daniel answered. "But everything that comes in comes from the west. We've got electricity, but no natural gas."

Kelly nodded. "I remember when it went out." The big pipe that fed Missoula came to it across the rest of Montana. Or rather, it had come across Montana. Now it lay squashed under God only knew how many feet of ash and dust and rock.

"Not much gasoline, either," Daniel went on. "We chopped down a hell of a lot of trees to get through last winter, and we'll chop down more this time around. We'll regret it one of these days, but people are too worried about not freezing now to give a damn about later."

"Welcome to America," Kelly said, and the other geologist spread his hands in resigned agreement. When this quarter's balance sheet decided whether you got promoted, you wouldn't care what happened a few years down the line. And when it really was a choice between fuel in the fireplace and a Missoula winter on steroids, you'd chop down the pines now and let the bare hillsides take care of themselves in the sweet bye and bye.

"So, when are you presenting your paper?" Daniel asked.

"Morning session tomorrow," Kelly answered. She was one of the world's leading experts on everything that led up to the supervolcano blast. Passing on what she knew . . . *probably won't matter one goddamn bit*, she thought. By the time another supervolcano went off, odds were they wouldn't understand English any more. And even if they did, you couldn't do anything about a supervolcano eruption anyhow.

"I'll be there," Daniel promised.

Kelly gulped a little; Daniel knew as much about the Yellowstone supervolcano as she did. At least partly to soften him up, she said, "You want to have breakfast tomorrow?"

"Sure. And when we talk shop in the restaurant downstairs, everybody can look at us like we're nuts." Daniel clucked and caught himself. "Nah. Most of the people in there'll be nuts the same way we are. Say, half past eight?"

"Sounds good. I'm scheduled for ten thirty. That'll give us plenty of time to eat, and then I can be nervous afterwards." Kelly knew she was kidding on the square. She'd critiqued other people's papers before, but this was her first big presentation on her own. The room would be packed, too. There wasn't anything more urgent in the field, and there wouldn't be for years, maybe centuries, to come.

"Okay. I know that song." Daniel grinned crookedly. He'd snagged a tenure-track job at Montana State while she was still in grad school. Had she been jealous? Oh, just a little, especially since he was younger than she was. Now he went on, "Let's meet in the lobby. That way, whoever gets here first can gawp at the ceiling till the other one shows."

"You do that, too? Oh, good! I wondered if I was the only one. Isn't it over the top?" Kelly said.

As it happened, neither one of them beat the other; they rode down in the same elevator. A couple of people were eating breakfast in the hotel restaurant, but only a couple. A sharp-faced, officious middle-aged woman in a fuzzy orange sweater waved away other would-be customers. "We can't serve you now," she said. "We're setting up for Sunday brunch."

"We don't want brunch. We just want breakfast," Kelly protested.

"There are people in there," Daniel added.

"We can't take you now," the woman in the orange sweater repeated, and she would not be moved.

Dejected, decaffeinated, and pissed off, Kelly and Daniel

walked up the stairs to the ornate lobby. "Where can we get something to eat in this miserable town?" Kelly growled at a desk clerk. "Your restaurant seems to be under a curse."

"A curse in an orange sweater," Daniel agreed.

The clerk blinked, but she said, "There's the Original, a block up Sixth."

"Let's go," Kelly said grimly. Out the revolving door they strode. Kelly was wearing long johns, and damn glad she'd put them on. The wind had knives in it. Snow crunched under her shoes. It drifted here and there. Not many cars were on the street. Chains made the ones that were rattle as they slowly went by. It was more like a scene from Duluth than anything anyone would have looked for in Portland before the eruption.

Decor in the Original lived up to its name. The paintings on the walls were of clowns and mayonnaise jars—together, not separately. Contemplating what use the swarms of Bozoids might have for all that Best Foods made Kelly queasy. Coffee and ham and eggs and hash browns worked wonders, though. Daniel had sausage and eggs instead.

When they were finishing up, he took his iPhone out of his pocket to check the time. Kelly looked a question at him. "Nine forty," he said. "Unless the grizzlies carry us off between here and the Benson, you're golden."

"Okay. Thanks. For a while there, I was too mad at that orange bitch to worry about what I'm going to say, you know?" Kelly said. "Maybe I owe her something after all."

"A kick in the teeth?" Daniel suggested.

"I'd love to. People might talk, though." Kelly sighed, as if to say there was no accounting for society's foibles. When the tattooed waiter brought the check, she grabbed it. Daniel started to squawk, but she cut him off: "Hey, how long did I spend at your place after things blew up?"

"I dunno, but I bet it seemed like forever," he answered,

which wasn't so far wrong. Even so, he let her put it on her Visa.

They walked back to the Benson through the arctic chill. Kelly changed into business attire. Pants hid the long underwear. A wool turtleneck under a jacket kept her top half tolerably warm. She grabbed the manila folder that held the paper and headed down the hall to the elevator again.

The packed function room intimidated her less than she'd feared it would. Standing up and lecturing her Dominguez Hills classes had burned the fear of public speaking out of her. And she'd have a much more interested audience here than she did there.

Her chairperson introduced her as "Somebody who knows the Yellowstone supervolcano better than anyone. If she'd been any closer to it when it did erupt, she wouldn't be here talking to us now." Geoff Rheinburg might have been stretching the first part of that. He sure wasn't kidding about the second half.

Kelly had to adjust the mike at the lectern before she started talking; Rheinburg was several inches taller than she was. "I am glad to be here—and you can take that any way you want," she said. In the second row, Daniel nodded emphatically. He knew how she felt, all right. And yes, Larry Skrtel and Ruth Marquez were here, too, farther back in the crowd. They'd also got out in the nick of time. And they were sitting side by side now, which was, or at least might be, interesting.

Interesting later. Now was business time. Kelly talked about everything the supervolcano had done in the runup to the eruption: the earthquakes all the way back to Hebgen Lake in 1959, the rising magma domes, the hot springs and geysers picking up, the premonitory volcanic outbursts in the southwest and northeast parts of Yellowstone, and finally the big kaboom.

"Even by supervolcano standards, it proved to be a large eruption: not quite the size of the one 2.1 million years ago, but close," she said. "Climatic effects have proved at least as severe as the models predicted." Her shiver underlined that. Even with all these bodies in the room, it was bloody cold. She went on, "So have other environmental impacts. Geologists did everything they could to alert the authorities to what a supervolcano eruption would mean. The authorities, unfortunately, didn't want to listen to us. At the time, I was furious. In retrospect, I don't think it mattered much. During the last big recession before the eruption, there was a lot of talk about companies and banks that were too big to fail. The Yellowstone supervolcano was a disaster too big to let us succeed. No matter what we did or didn't do, we were going to get overwhelmed. We grew up in the Golden Age. It's gone. It won't come back for decades or lifetimes, if it ever does."

It wasn't anything her audience didn't already know. They'd known it before the supervolcano went off, which was more than the rest of the world could say. But hearing it backed up with all the data Kelly'd presented was sobering all the same.

When she asked for questions, the ones she got were mostly technical—about the order and intensity of the precursor signs, about possible steps the government might have taken and what those could have accomplished, and the like. It was all academic, and everybody knew it. Yellowstone wasn't the only supervolcano. The one on Sumatra deserved careful watching, and so did the one on the Kamchatka Peninsula. There was even one near Mono Lake in eastern California. But none of the others seemed likely to erupt for thousands of years. The Midwest had drawn the short straw this time around. Well, so had the whole planet.

Professor Rheinburg beamed at Kelly as things broke up. "Good job! Very solid!" He clapped his hands with no sound.

"Thanks." She gathered up her papers. "I'm just glad it's over."

"I always feel that way, and I've been doing this about as long as you've been alive," he said. "So, how's your job?"

"Terrific," she replied. Having one was terrific. She had no doubt he was responsible for it.

He didn't let on. He never had. "How's everything else? How's your life? How do you like being married?"

"So far, so good. Better than so good," Kelly said. One day at a time. That was how you did anything.

VI

*T*hunk! The axe bit into the pine log. Rob Ferguson raised it and let it fall again. Little by little, trees turned into firewood. You could work up a sweat chopping wood even in a Maine winter. And the way Maine winters were these days, that was really saying something.

Thunk! Rob got the axe to do what he wanted now. When he'd first started with it, he'd counted himself lucky for not amputating anyone else's fingers or his own leg. These days, it was just a tool—a tool you had to respect, sure, but a tool all the same. *Thunk!*

Biff came out of the Trebor Mansion Inn. He held up his left wrist to display a windup watch. Rob wore one, too. They'd had electricity through what was laughably called the summer in these parts, but it was out again now that the Ice Age had returned. Without it, they had no cell coverage, and without coverage their phones were nothing but little plastic bricks.

To amplify the message, Biff said, "Town meeting's in half an hour."

"Gotcha." Rob swung the axe again. Another billet of what would be firewood jumped from the log.

Biff eyed it and the ones lying in the snow nearby. They were all of pretty much the same size and shape. "Dude, you're getting to be like Conan the Barbarian with that thing." The rhythm guitarist jerked a mittened thumb at the axe.

"Practice makes pregnant, same as with anything else." Rob hefted his implement of destruction. "What I think is, it's goddamn funny to be using a genuine axe for a change, instead of—" He mimed pulling hot licks from a guitar.

"Axe . . . axe . . . Yeah!" Biff grinned. You took the nickname for your instrument for granted until you did a compare-and-contrast with the real Craftsman article.

Rob went on chopping wood for another ten minutes or so. You had to earn your keep, all right. As soon as the power failed, Guilford and the rest of Maine north of the Interstate fell back in time to the land of Currier and Ives. What those nostalgia-filled prints didn't tell you was how much goddamn work that nineteenth-century life took. You had to find that out for yourself. Rob had, and his hands had new ridges of callus to prove it.

He walked to the town meeting with the other guys from Squirt Frog and the Evolving Tadpoles, and with Dick Barber and the swarm of his relations who lived on the family side of the inn. They'd had a couple of paying customers when some of the snow melted, but only a couple. Given that the all-time high summer temperature was sixty-one degrees, and that it snowed on August 3, ten days after that tropical afternoon, having any paying guests at all approached the miraculous.

Barber didn't seem to worry about it. "Are they going to foreclose on me and toss me out in the snow?" he asked, and answered his own question: "I don't think so! That kind of crap is all over, at least for now. Half the country isn't making any mortgage payments now, probably more. Hell, there are whole states where nobody's making any mortgage payments."

He was bound to be right about that. Nobody was living in Wyoming, for instance, much less keeping the bank happy about the loan on the condo. Montana, Colorado, and Idaho were almost as badly screwed, and it got better only in relative terms as you moved farther away from what had been Yellowstone National Park and was now the world's biggest, hottest hole in the ground.

The unwritten rule was that everybody shoveled the snow off the sidewalk in front of his own house or shop. The snow that got shoveled went into the street. Back in the day, plows had kept the roads cleared. They'd mostly given up on that now. If you wanted to go from town to town in wintertime now, you could take a sleigh or ski or snowshoe.

Children and people like the guys from the band amended the unwritten rule. If you were an old man with heart trouble or a woman with a bad back, you didn't shovel your own walk. You gave somebody something to do it for you: food or warm clothes or firewood or sometimes even cash. Even with the roads opening up in the alleged summer, it was an economy of scarcity. Things counted for more than money did. And Rob had got some of his calluses with a snow shovel.

Biff ducked into Caleb's Country Kitchen and came out with the waitress he'd fallen for. Cindy was a short brunette who hardly ever said anything. That had to appeal to Biff. Rob and Justin and Charlie were all full of themselves and full of their own opinions. So was Dick Barber. With Cindy, Biff could get a few words of his own in edgewise.

Caleb, the guy who ran and cooked for the diner, also came out. He turned the sign on the front door to CLOSED. "Won't do no business till the meetin's over, anyways," he said. He'd stayed open where the Subway, more dependent on outside supplies, went under. He raised chickens and a couple of pigs, and cooked lots of eggs. That improved the overall level of his cuisine; eggs were harder to screw up than some of the things that had been on the menu.

Guilford held its town meetings in the Episcopalian church, one of the few buildings big enough for the crowds. Everybody came; no one made noises about the separation of church and state. Locals nodded to the guys in the band as they came up. They were tolerated just fine, though they'd stay outsiders forever. Dick Barber had lived here for years. He remained an outsider, too, though not one who was shy about speaking his mind. As far as Rob could see, Dick wasn't shy about anything.

A fancy sleigh was hitched outside the church. Rob turned accusingly on Barber. "Why didn't you tell us Jim was in town?"

"Because I didn't know till just now," Barber answered with a broad-shouldered shrug. "The landline's out. I can do all kinds of things, but I don't read minds."

"It'll liven up the meeting, anyway," Charlie said, and no one was rash enough to try to contradict him. They walked inside.

"Boy, anybody'd think there were people here or something." Justin made like Phil Collins: "I can feel it in the air tonight. . . ."

Feel it wasn't quite right. But that didn't mean it wasn't in the air. Regular baths and showers were modern luxuries that had gone by the wayside along with so much else. If you wanted to get clean, you heated a basin of water over your fire and washed one body part at a time till the stuff in the basin got too frigid to stand. If you had the patience to do that once a week, you were about average.

Rob didn't notice how he smelled when he was by himself. He hardly noticed how the other people at the Trebor Mansion Inn smelled, either; he'd got used to them. But he sure did notice a whole bunch of strangers gathered together in one place. He noticed them for about five minutes, anyhow. After that, his nose forgot about them. When everybody was funky, nobody was funky.

The mayor of Guilford was a stocky, middle-aged fellow named Josh McCann. He also ran the local independent hardware store. Rob gathered that, before the eruption, it had been one step this side of a junk shop, and a small step at that. Since the supervolcano blew up and Maine north of the Interstate was mostly forgotten by the rest of the country, junk and being able to do things with junk suddenly became worth their weight in gold—sometimes, even worth their weight in pork spare ribs.

Swaddled in a bulky wool sweater, McCann took his place at the pulpit, where the minister usually stood. He brought down his gavel: once, twice, three times. People packing the pews quieted down, the way they would have at a church service. Democracy here was a secular faith, and the folks took it much more seriously than they did in SoCal. These towns were small enough that everyone knew or knew about everyone else. Money and slick advertising didn't matter the way they did in the big city.

"Meeting will come to order," the mayor rasped in a two-pack-a-day voice. Rob wondered how his habit was holding up. Tobacco had as much trouble getting here as everything else did. McCann went on, "First order of business is a little talk by Jim Farrell. He's come a ways to call, so it seems only fair to let him speak his piece."

Rob snorted under his breath. Nor was his the only amused or dubious voice rising to the heavens—or at least to the rafters. The next little talk from Farrell would be the first. He was a retired professor of Greek and Roman history who'd moved back to Maine after teaching for a million years at SUNY Albany. He was used to speaking in front of other people, in other words. And he was a man of strong opinions, and far from shy about letting the world know what they were.

Not long before the eruption, he'd run for Congress up here as a Republican. He'd got trounced. Dick Barber had helped run his campaign, and still grumbled about the way it turned out. The winner, a lawyer with an expensive haircut (Farrell's words), was down in Washington, where it was ... well, warmer, anyhow.

Maybe he was doing what he could for his district. You never could tell. What he could do, in this ravaged, ravished country, seemed vanishingly small. Farrell, who'd stayed behind, was the biggest cheese north and west of the Interstate.

The other difference was, the lawyer knew bureaucracy and politics and policy. When the Federal government touched this part of Maine only while the roads were open, and when they hadn't been open much this year, he became a cipher. Jim Farrell knew useful things, like which root vegetables had the shortest growing seasons and how to salt trout or make sauerkraut. He knew, and he talked. Oh, yes—he talked. And talked and talked some more.

He got to his feet now. Instead of the more common stocking cap, he wore a snap-brim fedora. His pearl-gray topcoat was of a cut reckoned elegant when FDR decided we had nothing to fear but fear itself: some years before he was born, in other words. He wasn't young, but he wasn't so old as that. He was a dandy with antique tastes.

He had a ruddy Irish face with a pointed nose and bushy eyebrows. The first time Rob met him, the winter before, he'd been reminded of a smaller version of John Madden, but only till Farrell opened his mouth. Madden had a mouth full of gravel. Jim Farrell's baritone was a very different instrument. He spoke in sentences that parsed and paragraphs where the sentences followed logically, one upon another. That should have ruled out a successful political career for him, and as a matter of fact it had— till the supervolcano erupted.

"Here we are again," he said as he took McCann's place at the pulpit. "Here we are again, all right, in this, the second winter of our discontent. The first one was pretty easy, as these things go. We chopped down the trees that stood closest, and we shot the nearest and stupidest moose."

People chuckled. It wasn't that Farrell was saying anything that wasn't so. They'd done exactly that the winter before. They'd got by with it, too, until things thawed out enough to remind the wider world for a little while that they were there.

"I'm serious," Farrell insisted, "or as serious as I'm likely to get, anyhow. I'm serious, and the situation is liable to turn critical. If we don't want to end up burning down our houses to keep warm and eating long pig so we don't starve, we'd better do some planning first."

Rob wondered how many of the men and women in the crowd understood what long pig was. Sitting next to him, Justin quirked an eyebrow, so he got it. Well, Justin knew all kinds of weird things. Knowing weird things was his specialty, maybe even more than playing guitar. And Dick Barber also grinned out of one side of his mouth. But he too was a man of parts, even if not all of them worked all the time. And he would have heard more from Farrell than anybody. For most of these folks, though, long pig would be caviar to the general. Then Rob wondered how many people here knew about caviar to the general. And then he quit worrying about crap like that and listened to Farrell some more.

"—got to organize and share what we can gather," the retired history prof was saying. "If we don't hang together, you can be sure we will hang separately."

That was Ben Franklin. Before Rob could even start to wonder how many people in the church knew that much, somebody called, "I thought you were a Republican, not a goddamn Commie!"

Farrell beamed. He loved hecklers, mostly because he loved demolishing them. Before Mayor McCann could gavel the loudmouth out of order, Farrell waved for him not to bother. "Right this minute, I think Moscow and Beijing and Pyongyang are a little too cold themselves to worry about Maine north of the Interstate." He got his laugh. Having got it, he went on, "At least, I don't *think* North Korea has a rocket that will reach all the way to such a dangerous place as Guilford."

That won him another one. "Washington doesn't worry about us, either. We've seen that. And I *am* a Republican, so I say that's a good thing more often than not. I don't want Big Brother watching me. But I also don't want my friends and neighbors squabbling like the Kilkenny Cats, and I don't want them starving or freezing, either. If we can take care of ourselves, we won't need to cry because Big Brother's falling down on the job. All politics is local, but some is more local than others. For about nine months out of the year, maybe more, ours looks as though it's going to be about as local as it gets."

He went on to talk about schemes for using the gasoline and fuel oil they did have, and about organizing hunts and woodcutting parties. He talked about parsnips and mangel-wurzels and Andean potatoes that ripened faster than the varieties of spuds Maine had been famous for.

"What the hell is a mangel-wurzel?" Rob whispered to Justin.

"You grab a wurzel and you hurt it real bad," Justin explained, so he had no clue, either.

"None of this will be exciting," Farrell finished. "But we're not talking about excitement now. Excitement is for good times. It's a luxury. We're talking about survival. Survival is what we'll be talking for the rest of my life, for the rest of your lives, and probably for the rest of your children's and grandchildren's lives.

I don't think Washington has figured that out yet, but it looks pretty obvious here, doesn't it?"

Nobody, not even the guy who'd yelled at him, tried to tell him he was wrong. No one applauded when Farrell stepped away from the pulpit—*the bully pulpit,* Rob thought—either. The thoughtful silence he got seemed higher praise than any mere handclapping could have been. And the agenda items following his talk seemed even duller than they might have otherwise.

After the town meeting adjourned, Rob waded through the crowd around Jim Farrell and waited his turn to talk. When it finally came, he asked, "Why *aren't* the Feds paying more attention to us? We're hit harder than any place that didn't get covered in ash."

"Well, for one thing, a lot of places *did* get covered in ash," Farrell replied, and Rob nodded. The older man continued, "And Washington is out for what it can get, much more than it is for what it can give. From us, that means it's out for nothing. You can't get blood from a turnip, or from a mangel-wurzel. So Washington shines the light of its countenance on the places that are still warm, or at least warmer."

That made more sense than Rob wished it did. He was less convinced than Farrell that being forgotten about by Washington was a good thing. But he wasn't nearly so sure it was a bad thing as he had been when Squirt Frog and the Evolving Tadpoles first got stuck in Guilford. He let someone else talk to Farrell and walked out into the sharp-toothed cold outside.

It was dark outside the church, too—no working streetlamps. Rob stepped on somebody's foot before he'd gone very far. "Sorry," he said, wondering who his victim was.

"No damage," came the reply: a woman's voice. She couldn't see him, either, because she asked, "Who are you?"

"Rob. I'm one of the fellows staying at the Mansion Inn."

"Oh, from the band!" she said. "You guys are good, even acoustic. I like it when you play in the park by the river. I go whenever I can."

"Cool," Rob replied. A fan—he recognized enthusiasm when he heard it. But which fan? "Um, who'm I talking to?"

"Oh. I'm Lindsey Kincaid. I teach chemistry at Piscataquis Community Secondary School," she answered. That was the high school not far from the inn.

Rob sortakinda knew who she was, the way he sortakinda knew an awful lot of people here. About his age, halfway between blonde and brunette . . . not half bad, all thing considered. How much considering did he feel like? "Where do you live?" he asked. "Can I walk you back there, wherever it is?"

If she said no, he wouldn't get shot down too badly. But she said, "Okay," and sounded pleased saying it. So maybe he'd find out how much considering he felt like.

"Attention! Attention! May I have your attention, please!"

When a man with a bullhorn shouted for your attention, you gave it to him whether you wanted to or not. He didn't even have to say *please*. Vanessa Ferguson wondered why he bothered. Vestigial politeness, was her guess. Like the human tailbone, it was shrunken and useless, but the FEMA guy out there still had that little bit.

He blared away: "Camp Constitution is being adversely impacted by the flood-type conditions currently obtaining in this geographical location."

That was so bad, Vanessa almost liked it. She couldn't imagine a more bureaucratic way to say *The flood here is screwing Camp Constitution to the wall.*

Things had been bad the spring before. Ash and dust covered the basins of the rivers that flowed into the Mississippi from the west. She still remembered what a pool-service guy had told her mother when she was a kid: "Your pool is the lowest part of your yard, lady. Anything that can get into it goddamn well will." He'd had a cigarette twitching in the corner of his mouth, and he was tanned as Cordoban leather. These days, he was probably dead of melanoma or lung cancer.

Which didn't make him wrong. The rivers were the lowest parts of their big back yards, too. They'd flooded last year from all the volcanic crud rain and melting snow and wind dumped into them. Now they were doing it again, still more crud going into riverbeds that hadn't yet got rid of everything from the year before. And so the rivers—including the Mississippi itself, which was after all the ultimate channel for half a continent's worth of gunk—were spilling over their banks and spreading out across the countryside.

It wasn't dramatic, the way the tsunamis in Indonesia and Japan had been. There weren't huge, speeding walls of water smashing everything in their path. But in the end, how much difference did that make? Whether you went under with a smash or merely a dispirited glub, under you went.

"Evacuation procedures are likely to become necessary for implementation in the nearly immediate future," the flunky with the bullhorn bellowed. Not just an evacuation, mind you, but evacuation procedures. That made it official, to say nothing of officious. "Gather your belongings and prepare to be in compliance with all instructional directives. National Guard personnel will assist in ensuring prompt satisfaction of requirements."

They'll shoot you if you don't do what we tell you. They would, too. The National Guard had opened fire in the camp several times. Like Vanessa, lots of refugees were armed, but not many had assault rifles or body armor or military discipline. The Guard outclassed them.

"What the fuck they gonna do to us now?" grumbled a middle-aged black man a couple of tiers of bunks over from Vanessa.

"Waddaya think, Jack?" a woman said in tones that came from Long Island, or possibly the Jersey shore. "They're gonna do whatever they damn well wanna."

And that was about the size of it. Vanessa hoped the waters would close over Micah Husak. She hoped crawdads and sticklebacks and little fish whose names she didn't even know would pick out his dead eyes and nibble the rotting flesh off his toes—and off his dick. All the while, she understood it was a hopeless hope. That kind of shit didn't happen to the people who ran camps. It happened to the people who wound up stuck in them.

Gathering her belongings didn't take long. Everything she owned fit in her purse and in a dark green garbage bag. That seemed fitting enough and then some, because most of what she owned *was* garbage.

Off in the distance, an M16 barked: a quick, professional three-round burst. Whoever'd been giving some Guardsman grief would just have discovered he'd made his last dumbass mistake. Or maybe he was too high on crank even to notice he was dead. Methamphetamines and weed fired people up and mellowed them out all over the camp.

The yahoo with the bullhorn ordered the people in the tent next to Vanessa's out to comply with his instructional directives. The middle-aged black guy moaned. "I didn't used to think there was no place worse'n this," he said. "But what you want to bet they went and found one?"

"Made one," Vanessa corrected. The difference sounded tiny, but seemed profound to her.

Then, half an hour later, the bell—or the bullhorn—tolled for them. "Tent 27B inmates, assemble outside the entrance in a single-file line," the guy with it boomed. Vanessa wondered if he would lead them to the Department of Redundancy Department. She didn't make the joke. She didn't think anyone else in good old Tent 27B would get it. Too bad, but there you were. And here she was.

Nervous-looking Guardsmen held their rifles in positions from which they could open up in a hurry. There were a lot of them. How much trouble had they had evacuating other great big tents? Quite a bit, by all the signs.

"Follow me toward the transportation that will transport you to the new provisional facilities," Bullhorn Boy continued. "Obey all commands immediately." That was so plain, it could only mean *Don't screw with me—or else.*

Off they went, at a retarded shuffle, garbage sacks slung over their shoulders. Up ahead, people were slowly filing onto buses ancient enough to have carried kids back in the days when Southern schools were still segregated.

Vanessa made up her mind right there that she didn't want to get transported to any provisional facility. Camp Constitution was bad. A half-assed version would only be worse. They said it couldn't be done, but as often as not they didn't know what they were talking about. This looked like one of those times.

Off to one side stood a much shorter row of newer, less decrepit buses. The people getting into those also seemed newer and less decrepit than the ones boarding the wrecks toward which Vanessa was heading. Pointing at the newer buses, she asked one of the Guardsmen, "What's up with those?"

He was a squarely built, blocky fellow with beard stubble so dark and thick he probably had to shave twice a day. "Oh, those are for the reclamation parties," he answered.

"Huh?" Vanessa said brilliantly.

"Reclamation parties," the Guardsman repeated. "You know, to go into the country the eruption fucked over and scavenge stuff from it and start cleaning it up so it's, like, worth something again."

"How do I get on one of those buses?" Vanessa asked. If

you were cleaning up the countryside, you weren't living in a camp. *Not* living in a camp seemed the most wonderful thing in the world to her, the way El Dorado must have to the conquistadors.

The guy looked at her. "You shoulda signed a volunteer sheet. They went around, like, weeks ago."

"Sign one? I never even saw one!" Vanessa yipped. She wondered if that was so. All kinds of stupid administrative papers circulated through the tents and FEMA trailers. Like most of the other poor slobs stuck in Camp Constitution, she ignored them. If she'd ignored the wrong one, she'd just screwed herself to the wall. But even if saying she'd never seen one might not be true, it was definitely truthy. She sure hadn't paid attention to one.

"If you didn't sign up, you can't go on those buses. You gotta get on these ones instead." The Guardsman pointed in the direction she was already going with the muzzle of his assault rifle.

Full of helpless longing, Vanessa stared at the newer buses. Helpless? God helped those who helped themselves. "I'd do anything to get on one of *those* buses," she said in a low, breathy voice she didn't remember using since before she threw out her last boyfriend.

If she hadn't taken care of Micah Husak that way, chances were she would have kept quiet. But after you'd done it once, the second time turned out to be a lot easier. She had a weapon, and she'd use it, the way the Guardsman would use the M16 if he needed to.

He understood what she was offering, all right. Well, he didn't exactly need to be Phi Beta Kappa to figure it out. "Yeah?" he said, as people not so young, not so cute, and maybe not so desperate trudged past so they could go from a godawful camp to one that had to be even worse.

"Yeah," Vanessa said. The fish had taken the bait.

"Joe-Bob, keep an eye on the parade," her Guardsman said to

the fellow next to him. Then he turned back to her. "C'mon in here." *In here* was into a tent that had already been evacuated. He beckoned to her as he undid his fly. "Let's just make it quick, okay?"

"Okay." She got down in front of him. Blowing him was better than fucking him. She wouldn't have to worry about dressing again—or about getting knocked up. He would have been better right after a shower, but he could have been worse, too.

And it would be quick. She could tell as soon as she started. "Yeah, babe," he muttered, shoving his hips forward and thrusting deeper into her mouth. Coughing, she pulled away a little, then went back to what she was doing.

He was about to go off. Just when she was going to jerk away so he'd spurt on the ground, he grabbed her head and held her to him while he came in her mouth. It was as bad as she remembered. She gagged and choked and almost puked on his sand-colored Army boots.

"All *right*," he said as he let her go. Eyes watering, she spat out as much of the gross, sticky stuff as she could. He chuckled and ran his hand through her hair: affection now, not brute strength. Why shouldn't he feel affectionate? She'd given him what he wanted. "You better hustle if you're gonna get on the reclamation bus," he told her.

"You bet I am," she said grimly. She spat again as she climbed to her feet and brushed dirt off the knees of her jeans. The Guardsman chuckled some more. He could afford to think it was funny. He hadn't been on the receiving end.

She fled the tent and hustled toward the newer buses before she realized they hadn't even found out each other's names. That came closer to the famous zipless fuck than she'd ever dreamt she'd get. She hadn't got fucked, though. She literally hadn't even got kissed.

She spat one more time before she got into the boarding line.

She wished for a jug of Scope, but wishing failed to produce one. The taste lingered. As she took her place, the woman in front of her—a gal about her own age—gave her a curious look, but didn't say anything.

A man with a clipboard was making checkmarks on the paper it held. A roster sheet? Vanessa's heart sank. If she'd sucked off that National Guard asshole for nothing . . . "Ferguson," she said with more confidence than she felt.

He frowned. "You aren't on the list."

"I'm supposed to be," she declared—again, at least truthy if not true.

He inspected her. Was she going to have to do him, too? Pretty soon she'd be swimming out to meet troopships if she wasn't careful. But all he said was "Well, get on. We're a couple people short, and you look like you can do the work. Ferguson, your name was?"

"That's right. Vanessa. Thank you." She didn't usually dole out gratitude so casually, but she made an exception here. As the man added her to the roster, she happily hopped into the bus. She didn't care where it took her. She was out of Camp Constitution at last!

When Marshall Ferguson wasn't babysitting his little half-brother, he had the family house pretty much to himself. His father went to the cop shop early every morning, and Kelly—Marshall couldn't think of her as a stepmom, not when she was as close to his age as to his old man's—headed for CSUDH not a whole lot later. Peace. Quiet. If he wanted to make like a writer, all he had to do was sit in front of the screen and let the words pour out.

In theory, anyhow. Theory was wonderful. Practice, he was discovering, was a little different. Yeah, just a little. Theory was all about inspiration and how to court it. As he was discovering, practice turned out to involve a lot more of figuring out what the hell you did after the fickle bitch upped and left you.

Because she damn well would. Inspiration had launched Marshall into a couple of stories that seemed like surefire winners. Inspiration took him 1,500 words into one of them, maybe 2,500 words into the other. Then he had to work out what happened next and what, if anything, it meant. And he had to work out how to put it across without being obvious or boring.

Somehow, neither of those masterpieces of Western literature ever got finished.

But Marshall did finish one piece he started with no inspiration whatsoever. Well, almost none. His father's dubious stare at the dinner table every evening kept Marshall busy. Where art and brilliance failed to serve, stubbornness and craft got him to the end.

Then he had to put the story on the market. Being forced to submit by Professor Bolger at UCSB was one of the best things that ever happened to him: he'd started early on getting hardened to rejection. The prof said straight-out that some people would rather submit to a root canal than to an editor.

Marshall had never had a root canal, but he understood the feeling. He'd sold a story during that quarter, which freaked him and the prof almost equally. But you didn't sell every time. And getting rejected sucked.

He tried to think of it like dating. If you didn't hit on girls, you'd never get laid. Yeah, sometimes they shot you down. That didn't mean you didn't pick yourself up and ask somebody else out. It might not even mean you didn't try again with the girl who'd told you no before.

Or with the market that told you no. Marshall's stubborn story went out and came back five times before it found a home at a Web site that put the munificent sum of two and a half cents a word in his PayPal account.

Two and a half cents a word wouldn't make anybody rich. Marshall knew that only too well. In case he didn't, his father rubbed his nose in it: "I don't think you'll have Tom Clancy or Bill Gates trimming your oleanders any time soon."

"Right," Marshall said, and then, "Pass the potatoes, please." Was Dad cynical because he'd been a cop for too long, or had he become a cop because he was already cynical? Could you answer *all of the above*? That was how it looked to Marshall.

"He sold it," Kelly said. "Two and a half cents a word is better than nothing. It's more than I've ever got for an article. In academic publishing, all they give you is the glory of your name in print—usually with a raft of coauths."

"Yeah, well, you're advancing human knowledge," Colin Ferguson said, "not just—" He stopped short.

"Bullshitting?" Marshall suggested.

"You said it. I didn't." Dad wouldn't, either, not with Kelly across the table from him. Which didn't mean he wasn't thinking it.

Kelly was less touchy about that kind of thing than her husband. "God knows there's plenty of bullshit in the academic journals," she said. "How about the ones for criminal justice?"

One reason you had to respect Dad was that he would 'fess up when you caught him out. "Well, you've got me there," he admitted now. "You read those things, you'd think we caught every perp, and that about day after tomorrow we can talk all the bad guys into staying good guys and put ourselves out of business forever." He smiled crookedly. "And rain makes applesauce."

"Is that what they call pie in the sky?" Marshall had run into the phrase, but he wasn't sure exactly how it worked.

His father nodded. "That's what they call it, all right. Come the revolution, they used to say. Then the revolution came, and things were just as nasty afterwards as they were before. Meet the new boss, same as the old boss." He got that from some old rock song.

"All animals are equal, but some are more equal than others," Kelly said, which sounded like agreement.

It also sounded familiar. "That's from *Animal Farm*!" Marshall exclaimed. "I had to read it in Western Civ. It's by the guy who wrote *1984*, back when 1984 seemed a long way away." It seemed a long way away to him, too—lost in the distant past like 1945 and 1865 and 1776 and 1066.

"The 1984 we got wasn't too great, but it was better than the one Orwell wrote about," Dad said.

"If you say so," Marshall answered. He had no memories of 1984. Kelly would have been a little kid back then, so she wouldn't remember much, either. For Dad, it seemed to feel like the week before last. Getting old, having all that stuff to remember, to try and keep track of, had to be a terrible thing.

Thinking about what a terrible thing it was and trying to work out exactly what kind of terrible thing it was must have shown on Marshall's face. Kelly murmured, "He's getting an idea for a story."

"Or indigestion, one." But Dad didn't sound disgusted. Coming out with snide cracks was as much a reflex with him as breathing was. All the other cops Marshall knew—and he naturally knew more cops than most stoners ever wanted to—talked the same way. It had to help shield them from some of the nasty shit they ran into on the job.

"Well . . ." Marshall stood up.

He paid rent—a third of what he grossed. Not netted: grossed. Between babysitting and writing, he wasn't grossing one whole hell of a lot. But he was a cash customer, so his old man didn't ride him too hard. With most of his high school buddies scuffling even harder than he was, he didn't feel embarrassed about living at home. Misery really did love company.

He went up to his room. He kept it tolerably clean and neat; he'd learned how taking care of himself at UCSB. It wasn't so much for his sake. Like a lot of young males on their own, he didn't mind living like a slob. What guys didn't mind, though, grossed girls out. Some guys were too dumb to learn from failure and frustration. Marshall wasn't.

No one in the house minded if he brought a girl upstairs. No one was going to pound on the door with the crime-scene tape while he had company. Things could have been worse. He kept telling himself as much. He kept looking at apartments, too. Unfortunately, landlords were less adaptable about rent than Dad was.

Earbuds and his iPod made the outside world go away. Or they would have, but the first song that came out was from Squirt Frog and the Evolving Tadpoles: a strange, droning chant called "Justinian II," an Emperor of Byzantium who got his nose chopped off. Listening to it reminded Marshall how much he missed his older brother. He hadn't seen Rob since before the supervolcano blew. Maine? OMG! Maine was the Devil's personal icebox these days.

In the song, Justinian II came to a bad end. Singing about it, Justin Nachman sounded unwholesomely amused. He had a knack for that. Something more innocuous but less evocative shuffled onto the iPod next. Marshall closed his eyes and listened.

After a while, he shut it off and started noodling on a story. Not much inspiration, no. Maybe perspiration would do. One thing sure: the elves wouldn't write it for him, no matter how much he wished they would. Wondering why they didn't make elves the way they used to, he soldiered on. Once he finished the first draft, he could read it over and see just what he had, or if he had anything at all.

VII

Dwip. Dwip. Dwip. Bryce Miller didn't know whether everybody who worked for the Department of Water and Power sounded like Elmer Fudd impersonating a leaky faucet. He did know he wasn't the only one, though.

And he knew the noise fit the weather much too well. The dirty-gray heavens dwipped dwizzle as he pedaled his bicycle toward the bus stop. He couldn't afford to drive downtown, not with gas through the roof and into the ionosphere—and not with most stations showing red flags to let people know they had no gas at any price. Long, long lines—old farts talked about 1979—marked the ones with a little to sell.

It wasn't supposed to rain in L.A. in June, not even a little bit. Well, it hadn't been supposed to. Mother Nature was reading a new rulebook these days. Bryce rode on, keeping a wary eye out for cars. Not so many of them on the road these days, and a lot more bikes like his. Some of the people on the two-wheelers were as nonchalant as if they'd been doing it for years. A few might even actually have been doing it before the eruption—a few, but not many. Others looked as if they'd borrowed some kid's bike they almost remembered how to handle.

Bryce figured he fit somewhere in the middle. It *was* his bike, and he *had* ridden it before the supervolcano blew. He hadn't ridden it to work, though. And he wouldn't have ridden it in the rain. Biking was supposed to be fun, right?

The bus stop on Braxton Bragg Boulevard had a big new parking rack bolted to the sidewalk next to the bench. Bryce chained his bike to the steel. The stop, like a lot of others, also had a new armed guard: a guy who looked as if he was recently back from combat on distant shores and had had trouble finding work here in the States. Bryce nodded to him. The guard gravely dipped his head in response. No, he wouldn't have got that polite anywhere but in the military.

Other people already stood at the stop. Bryce nodded to them, too; he saw a lot of them several times a week. The rather cute Hispanic chick, the hulking black guy, the Asian fellow who never quit texting . . . They'd been regulars on this route longer than he had.

Up grumbled the bus. People stepped away from the curb as it neared, not wanting to get splashed. The doors hissed open. They filed aboard. The black guy found a seat, then lifted his hat. He had a half pint of Southern Comfort under there. *Sudden Discomfort,* Bryce thought, remembering a collection of *Mad Magazine* pieces older than he was but still funny. The guy took a quick knock, then stowed the booze again.

The bus took off. A couple of blocks later, of course, it stopped again. More people got on. By the time it reached the Red Line station near the Harbor Freeway, it was packed. Most of the passengers climbed off there, Bryce among them.

He got his ticket from the automated kiosk. He felt automated himself; once you'd done it a couple of times, boarding took next to no conscious thought. He walked out onto the platform—which did boast a roof—and waited for the next train to pull in.

Along with the other commuters, he got on when it did. The train headed north, toward downtown. The tracks ran along the middle of the 110. In other words, they went straight through South Central L.A. People—most of them either African-American or Hispanic—got on and off at several stops.

Bryce kept his head down and his nose buried in the *Times*. Like most white kids raised not far from South Central, he'd heard a lot about the area—none of it good—and had gone there never. The most horror he'd experienced on the train was a couple of guys a little younger than he was yelling at each other in Spanish. The yells soon subsided to dirty looks. Neither young man pulled out a Glock and shot up the car, or seemed likely to. Yells and glares Bryce could live with.

No yells today. Nobody even fired up a joint. That happened now and again, although you weren't supposed to smoke anything inside the train. Funny—he'd never seen anybody light up an ordinary cigarette. People always waited till they got off for that. Harder to wait to get baked, evidently.

He left the train and headed for the DWP building. Skyscrapers—some office complexes, others hotels—turned the streets into corridors. His mother and Colin Ferguson talked about their childhood days, when, for fear of earthquakes, City Hall was the only building allowed to rise higher than twelve stories. Modern architects and engineers had convinced the powers that be that their efforts would stay up no matter what the San Andreas Fault did.

Even if they were right, Bryce wouldn't have wanted to be where he was when the Big One hit. The skyscrapers might not topple. Sure as hell, though, razor-sharp spears of glass would rain down from their sides. And the glass would slice anybody walking along here into hamburger in nothing flat.

"Hey, guy?" A homeless woman of indeterminate age tried to look alluring. What she looked was skinny and dirty and strung out: desperate, in other words. You'd have to be even more desperate yourself to want to go to bed with her. But turning tricks was probably the only way she could get the cash for whatever drugs had washed her up on life's lee shore—and maybe, if she was lucky, for a little food, too.

Bryce walked by as if she weren't there. He wasn't particularly proud of it, but what could you do?

"Stinking fairy!" she whined after him. He could see the logical fallacy. That was what he got for doing classics in grad school. Just because he didn't want her, that didn't mean he didn't want any woman. Plato would have tried to convince this gal that she'd understood the flaw in her own thinking all along.

She wasn't likely to care much for philosophy, though. All she cared about was the next fix. And if she could wound him a little for ignoring her charms, such as they were, so much the better. No doubt she'd come on to someone else in a little while, and then cuss him out, too.

DWP headquarters wasn't in a skyscraper: just an ordinary blocky office building at the edge of the fancy-shmancy built-up area. You could walk past it without noticing it was there. No doubt thousands of people did every day. Bryce would have if he'd worked anywhere else.

He showed his ID to the security guard at the front entrance. The man had been seeing him five days a week for several months now, but still carefully inspected it. Only after he was satisfied did he nod and say, "Morning, Dr. Miller."

"Morning, Hank." Bryce didn't know how Hank knew he had his Piled Higher and Deeper. He didn't go around calling himself Dr. Miller. As far as he was concerned, *Doctor* was the right title for M.D.s, dentists, and veterinarians; people with Ph.D.s who glommed on to it were pompous asses.

That wasn't the DWP mindset. Here, if you had a doctorate you flaunted it like a well-built girl in a spandex tank top. Somebody must have tipped Hank off about Bryce's sheepskin. He became *Dr. Miller* to people here almost in self-defense, even if he didn't use the title himself; otherwise, he would have seemed like a security guard.

He climbed the stairs to the fourth floor. *Have to keep my girlish figure,* he thought vaguely. He didn't boast one of the offices with windows around the outside of the building. Nope. He had himself a cubicle with fuzzy walls in a big room in the middle, straight out of Dilbertland.

Jay Black was already hard at it in the Skinner box next to Bryce's. He was a computer whiz, a balding, fortyish guy who wondered why he had trouble finding a girl he liked. *Because all you're looking for is a twenty-five-year-old supermodel* didn't seem to have crossed his mind. Finding one who also appreciated the fine points of iPhone app-writing (to say nothing of a cross-stitched sampler on the wall that read CUBICLE, SWEET CUBICLE) would take some doing.

He looked up from what Bryce hoped was his first Mountain Dew of the day. Sugar in the morning, sugar in the evening, sugar at suppertime—you'll get diabetes, and you won't be worth a dime.

"Welcome to another day in paradise," Jay said.

"Could be doing anything out there. We'd never know it," Bryce answered.

"Used to be, that was a crying shame," Black said. "The way things are now, we're lucky to be in a building where the lights and the heat work." He grinned crookedly. "This is the last place in town that'll go cold and dark."

"Yeah." Bryce hadn't looked at it that way, which didn't mean Jay was wrong. The coffee machine by the copier still worked, too. Bryce got some caffeine and a little sugar of his own, then sat down at his desk for the day's important project. *And other fantasies,* he thought—he'd sure had plenty that were more enjoyable.

He cut down the text on a newsletter so it would fit on one sheet of paper. He did his best to translate a brochure from bureaucratese into English. He changed the small print on DWP electric bills to keep up with revised state and city conservation rules. When nobody was paying attention to him, he fiddled with a new pastoral: Theocritus meets the supervolcano, in effect. When he finished, he planned to send it to the *New Yorker.* After they told him no, he'd start going through all the markets that didn't pay. Marshall Ferguson wasn't getting rich, but he was selling things now and again. Bryce wished he could say the same himself.

Since he couldn't, he had this day job. The DWP was the kind of place where you could look up after a quarter of a century and wonder where the hell the best years of your life had gone. Jay hadn't been here that long, but he was starting to get those moments.

Bryce hoped *he* wouldn't stick around long enough to have them. You'd never go toe-to-toe with the Donald or Bill Gates on what they paid you, but you could live and even raise a family on it. Medical, dental, vision, retirement plan . . . When you got all that good stuff, would you really worry about where the time was going and why you were bored out of your skull?

A lot of people wouldn't. Hell, a lot of people didn't. They put in their hours and used the company Xerox to copy their own stuff and stole paper and pens and anything else that wasn't nailed down and did what was required of them and not a speck more. Bryce sometimes found himself slipping into that easygoing slothfulness. He wondered how different it really was from going nuts in a quiet, polite way.

After lunch, someone put an RFP on his desk with a Post-it

note: *What do you think our chances are for getting ahold of some of this grant money?* Evaluating an RFP, especially one from the Federal Department of Energy, was a little more fun than passing a kidney stone, but only a little.

Could I do this for twenty-five years? he wondered as he scribbled notes. *Would anything be left of me if I did?*

Somewhere in Kansas. That was as much as Vanessa Ferguson knew about where she was. Probably somewhere in eastern Kansas. The dust and ash got thicker as you moved toward the Colorado border. That meant things got more screwed up. She didn't think anybody had actually gone back into Colorado yet. There was plenty of disaster to go around here closer to the edges of the ashfall.

She didn't care. She'd escaped Camp Constitution, and escaped whatever sorry-ass place the suckers flooded out of Camp Constitution had gone to instead. She would never see Micah Husak again. If by some misfortune she did, she could kick him in the nuts or plug him instead of sucking him off.

And all her freedom had cost her was one more quickie blow job on that nameless National Guardsman. Her self-respect? As a matter of fact, no. You did what you had to do and you counted up the tab later on. Or else you didn't worry about it at all. Most of the time, she didn't.

Some stretches of ground in these parts were free of volcanic crud. Rain and wind had blown it away or washed it into rivers—which was why the floods were so horrendous. But there was genuine, no-shit green in those places. Robins hopped around, probing the ground for worms. Every so often, they even found some. Worms had to be tougher than Vanessa had imagined.

But where the ash and dust had drifted . . . In the lee of houses and fences, in places where the wind didn't reach, in hollows without streams running through them . . . In spots like that, the ground was as gray and lifeless as it had been right after the eruption, going on two years ago now.

No people had been found alive. Not everybody had fled to the camps, maybe, but the people who hadn't fled hadn't made it. Lung diseases brought on by inhaling all the abrasive ultramicroscopic crud in the air did them in. It wasn't quite as if they'd smoked twenty packs a day for fifty years, but it might as well have been.

Cows? Sheep? Pigs? Chickens? Horses? Gone, gone, gone, gone, and gone, for the same reason. Those worm-hunting robins must have flown here from somewhere else. Livestock couldn't fly away like that.

No crops in the ground the past two years, either. Where anything grew up in the fields, it was weeds pushing up through dead cornstalks. No trace at all was left of year before last's wheat. It was only a memory. This country was importing as much grain as it could these days, along with oil and so much else. The dollar was sinking like a stone. It would have sunk even faster if Europe and Japan and China weren't hurting, too.

Except for the ruined farmlands all around her, Vanessa didn't have time to think much about the battered economy. Washington talked about sending work crews into ashfall country to reclaim it. Washington, though, was a thousand miles away. Nothing would reclaim this country except time.

"So what are we doing here, then?" she asked the boss to whose crew she'd been assigned.

Merv Saunders looked like something out of a Grant Wood painting. He was tall and thin and bald, with wire-framed glasses and a long face made up of vertical and horizontal lines of disapproval. "Scavenging," he answered matter-of-factly. "Lots of stuff got left behind when people had to run. Quite a bit of it'll still work—or we can make it work with a little cleaning and tinkering. There's an awful mob of folks out in the camps who need anything we can get our hands on."

Ashley Pagliarulo let you know at any excuse or none that she had a law degree. That didn't mean she wasn't wearing somebody else's old clothes like the rest of the work crew, or that she didn't need a shower as much as her comrades. But it did give her an attitude. Now she said, "Under most circumstances, this would be theft." By the way she said it, she expected cop cars to roar up with sirens blaring any second now.

It wasn't gonna happen. If there were any cop cars within a hundred miles, Vanessa would have been amazed. And Merv Saunders sounded as calm as Valium as he answered, "The Abandoned Property Act makes it legal, as you know perfectly well."

Ashley only sniffed. Either Pagliarulo was her married name or her ancestors came from some part of Italy that produced petite blondes. "The Abandoned Property Act will never stand up under judicial review," she predicted.

Saunders shrugged. "If you feel that way about it, how come you're here?"

"Because I was gonna go bonkers if I stayed in that lousy camp another minute," the attorney snarled, a sentiment Vanessa completely understood.

"Well, okay." Saunders got it, too. "But we honest to God are doing something useful for the country here. A lot of the stuff that we're getting out won't be worth having if we leave it here for another few years. And most of the people we're taking it from are dead."

"Some aren't. Some wound up in camps the same way we did." Ashley was always ready to argue. Any time, any place. She was a lawyer, all right. She went on, "And even the dead people have heirs. We're plundering their estates."

The crew boss looked at her. "You can always go back to a camp, you know." He didn't say *whether you want to or not*, but anybody with two brain cells to rub together would hear it in his voice. Vanessa sure did. She'd given him some static, too. Now she decided keeping her mouth shut for a while might be a pretty fair plan. Going back to a camp was the very last thing she wanted to do.

Ashley Pagliarulo also got the message loud and clear. She said not another word. She looked miffed. Hell, she looked righteously pissed off. But she was plainly of the same opinion as Vanessa: that going to a camp was like going to jail, only with worse food and accommodations.

Not that being in the middle of ruined Kansas was any bargain. Whenever the wind blew out of the west, as it did a lot of the time, it picked up dust from the thicker layers in those parts and did its best to re-cover what time and rain had started to clear.

They all had pig-snouted gas masks. When the wind blew from the west, they wore them, too. Hundreds of thousands of people had already died from HPO and other lung ailments brought on by breathing that crap. Nobody could guess how many more would prematurely follow them into the grave. And, as Vanessa knew from the dreadful days right after the eruption, being out and about with the dust blowing around was like trying to carry on after you'd had a handful of grit thrown in your eyes. Wearing a gas mask was a metaphorical pain. Doing without one was a literal pain. Reality trumped metaphor every goddamn time.

Here was another farmhouse with the front door standing open. Maybe the people who'd lived here hadn't bothered closing it when they got the hell out. Maybe looters had hit the place after the owners bailed. If they had, Vanessa hoped the time they'd wasted plundering meant they came down with one of the zillion lung diseases the dust could give you. As far as she was concerned, looters deserved all the bad things that happened to them and a few more besides. Her father, no doubt, would have sympathized with the attitude.

Looters *had* hit the place. The TV was gone. There was no computer anywhere. Pulled-open drawers, everything in them now gray with dust, said there wouldn't be any jewelry, either.

But there were shoes in the bedrooms and clothes in the closets. Before long, some refugees would be wearing these people's castoffs. Vanessa was in clothes like that herself. So were her colleagues. Demand still exceeded supply. Like her, plenty of people in the camps had no money to buy anything new. They depended on charity—and on the fruits of the Abandoned Property Act.

The wearables went into black trash bags. Vanessa wondered out loud what people had done before they had plastic bags to stash stuff in.

She didn't particularly expect an answer, but she got one. "Burlap," Merv Saunders said. "It was cheap, and there was lots of it. They still use it for sandbags because of that. Feed sacks, too."

They found feed sacks out in the barn. No livestock remained in there. These people must either have taken their animals with them or, if they couldn't do that, turned them loose and hoped for the best. Those hopes were doomed to disappointment, but they couldn't have known ahead of time.

Vanessa had had to turn her cat loose before they let her into a refugee center. She'd hoped for the best, too, but . . . Poor Pickles! Tears stung her eyes. She blinked them back. Crying inside a gas mask was a bad idea, because tears had nowhere to go and fogged up your lenses like nobody's business.

But the barn did have those sacks of feed—some made from plastic-impregnated paper; others, sure as hell, of good, old-fashioned burlap. And feed, even feed that was past its sell-by date, was precious. The Midwest's endless abundance was dead, smothered in supervolcano ash and dust. Those sacks of corn and soybeans and whatever wouldn't be coming out of America's breadbasket by the millions any more, not for God only knew how many years. Animals that had survived elsewhere in the country still needed to eat. If the food was stale, well, stale feed was a hell of a lot better than no feed. People weren't so fussy now as they had been when times were flush.

The crew lugged the feed sacks to their truck. It wore the mechanical equivalent of a gas mask. It sported an enormous, heavy-duty air filter that sure as hell wasn't part of its original equipment. The engine compartment and transmission were much better sealed off than was necessary in most of the country, to keep grit from getting into the moving parts.

Vanessa remembered how her own Toyota had crapped out on the road while she was trying to get away from the eruption. She just thanked heaven she'd got her hands on some surgical masks before then. Otherwise, she'd be coughing her lungs out now, if breathing in that garbage hadn't made her kick the bucket.

Then she thought of Pickles again. She'd had to turn him loose to die. This time, she wasn't fighting tears but killing rage. If she ever ran into the prune-faced bitch who'd made her get rid of the cat . . . That gal wouldn't last fifteen seconds, and there was the long and short of it.

And here she was, straining her back to lug feed sacks over to a truck kitted out like something from a Mad Max movie. And she was glad to be doing it, too, because all her other choices looked worse. If that wasn't a bastard and a half, she was damned if she knew what would be.

When they'd emptied out the barn, Merv Saunders checked a printout he'd got before they started this grave-robbing expedition. "Way to go, people," he said. "Our next stop is Arma, Kansas."

"*Arma virumque cano,*" Vanessa said. It was a leftover from Bryce, and damn near the only bit of Latin she knew.

Everybody else in the crew looked at her. Saunders rolled his eyes.

"It's from Vergil," she said. "Means 'Of arms and the man I sing.'"

They didn't care. Their stares, some black and others suspicious (as well as she could guess by reading expressions through gas masks), showed that only too clearly. She wished she could have done three or four more lines, but that probably would have just made matters worse. She spread her work-gloved hands.

"Our next stop is Arma," Saunders repeated, every line of his body saying *Wanna make something out of it?* Vanessa gave up and stood there, waiting. The crew boss went on, "It's a decent-sized town—more than fifteen hundred people, when it had people. It's got a gas station. If the underground tanks are anywhere close to full, that's even more important than bringing back feed."

The crew nodded. Vanessa found her own head going up and down. Any gasoline or diesel fuel that you could get your hands on was more precious than rubies these days. The dollar was hurting. Countries that hadn't been trashed could afford oil imports better than the USA could. Not that the oil business was in great shape itself. The sputtering wars in the Middle East made sure of that.

So . . . grave-robbing. And it was important enough that even Vanessa couldn't get—too—cynical about it.

Louise Ferguson pulled into her parking space in the condominium complex. She wondered how much longer she'd be able to keep driving to the ramen headquarters on Braxton Bragg Boulevard. It wasn't all that far from here, and she didn't use very much gas going back and forth. But the stuff was ridiculously expensive—when the stations had any, which they did less and less often. Back before the supervolcano erupted, Europeans would have rebelled at paying prices like these. They were paying even more than she was now, not that that made her happy. Misery, here, didn't love company. Misery was just miserable.

She walked to the mailboxes at the front of the complex. A cable bill. A catalogue from a clothing company—NEW FASHIONS FOR COOLER CLIMES! the cover said, sounding more cheerful than it had any business being. A notice from the electric company, warning that reduced generating capacity might mean intermittent service. That translated into English as rolling blackouts. *The governor threatened them before. Now they're here,* she thought as she went back toward the condo that had been Teo's and was now hers.

It really was hers. The lawyers had done their dance over title to the place, dotting every *t* and crossing every *i* and doing whatever the hell they did: probably lifting their legs and peeing on the papers till the miserable things smelled right. Whatever it was, it hadn't come cheap. Nothing did, not in this day and age.

Up the stairs she trudged. She remembered how Teo had bounded up them, and how her heart had jumped when she heard his energetic strides. She would have loved him still if only he could have handled the idea of having a kid. She had the kid. She had the condo. She didn't have Teo—and if he showed up now, she'd spit in his eye.

When she walked in, Marshall was holding his little half-brother. The baby's smile at seeing his mother was so wide it almost made the top half of his head fall off. "Da-da-da-da!" he squealed.

"That's your mama," Marshall said. "Mama."

"Da-da-da-da!" James Henry repeated, even louder than before.

"He'll figure it out," Louise said. "All of you guys went 'dada' before you went 'mama,' too." That had made Colin proud and irked her, not that either one of them would ever have admitted it.

"Whatever." Usually, Marshall bailed out of the condo as if his Nikes were on fire when Louise got home. That was partly because he liked babysitting no better than any other single guy his age, partly because he remained pissed off at his mother for ending the marriage that had brought him into the world. He didn't—by the nature of things, he couldn't—understand how dead the marriage was before Louise ended it. (That Colin hadn't had the first clue it was dead said nothing good about him: not if you listened to Louise, anyhow.)

Today, though, Marshall didn't go anywhere. He just stood there. Louise gradually recognized the look on his face as expectant. With a sigh, she remembered why: she was supposed to pay him today. She fumbled in her purse till she found her checkbook and a pen. She wrote rapidly, tore off the check, and handed it to him. "Here you go."

"Thanks." He put it in the pocket of his Levi's. That he wouldn't help his mother for free never failed to annoy her, but he wouldn't. If you listened to Colin, you couldn't reasonably expect anything else, but Louise made a point of not listening to Colin.

"Wait!" she said suddenly when Marshall was already halfway to the door.

He paused. "Wazzup?"

"Let me see that check again."

He handed it to her. She scribbled the amount in her register. She used to forget to do that about one time in five. It had driven methodical, organized Colin straight up a wall. Louise always figured she had more creative things to worry about . . . till she was on her own, and had to balance the checkbook herself instead of letting somebody else worry about it. The hassles a couple of unexpected bounced checks put her through did more to make her note every single one of them than Colin's sarcasm had ever managed.

She gave back the check. "Now you can escape."

"Whatever," Marshall said again, and did just that.

Dealing with the register meant Louise had taken her eyes off James Henry for a few seconds. She couldn't safely do that any more, not when he was crawling. He'd got something in his mouth. She grabbed him, reached in there, and pulled it out.

A little scrap of paper. It wouldn't have hurt him even if he'd swallowed it, but you never wanted to take chances like that. Most of the time, she wouldn't have wanted to stick her finger into somebody else's mouth, either. A mom with a baby got used to all kinds of things she wouldn't have wanted to do most of the time.

She nursed him. She gave him some rice cereal and some carrot goop. His diapers had got more revolting since he started eating solid food. Colin used to say a rug rat wasn't human till it was potty-trained. Like a lot of things Colin had said, that held just enough truth to be annoying.

Louise found herself thinking of her ex-husband a lot more often than she thought about the departed father of her latest child. Yes, she'd been together with Colin a lot longer than she had with Teo, but that wasn't it, or not all of it. Colin said and thought more interesting things than Teo.

Which mattered only so much. Teo'd been a hell of a lot better in bed and easier to get along with . . . till he freaked out when she found herself pregnant.

James Henry was trying to catch his toes and stuff them in his mouth. "I love you," Louise told him, "but you are such a damn nuisance."

"Da-da-da!" the baby said happily. His tummy was full. His diaper was dry. His onesie kept him warm. His mommy was there. He didn't care about anything else in the whole wide world.

I should be so lucky, Louise thought.

Kelly lay next to Colin. Once upon a time, Louise had lain with him on the same mattress. Kelly mostly didn't think about that. Expecting somebody to get a whole new bed after a breakup would have been way over the top. Now, though, it forcibly came back to her mind.

Maybe it came back to his, too. "You sure you wanna go through with this?" he asked in a low voice. It was dark. The door to the master bedroom was locked *and* latched. Marshall's door was locked, too, and he probably wouldn't come out for anything this side of the crack of doom, anyway. And if he did, he wouldn't worry about his dad and his dad's new wife. Colin kept his voice down just the same.

"Darn right I do," Kelly said. She nodded, too. It was so dark, Colin might not see that. She reached for him. And go through with it they did.

Afterwards, Kelly sprawled on her side, lazy in the afterglow. Colin said, "Boy, I don't remember the last time I did that without protection."

"Me, neither," Kelly said. One of the reasons she didn't remember was that she'd been seriously drunk when it happened. And she'd let out a long, loud sigh of relief when her next period came right on schedule.

This, though, this was different. You could joke about biological clocks. It wasn't as if she never had. But things got less funny when you listened to your own ticking—and when you knew it would wind down for good in the ever-less-indefinite future.

Oh, sometimes you got a surprise later than you thought you could. Colin's ex sure had, and now his kids had an altogether unexpected half-brother. *And here I am, thinking about Louise again.* Kelly was annoyed with herself, which didn't mean she could keep from doing it. Which was part of what she got for marrying a man with a considerable past. Of course, when you got up to her age the only men without considerable pasts were the ones who'd never moved away from their mothers. They presented different—and usually worse—problems.

She shook her head. "What?" Colin asked, feeling the motion.

"Nothing," Kelly answered, which wasn't quite true, but it was nothing she wanted to talk about with him. After a moment, she went on, "If we can make something together—make a baby together—what could be more special than that?"

"That's why we're doing it. And besides, even trying is fun," Colin said. Kelly poked him in the ribs. She was usually more ticklish than he was, but she must have hit the bull's-eye, because he jerked.

"Serves you right," Kelly told him.

"What? You *didn't* have fun trying?" When he decided to be difficult, he was difficult as all get out. But then he said, "Y'know, after Louise and I had our three, she was always after me to get a vasectomy so she wouldn't have to go on using her manhole cover."

"Her what?" Kelly was glad Colin couldn't see her blank stare.

"Diaphragm," he explained.

"Oh." She poked him again, less successfully this time. He *would* make a bad joke like that. He not only would, he had.

"Yeah, well," he went on, "I didn't feel like doing anything where the odds of undoing it weren't so great. I didn't think anything was wrong—which only shows how much I knew, doesn't it? But I even used condominiums every once in a while so she wouldn't need the Frisbee."

To do that justice, Kelly would have had to poke him eight or twelve times. She contented herself with snorting instead. Colin hadn't made the smallest of sacrifices, though, not from the male point of view. Guys used condoms, but the next man she found who liked them would be the first. Then again, she hoped she wouldn't have to do any more looking for men—or why had she just made love wanting to get pregnant?

Colin turned on the lamp on his nightstand. He smiled over at her. "I definitely got lucky," he said.

"Oh, foosh!" she replied. She wasn't anything special, not with the way her tummy pooched out and her seat spread. She'd never actually met Louise in person, but she'd seen photos. Louise was elegantly slim, and her sculpted features reminded Kelly of some actress whose name she couldn't quite come up with. When she added, "I don't know what you see in me," she wasn't making idle talk.

"Somebody I love, that's what," Colin said, which was always the right answer. He went on, "Somebody who loves me, too, and who wants to be here with me."

Kelly kissed him. "You better believe it, mister."

"Oh, I do. For a while, I didn't think I would ever believe it, but I do." This time, he kissed her. "Thank you."

"My pleasure." She meant it.

He grinned a male grin. "Not all of it, lady. And the other thing I see is, I see this darn sexy broad naked in bed with me, and what could be better than that?"

Kelly didn't think of herself as a darn sexy broad. She thought of herself as a geologist. Being thought of as a sex object kind of weirded her out. Then again, if you weren't your husband's sex object, you had other worries. Colin didn't *just* want her for that. She never would have married him if he had. Since he did want her for that . . . "Turn off the light again."

He was in his fifties. Second rounds didn't happen quickly, the way they would have when he was younger, or sometimes at all. That didn't make fooling around any less enjoyable. And even if he didn't rise to the occasion right away, he wasn't shy about using fingers and tongue to bring her along.

"I don't think I can walk to the bathroom," she said after a while. "My knees are all loose."

"That's nice." If he sounded smug, he'd earned the right. "You could just roll over and go to sleep."

"That's your department," Kelly retorted, though Colin didn't live up to—or down to—the male cliché very often.

"Huh!" This time, he poked her in the ribs. She squeaked. He chuckled. "I'll go, then," he said, and he did. When he got back, he added, quite seriously, "I do love you, you know."

"I noticed," she answered. "If I remember straight, that's how my knees got all loose."

"Nah." He shook his head; the mattress sent her the vibration in the dark room. "That's just fooling around. Fooling around is great—don't get me wrong. But I mean, I really love you. That quake in Yellowstone was the best thing that ever happened to me."

Well, I got some good data from it, too. The thought went through Kelly's mind, but died unsaid. Another time, another place, she would have come out with it. Colin appreciated dry—you didn't know him at all if you didn't know that. Not right this minute, though, not when they'd been trying to start a child together. "I love you, too," she said, and leaned over and kissed him. "And now I am gonna go to the john, loose knees or not."

She burrowed under the covers when she returned. It wasn't warm. It hardly ever was any more. "Good night," Colin said, so he hadn't gone to sleep.

"G'night." A few minutes later, she did.

VIII

It wasn't snowing. There was still snow on the ground, but not everywhere. Rob Ferguson savored the sun shining wanly down out of a sky exactly the color of a high school girlfriend's gray-blue eyes. Here and there, hopeful green grass sprouted through the dead yellow tangle of last year's halfhearted growth. A few deciduous trees showed new little leaves.

It should have been April, or maybe early May—Rob wasn't a hundred percent sure how the weather had worked in Guilford before the supervolcano went off. It was . . . the middle of August. It was the second year in a row without a summer, the second of nobody knew how many.

The roads were open. For the time being, till the blizzards clamped down again, Maine north and west of the Interstate was reconnected to the rest of the country. The Shell station down the street from the Trebor Mansion Inn had gas—not a lot of gas, and twelve bucks a gallon, but gas. Squirt Frog and the Evolving Tadpoles could have got the hell out.

Plenty of people had. Most of the ones who'd left had relatives in warmer parts of the country. (There weren't many colder ones, not in the Lower Forty-eight. What was happening to places like Fairbanks and Nome and Anchorage, Rob didn't want to think about.)

Dick Barber was glad to see individuals and families pull up stakes. So was Jim Farrell. "The fewer mouths we have to feed when we're on our own again, the better off we'll be," he declared to anyone who would listen. Barber spread the gospel of flight, too—without packing up and leaving himself.

The band was still here, too. Every once in a while, Justin would make wistful noises about hitting the road again. Sometimes Charlie Storer would nod, but not in a way to make anybody think he really meant it. One reason he didn't was that Biff wasn't going anywhere. Biff cared more about Cindy down at Caleb's Kitchen than he did about touring. Well he might: she was going to have a baby. They hadn't tied the knot yet, but that also looked to be in the cards.

And Rob wasn't eager to vamoose from the land of moose, either. He'd been going with Lindsey ever since they literally bumped into each other outside the Episcopal church. She wasn't carrying his child, but not for lack of effort. If it came down to a choice between her and the band ... Rob was glad it hadn't come down to that.

Justin and Charlie had also found friends of the female persuasion. That, no doubt, was one reason why they didn't sound more serious about bailing out. Yes, they were musicians. Yes, they were used to temporary attachments. But, whether or not they'd intended to, they'd put down roots here.

Roots ... Every house had a garden. All the gardens were trying to grow potatoes and parsnips and turnips and mangel-wurzels and anything else that had a prayer of maturing in a growing season abbreviated even for Maine. Extravagant mulch and plastic sheeting fought the cold as best they could. And maybe there would be a crop and maybe there wouldn't. Everyone would find out when the weather turned really bad again.

In the meantime . . . In the meantime, Rob ambled down the semigrassy slope to the Piscataquis. The stream had thawed out enough to chuckle over its rocky bed. It had probably been born from glacial runoff. Rob stuck his finger into it, then jerked the digit out again. "Brr!" he said. By all the signs, the river was getting back to its roots.

A blue jay scolded him from a pine tree. A lot of birds had flown south for the winter and not come back. Jays and robins and ravens lingered. So did ospreys—one plunged into the frigid water and came out with a fish clamped in its talons. Another jay flew after the fish hawk, screeching.

Some kids threw a football around. The slope that led to the river meant only sidehill sheep could have played any proper kind of game. The kids didn't care. They threw and kicked and yelled and laughed. It was summer vacation, even if it was summer only by the calendar.

They'd missed a lot of school even when it wasn't vacation. Lindsey made sorrowful noises about that. Sometimes it was because they couldn't get to class themselves. When the snowdrifts were taller than they were. . . . More often, though, their teachers couldn't make it. Not all the teachers lived in Guilford. The ones who didn't had relied on the quaint concept known as motor transportation. Here and there in the U.S. of A., roads still stayed open. Not in this part of the country, though. Nowhere close. The joke for Siberia had been ten months of winter and two of bad skiing. The joke, these days, applied all too literally to this part of Maine.

As he had with Alaska, Rob wondered how things were in Siberia right now. Cold: the one-word answer immediately supplied itself. Bloody fucking cold, if you wanted to get technical.

Though it might seem hard to believe, there had been places with climates worse than the one Guilford didn't enjoy. If Guilford had turned into a pretty fair approximation of Siberia, what had Siberia turned into?

The South Pole, Rob thought. Then he tried to imagine penguins roaming the tundra. It made him want to giggle.

A kid missed the football. It took three crazy bounces and stopped right at Rob's feet. "Throw it back, man!" the kid yelled. He was about twelve—no beard on his cheeks, and his voice hadn't broken.

Rob picked it up. "I'll do better than that," he said. The shape and the pebbly feel of the leather or rubbery plastic or whatever the hell it was combined irresistibly. Like a certain deranged beagle, what red-blooded grown-up doesn't want to be the Mad Punter, even if only for a moment?

He let fly. He hadn't played football since PE in high school, and he hadn't been the punter then. By rights, he should have squibbed it off the side of his foot. By dumb luck, he caught it square. It flew long and straight. It would have been a forty-yarder on any NFL gridiron—well, any NFL gridiron except Mile High Stadium, which was still deeply buried in volcanic crap.

"Wow!" The kid who'd called for the ball wasn't the only one to stare at him, wide-eyed. He tried not to preen. Damned if he hadn't had standing O's at club gigs that he'd enjoyed less. Being applauded for skill was one thing. Being applauded for skill and strength . . . He felt as if he'd grown shoulder pads under his flannel shirt.

After the kids retrieved the ball, they brought it back to him. One of the kids flipped it his way. "Do it again!"

He didn't think he could do it twice in a row. Hell, he hadn't thought he could do it once in a row. But he'd always been able to resist anything but temptation—a line his old man had used more than once. He punted again. It wasn't as good as the first try, but it went a lot farther than any kid who hadn't reached puberty could manage.

They swarmed after it and brought it back like retrievers. He didn't want to play punting machine. If once was experiment and twice was perversion, what was three times? Boring, that was what.

They didn't ask him for another punt, though. Instead, one of them said, "When are you guys gonna play again?"

"I dunno," Rob answered. "Next town meeting, maybe, if they want us to." That was a week away.

When you were eleven or twelve, a week was as good—no, as bad—as forever. "Wish you'd play here in the park again, sooner than that," the boy said.

"In the daytime," one of his friends added.

There was a lot of daytime at this season of the year, just as nights here stretched like Silly Putty during wintertime. More than just the weather told you Maine lay a lot farther north than L.A. or Santa Barbara, which were Rob's standards of comparison.

"Well, we'll see," he said.

"Puhleeze!" Three of them squealed it at the same time.

Hearing them, he realized how starved for entertainment they were. They'd grown up with TV and the Net and PlaySta-tions and Wiis and Xboxes. All of that stuff took electricity, though. Guilford had power for three or four hours a day during the summer. During the winter . . . Well, people tried—you had to give them that. But it was mostly no go, and no juice.

If they wanted to listen to a band they'd surely never heard of before it washed up on their frozen shore—and wanted to badly enough to beg for music—they really had it bad. If Squirt Frog and the Evolving Tadpoles could tour the local towns, towns that hadn't had an almost-rock band get stuck in them, it might clean up. It might clean up as much as anybody in this part of Maine could right now, anyhow.

"We'll see," Rob repeated, but in a different tone of voice this time. Biff wouldn't mind that kind of tour. Rob wouldn't mind it himself. It might work. It was definitely worth talking about.

The kids caught the difference. "Yeah!" they said, or rather, "Ayuh!" It was Maine, all right. One of them waved for another to go out on a pass pattern. The ball spiraled after him. The boys raced away.

But when Rob looked out the windows of his tower garret in the Trebor Mansion Inn the next morning, the sky had gone gray and gloomy and dark. Snow swirled through the air. It wasn't a blizzard, but it also wasn't the kind of weather that would let the band draw a crowd, even from the hardy folk who'd stayed in Guilford. He still intended to talk about playing, but this wasn't the day for it.

Colin Ferguson looked wistfully at the Taurus in his driveway. It still ran. He fired it up every now and then and took it around the block to keep the battery alive and to make sure the tires stayed round. He'd drive it if he went out to dinner with Kelly, especially when it was raining. And these days it rained more often in the L.A. basin than he'd ever dreamt it could.

But he didn't go to work in the Taurus every day any more, even though it wasn't far. Gas was too hard to come by, and too expensive for anyone on a civil-service salary to use very much. A San Atanasio police lieutenant made a pretty good civil-service salary. What Kelly brought in from Cal State Dominguez didn't hurt, either. All the same . . .

All the same, he put his briefcase in his bike's cargo basket, climbed aboard, and pedaled away. He hadn't ridden a bicycle very often between the time when he was fifteen or sixteen and the day the supervolcano erupted. They said you never forgot how. Like a lot of things they said, that had holes that would have sunk it if it were a boat. He'd wobbled all over the place when he started riding again. He'd had a good fall, too. Luckily, he'd blown the knees out of an old pair of sweats, not the pants from any of his suits. Even more luckily, though he'd pedaled home scraped up and bruised, he hadn't broken anything.

It did come back in a hurry. The mysterious *they* were right about that much. Colin had got to the point where he enjoyed the wind in his face as he rode. (The rain was a different story. He'd quickly bought a plastic slicker that covered him from head to foot, and a broad-brimmed hat to keep most of the raindrops off his bifocals. Bicycling with an umbrella, he'd rapidly discovered, was an invitation to suicide.)

He wasn't the only two-wheeled commuter. Oh, no—not even close. Bikes, and especially bikes with adults in business attire on them, had been uncommon sights on L.A.–area streets before the eruption. No more. As gas prices zoomed up like a Trident missile, more and more people said to hell with their cars and started doing without infernal combustion.

Colin had dropped five pounds since he started biking more than he drove. His wind was better than it had been. That was the good news. The bad news was the San Atanasio PD's Robbery Division was trying to deal with an explosion of bicycle thefts. So was every other police department in Southern California—and in a lot of other places, too.

A car whizzed by. It didn't come particularly close, but he sent it a resentful stare even so. Now that he rode the bicycle, he looked at automobiles in a whole new way. The goddamn things were dangerous. If you tangled with one, you lost. It was as simple as that. And so many people drove with their heads up their asses. *Bike? What bike?* they might have been saying.

He'd probably driven that way himself. As a matter of fact, he was sure he had. How many times had he almost creamed some green ecofreako with delusions of Lance Armstrong? Plenty—he knew as much. And he'd blamed the skinny morons on the bikes every single time.

He stopped at a light, then turned right onto Hesperus. That was a bigger street. It had more cars on it. Not a whole lot more, though. Even L.A. and its auto-based suburbs could do without the sacred conveyance if they had to. They sure were trying to make like they could, anyhow.

"Pothole coming," he muttered, reminding himself. It was right in front of a tropical-fish place run by a Japanese couple who, he happened to know, also owned about a quarter of the real estate down in Torrance—a bigger, richer burb than working-class San Atanasio. But they just plain liked tropical fish, so they went on selling them.

The pothole was a doozy. He would have felt it in the Taurus. On the bike, it might have sent him ass over teakettle. Not for the first time, he told himself to call Street Maintenance and give them hell. One of these days. In his copious spare time.

He had to get out into the middle of the street to turn left into the police station parking lot. The bike rack there was new since the eruption. Colin chained his mount to a hitching post. The bike was secondhand, and had seen better times. The chain was new, and industrial-strength. Marshall had had a bike disappear from a UCSB rack on account of an el-cheapo chain. Colin made his share of mistakes, but usually not the ones he could see coming six miles down the road.

Gabe Sanchez was standing outside the door poisoning his lungs. Colin nodded to the sergeant. "What do you know?" he called.

"I know I'd rather do this inside," Gabe answered. "It's cold out here, dammit."

Colin didn't feel cold. "You must have driven this morning," he said. No, he didn't feel cold at all. Antiperspirant was still getting into SoCal. The world would turn less pleasant if that supply ever failed.

"Way to go, Sherlock," Sanchez said. "Anybody would guess you were a cop or something."

"You think maybe?" Colin said. He looked like a cop. He dressed like a cop. He talked like a cop. He thought like a cop. So what was he gonna be? A tropical-fish merchant? An auctioneer? Like Popeye, he was what he was, and that was all that he was.

Well, almost all. If he hadn't been a post-divorce tourist, he wouldn't also be a middle-aged guy trying to start a second family. Rob, Vanessa, and Marshall might end up with a new half-brother or half-sister. *Another* new half-brother or half-sister, that is. And one with exactly zero biological relationship to their last new half-brother.

"Life gets fucking weird sometimes, you know?" Colin said: no great originality there, but plenty of feeling.

Feeling or not, Gabe shook his head. "Unh-unh, man. That's a negative. Every once in a while, life *stops* being fucking weird. That's when you think it starts making sense. And when you do, it drops the hammer on you but good. Because the rest of the time . . ." He shook his head again, and crushed the coffin nail under his heel. Then he looked mournful. "I want another one, dammit."

"I'd go easy, if I were you." Colin left it there. Like antiperspirant, tobacco reached L.A. from points east. Like antiperspirant and everything else coming in from points east, it reached L.A. in limited amounts, with prices inflated to match. Or maybe to more than match. People who had the cigarette jones had it bad.

Take Gabe Sanchez, for instance. He looked more sorrowful still. "Tell me about it. I'm smoking, like, half as much as I used to. That means I always need the next one twice as bad." His laugh was singularly—almost plurally—devoid of humor. "The weenies who get on your back for liking the shit at all say you'll live longer if you smoke less. It sure as hell seems longer—I'll tell you that."

"Ready to earn your next pack?" Colin asked, stepping toward the door.

"Way prices are now, that's about two weeks of work." Gabe exaggerated, but less than he would have a year earlier, and a lot less than he would have before the eruption. He followed Colin into the station.

Before long, Colin wasn't so warm as he had been right after he chained his bike to the rack. You couldn't crank up the heat the way you had in the old days. You also couldn't roll the AC like nobody's business on a scorching summer day. That turned out not to be such an enormous issue. The next scorching summer day here after the eruption would be the first.

Supervolcano or no supervolcano, people still robbed banks and liquor stores and even a laundromat. That one croggled Colin. The perp had escaped with over a hundred pounds of quarters in four large sacks.

"What the hell's he gonna do with all of 'em?" he asked, not at all rhetorically. "You can't spend 'em more than maybe five bucks at a time. Take your girlfriend out to a fancy restaurant and pay in rolls of quarters, people will talk."

"Watch out for some dude buying everybody games at the arcade," Rodney Ellis suggested. The black detective mimed working a joystick.

"There you go," Colin said. "Makes more sense than anything I thought of."

"Perp was in his forties, the crime report says," Gabe pointed out. "So that's kinda less likely, know what I mean?"

"Maybe yes, maybe no," Rodney answered. "But what did that guy say? You're only young once, but you can be immature forever."

Colin thought of Louise, and of her adventures and misadventures with her younger man. But if he told her anything like that, she'd go off the way the hot spot under Yellowstone had. Except in the line of duty, he tried not to talk to her these days.

Back to business. "What are we going to do about this asshole?" he said. "It's not what you'd call a good description."

"Wait till he hits the next Stop-and-Rob," Rodney said. "And if he gets away with quarters again, right after that he'll show up at the San Atanasio Memorial ER with a double hernia."

"Everybody's a comedian," Colin said, but he and Gabe were both laughing.

It had started raining by the time they went out to lunch in Gabe's car. The Honda stank of cigarette smoke, but that was better than getting drenched. "You're gonna have fun riding home tonight," Gabe remarked.

"Tell me about it," Colin said gloomily. Poncho or not, he'd get wet. Sighing, he went on, "Once upon a time, it didn't rain this time of year."

"Yeah, I know." Gabe nodded. "We'll keep saying that till they shovel dirt over us. All the kids too young to remember what it was like back then will think we're a pathetic bunch of old farts for all the pissing and moaning about the good old days we do."

"Yup." Colin contented himself with the one word. The prediction sounded altogether too likely.

"Your wife knows about this shit, right?" Gabe said. "So, how long is the weather supposed to stay fucked up?"

Colin only shrugged. "From what she tells me, nobody can say for sure. Twenty years? fifty? A couple of hundred? A couple of thousand? We all get to find out." He didn't say that Kelly feared things would stay bad for the long end of the guesses— estimates, if you wanted the more scientific term. She didn't think a short cold snap would have put *Homo sapiens* through such a wringer 75,000 years ago, after Mount Toba went kablooie.

No point passing that on to Gabe. Kelly admitted it was nothing but speculation. If Gabe wanted to think his kids would see the good old climate again, he could. Nobody could prove he was wrong for thinking so. And optimism, like so many other things, came where you found it.

The rain had grown more serious, more sure of itself, while they were eating. They ran to Gabe Sanchez's car. "Boy, this is fun," Sanchez said. He pulled out a pack of Camels from his inside jacket pocket and held it up. "You mind?"

"You think I'm gonna tell you what to do here?" Colin said. "I'm rude, but I ain't that rude, dude." Gabe lit up and started the car. Colin knew secondhand smoke from one cigarette wouldn't give him lung cancer. He also knew it would make his clothes—and his skin, too—smell like burnt tobacco. Kelly would wrinkle her nose when he came home tonight. Maybe if he got there ahead of her, showered, and changed into something else . . .

"One thing," Gabe said as he pulled out of the parking lot and onto the street. "South Bay Strangler's been quiet lately."

"Probably had to pull overtime at his day job," Colin answered. For all he knew, it was the exact and literal truth. If he'd known more . . . If he'd known more, he would have dropped on the son of a bitch a long time ago.

The sign was dusty. It could have used a fresh coat of paint. But it was still easy enough to read. KEEP OUT! it said in big red and blue letters on a white background. THIS MEANS YOU! Below that was a line of slightly smaller words: TRESPASSERS WILL BE VIOLATED!

Vanessa Ferguson eyed the sign with something less than enthusiasm. "Nice friendly asshole, wasn't he?" she remarked.

"Or maybe, isn't he?" Merv Saunders pointed to the farmhouse in the middle distance. "Somebody might still be holed up in there."

"I don't think so!" Vanessa wasn't shy about talking back to the scavenging crew's boss. Vanessa had never been shy about talking back to anybody. She'd had a checkered work life and a checkered love life because of it, but she was one of those people who counted costs afterwards, if they counted them at all.

"Do we want to find out?" Ashley Pagliarulo pointed to another sign, maybe fifty feet closer to the farmhouse.

That one showed a black skull and crossbones, with a blunt warning in red below it: ACHTUNG! MINEN! Not DANGER! MINES! No, not that, but *auf Deutsch*. Vanessa's lip curled in disgusted scorn. "Neo-Nazi shithead," she said. "I hope he did cough his worthless lungs out. He deserved it."

"It's likely just bullshit," Saunders said, but he made no move to approach the farmhouse. "And if people are alive in there, we're supposed to make contact with them no matter what kind of dumbass politics they've got."

No one was supposed to be living in this part of Kansas. The mandatory evacuation order had gone out soon after the supervolcano erupted. Vanessa had been stripping farms and little towns of whatever might prove useful to survivors for months now, her team steadily working its way deeper into the ruined state. She'd helped bury more bodies than she cared to remember. That was one reason her palms were hard with callus. As for livestock carcasses . . . No point even trying to count those. The scavengers didn't try to put them underground.

She did wonder what the country could do for meat with so many of its cows and sheep and pigs and chickens as one with the extinct animals that had died in earlier eruptions and fossilized. One of these millions of years, funny-looking archaeologists digging up ash-covered cattle ranches might write learned papers about what they found.

In the meantime . . . "I'd just as soon go on to the next place down the road," Vanessa said. "I don't care if we are supposed to make contact with people. If they don't want to make contact with us, the hell with 'em."

Several of her comrades in vulturing nodded. Saunders frowned, though. "We *are* supposed to get in touch with them, assuming they're alive."

"Harder if they're not," Vanessa agreed sweetly.

He gave her a dirty look. "I don't think it's real likely that they are, though," he said, as if she hadn't opened her mouth. "I think the chances are that that sign is a bluff, too, or was a bluff when there were people here."

As if to prove as much, he took a few steps past the KEEP OUT! sign, toward the one that warned of the mines. He hadn't gone far before something in or near the farmhouse opened up with a stuttering roar. Tracers zipped past overhead, but not too far overhead.

The machine-gun fire stopped. "Get the fuck off my land, bastard!" an amplified voice bellowed. "I won't shoot to miss next time."

Maybe he had a generator in or near the farmhouse, even if Vanessa couldn't hear one chugging. Maybe he just had a battery-powered bullhorn, though batteries were drawing ever closer to their shelf life. Whatever else he had, he had the goddamn machine gun. Vanessa had used firearms often enough. Having the bullets coming in instead of going out was a whole different feeling, though. Fear tasted like a copper penny under her tongue. She didn't piss herself, but she had to clamp down hard to keep from having that accident.

Merv Saunders didn't argue with the survivalist or whatever the hell he was. Whatever he was, he *had* survived. Was he living on stashed food? Did he go out to do some freelance scavenging of his own? Had he somehow kept his livestock alive along with himself and whoever else he had in there?

At the moment, all that was academic. The government-sanctioned scavengers retreated with more speed than dignity. Saunders got on the radio to points farther east. Except for the satellite variety, cell phones didn't work in these parts. Power remained out through most of the country's midsection. When it would come back, nobody could even begin to guess.

"Can you call in helicopter gunships?" Vanessa asked eagerly. "Or at least soldiers with mortars and grenades and things?"

The crew boss looked at her. "Have you been eating raw meat again?"

Her ears burned. "We ought to kill that son of a bitch!" she said.

"Go ahead," Saunders answered. "You first."

That made her ears flame hotter. Her pistol seemed mighty small potatoes when you set it against the concentrated essence of infantry a machine gun represented. "They can get him on a weapons rap." Machine guns weren't legal anywhere that she knew of. Then real inspiration struck: "Or for taxes! I bet he hasn't paid a dime since the supervolcano went off."

"And you have?" Saunders inquired.

He was being as difficult as he could. It sure felt that way to Vanessa, anyhow. "No, but I haven't had any money, either," she said, which wasn't provably false. What followed was actually true: "My stupid little credit union's servers are back in Denver, and they're dead as King Tut."

"Denver. That's right." He nodded, as if reminding himself. "Not many got out from that far west."

"Tell me about it." Vanessa knew how lucky she was to have fled far enough and fast enough. She was as stubborn as she was lucky, too: "Taxes work. That's what they finally hung on Al Capone, remember."

"The guy probably figured we were bandits, not I'm-from-the-government-and-I'm-here-to-help-you," Saunders said. Vanessa inhaled sharply. The gang boss must have psyched out what she was going to say, because he beat her to the punch by continuing, "But if it makes you happy, I'll pass the suggestion along. Maybe someone in authority will do something about it."

Fuck off. Get out of my hair. That was what he meant. If she pissed him off badly enough, he could send her back to whatever had replaced the soggy Camp Constitution. If that wasn't a fate worse than death, you could sure see one from there. She would have done almost anything to keep from ending up in a refugee camp again.

Her mouth twisted. Micah Husak had given her a most unwelcome education about what doing almost anything to get out of something else really meant. If Saunders made it plain her choice was between coming across and going back to a camp . . . She'd already had to make that kind of choice twice now. She'd yielded both times, and loathed herself whenever she had to remember. She also would have loathed herself had she chosen the other way; she knew that only too well.

Sometimes you couldn't win.

Sometimes you couldn't even play. The scavengers' boss had shown exactly zero interest in her fair white body. That irked her, too. There weren't a whole lot of things that didn't irk Vanessa.

For now, though, unless she really wanted to piss Saunders off, she needed to leave him alone. She could see that. She didn't like it for hell, but she could see it. With poor grace, she walked away. Dust and volcanic ash that would be dirt one of these years scuffed up under her feet.

IX

A bus up from downtown. The subway out to North Holly-wood, which was on the fringes of the Valley. An express bus out to the heart of darkness (actually, in Los Angeles, the Valley was the heart of whiteness). Bryce Miller wondered if he should have taken his car, expensive though that was. Getting out here this way was a royal pain.

He could have used the car this once, yeah. If he had to do it every day . . . He shook his head. Not a chance. From San Atana-sio to here and back again was about seventy-five miles. Multiply that by Monday through Friday by gas at prices that would have made a European blanch before the eruption by the fact that half the time you couldn't buy gas at any price at all, and what you got was *Not a chance* one more time.

If he did end up doing this, he'd have to move to the Valley. He couldn't afford or manage to drive. For the third time, *Not a chance*. And this was a Saturday, and he'd left his apartment al-most two hours ago, and he still wasn't where he needed to be. Add four hours of daily commuting to a job and you'd be nutso in nothing flat.

Before the supervolcano went off, he wouldn't have moved to the Valley on a bet. When you lived in the South Bay, the sea breeze spoiled you. It wasn't quite perfect Santa Barbara, but it rarely got too hot or too cold. No sea breeze in the Valley; the Santa Monica Mountains blocked it off. Hard freezes during the winter? Temps that went up past 110 in the summertime? If you were a South Bay guy, you didn't want thing one to do with any of that crap.

But that was before the supervolcano went off. The South Bay hadn't just got hard freezes; it had got snow. So had the rest of the L.A. basin. And no way in hell any part of the basin would see 110 again any year soon. Hard to imagine you could get nostalgic for sweat, but human nature argued you could miss anything you didn't have any more.

Christ, there were times he still missed Vanessa. It wasn't that he wasn't happier with Susan. In all the time they'd been together, he'd quarreled with her less than he had with Vanessa in a bad month—and they'd had several bad months in a row before she invited him to get lost.

And once in a while he missed her anyway. Part of it, he supposed, was that he hated getting anything wrong. Part of it was that she was the first one he'd fallen for hook, line, and sinker. And she'd fallen for him the same way.

When it was your first time, of course you thought it would last till the end of time. They'd gone to a wedding not long after they got together: a couple of her friends were tying the knot. A high school English teacher of hers who was there had asked them what they were going to do. Bryce remembered that very clearly.

He remembered what he'd answered, too: "We'll live happily ever after." And he remembered how that English teacher had laughed her ass off. He'd been pissed. Vanessa had been furious—almost furious enough to make a scene at Jack and Katarina's reception.

Well, prune-faced Miz What's-her-name got the last laugh. Happily ever after Bryce and Vanessa did not live. As for Jack and Katarina, they broke up before Vanessa showed Bryce the door. Shit happened. Boy, didn't it just?

The bus stopped, liberating Bryce from his gloomy maunderings. The doors hissed open. He got off and looked around. If the guy wasn't here . . . Well, that was why God made cell phones—when the power let them work, anyhow. Today, it was on.

But a stocky man in his late thirties who'd been standing in the little bus station came forward with his hand stuck out. "You're Dr. Miller, aren't you?" he said. "I went to your Facebook page to see what you looked like. I'm Vic Moretti."

"I'm Bryce Miller, yeah." Bryce shook hands with Moretti, who, by his grip, might have been a construction worker when he wasn't teaching. He wasn't comfortable with *Dr. Miller* at the DWP, and he wasn't comfortable with it here, either. After a longish pause, he managed "Good to meet you." If this guy wanted small talk from him, he was in trouble.

"And you." Moretti seemed very much at ease in his own skin. Maybe that was personality, maybe just years. Whatever it was, Bryce envied it. The older man went on, "My car's right around the corner."

It was a Prius. Bryce envied that, too. The less gas you used these days, the better. But some of the envy went away when he got into the hybrid. His knees banged the glove compartment. He might have been able to fit his legs around the steering wheel. He didn't think he could have got them under it.

Moretti chuckled as he fastened his seat belt and started the car. "Helps if you're not a big tall guy," he admitted. "Me, I'm five-nine, and I'm fine in here." He pulled out into what traffic there was. "So how much do you know about Junipero High?"

"Not a whole lot." Bryce was sandbagging a little; he'd done his online homework, too. No point not showing that: "Your

Web site says you're one of the leading Catholic high schools in the West Valley. And Craigslist says you're looking for somebody who can teach Latin and history. I can do Greek, too, if you want me to." He liked Greek much better than Latin, though he wasn't about to say so when Junipero was looking for a Latin teacher.

"Well, we can look into that a little further down the line," Moretti said smoothly. He had to mean something like *Greek? In a high school? You've got to be shitting me.* Bryce didn't get his bowels in an uproar about it. No matter how interesting he thought Greek was, only a handful of prep schools did offer it.

The Prius purred west. The Valley looked like any other part of the Los Angeles urban sprawl: houses, apartment buildings, shops, strip malls. Some of the billboards were in Spanish. So were some of the ones in San Atanasio.

Moretti took a couple of turns that got him off the big streets and onto little ones. Mountains loomed against the western horizon: not great big mountains, but a lot closer than the smudges on the horizon that were all you saw in the South Bay. Those couldn't be the Santa Monicas. What were they, then? The Santa Susanas? Bryce realized how little he knew about the local geography. Back East, this might easily be a state or two away from him. Here, it was in the same county. The scale on this side of the country was different.

"Here we are." Moretti swung into a parking lot. He stopped the car under the overhanging boughs of some pines that sprouted from the grass by the lot. When Bryce got out, he heard woodpeckers drumming in the trees. He glanced around. Some of the buildings looked as if they'd gone up earlier this morning. Others had probably stood there for fifty years or more, which made them ancient by Southern California standards.

"Nice campus," he offered.

"It is, isn't it?" Moretti agreed. "That's one of the compensations for teaching here." Bryce knew exactly what that meant:

they paid bupkis. He'd have to take a serious cut if he bailed from the DWP.

Moretti led him to one of the blocks of classrooms. A key opened the room that turned out to be his. It looked like, well, a high school classroom. Instead of sitting behind his big wooden desk, he plopped down into the nearest steel-tube-and-plastic jobs the kids got stuck with. He waved Bryce into the one in the next row over. The easy assumption of equality made Bryce like him better.

"You've got a steady job that pays you more money," Moretti said. "Why would you rather do this?"

Bryce had been wondering the same thing. When you got out into the real world, cash often seemed the most important thing there was. But he answered, "I can do the job I've got, but I'd sooner use some of what I studied and pass it along. There aren't any university positions out there—the way things are these days, they're shutting down classics departments, not hiring new people for them. So this looks like my next best bet."

"I see." Vic Moretti steepled his stubby fingers. "If a university post did come along, would you take it?"

"Of course I would." Bryce wasn't going to lie to him, not when he already had a job and wasn't desperate to grab any spar in the sea. He did go on, "But I don't think that's likely. I only wish I did."

"Hmm." Moretti wrote something down. "You're up front, anyhow. I'll say that for you."

Is he saying it for me or against me? Bryce wondered. Aloud, he said, "You may as well know where I'm coming from."

"That's true. We also needed to know whether your degree was genuine. We've had a couple of applicants who knew just enough Latin to order a pizza—if they didn't want pepperoni on it." The Junipero teacher looked thoroughly grim.

"Oh, wow," Bryce said.

"Yeah." Moretti nodded. "You were talking about how things are these days yourself. Some people watch too much poker on TV. They think they can bluff their way through anything. Maybe they hoped they could stay half a chapter ahead of the kids the first year, and then they'd have it psyched out. With priests on the faculty, though, that doesn't fly."

"I guess it wouldn't," Bryce allowed. "I can do the Latin. I can do the history, too. They make you learn it at UCLA." He probably would have to stay half a chapter ahead of the kids for some of the more modern stuff, but that was one more thing he didn't say.

"Professor Harriman thinks you can," Moretti said.

Even though Bryce hadn't expected anything else—he wouldn't have listed his chairperson as a reference if he had—hearing that still warmed him. It also told him his chances of landing this job were pretty decent. Sure as hell, Moretti started talking about money, and about benefits. No, neither was on a par with what Bryce had now.

"When will I hear back from you?" he asked. *Do I really want to do this?*

"Within a week, I expect," the older man replied. "We do have two or three other people who we think are legit, and we need to talk to them, too."

"Okay. Fair enough." Bryce said the polite thing. Whether he meant it . . . As far as he was concerned, all those other people could *geh kak afen yam*, one of the handful of Yiddish phrases he knew.

Or could they? *Do I really want to do this?* he wondered again. He would be doing something he enjoyed a lot more than sitting in the DWP's cubicle farm. And they would pay him a lot less for doing it, too. Could he scrape by on what they did pay him? If he didn't think so, what was he doing here? Besides wasting his time and Vic Moretti's, that is?

"Let me run you back to the bus stop," Moretti said. "Boy, that'd be a hellacious commute from the South Bay. It wouldn't be any fun if you could drive it, and bus and subway are a lot slower."

"Unless the 405 clogs up," Bryce answered dryly.

The teacher chuckled. "Yeah, there is that. But you probably would think about moving up here, huh?"

"It has crossed my mind," Bryce said. As they walked down to the Prius, he went on, "I never thought I might end up at a Catholic school." He didn't say he was Jewish. Miller could be anything. Some people knew at a glance he was a *Landsman*. Others, especially the ones his red hair threw off, hadn't a clue.

"It's a Catholic curriculum, yeah," Moretti said. "The kids— the kids are Valley kids. We're maybe ten percent Jewish, including the quarterback on the football team. We've got Sikhs, Muslims, Hindus, Koreans. You name it, they're here. Anybody who figures the Los Angeles Unified School District stinks—"

"Which means just about everybody," Bryce put in.

"How right you are. And there's a reason for that: LAUSD *does* stink. It's great if you shuffle papers. But if you're a student and you actually want to learn something . . . I spent six years working at L.A. Unified. The nonsense you've got to put up with made me glad to take the cut that went with coming here. I can accomplish something here, you know?"

"That'd be nice." Bryce wondered if he'd accomplished one single goddamn thing at the DWP. He'd kept a roof over his head and food on his table. In the larger scheme of things? Not so you'd notice.

He talked things over with Susan that night. They ate at a Chinese seafood place a couple of miles from his apartment. That was the kind of thing people used their cars for these days. "Whatever you want to do is fine with me," she said. "Money . . . If I worried about money, would I be messing around with the Hohenstaufens?"

The Western medieval world was a lot closer in time to the here and now than Bryce's period was. In attitude? He doubted it. The Hellenistic Greeks could seem amazingly modern—and amazingly cynical. Of course, from what Susan said, so could Frederick II. But the Holy Roman Emperor spectacularly didn't fit into his own time. Chances were he would have been right at home amongst the clever cutthroats who ruled Ptolemaic Egypt, Seleucid Syria, and Antigonid Macedonia.

Their food came. Seafood was local. Next to beef or lamb or chicken, it was also a bargain. People screamed about that all the time. They wanted Washington to Do Something. They wanted it louder every day, too. Just what Washington could do, they didn't seem so sure. Retroactively declare the supervolcano hadn't erupted, maybe.

People like that probably ordered unscrambled eggs when they sat down to breakfast at Denny's, too.

All of which was beside the point. Bryce swallowed a tiny squid braised in hoisin sauce and came to the point: "If I take the job, looks like I'll have to move up to the Valley. Will you come up there with me?"

"Live with you, you mean?" she asked. A squid of her own paused halfway between her plate and her mouth. She frowned a little; a vertical crease formed between her eyebrows. They never had lived together—she was old-fashioned about that. She'd spend the night at his place, and let him spend it at hers, but no more.

Bryce nodded, anyhow. "Uh-huh. It's no farther to UCLA from there than it is from the South Bay. Closer, I think."

She ate her squid. Then she said, "I don't know," in a way that told him she did know but was still looking for a way to soften the blow.

He took a deep breath. "It'd be okay if we got married, right?" He'd figured he would propose to her one of these days.

He hadn't figured this would be the one. Sometimes his mouth lived a life of its own, wild and free.

By the way Susan's eyes widened, she hadn't figured this would be the day, either. "Are you sure?" she asked.

Weren't women trained not to give men a second chance when they popped the question? But if Bryce said he wasn't sure now, they were finished. He nodded. "You bet I am." He meant it, too. "Even if it means telling your dad I proposed at the same time as I was talking about taking a job that didn't pay so well."

"Could be worse. You might not have a job at all—plenty of academics these days don't. Pop would really love that." Susan paused, as if remembering she hadn't answered the relevant question. She took care of that: "Yes, I'll marry you, Bryce. You can even invite Lieutenant Ferguson if you want to—but not Vanessa, thank you very much."

Not inviting Colin to his wedding had never occurred to Bryce. Neither had inviting Vanessa, even if she were in this part of the country. Had he been rash enough to invite her, he knew she would have said no. Actually, chances were she would have told him to fuck off and die. Once Vanessa was through with somebody, she was *through* with him. Forever and twenty minutes longer.

But thinking about one girl when he'd just successfully proposed to another one wasn't the smartest thing he could do, even if Susan had been the one to bring up Vanessa. He reached across the table and took her hand. "I love you, you know," he said. "The best I can."

She nodded. "I know," she said, accepting the qualification. "And I know that if you keep working for the DWP much longer, you'll go right out of your tree. So if Junipero calls and tells you they want to teach their kids Latin, you do it, you hear?"

Bryce sketched a salute. "Yes, ma'am!"

Susan stuck her tongue out at him. "Just don't let your eyeballs stick out on stalks when you stare at the cute ones."

She tried to sound severe, but he knew she was kidding.

They went back to his apartment. He did his best to show where she satisfied his appetites. By all the signs, he satisfied hers, too. And wasn't that the point of the happy exercise?

Vic Moretti called back five days later. He considerately waited till Bryce was home from the DWP. "You want the position, it's yours," he said without preamble.

"I want it," Bryce said.

"You sure you know what you're getting into?" Moretti asked. Maybe he was joking, and then again maybe he wasn't.

Bryce didn't care . . . too much. "I know what I'm getting out of," he replied.

Moretti paused. "Yeah, that counts, too," he agreed thoughtfully. "Well, semester's starting soon. It's good to have the slot filled."

"Good to fill it." Bryce wondered whether he'd mean that five years—or even five weeks—from now.

James Henry Ferguson sneezed. Yellowish snot leaked from his right nostril. Dried, crusted boogers clogged the left one. He coughed and almost choked, but then didn't quite.

"You poor thing," Louise said. If anything was more pathetic than a sick baby, she had no idea what it could be. James Henry didn't know what was wrong with him. He didn't know he'd be okay again in a couple-three days. He didn't know what a couple-three days were, or how to wait them out. All he knew was that he felt crappy.

"Mama!" he said, and started to bawl. That did nothing to improve the situation. His eyes leaked tears. His snot got runnier, which meant it oozed from both nostrils. Looked at objectively, he made a most uninspiring spectacle.

Louise wasn't objective—nowhere close. Mothers weren't equipped to be. If they had been, the human race would have died out long before it ever escaped from the caves.

Colin, now . . . She remembered Colin surveying a sick kid—had it been Rob or Marshall? why couldn't she remember?—and going, "Boy, he's an ugly little son of a gun, isn't he?" She remembered the clinical interest in his voice, and how much it had infuriated her.

If she'd been in touch with her feelings then, she would have walked away from the marriage on the spot. And if she had, her life now would sure as hell be different. Better? Worse? She hadn't a clue. Different she was sure of.

The other thing she was sure of was that the OTC meds she was stuffing into James Henry weren't worth shit. She was definitely in touch with her feelings about that. It made her mad, was what it did. Back when her other kids were little, you could buy stuff that actually made snot dry up. Sure, it'd come back as soon as the dose wore off, but it went away for a while.

No more, dammit. The FDA, in its infinite wisdom, had decided that the drugs that helped most kids also messed up fourteen in a million, or whatever the hell the number was. And so, to keep the fourteen in a million safe, the other 999,986 sniffled for a solid week whenever they caught a cold.

And they did catch them. Boy, did they ever! Babies and colds went together like ham and eggs. All the cold medicines on the drugstore shelves looked pretty much the way they had back when Louise was taking care of Rob and Vanessa and Marshall. Their boxes said things like SAFER THAN EVER! What that meant was, they didn't do squat.

She cuddled James Henry. "Mama!" he said mournfully. He got snot on her shoulder even though she'd put a cloth diaper there to try to block that mucus. One more blouse she'd have to wash. At least snot didn't stink the way spit-up did.

Her phone rang. James Henry jerked. He wasn't as jumpy about the phone as a cat was, but he didn't like it. The phone made her pay attention to something besides him, and he didn't like that, either.

She fished the phone out of her purse. Marshall's number was showing. "Hello?" Louise said.

"Yo." That was Marshall's way of talking, but it didn't sound like him. It was too deep and too slow, and punctuated by a sneeze: "I better not come over there tomorrow. I'm—*ah*-choo!—sick."

"So is James Henry," Louise said. She didn't quite remember how she'd got into the habit of always using both his first and his middle name, but she had. "Did you give him the cold, or did he give it to you?"

"Probably," Marshall said. Again, the answer sounded like him even if the voice didn't. Again, he sneezed. This time, he blew his nose right afterwards: a long, sorrowful honk. *I wish James Henry could do that,* Louise thought. Her older son went on, "Either which way, I feel like dog shit."

Unlike his father, he wasn't shy about swearing where women could hear. Chances were he hardly noticed he *was* swearing; to people of his generation, it was just the way they talked. Louise wasn't offended. As far as she was concerned, Marshall's casually foul mouth only proved Colin had wasted time and temper smacking him for cussing.

Right this minute, that was beside the point, no matter how gratifying it might have been some other time. Louise didn't want to think about Colin, not when she could—and needed to—think of herself instead. "What am I supposed to do?" she asked. "How can I go to work tomorrow if James Henry's sick and you can't come take care of him?"

"Beats me, Mom." Marshall sounded nearly as chilly and indifferent as his father might have. Maybe the cold helped, or maybe it was the triumph of one heredity over another. Then he added, "Don't forget—I'm sick, too."

Lost in her own worries, Louise *had* forgotten. She was briefly embarrassed, but only briefly. "What am I going to do?" she said—not quite a repetition, but close enough.

"Whatever it is, don't put me in it." Yes, Marshall could sound too damn much like Colin. And he'd always blamed Louise for walking out and getting free. He got only the first part, not the second. He took care of James Henry for money. He didn't really care about his little half-brother. As if to underscore that, he went on, "I'll check with you when I'm not so rancid any more. 'Bye." Silence echoed in Louise's ear: the Zen sound of a seashell that wasn't there.

"*Shit!*" she said, most sincerely.

James Henry looked at her. "Shit," he echoed, the way babies will.

She laughed so hard, she almost dropped him. He laughed, too, till he coughed and choked and sprayed boogers all over his cheeks. She wiped him off, saw he could have more of the worthless decongestant, and spooned it into him. He made a horrible face. It all seemed so unfair. If the crap didn't do any good—and it didn't—couldn't it at least taste halfway decent?

She still didn't know what she was going to do tomorrow. She couldn't take James Henry to the ramen works. He'd only make everybody else sick. *That*'d thrill Mr. Nobashi, wouldn't it? But she didn't want to stay home, either. Waste a vacation day? She didn't get enough of them to be happy squandering one on a sick kid.

Which left . . . what? Anything? The Yellow Pages weren't worth shit those days. She wouldn't find a babysitting service there. She went online instead. She came up with several in the area. All of them said *Se habla español*. Which was great, no doubt, but how about *inglés*? Well, the only thing she could do was start calling and find out.

So she did. Sure enough, most of the people she talked with had accents flavored with Spanish. You got used to that in Southern California. What she had more trouble getting used to were the prices they wanted. If Marshall ever found out what they were asking, he'd yell for more himself.

"That's just about what I bring home!" she yelped to one service that was particularly outrageous.

"Sorry, ma'am. We got to make a living, too," replied the woman on the other end of the line. That might have been politer than *Fuck you, lady*, but it amounted to the same thing.

She ended up burning the vacation day. The professional babysitters were too goddamn professional for a mere human being to afford. Then she had to burn another one, because Marshall was still sick the next day. That got her through Friday. She dared hope things would be at least near normal by Monday.

Back when she first found out she was pregnant, her OB had asked her if she would take it out on the baby for blowing up the life she'd had. She'd denied the possibility—denied it indignantly, in fact. Now . . . Now she would have been a liar if she said the idea of punting James Henry didn't cross her mind.

She didn't do it. By Saturday afternoon, the baby was pretty much his old cheerful self again . . . and Louise had a scratchy throat and a tickle in her nose. You couldn't win. The way things looked, you couldn't even break even. That crossed her mind just before she started sneezing.

There were times when Marshall Ferguson felt as if he'd never gone to college. Here he was, in the house where he'd grown up—in his old room again, for God's sake! He had more money in his pocket than he'd enjoyed before he went up to Santa Barbara, but not enough more to move out on his own. If his mother hadn't had her little bastard, he wouldn't even have had that. The economy had fallen, and it couldn't get up. He wondered—and wondered seriously—whether he'd die of old age before it managed to climb to its feet again.

And there were times when he thought he'd fallen into the looking glass, just like Alice. Dealing with his mother as a near-enemy would do that to him. However much he tried, he couldn't think of her any other way now. She'd blown up the family. What else was he supposed to think about her?

His dad's new wife . . . He liked Kelly. He liked her better than he liked the woman who'd given him birth. But she didn't seem like a mother to him, or even like a stepmother, however a stepmother was supposed to seem (what he knew about stepmothers was a weird mash-up of fairy tales on the one hand and friends and acquaintances whose folks had divorced and remarried on the other).

What she really reminded him of was a new older sister. He also liked her better than he'd ever liked Vanessa, though. Why not? She didn't try to boss him around the way Vanessa always had. She didn't make as if she knew everything there was to know, either. She just . . . got along with him. He wasn't remotely used to that.

He would have liked to talk it over with Dad. His father was the one unchanged point in his life. Dad might be a little grayer, a little jowlier, than he had been when Marshall was in high school, but how often did you notice that? His style hadn't changed, not a nickel's worth. And wasn't the style the man himself? Somebody'd said that. Marshall couldn't remember who. So much for the bachelor's degree they'd finally made him take.

But, because Dad *was* Dad, Marshall couldn't imagine talking to him in any serious way. Dad would listen. He'd listen hard, like the cop he was. And then he'd give forth with something that might as well come from Mars. Which was one reason Marshall didn't try talking with him: he'd had that happen before. The other reason, of course, was much older and more basic. Marshall had expended a lot of time and testosterone gaining such flimsy independence as he had. Was he going to risk that for the sake of *conversation*? Like hell he was.

And so he had to find some other way to channel his confusion. He put it into a story. Not only was he channeling it, he was giving himself a chance to make some money from it. He did sell things—less often than he wanted to, but he did. The money was nice, but he couldn't begin to live on it. Nobody could live on what you made from short fiction. Everybody said so, and for once everybody seemed right.

He could talk about that with Kelly: no testosterone involved there. She thought for a little while, then said, "Maybe you should write a novel."

"A novel? Are you nuts?" Marshall made a cross with his two index fingers, as if trying to protect himself against vampires. "I couldn't write a novel!"

"Why not? You sell some of what you write." Kelly was painfully precise—even more so than Dad. Did that go with being a geologist or just with being her? Marshall wasn't sure, but either way . . . She went on, "That's got to mean you're good enough, right?"

"Jeez, I dunno," Marshall muttered. What he did know was that the idea of tackling a novel scared him shitless.

Kelly didn't want to let it go. "You can make a living on novels, can't you?" she asked.

"If you're lucky enough, maybe." Marshall didn't want to admit anything. But she had a point, or the blogs and Twitter feeds and bulletin boards he haunted made him think she did. You wrote short stories for glory or experiment or because you liked a little idea so much you couldn't *not* write it. Novels, now, novels paid bills—except when they didn't.

"So go for it. What have you got to lose?" Kelly could be most infuriating when she sounded most reasonable.

"My mind?" Marshall suggested. One more thing everybody always said was *Don't quit your day job*. Considering that his day job was taking care of his half-brother, dumping it didn't seem half bad. It wasn't that he had anything personal against James Henry. The baby was probably as nice as a baby was gonna be. He couldn't help it that, just by coming along, he'd fucked up a whole bunch of lives.

Being able to tell Mom to find somebody who really was a babysitter, though? *That* sounded pretty good. If he never messed with another poopy diaper as long as he lived, he wouldn't shed one single, solitary tear. Dad always claimed babies weren't really human till they got potty-trained. Marshall hadn't known about that one way or the other before. He believed it now.

Making real money, grown-up money, sounded pretty good, too. Zero chance of doing that with short stories. Your chances of doing it with novels weren't what anybody would call good, but they weren't zero, either. People *did* make a living writing novels. One or two of them even got rich.

All the same . . . "I mean it, Kelly. I've never had an idea that big."

"How hard have you looked?" she asked.

He didn't answer that. He had no idea how or why ideas came, or why sometimes they didn't. Maybe the Idea Fairy was spending a couple of weeks on the beach at Maui, working on her tan. Maybe the bulb in his story-detector light burned out, and he didn't notice it for a while. He had no clue.

"Um, Marshall . . ." Kelly's voice changed. It was as if she'd suddenly realized she didn't know everything there was to know. So Marshall thought, anyhow, but he was feeling harassed right then.

"What is it?" he asked, more roughly than he might have.

She bit her lip. "Just so you know, your father and I are trying to have a baby. So there may be another half-brother or half-sister on the way for you. I didn't think it should be a surprise if it happens."

"How about that?" Marshall said, which was safe almost all the time. His first reaction was *Oh, Christ! I'll never get away from diapers!* His second reaction made him giggle. Kelly raised an eyebrow the way Dad would have—damned if they weren't rubbing off on each other. Marshall explained: "Here I'd have two new half-sibs, and they wouldn't be related to each other at all. How bizarre is that?"

"Pretty much," Kelly allowed. "Your father said the same thing about you and Rob and Vanessa when we started trying."

"Oh, yeah?" Marshall pondered that. Nothing he could do about it, he decided—Dad had had a lot longer to rub off on him than on Kelly.

"Uh-huh." Kelly got back to the main track: "Is it bizarre enough to be a novel idea?"

It was novel to Marshall, all right, whether it was to his father or not. Then he realized that wasn't what she meant, or not all of what she meant. He shrugged. Maybe it was. Maybe.

X

The last time Kelly'd seen Missoula, Montana, she'd left it behind in a GI-issue Humvee with a super-duper desert air filter and a pintle-mounted .50-caliber machine gun. That was what the Idaho sheriff—an old buddy of Colin's—who'd taken her away had called it, anyhow. Kelly didn't know from pintles. She'd never heard the word before—or since, either.

But now she was back in Missoula, looking at more Humvees with super-duper air filters and pintle-mounted guns. When she climbed into one of them this time, she'd be heading east, not west.

Missoula was the edge of the world these days. The edge of the habitable world, anyhow. Everything closer to the supervolcano was buried in ash. Missoula had got ashfall, too, but it wasn't buried. Plenty of places much farther away had had a lot more dumped on them. The prevailing winds kept most of the ash away from here.

And so, if you wanted to examine the new caldera, Missoula made a good place to start from. That you had to be out of your frigging mind to want to do any such thing . . . Colin had said as much to Kelly. He'd been as emphatic as he could manage without using profanity—enough to impress her quite a bit, in fact. And then, when he saw she *was* out of her frigging mind, at least that particular way, and had been for years, he threw his hands in the air and said, "Well, if you're gonna go, I hope to God you learn something worthwhile."

If that wasn't love, what was it?

Kelly'd signed as many releases for this little jaunt as she had when she flew over the enormous zit the supervolcano blew on the Earth's face. If anything happened to her while she was exploring—anything at all, from dandruff to unasked-for rattlesnakes or bears to getting charbroiled in a lava burp—she admitted in advance it wouldn't be the government's fault.

This time, the Humvees had U.S. GEOLOGICAL SURVEY stenciled on their sides. The guys sitting behind the machine guns, however, didn't look like USGS personnel. They looked like soldiers. There was a good reason for that, too: they were.

One of them had two little black stripes on each collar point of his camo uniform. "Uh, Corporal, are we really gonna need all of that firepower?" Kelly asked him.

"Ma'am, I just don't know," he answered with unsmiling—and unyielding—seriousness. That *ma'am* grated, but only for a moment. He was more than half Kelly's age, but he couldn't have been much more than half her age. To him, that would make her a walking antique. He went on, "Better to have it and not need it than to need it and not have it."

"I guess." Kelly didn't feel like a walking antique, no matter what the corporal (who had zits of his own, though not supervolcano-sized ones) thought. Nobody truly antiquated could have a baby, right? She wasn't going to have one now, or they wouldn't have let her do this no matter how many releases she signed. But she was trying. She took another shot here: "I didn't know anybody was left alive very far east of Missoula."

"Well, ma'am, nobody's quite sure—that's what our briefing says." The corporal was relentlessly polite. "Some of the ash has washed away since the eruption. Some of the land toward the crater may be habitable, and some people who kind of want to get out from under may have taken up residence there."

People who kind of want to get out from under. That was an interesting way to put it, but not a bad one; for the first time since Wild West days wound down, the government of the United States didn't fully control all the land from sea to overfished sea. You saw CNN stories about squatters and homesteaders and survivalists and cultists founding their own little communities inside the devastated areas off to the east of the eruption. They didn't always like it when the government found them again. Sometimes they didn't like it with guns.

You didn't see stories like that about Montana, or at least Kelly hadn't. But since when had CNN given a flying fuck about Montana? Kelly wouldn't have bet CNN had ever heard of it. And some people had always lived in these parts because they wanted the government bothering them as little as possible. Some of those people did have guns, too. Lots of guns, in fact.

Which meant the pintle-mounted .50-calibers probably weren't the worst idea in the world. That world wasn't the way you wished it were, or the supervolcano never would have gone off to begin with. The world was the way it was, dammit, warts and zits and all.

Her breath smoked. Missoula in autumn hadn't been a place where anyone would go to loll around in a bikini even before the eruption. Since? Places like Moose Jaw and Novosibirsk came to mind. What Moose Jaw and Novosibirsk were like these days . . . *Is someone else's worry, thank God,* Kelly told herself firmly.

"All ashore who's going ashore! Everybody else, all aboard!" Larry Skrtel didn't have a bullhorn. Then again, the USGS geologist didn't need one, either. He was as close to an unflappable man as anyone Kelly'd ever met, but he'd never had trouble making himself heard.

He walked up and down the convoy of Humvees, impersonating a liner's chief steward or a train conductor or a mother hen or whatever the hell he was impersonating. When he neared Kelly, he dropped his voice to talk in more civilized tones: "Won't be quite such a mad dash along I-90 this time . . . I hope."

"Jesus, so do I!" Kelly blurted. They'd roared west from Butte to Missoula in a Ford they'd piled into at the Butte airport right after the supervolcano blew. That impossibly huge cloud of dust and ash swelled and swelled behind them, and Kelly'd thought it would catch them and eat them no matter how big a jump they had on it. This was the way the world ended—not with a whimper but with a bang.

Skrtel grinned at her. "We're still here. The caldera's still here. Of course we'll go take a good look at it. Doesn't the Bible say something about a dog returning to its vomit?"

"Beats me." Kelly had only the most limited acquaintance with the Bible. If it went on about puking dogs, she wasn't sure she wanted any more.

Geoff Rheinburg climbed into the Humvee right behind hers. Her chairperson waved and winked when their eyes met. Kelly hoped he didn't notice how halfhearted her answering wave was. Even more than she had at the geologists' conclave in Portland, she felt as if she'd fallen back into grad school.

They headed east about an hour later than they'd planned to. Used to the ways of geologists, Kelly thought that was a miracle of efficiency. The soldiers who manned the machine guns all rolled their eyes and shook their heads. They defined efficiency in military terms. It took more than surgical masks (Kelly wore one, too) to hide their scorn.

For the first fifteen or twenty miles on I-90, things seemed close to normal. The Interstate was, well, the Interstate. There were a few vehicles on it besides the USGS Humvees. There were even a couple heading toward Missoula from the east. Missoula might not have been the end of the known world after all, then, even if you could see it from there. When would they reach Here Be Dragons country?

It didn't take long. Even before they got out of Missoula, she saw patches of ash and dust that a couple of years of rain and snowmelt hadn't cleared away—they looked like nothing so much as the Jolly Green Giant's spilled sacks of Ready-Crete. A giant had spilled that junk over the continent's midsection, all right, but it wasn't jolly and it wasn't green.

Halfway between the mighty metropolises of Clinton and Bearmouth, neon-orange highway signs warned ROAD PAST THIS POINT NOT PLOWED. PROCEED AT YOUR OWN RISK. It wasn't quite *All hope abandon, ye who enter here,* but it was—literally—close enough for government work.

Odds were those signs had been made with snow in mind. What they'd been made for didn't matter, though. They could, and did, also warn of other trouble ahead. Even in the jaunt from Missoula to here—the easy part of the trip—Kelly had watched those spilled-cement patches getting bigger and coming closer to the road.

Then there was more grit on the Interstate than blowing wind could account for. She could feel it in the Humvee's motion and hear it scritching under the tires. "Fuck," said the corporal behind the machine gun. "Signs weren't bullshitting, were they?"

Bearmouth still had people in it: ghosts wouldn't have needed to burn stuff and make smoke pour out of chimneys. The whole tiny town looked as if someone had smacked it in the face with a dirty-gray powder puff about the size of the Superdome, though. Kelly wondered if the locals would be as gray as their town, but she didn't see any of them.

Pine forests were gray, too. Under that gray, how many of

those trees were dead or dying? Most, unless she missed her guess. Rivers ran gray. Ash covered their beds and swirled along in their turbid waters. Ash did such a job of clogging rivers that the floods throughout the Midwest had been horrendous. They would have been even more horrendous if so much of the Midwest weren't currently uninhabited.

Super-duper desert air filter or not, one of the Humvees crapped out only an hour and a half into the journey. Everybody stopped. People who knew about engines, or thought they did, huddled about under the hood. After a while, they threw their hands in the air and gave up. Once upon a time, Kelly'd seen a World War II cartoon of a tough sergeant looking away as he gave his mortally wounded Jeep the coup de grâce with a .45. She'd never run into anything in real life to remind her of that, not till now.

They shifted people and supplies to the surviving Humvees and went on. The Interstate became more and more a matter of opinion. There were times when Kelly couldn't tell whether they were on the road or not. Only when they went under an overpass—or had to go around one that had collapsed under all kinds of strains its designers never worried about—was she sure.

The Humvees' big, heavy-treaded tires began throwing up wakes of dust and ash. "Fuck," the corporal said again. "This shit makes Iraq and Kuwait look like a walk in the park, and I thought they were just about all sand when I was there."

When they camped that night, their site precisely defined the middle of nowhere. Kelly'd chowed down on MREs before. The one she had there did not improve her opinion of them. Back in the old days, hadn't men joined the Army to get three square meals a day? Since then, the people who fed soldiers seemed to have forgotten the difference between a square meal and a meal that came in a square box.

Water had turned some of the ash and volcanic dust into

something halfway between dried mud and cheap concrete. Except for the geologists, Kelly was hard-pressed to find anything alive. Everything was grayish brown. Well, almost everything. One of the machine gunners brought in a small plant and said, "This here is a dandylion, ain't it?"

"It sure is," Skrtel agreed. After popping the dandelion into a specimen jar, he checked the GPS on one of the Humvees to find out exactly where they were. He wrote it down. They had laptops and iPads, but the only way to recharge them in the field was from the Humvees' batteries. Keeping their use down was a good idea, in other words.

Kelly's chairperson did some poking around of his own. After perhaps ten minutes, he grunted in triumph and plucked a specimen of his own. He carried it over to Kelly. "Can you identify this?" Professor Rheinburg asked, as if she were still his student.

Her heart thumped in alarm. As if she were still his student, she didn't want him to think she was dumb. She peered at the plant in the palm of his hand. Whatever it was, a dandelion it wasn't. She nervously licked her lips. She knew a hell of a lot more about rocks and soil than she did about the plants that grew on them. Still, considering where they were and what this one looked like . . . "It's a lodgepole pine sapling, isn't it?"

He beamed at her. "That's just what it is! The damn things can grow in the crappiest soil there is. That's why there are—were—so many of them in Yellowstone. They're the first squatter trees to come back after an eruption—even after this eruption."

"Except this one won't grow now," Kelly pointed out.

"Nope." Rheinburg didn't sound upset about it. "If I can find one after a few minutes of poking, there are bound to be millions of them popping up all over the ashfall."

"I guess." That made Kelly more cheerful, but not for long. Millions of lodgepole pines scattered over hundreds of thousands of square miles meant maybe ten trees per square mile. Ten saplings per square mile, that was. Not all of them would live to grow up. Even if all of them did, the result wouldn't be what anyone in his right mind could call a forest. It would look a lot more like a bald man's comb-over.

She said as much to Rheinburg. He laughed. "There's a difference," he said. "A bald guy's comb-over gets worse and worse as time goes by, 'cause he's got more and more scalp showing and less and less hair to cover it with. Here, there will be more and more trees and bushes and whatnot to patch over Mother Earth's bald spot."

Kelly found herself nodding. "Well, you're right," she said.

Her chairperson beamed at her. "You can say that. It's one of the reasons I enjoyed having you in the program so much. Most people would sooner be drawn and quartered than admit they're wrong." He briefly—only briefly—looked sheepish. "Lord knows I would."

"How come you never told me you enjoyed having me in the program till I wasn't in the program any more?" Kelly asked pointedly.

"How come? Because grad students are supposed to worry, that's how come. It makes them work harder. If you thought everything was cool, you'd try to skate through your research, and then I wouldn't enjoy having you around so much. Nope— you need fear and deadlines. And so did I."

Kelly would have liked to tell him he was full of it. She didn't even try. She knew too well he wasn't. What had kept her cramming her head with facts and formulas before her orals but fear of failing? If she'd been sure she would pass, she wouldn't have studied so hard—and she would know less now.

"Wait till you have grad students of your own," Rheinburg said. "You'll find out what I mean. Oh, will you ever!"

People were slithering into sleeping bags. Kelly hadn't done that in a while. She was used to sleeping on a nice, soft bed with a nice, warm husband. In spite of a foam pad between her and the ground, she tossed and turned, trying to get comfortable and not having much luck.

She couldn't go off behind a bush the next morning: no bushes to go behind. The geologists went behind Humvees instead, pointers and setters choosing different vehicles. Eventually, the Humvees wouldn't be able to go any farther. What would they do then? Turn their backs, she supposed. Or, more likely, they'd be able to go behind boulders by then. The supervolcano had thrown great big rocks a hell of a long way.

In fact, the Humvees lasted till late that afternoon. They were tough critters. They kept going for quite some time after the eruption had destroyed any sign that human beings had ever lived or built things in these parts. Had they been half-tracks, they might have gone farther yet. Or they might not have; wouldn't tracks be even more susceptible to grit than wheels were? Kelly didn't know one way or the other. When she asked at the stop for supper, the soldiers, who thought they did know, got into a hellacious argument, some saying one thing, some the other.

They were still close to eighty miles from the crater when even the valiant Humvees couldn't force their way through the dust and volcanic ash any more. "It's a shame we couldn't get helicopters to take us all the way in and out," Kelly remarked the next morning as the geologists got ready for the trek that would follow if they wanted to—and if they could—see the caldera up close and personal.

Larry Skrtel clapped a hand to his forehead: as much emotion as she'd ever seen him show. "Helicopters, she says!" the USGS veteran exclaimed. "Kelly, it took hand-to-hand bureaucratic combat to get the Humvees. The way things are, the way they're gonna stay for as long as anyone can see, nobody will spend a dime on anything the computer geeks and bean counters call unessential. Like I just told you, it took a special miracle to get 'em to spend a nickel."

Mounting the expedition had cost Uncle Sam and however many taxpayers were still paying taxes a pretty fair pile of nickels. Skrtel was bound to be right, though: to a bean counter, it looked like small change. What did they say about the Feds? *A billion here, a billion there, and pretty soon you're talking about real money.* That was the line. That was the attitude, too.

But something else Skrtel said raised Kelly's hackles, even if she wasn't sure what hackles were. "Who says this is unessential?" she demanded irately. "What could be more important than understanding how the supervolcano did its number on us?"

He spread his callused hands in resignation. "Darn near anything," he answered. "It's not gonna go off again, not the way it did—the magma pool takes a long time to fill up again after it blasts out. Ordinary volcanic eruptions? After what we've already been through, those are a piece of cake."

Some of the ordinary eruptions that would come would be enormous by the standards civilization was used to. Enormous, yes, but not humongous: the technical term geologists used for a major supervolcano blast. And Skrtel's words brought back Kelly's old worry—if studying the supervolcano was obsolete, wasn't she?

Well, it wasn't quite. There might be hope for her yet. And she had more urgent things to worry about. One was a volcanic hiccup, the equivalent of an earthquake aftershock, only with lava. Another was getting lost in this literally tractless wilderness and not making it out again.

MREs and plastic water bottles made her pack feel as if she were carrying another person piggyback. Everybody who was going forward had a GPS set. That ought to make getting lost less of a worry. And it did . . . up to a point. Everybody had a compass, too, but the damn things swung at what looked like random. The supervolcano hadn't belched out much iron in relative terms, but there was plenty to confuse anything that relied on the Earth's magnetic field.

GPS systems didn't, of course. That didn't mean Kelly trusted hers completely. When sorrows came, they came not single spies but in battalions. She laughed at herself. Where the hell had she come up with that bit of Shakespeare from an undergrad lit course? Only showed that general-ed requirements didn't always go to waste.

Off she went with her colleagues. The dust and ashes scrunched under her hiking boots. She'd let herself fall out of shape since she got married, too. Well, things could've been worse. She could have been slogging through mud as deep as she was tall.

Still nothing man-made visible. Gone—all gone, buried, on the way to fossilization. She looked ahead. Even the mountains seemed strange. So much volcanic rubbish had fallen on them, it had changed their heights and their shapes. That should have been impossible. It wasn't, not to the supervolcano.

Scanning the mountainsides with binoculars, she did spot a few dead pines sticking up through the dust and ash. Back in the day, you could see dead trunks from the big fires of the 1980s sticking up through snow. Colin said those reminded him of the stubble on a corpse's cheek. Kelly never would have thought of that herself, which didn't mean it didn't fit.

Larry Skrtel called back to Missoula. He had a satellite phone. Like the GPS, those still worked. They also carried little radios, whose signals would cross the ruined land. Geoff Rheinburg called them Dick Tracy wrist radios. They weren't quite, but that came close enough.

Except for the noises the geologists made, the world was eerily quiet. No insects buzzed or chirped. No birds called. No hawks or vultures glided overhead. At night, no coyotes yipped and yowled. No dogs howled at the moon. No cats screamed. No mosquitoes imitated tiny dentists' drills. It wasn't the worst of the mosquito season, nowhere near, but there should have been a few.

"You're right!" Larry exclaimed when Kelly mentioned that. He made as if to slap himself upside the head. "I didn't even notice."

"Hard to notice something that isn't there," Professor Rheinburg said.

"Now we know what the supervolcano really was," Kelly said. When her comrades sent her blank looks, she explained: "The world's biggest bug bomb—what else?"

They groaned. She'd been sure they would. "Now that's what I call overkill!" Skrtel said. Then he paused thoughtfully. "Or is it? Nothing smaller than a supervolcano could even slow the bastards down."

"It's not just the world's biggest bug bomb," Rheinburg said. "It's the world's biggest people bomb, too."

No one said anything to that for some little while. The United States, one of the most thoroughly measured and counted countries in the world, couldn't come close to being sure how many people the supervolcano had killed, not even two years after the eruption. Somewhere between two and three million: that was the best guess. Somewhere between five and ten times that many were still homeless.

Refugee camps were a staple of stand-up comics and late-night talk-show hosts. They weren't so funny if you were stuck in one. And if you'd ended up in one after the supervolcano blew, odds were you remained stuck there. You could get out if you landed a job somewhere, but plenty of other people, most of them not from camps, were chasing that job, too. And there were hardly any jobs to land to begin with.

Colin's daughter had managed to get out. Kelly had never met Vanessa Ferguson. Colin was tight-lipped about her. Kelly gathered that the guy for whom she'd moved to Denver, the guy who was indirectly to blame for her landing in Camp Constitution, was his age, maybe older. What that said about Vanessa, Kelly didn't want to know.

But she *was* out. She was doing some national-service gig, salvaging what could be salvaged from the eastern fringes of the eruption zone. There was a government program that did make sense, no two ways about it. Because the supervolcano wasn't done causing casualties. Oh, no. It was just getting started.

This would be the third harvest in a row that didn't happen in what used to be the world's breadbasket. Well, the world's breadbasket had taken one in the breadbasket. How many people would go hungry on account of that? No way to know, not yet, but the number wasn't small.

And how many would freeze on account of climate change from the supervolcano? Some already had frozen. But that would only get worse. Canada, the northern United States, Scandinavia, England, Russia . . . Drop Los Angeles' average temperature by five degrees Celsius (nine in the scale she still used when she wasn't being scientific), and you could still live there. Drop London's or Moscow's or Toronto's? Living in any of those places after the climate change fully kicked in didn't strike her as a whole lot of fun.

Besides, how hard would the sudden cooling hit all the big agricultural areas that weren't caught by the ashfall? Again, nobody knew for sure. Everybody would find out, probably the hard way. Kelly did know the computer models weren't encouraging.

Easier to lay your worries aside when you were exhausted. Which she was. And she, and everyone else, would only get tireder as they slogged on toward the caldera. *Maybe I should have listened to Colin and stayed home*, she thought. But that was bare heartbeats before sleep dragged her under.

She felt more like going on the next morning. She felt enough more like going on, in fact, that even an MRE for breakfast didn't discourage her ... much. The instant coffee was nasty, but it packed a caffeine punch.

Away they went. The wind was at their backs, blowing toward the crater. All the same, Kelly got whiffs of sulfur in the air. It was as if the Devil had set up shop in the phenomenal world. She shuddered. Yeah, it was just like that.

Every so often, the geologists stopped to collect specimens. Mass spectrography of samples of dust and rock and ash from varying distances from the caldera would tell them all kinds of interesting things about what went into the magma pool deep underground. That was the hope, anyhow. Right this minute, Kelly was just glad the technology had come far enough that the samples could be little tiny ones. She didn't want to carry one more thing than she had to. For that matter, she didn't want to carry the stuff she did have to. Her backpacking muscles were as out of practice as her hiking muscles.

When she complained about it, Daniel Olson gave her a crooked grin. "It'll get light faster than you wish it would," said the geologist from Missoula. "Trust me on that one."

"Yeah, yeah," she said. Much of what she was carrying was food and water. She had enough to get her through the planned length of the trek, and a little more besides. If something went wrong, though, they were liable to find out how far they could go on empty.

In due course, Larry Skrtel consulted his GPS and announced, "Well, we're inside Yellowstone National Park."

"I hate to tell you, but it's not worth the price of admission any more," Kelly said. That was definitely in the running for the understatement-of-the-year prize. The ground here was as ugly a gray-brown mash-up of dust and ash as it had been half a mile farther northwest. Here and there, igneous boulders—yes, there were plenty—gave the landscape variety: they made it ugly in a different way.

Daniel tugged on Larry's sleeve like a spoiled six-year-old. He sounded like one, too, squealing, "I wanna see the buffaloes! And the grizzly bears! And the wolves and things, too!" in a high, thin voice.

Kelly laughed. If you didn't laugh, you'd cry. The USGS geologist's face was only half visible, what with his breathing mask and hat, but he seemed closer to tears than to mirth. "So do I, man," he answered softly. "So do I."

Yellowstone's wide-open spaces—its wide-open, protected spaces—had saved bison from extinction at the end of the nineteenth century. It hadn't quite been the only place where grizzlies still lived in the Lower Forty-eight, but it had held more of them than any other area of similar size. Wolves had been a recent re-introduction here, but they'd done well enough to leave the park and start raiding nearby farmers' flocks and herds.

All gone now. Buffalo herds? Grizzlies? Wolf packs? Gone, gone, gone. Hell, the whole park was gone, and it was—or had been—bigger than several states. So were the nearby flocks and herds and crops . . . and the ones not so nearby, too.

"I loved this place," Kelly said.

"We all did," Geoff Rheinburg agreed.

"I loved it," she repeated. "I did, but there's nothing left, not even the parts that didn't fall into the caldera. It's off the map—I mean, literally off the map. You can still figure out what some of the mountains are, but even that's not easy."

"Tell me about it," her chairman said. "I've been photographing them as we go by, to help work out the changes in the local geography."

Something far overhead made *grukking* noises. "A raven!"

Kelly exclaimed in amazement. It was the first one they'd seen. "I feel like something out of Edgar Allan Poe—I want it to go 'Nevermore.' "

"Not me," Daniel said. "During the Civil War, when Sherman was marching through Georgia, he said he'd wreck it so well that even a crow flying across it would have to carry provisions. I was looking to see if the raven had a backpack."

"You suppose it's carrying MREs?" Kelly asked.

"Wouldn't that be cruelty to animals?" Rheinburg put in. They could always bitch about their alleged nourishment.

"Seriously, though, something may sprout where it craps," Daniel said. "Seeds in the shit, a little extra fertilizer . . . That's one of the ways life starts up again after big eruptions."

A million ravens crapping for a million years. . . . Kelly shook her head. It wouldn't take anywhere near so long. A million years from now, the supervolcano probably would have gone off again and mellowed again afterwards. In geological terms, these things healed fast. It was only in terms of human lifetimes that they seemed long-lasting.

Only? She shook her head again. Scientists had invented all kinds of other time frames to help them grasp things that happened very slowly or very quickly. But a human lifetime and its smaller divisions—those were what they lived in, the same as other people.

They reached the crater at the end of the fourth day. The air smelled of brimstone and metal. It smelled *hot*, too, or Kelly thought so, even if no thermometer showed a rise in temperature till they got very close to the edge.

When they did . . . When they did, it was with a certain amount, or more than a certain amount, of trepidation. One little burp from the supervolcano, something so small as to be unnoticeable next to the eruption that dropped so much of Yellowstone into the frying pan, would be plenty to make sure the presumptuous geologists didn't make it back to the Humvees.

No doubt about the heat at the edge. Kelly could see the air shimmer, the way it did above a desert highway in the summer—or, more to the point, above a burner on a stove. The odor of sulfur was stronger now. Had people got the idea for hell by staring down into active volcanoes? Kelly wouldn't have been surprised.

With the others, she collected mineral samples from the caldera lip. She carefully labeled them, using the GPS to get her exact position. *One of these days,* she thought, *I'll have to see where this would have been in Yellowstone before the supervolcano went off.* Like the others, she'd loved the great park and mourned its loss—along with so much else.

But that would be one of these days. She had no idea when she'd come back to the caldera, or whether she ever would. She stepped forward till she could look down and look across.

It was like sticking your head into an oven on high. You could do it for a little while, but not long. More of the lava half a mile down had congealed into rock than had been true when she flew over the crater in a Learjet. She snapped a few photos. Then she had to step back and cool off for a bit.

The rest of the geologists were doing the same thing. Awe softened Larry Skrtel's features as he drew back from the very edge. Kelly knew he wasn't a man who awed easily. "The scale of the thing!" he said.

"It's amazing," Kelly agreed. It was too big for anything so mundane as mere words. More than heat shimmers blurred the caldera's far wall. It had to be thirty-five or forty miles away: this was a bigger eruption than the one that had created Yellowstone. More than half an hour at freeway speeds. How many thousands of years would it be before there were any roads here again, much less freeways?

Kelly stepped up for another look. Something out there on the crater floor geysered upward. But that wasn't boiling water. It was melted rock. She got a pic: a good one, she saw when she checked her viewfinder. Gold and red against the gray—no, things down there hadn't calmed down, nor would they for a long time to come.

Anywhere on earth but here (except maybe on the Big Island of Hawaii), that would have been spectacular, astonishing, even newsworthy. In this place, what had gone before utterly dwarfed it. Such minor spurts happened all the time. Satellites recorded some of them. Others just made small squiggles on seismographs. Too many trees had fallen in this forest. No one cared if the next one was noisy.

After a while, Geoff Rheinburg said, "People, we have done what we came to do. Now let's get the hell out of here." Kelly couldn't remember hearing an idea she liked better.

XI

Winter. Back in his SoCal days, Rob Ferguson had thought the season a bummer, yeah. It got kind of chilly, yeah. Sometimes it rained. When it did, the freeways clogged. There were landslides if it rained a lot. Every once in a while, one would squash a car on Pacific Coast Highway.

That was SoCal. That was SoCal before the supervolcano erupted. This was Guilford, Maine, in the third winter after the eruption. Comparing one to the other was like comparing O'Doul's to Everclear.

He carried a rifle through pine woods. During the Second World War, the Germans and Russians who'd fought in front of Murmansk might have carried rifles through weather like this. Or maybe it had been warmer and less windy up there.

Just for a moment, he wondered what Murmansk was like these days. This particular shiver had nothing to do with the deep freeze in which he walked. Better *not* to think about something like that. Or maybe it wasn't. The only reason Murmansk had ever been even slightly habitable was that it got the Gulf Stream's last gasps. If it was still getting them, it might have stayed slightly habitable.

But the Gulf Stream was supposed to be in trouble, too. He'd heard that, with the Gulf of Mexico and the Caribbean suddenly so much cooler, less water was going out from them into the Atlantic. If that was true, Murmansk wouldn't be the only place getting the shaft as a result. All of northwestern Europe would go up against the wall—a wall made of blocks of ice.

That was northwestern Europe's worry, though. *His* worry was shooting something to help Guilford through this latest winter of its distress. The few summer months had let the government send in what supplies it could. But even the government was running out of things, and couldn't get more for love or increasingly worthless money. If people up here were going to make it, they would have to make it on their own.

I could go back to California, Rob thought. He'd been telling himself the same thing since Squirt Frog and the Evolving Tadpoles found themselves stranded in the middle of Maine. The advantages were obvious. Rain, not snow—at least not snow all the goddamn time. Electricity. TV. The Net. He hadn't sent or got an e-mail in months.

Only one thing was wrong with that picture: he liked it here. He couldn't imagine any place he'd rather be. Guilford would have been a neat place to live even before the supervolcano cast it back on its own resources. Everybody knew everybody else's business, and all the people figured they had a right to know. And everybody chipped in to help everybody else, too. It wasn't like SoCal, where half the time you didn't even know the name of the people who lived next door to you.

And there was Lindsey. He'd never figured himself for the sort who fell in love, which made him slower to recognize it when it happened than he might have been. But he knew what was what now—knew it and liked it, which surprised him all over again.

The wind howled down from the northwest. Snow flew almost horizontally. Even in his extra-heavy-duty L.L. Bean winter gear and a bright vest over it, Rob was chilly. But he wasn't any worse than chilly—well, except for the few square inches of face he had to expose to the blizzard.

What he really hated about weather like this was that a Super Bowl crowd of moose could amble by a hundred yards away and he'd never know it. Unlike so many things, that really mattered. Moose were lots of meat on the hoof. You couldn't afford to miss them if they were around.

If. Sooner or later, Maine would run out of them. If people north and west of the Interstate had to get through every winter on moose meat, it would be sooner. Rob didn't know what they'd do about that.

They were doing what they could. Lots of people were raising pigs and chickens. Unlike other livestock, those made do at least in part on human garbage. With greenhouses and sometimes even in carefully tended ground outside, some of the root vegetables of the far north got enough of a growing season to mature. Rob had never tasted, or heard of, a mangel-wurzel before he got to Maine. The food in California had to be better than this.

Something shot past him, seen and then gone. He started to raise the rifle, but lowered it again a moment later, feeling foolish. You needed a shotgun to go after a flying goose. Trying with a rifle only wasted ammo. Waste, these days, felt criminal.

He laughed at himself. *Two years here and you're turning into a New Englander,* he thought. But what he felt wasn't really old-fashioned New England frugality. No, it was post-supervolcano desperation. When you used something these days, you could never be sure you'd be able to replace it.

That flurry of motion was a fox. He took them for granted now, though the first one that darted in front of his SUV had freaked him out. He supposed there would always be foxes and weasels and mice and squirrels. They'd find enough to eat, whether people could or not.

Sure as hell, a squirrel chittered at him from high in a pine. If he'd had a .22 instead of a .30-06, he might have knocked it down. Rob had nothing against squirrel meat, one more delicacy (if that was the word) he'd met here. But hit a squirrel with what was originally a military round and you didn't commonly leave enough to be worth salvaging.

He'd had to walk farther to reach the woods than he would have at the start of the winter before, and quite a bit farther than he would have the winter before that. Like the moose, the firewood had held out so far. What would they do when it ran out? You couldn't raise baby pines to a useful size on table scraps in a few months.

The wind eased up. The snow kept falling, but more nearly vertically. Rob could see farther that way, or thought he could. Maybe his eyebrows were just a little less frozen. That over there in the electric-orange vest was another hunter. Moose hardly ever wore vests like that.

Someone had got shot near Dover-Foxcroft in spite of a Day-Glo vest. He'd lived. Officially, it was listed as an accident. Unofficially . . . People said the guy who'd plugged him didn't get along with him. Still as near a stranger as made no difference even if he'd been here more than two years, Rob didn't know about that one way or the other.

More motion, this time straight ahead. Damned if that wasn't a bull moose, sure as the ghost of Teddy Roosevelt. Rob did his best to impersonate a bright orange pine sapling. The moose dug at the snow with a big splayed hoof. Not much grass had come up during this abbreviated sortasummer. Rob would have bet the moose'd come up empty. And he would have lost the bet, too, because it lowered its dewlapped head and started pulling up whatever it had found.

"Yeah, you go ahead and chow down." Rob's mouth silently shaped the words. Fog gusted from his lips. If he'd worn glasses, it might have screwed him up. Not a sound came out to spook the moose. Slowly, smoothly, he raised the rifle to his shoulder.

A gunshot.

Next thing he knew, he was lying in the snow. He couldn't figure out how he'd got there. He didn't hurt or anything—and then, all of a sudden, he did. Quite a bit, as a matter of fact. "Fuck!" he said, in lieu of howling like a wolf. No wolves in Maine yet, or none anybody knew about, anyhow. From how far up in Canada would they have to come? However far it was, they hadn't got here.

And Rob had other things to worry about. It felt as if one of those wolves that weren't here was gnawing on his left leg. He wondered if he wanted to look down. If that bullet had shattered tib and fib, they were liable to have to take the leg off. *A cripple in the Ice Age—just what I always wanted to be.*

Blood on the snow, more of it every second. It steamed like his breath. Breath, blood—both showed life going out. He hiked up his jeans and his long johns. Each had a neat piece bitten out.

His stomach lurched when he saw that his leg had a piece bitten out, too. But then he realized the wound was a groove. It had got the muscle on the inside of his calf, but it hadn't—he didn't think it had—smashed the bones to smithereens. He yanked a hanky out of his pocket and packed the bleeding gouge with it. Not exactly sterile, but he'd worry about that later. Little by little, he realized he'd probably be around *to* worry about it.

The other hunter lumbered over to him. The moose was long gone. "Dude! What happened?" the other guy said brilliantly.

"Some dumb asshole went and shot me," Rob answered. "The fuck you think happened?" His wits began to work again, after a fashion. "You got anything I can use to hold this bandage in place?"

"Sure do." The other hunter pulled a fat rubber band out of his trouser pocket. What he was doing with it in there, God only knew. Rob took it gratefully any which way. In the war, he would have dusted the wound with sulfa powder. He would have done it now, too, if only he'd had any.

Another man came up. "I'm so sorry! I was aiming for the moose." He had to be the guy who'd nailed Rob.

"Yeah, well, you got some long pig here," Rob said. The local only stared at him, so he had no idea what long pig was. *Clueless git,* Rob thought. Aloud, he went on, "Look, I don't think it's too bad. Can you guys get me back into Guilford and let them patch me up?"

He had one good leg. The hunters made animated crutches. The fellow who'd shot him turned out to be Ralph O'Brian, who worked at the Shell station down the street from the Trebor Mansion Inn when he had anything to do there. "I'm so goddamn embarrassed," he said. "I never done nothing like that before, swear to Jesus I didn't."

"Believe me, once is twice too often," Rob said through clenched teeth. The leg hurt like a mad son of a bitch now, and sparklers of pain burned him whenever it touched the ground or bumped O'Brian, who was on that side of him. *He would be,* Rob thought. It didn't hurt enough to make him want to pass out or anything. He rather wished it would have.

They were almost back to town when they came upon a middle-aged woman hauling a big sack of rice to her outlying house on a sled. In a matter of moments, the rice was off the sled and Rob was on it. The woman put the sack on her back and trudged away.

The clinic did what it could for Guilford. There was a real hospital in Dover-Foxcroft—a little one, but still. Rob hoped he wouldn't have to go there. At the clinic, Dr. Bhattacharya said, "Oh dear me! How did this happen?" The small brown man sounded like somebody who did tech support from Mumbai.

"Damn Venezuelans are giving the moose AKs," Rob answered, deadpan.

For a split second, the doctor took him seriously. Then he snorted through his bushy mustache. "You are probably not at death's door," he said in his lilting English, sending Rob a dirty look.

"Good," Rob said. "What really happened was—"

"I'm a crappy shot," O'Brian broke in.

"Yeah, well, listen, Mr. Crappy Shot, go on over to the school and let Lindsey know what happened to me, okay? And stop at the Mansion Inn and tell the guys, too," Rob said. Ralph O'Brian nodded and scurried away, seeming relieved at the excuse to be gone.

Dr. Bhattacharya brandished a needle. Rob wished he had an excuse to get the hell out of there, too. "I will give you the local anesthetic," the doc said. "It will sting, then you will grow numb. Then I will clean the wound and I will suture it. You will experience some pain when the local anesthetic wears off. I will give you pills for it. They will help less than you wish they would. I will also give you antibiotics."

"Have any more good news?" In spite of the way Rob's leg was yelling at him, he felt the needle go in and the sting of the local. He felt them several times, in fact, because Dr. Bhattacharya stuck him again and again. Then, blessedly, he stopped feeling anything south of his knee. The doctor went to work.

When he finished, he said, "Let me see if we have a set of crutches that will fit you. Your height is . . . ?"

"I'm six-one," Rob answered. Using crutches through snow didn't sound like something he much wanted to do. The alternative seemed to be staying right here till he healed, though. Crutches, then, if they had them.

Dr. Bhattacharya pulled a pair from a closet, shook his head, and put them back. "Too short," he muttered, and tried again.

The next set he found made him nod. "Yes, these will do." He used set screws to adjust their length. "Six feet one, you said."

"Uh-huh."

"See how you do here, then."

Rob tried. He'd used crutches before, but that sprained ankle was half a lifetime ago now. The knack didn't come right back. He swung himself across the linoleum of the clinic floor. Dr. Bhattacharya gave him a vial of Vicodin and one of amoxycillin.

What doesn't kill me makes me stronger. Somebody said that. Who? He couldn't remember. If it was true, he'd just gained some serious strength points. And, if he could make it back to the Trebor Mansion Inn without breaking his other leg or his neck, he'd pick up some more.

Then the local would wear off. He wasn't looking forward to that, even with drugs in his anorak pocket. Maybe it would make him stronger, too. Somehow, he couldn't work up much enthusiasm for finding out.

Lindsey rushed in just before he was going to leave the clinic. "I got Marya to cover my class for me," she panted. "Ralph said you got shot! My God!"

"Ralph said I got shot?" Rob echoed. Something in the way that was phrased made him go on "Did he say who shot me?"

"No. Who?"

"He did."

Her face was a study—disbelief, amazement, and rage chasing one another across her features. "I'll murder him!" she said when her mouth stopped hanging open.

"Don't," Rob said wearily. "It was just one of those stupid things. It wasn't like he meant to do it—and I'm not too badly damaged, anyway."

"For a gunshot wound, it is very minimal," Dr. Bhattacharya agreed.

"For a gunshot wound," Lindsey said. "Not for any other kind of wound." The doctor didn't tell her she was wrong.

"Would you break trail for me while I go back to the Inn?" Rob asked her. "That'd help."

"Come to my place instead," she said. "It's closer, and you won't have to climb stairs and a ladder to get to your room."

"I'll do that," he said. "You bet I will. I should get shot more often." She snorted and held the clinic door open for him.

Bryce Miller's alarm clock went off like a bomb. It was a windup Timex of uncertain but ancient vintage. Its ticking was loud enough to be annoying when he noticed it. It kept rotten time. He'd bought it for two bucks at a Goodwill store right after he landed the job at Junipero High.

That was six months ago now. These days, one like it would cost at least ten times as much, likely more. Six months ago, power in L.A. had been pretty reliable. Now . . . Now all the supervolcano sludge in the Columbia had screwed the fancy turbines up there but good. The grid had other problems, too, but that was the juicy one.

So L.A. had power a few hours a day, a few days a week. Bryce vaguely remembered reading Bucharest had been like that, back when the Communist dictator, old nutty What's-his-name, ran Romania. The Cold War was only history to him, and seemed almost as far removed from the here and now as his pet Hellenistic poets.

The Cold War here and now was the war against real, physical cold. The world's politics were still screwed up, but not that particular way. Los Angeles remained lucky. It might get chilly here, but chilly wasn't arctic.

And Bryce was awake. Once that alarm started clattering, he would have had a hard time staying dead. With a rented truck, he'd spent a small fortune moving up to what they called West Hills. He was only a couple of miles from Junipero High here. These days, that was walking distance.

He had a gas stove. He could light a burner with a match when the electric flame-starter didn't work. That let him boil water to make coffee to go with his bagel. He liked real cream in his coffee, but he used Coffeemate with sugar. Coffeemate kept basically forever. Cream didn't keep at all without refrigeration. The apartment had a refrigerator. It made a fair icebox when he could get ice, which wasn't often enough.

Out he went, carrying a briefcase and an umbrella. It wasn't raining right this minute, but you couldn't trust it even in summer after the eruption, let alone in winter. He'd work up a sweat by the time he got to school, but he didn't worry about it. He wouldn't be the only one.

When he got to the campus, the first thing he did was check his box. With e-mail scarce and unreliable, paper was making a comeback. A typewriter—an ancient manual, dredged up God knew where—clacked on a secretary's desk. When you lacked what you'd had before, you did the best you could with what you could find. Or, welcome back to the turn of the twentieth century.

Bulletins and orders might be typewritten, but they got Xeroxed when the power did come on. Junipero dished out less bullshit than he'd heard public schools had to endure. All the same, the administration had some pretty good fascists in training—or would they be inquisitors here?

Bryce taught Latin, world history, and U.S. history (in the latter, he was indeed staying a chapter ahead of the kids). Maybe next year, if the world hadn't ended by then, the powers that be honest to God would let him take a swing at Greek. Or maybe they wouldn't. And if they didn't, maybe he wouldn't be so very upset. Seeing what tough sledding the students made of Latin, they might not grok Greek at all.

U.S. history first period. In he walked, to go over the causes of the Civil War one more time before the kids showed up. By Junipero standards, it was a big class: twenty-three students. No, public school wasn't like this.

The kids were totally SoCal, which was to say, almost everything under the sun. Hispanics. Irish. A very bright Jewish kid named Perry Ginsberg, who seemed to be stoned most of the time. A dark, pretty girl named Singh, which probably meant she was a Sikh. A Vietnamese kid. A Korean.

No African-Americans, though. There weren't many at Junipero—fewer, Bryce thought, than there were Jews. It would have been funny if it weren't sad. Fewer black parents than Jewish ones trusted a Catholic school not to mess up their children.

He covered the points he needed to cover. "Slavery," he said. "That's the biggest cause. All the talk about states' rights and other stuff, it's just a smokescreen for slavery. The South wanted to keep it and make it grow. The North wanted to stop it and eventually roll it back."

Most of them took notes. A few didn't give a damn. Their parents were wasting the cash they spent here. What could you do, though?

"Question?" Bryce nodded towards a raised hand.

"Yes." The Sikh girl nodded. "How do you know it was slavery most of all? What is the evidence?"

Would she be a lawyer when she grew up, or a biochemist? Bryce was just glad he'd done his review before the class started. He had the answer at his fingertips. "Well, let's look at South Carolina's Ordinance of Secession. South Carolina was the first state out of the Union, remember. When the ordinance talks about why the state's leaving, it says 'These States'—the free ones—'have assumed the right of deciding upon the propriety of our domestic institutions, and have denied the right of property established in fifteen of the States and recognized by the Constitution; they have denounced as sinful the institution of Slavery; they have permitted the establishment among them of societies, whose avowed object is to disturb the peace and eloin'—that means *steal*—'the property of the citizens of other States. They have encouraged and assisted thousands of our slaves to leave their homes; and those who remain, have been incited by emissaries, books, and pictures, to servile insurrection.' It goes on for several more paragraphs after that.

"Instead of reading them, though, let's look at the Confederate Constitution. That was the law the South set up for itself to live by. A lot of it's modeled after the U.S. Constitution, but some isn't. Here's Article One, Section Nine, Part Three: 'No bill of attainder, *ex post facto* law, or law denying or impairing the right of property in negro slaves shall be passed.' The Confederate Constitution talks about the right of slaveholders to keep their property in a couple of other places, too."

He looked at her. "So. Is that evidence?"

"It is." She nodded gravely.

Right then, he was a little relieved to have no black kids in the class. Reminding them Southern whites had been sure enough that their ancestors were no more than cattle with hands to fight a war about it wouldn't have been comfortable, which was putting things mildly. Easier to sound dispassionate about it while they were out of the room, so to speak.

Or maybe the fact that he still worried about it meant the country had taken longer to dig out from under the burden of slavery than it would to clean up after the supervolcano eruption. And if that wasn't a scary thought, he didn't know what would be.

Latin was cleaner. It didn't seem so intimately connected to the world they lived in. (Well, yes, the Romans were slaveowners, too. Well, yes, the Hispanic kids, or most of them, spoke a language that was one of today's versions of Vulgar Latin. Details, details . . .)

Trying to explain what cases were all about took up a lot of his time. When he was in college, he'd taken German before Latin, so the dead language had confused him less, anyhow. The kids might well have had an easier time with calculus. Some of them *were* having an easier time with calculus.

Then there was Sasha Smyslovsky. He spoke Russian at home, and Russian had more cases than Latin. His trouble wasn't grammar—it was vocabulary. People who grew up with English (and, even more so, people who grew up with Spanish) could figure out a lot of Latin words from their modern cognates. Russian, though, didn't have that kind of relationship to Latin.

Sasha was a junior, so he was sixteen, maybe seventeen. To Bryce, he looked about thirteen. All the boys in his classes, even the football players who could have cleaned his clock without breaking a sweat, looked like kids to him. He worked hard not to show it. He'd hated his teachers condescending to him when he was in high school. That had to be a constant of human, or at least teenage, nature.

Some of the girls in his classes looked like kids to him, too. Some of them struck him as seventeen going on thirty-five. He also worked hard not to show that. He didn't want to give them ideas, and he didn't want some of the ideas they gave him. More than he ever had before, he understood how high school teachers slipped every once in a while.

He never said word one about that to Susan. He didn't want to give her ideas, either. If he had, he knew what she would have given him: a piece of her mind, and a sharp-edged one at that.

World history struck him as an exercise in political correctness. Every ethnic group made its contribution—its *important* contribution, its *wonderful* contribution—to the way things ended up working out. Kalmuks? Papua New Guineans? You betcha, and you'd better be able to give them back on the test.

Female Kalmuks? Gay, lesbian, and bisexual Papua New

Guineans? Of course there'd be a question about them. Two questions, more likely.

Maybe history courses had been all about dead white males once upon a time. No, certainly they had. World history was supposed to be the antidote to that. From time to time, Bryce wondered if the cure wasn't worse than the disease.

They were paying him not to wonder about such things. No, they were paying him to keep his big trap shut if he did wonder about them. And keep it shut he did—where the students and the people who were paying him could hear, anyhow.

Susan got an earful, though. When his cell phone had power, so did Colin Ferguson. The police lieutenant laughed his gruff laugh. "Didn't you take Hypocrisy 101 in college?" he said. "Well, even if you didn't, this is your postgraduate course."

"Tell me about it!" Bryce exclaimed. "Is the whole world like this?"

"Pretty much." Colin wasn't laughing any more. Bryce remembered he'd been passed over for chief of the San Atanasio PD not least because he had the dangerous habit of saying what he thought. *And I just stuck my foot in my face,* Bryce thought unhappily. After a beat, Colin went on, "You get used to it after a while . . . most of the time, anyhow."

"I guess." Bryce wasn't nearly sure he wanted to get used to it. He wondered if he had any choice. No, there were always choices. Socrates had made his. *Sure, and look what it got him.* Changing the subject looked like a good idea: "You ever hear anything from Rob and Vanessa?" He asked about his ex with no more than a momentary twinge.

"Well, Rob got shot," Colin answered.

"Shot!" That was the last thing Bryce expected to hear. "Jesus! What happened?"

"I got a card from him a few days ago. He says somebody mistook him for a moose. He says he isn't eating that much. He says there isn't that much *to* eat where he's at in Maine. And he says he's healing up, which is the most important part."

"Uh-huh." Bryce nodded, not that Colin could see him. That sounded like Rob, all right. It also sounded quite a bit like Colin himself. His firstborn would have got pissed off had anyone told him so, though. Bryce tried again: "And Vanessa?"

"Still on the scavenger circuit. She doesn't write much, and she's not any place where she can power up her phone—or where she can get bars even if she does. I keep reminding myself she's good at landing on her feet. You know about that."

"Now that you mention it, yes." Bryce tried to sound light, and feared he made a hash of it. On the way to one of those landings on her feet, Vanessa'd kicked him in the teeth. The Bulgarian judge gave her a 9.85 for technical ability when she did it, too, and 9.9 for artistic merit.

Well, what could you do? She'd walked out of his life four and a half years ago now. He couldn't do a damn thing, that was what. What he ought to do was forget he'd ever known her and spend all his time thinking about Susan, who actually wanted to be with him. Much as he would have liked to, he'd long since discovered he couldn't do that, either. Colin still had Louise on his mind, too, even if he wished he didn't. No wonder they'd stayed friends. No, no wonder at all.

What Bryce could do now was grade papers. As a matter of fact, that was what he had to do. And so, as soon as he got off the phone with Colin, he went ahead and did it.

The late, not so great town of Fredonia, Kansas, wasn't quite in the middle of nowhere. It was in the southeastern part of nowhere, or at least of Kansas. Since the supervolcano blew, Kansas and nowhere had become effectively synonymous.

As far as Vanessa Ferguson was concerned, Kansas and nowhere were synonymous long before the supervolcano blew.

Since she'd escaped Camp Constitution to pick the bones of people who'd made the mistake of feeling otherwise, she kept quiet on that score.

Fredonia, Kansas, also wasn't in the middle of a Marx Brothers movie. Vanessa made the mistake of mentioning it to the rest of the refugees from the refugee camp she worked with. They all looked at her as if she'd just sprouted an extra head, even—no, especially—when she started singing "Hail, Hail, Fredonia!"

"Vanessa, we already know you're weird," Merv Saunders told her with what sounded like exaggerated patience. "Do you have to go and advertise it?"

"Oh, give me a fucking break," she snarled. He was close to twenty years older than she was. Shouldn't that have been enough of a head start to give him some kind of clue about the Marx Brothers? Evidently not.

What really pissed her off wasn't that he didn't have a clue. What really pissed her off was that he didn't *want* a clue. He wasn't just a yahoo. He was proud to be a yahoo. He was the kind of yahoo who didn't know what a yahoo actually was, too. If he didn't know about Groucho, Harpo, Chico, and hapless Margaret Dumont, he for sure wouldn't know about Lemuel Gulliver's last voyage.

Winter in Fredonia wouldn't have been a picnic before the eruption. Winter in Fredonia since the eruption reminded Vanessa of what she'd heard about Fargo, or maybe Winnipeg. Sometimes it got up into the twenties. Sometimes it warmed up to zero. And sometimes it didn't.

Fredonia hadn't had a whole lot of trees when the supervolcano was biding its time. This was Kansas, for crying out loud. Just about all the trees it had had were dead now. If the ashfall hadn't done for them, those upgraded winters bloody well had.

So they were bare-branched and graying. They reminded Vanessa of human corpses—you could tell right away that they wouldn't spring back to life when (or, nowadays, if) spring came around again. And their gray starkness, and that of the rest of the local landscape, just made the cell phone relay towers all the more obvious—and obtrusive.

The towers here, like the ones in L.A. and Denver, had been disguised as trees, with brown plastic trunks and green plastic leaves. They hadn't made what you'd call convincing trees: neither colors nor shapes were spot-on. But they looked better than bare aluminum scaffolding and wires and whatever would have.

Because they were only approximations of trees, Vanessa and her family and friends had noticed them every so often, mostly when out driving. Somebody (as a matter of fact, it was Bryce, which Vanessa had deleted from her internal hard drive) tagged them alien listening devices. The name stuck in her little crowd.

Here in drab, abandoned Fredonia, Kansas, the relay points honest to God did look alien. Their plastic leaves were still green (snow-speckled green right now), their plastic trunks still brown. Sooner or later, the sun would fade them. With the sun so feeble nowadays, it was likely to be later.

No matter how out of place they seemed, their wiring and electronics remained valuable. The salvage team methodically cut them down and cut them up. "We'd better be careful," Vanessa said. "We don't want the aliens to find out we're messing with their stuff."

She meant it for a joke. She was going to explain how her friends had called the relays alien listening devices. Had the rest of the team liked her better, she would have got a laugh.

But the others disassembling the relay only scowled. "Aliens! Give me a fucking break!" one of them said.

"Bite me," Vanessa answered sweetly.

"Knock if off, both of you." Saunders sounded weary. One of his jobs, along with this government-sponsored graverobbing, was putting out little fires in his crew before they turned into big ones. Nobody'd murdered anybody yet, or even assaulted with intent to maim, which proved he was good at what he did.

Vanessa wanted to yell *He started it!* How many times had she done that back home, with one brother or the other? Sometimes it worked and sometimes it didn't, but it was always worth a try. Not here. Merv Saunders didn't care who'd started it. He just wanted it to stop.

And he had the power to bind and to loose. He could kick somebody off the team. If you got kicked off, you went out of the devastated zone on the next truck that came in to pick up salvageables. You didn't get to go off on your own once you left the devastated zone, either. Oh, no. The powers that be were crueler than that. If you got kicked out, you went straight back into a refugee camp.

Staying in a camp was punitive. The authorities could see that (so could anybody who'd ever been in one). But millions of people remained stuck in them. The authorities couldn't see how to put them anywhere else.

Not enough houses. Not enough money to build them. Not enough money for anyone to afford them even if they got built, either. The economy had been rotten before the supervolcano went off. With the Midwest essentially gone, it wasn't just rotten any more. The vultures had eaten the meat off its bones. And the rest of the poor, chilly world wasn't much better off. The USA had been the engine that pulled the train. Well, the engine had gone off the rails.

They slept in the best quarters Fredonia offered. It wasn't a Motel 6, but it might as well have been. A motel with no electricity and no running water. Happy fucking day! The bed was more comfortable than a sleeping bag. The windows in Vanessa's room weren't broken, either, so they shielded her from the freezing wind. And that was about as much good as she could find to say about the place.

Her father had stayed at a Motel 6 when he went to Yellowstone. She remembered him bitching about it. That was back in the days when things still worked, though. Now ... Now she was stuck in this cold, miserable place with a bunch of people who couldn't stand her.

She'd blown that National Guardsman so she could end up in a place like this, no matter what the people with her thought of her. She nodded to herself. *I'd do it again, too,* she thought. Next to Camp Constitution, this wasn't half bad. There was a judgment for you! Nodding again, she rolled over and fell asleep.

XII

Colin Ferguson took his left hand off the bicycle's handlebars and held out his arm with the hand pointing up: the signal for a right turn. He lived on a small, lightly traveled street, but he was getting into the habit of using hand signals all the time, the way he'd hit the flicky-doodle in his car whenever he changed lanes or turned.

He swung into his driveway. The Taurus still waited there. So did Kelly's old Honda. Marshall's little Toyota sat by the curb. They all ran. Colin thought they did, anyhow. None got used much, even in weather like this. Whose cars did?

With a sigh of relief, he swung off the bike and walked it onto the porch. He stood there a few seconds, letting the rainwater drip from his slicker. He slipped off his galoshes. He'd never worried about galoshes before the supervolcano. Who had, in SoCal? People did now, by God!

Before he could open the door, Kelly did it from the inside. They kissed briefly. "How are you?" she said as he brought the bike into the front hall. Hers already stood there, parked on old towels. He lowered the kickstand on his and put it next to hers.

"I've had days I liked better." He walked back into the kitchen and pulled a green bottle out of the pantry. After he poured himself a fair knock, he asked Kelly, "Want some?"

"That's okay. You know me—far as I'm concerned, Laphroaig is Kermit's last name." Instead of drinking scotch, Kelly popped the cap on a Red Trolley ale. She clinked the bottle against his glass. "Sympathies."

"Thanks." He let smoky fire run down his throat. She'd improved his taste in beer, but he'd never been able to persuade her that scotch tasted like anything but medicine. *More for me*, he thought.

"What went wrong?" she asked.

"Stupid judge let a perp off. Not enough evidence to keep him, he said. The video didn't quite show his fingerprints, so we had no grounds for the arrest. My—"

"Ass," Kelly said helpfully when he stalled.

"Yeah. That. It was a good bust. Honest to God, it was. That jerk in a robe, he—" The complaint dissolved into a disgusted growl. Colin drank more Laphroaig. "How are *you*? Better'n that, I hope."

"Me? I'm tired. Long way to Dominguez on a bike. They say the buses are supposed to get more fuel next week, but I'll believe it when I see it."

"Mrmm." Colin made a different kind of unhappy noise. "We're getting low on gas ourselves. What we hijacked from LAPD is pretty much gone, and we aren't getting as much as we still want to use. Pitcavage isn't what you'd call happy about it." He drained the glass and filled it again.

Kelly raised an eyebrow. "You don't do that very often."

"Not as often as I did before I started hanging around with you, and you can take that to the bank." Despite what he said, Colin drank from the refill. "You've got no idea how wrecked I was the morning we met in Yellowstone—and that was after the aspirins and the coffee kicked in. But I don't need it so much now."

"Good. I'm doing something right, anyhow." Kelly wasn't halfway down her beer yet. She liked the taste and a little buzz. Colin didn't think he'd ever seen her smashed, though. The reverse? The reverse wasn't quite true.

"Darn right you are," he said. "I wish you were chief, and doing things right in that chair. Pitcavage . . ." Some of the beat cops called their big boss Shitcabbage. Colin hadn't heard any of the detectives use that particular endearment, but they had others for the chief. And they had their reasons for using them, too.

"What now?" Kelly knew there were things he hadn't said yet.

"His worthless kid," Colin answered. "I mean, you try to make it easy on 'em. I never busted mine for smoking dope, and God knows I could have a million times."

"You never busted me, either," Kelly pointed out.

"You never smoked it in front of me to get my goat."

"No," she agreed quietly. "I knew you didn't like it, and it never was that big a deal for me. I don't miss it—beer's fine."

"Okay. Good, even," Colin said. "If you'd thrown it in my face the way my kids did, I don't suppose I would've busted you, either. But I wouldn't've wanted to marry you, or I don't think I would."

"I sorta figured that out," Kelly said, quiet still.

"Uh-huh. You're no dummy." Colin nodded and made that unhappy noise again. "Darren Pitcavage, though—" He took another sip of scotch, as if to wash the taste of Darren Pitcavage out of his mouth. "My kids aren't mean. Mm, Vanessa is sometimes, I guess, but she's snarky mean, not bar-brawl mean. If the chief hadn't done some fancy talking, there've been a couple of times his precious flesh and blood might've found out more about the inside of a jail than he ever wanted to know."

"Ah. Okay. Now I know where you're coming from," Kelly said. "This just happened again?"

"Too right it did," Colin agreed. "There's a bunch of bars and strip joints on Hesperus up near Braxton Bragg, and Darren thinks it's cool to hang out in 'em. Maybe he picks up the girls. Maybe he just watches. I dunno. But the people who run those places, they sure know who he is—and who his old man is. Does he get free drinks?"

"Ya think?" Kelly said sarcastically.

"Yeah. Like that. And the bouncers cut him slack. For all I know, some of the girls give him a throw to keep him happy. But not everybody who goes to those joints knows who Lord Darren Pitcavage is."

"Or cares," Kelly said.

"Or cares. That's right," Colin said. "Some of those guys, they'd want to rack him up good if they did know. This latest fight he got into wasn't like that. He was drunk, and so was the other fellow. The guy said something, and Darren coldcocked him. He's got a nasty left hook—he knocked out two teeth and broke another one."

"Let me guess—they called it self-defense?" Kelly asked.

"Right the first time," Colin said heavily. "But if that Mexican'd hit Darren, then it would have been assault with intent to maim. Bet your sweet wazoo it would." He gulped down the second drink.

Kelly reached into the refrigerator—which was, like most people's these days, half-full of ice to keep things fresh when the power was out. She grabbed some steaks. "Here. I'll pan-broil these. That'll help get the taste of today out of your mouth."

She does know how I work, Colin thought. The power wasn't on right now, which meant the stove's fancy electronic brain was useless. But natural gas still flowed when Kelly turned the knob.

She started it with a match. Not elegant, but it worked . . . till the gas stopped coming, if it did. When it did.

Marshall must have had some radar that told him when supper was ready. He walked in the front door right when Kelly took the pan off the fire. "Smells good," he said.

"Sure it does—it's food, isn't it?" Colin said. "You can drag up a rock and help us eat it. And you can tell us how your little brother's doing." Morbid curiosity? Probably. But he had it, morbid or not. And it gave him and Marshall something to talk about. Fathers whose grown sons lived their own lives understood how important that could be.

The rock in question was a chair at the dining room table. "He's, like, at the age where everything is *no* all the time," Marshall said as he planted his hindquarters on it. "I mean, everything. You want to take a nap? No! You want me to read a book? No! You want to play outside? No! You want to turn into a centipede and crawl up the wall? No!"

"I remember those days," Colin said, realizing he'd probably see them again himself, at least if he hadn't started firing blanks. "You all went through 'em. Vanessa especially."

"Why am I not surprised?" Marshall said with a crooked grin. "Anyway—"

Before he could get to *anyway*, Kelly broke in: "Did you really ask him if he wanted to turn into a centipede?"

"Sure," Marshall answered. Colin believed him. His youngest would never set the world on fire when it came to foreign languages, but he was the one who'd translated *An elephant is eating the beach* into Spanish in high school. He had that surreal turn of thought—or else he was just flaky. He might be cut out to make a writer after all.

"When Vanessa had it worst," Colin said reminiscently, "I went and asked her if she wanted a cookie. 'No!' she said, the way she did for everything for a couple of months there. Then what I said sank in, and she started to bawl." After more than a quarter of a century, he could call up the expression of absolute dismay that had filled her face.

"You're mean!" Kelly exclaimed, plopping steaks and green beans onto plates. But she was fighting laughter, fighting and losing. As she set his supper in front of him, she added, "You ended up giving her the cookie, didn't you?"

"Who, me?" he returned.

She started to stare at him as if he were Ebenezer Scrooge in the flesh, even without bushy Victorian side whiskers. Then she realized he was having her on. "You're impossible," she said, more fondly than not.

"Well, I try," he replied, not without pride.

If he hadn't fed Vanessa that long-ago vanilla wafer, would his cruelty have warped her for life? Left her sour and embittered and suspicious, for instance? You never could tell. People went off the rails some kind of way, and half the time parents and priests and shrinks had no idea why. More than half the time.

But he had given her the goddamn cookie. She'd wound up sour and embittered and suspicious any which way. Sometimes you couldn't win. Hell, sometimes you weren't sure what game you were playing, or even whether you were playing a game at all.

He washed dishes while Kelly dried. Getting stuff clean with cold water took elbow grease. In his wisdom, he'd got an electric water heater here. It had been pretty new when the supervolcano erupted. Now, when it worked, they saved the hot water for bathing. A gas one would have been better . . . or maybe not. These days, everything had some kind of electronic controls. And when the power went out, that probably would have fouled up the whole unit.

Marshall went upstairs to his room. It got quiet in there. He had a battery-powered lamp with LEDs that used next to no electricity, and he was writing in longhand when the juice was off. Colin wondered if he could scare up a typewriter from somewhere for the kid.

He lit a candle. You could get those without too much trouble. He wouldn't have wanted to write or read or even play cards by candlelight, but it was enough to keep you from barking your shin on a table or tripping over a footstool and breaking your fool neck.

Kelly came and sat down beside him on the couch. He put his arm around her. She snuggled against him, for companionship and no doubt for warmth as well. The heating system was gas. But, again, the thermostat had a built-in computer chip. The people who'd designed all this stuff had assumed there'd be electricity 24/7/365. Well, Colin had assumed the same thing. Which only went to show that you never could tell, and that assuming wasn't always smart.

"I tried to use a manual typewriter in the library at Dominguez Hills on a paper the other day," Kelly said, echoing his thought of a little while before. "They put them out where the light's good so people can, you know? But I don't have the touch for it. You've got to hit the keys so hard! I felt like a rhino tap-dancing on the keyboard."

"Ever mess with one before?" Colin asked. She shook her head; he felt the motion against his shoulder. He went on, "I did—I had one when I was a kid. But I didn't miss 'em a bit when computers came in. Typewriters aren't—waddayacallit?—user-friendly, that's it."

"No shit, they aren't!" Kelly burst out. Colin gave forth with a startled laugh. He wouldn't have said that himself, not where she could hear it (though he wouldn't've hesitated for a second if the intended ear belonged to Gabe Sanchez or to Chief Pitcavage). She laughed, too, but the amusement quickly left her face. She went on, "The world's not user-friendly any more, you know?"

Colin started to laugh again. This time, the laugh didn't pass his lips. Gasoline was a king's ransom a gallon when you could get any. Most of the time, you couldn't, not for money or for love. (Sex was a different story. The Vice Unit had closed out a pimp's stable of hookers, who'd been turning tricks to keep his Lincoln Navigator's tank full.) Power came on when it felt like coming on, which seemed less and less often day by day.

Not much TV. Not much Internet. Cell phone connections rare and spotty. Even good old-fashioned radio took electricity, for crying out loud.

"Well, we've still got books," Colin said. His arm tightened around her. "And we've got each other, and maybe in a while we'll have a baby to keep us too busy to worry about all the stuff we don't have."

"Marshall's probably writing now," she said. "Want to go upstairs and see what we can do about that?"

"The wench grows bold," Colin said, and squeezed her again. Up the stairs they went. He closed the door to the master bedroom behind them.

Every once in a while these days, you read a newspaper story about somebody who killed himself because he couldn't write on his Facebook wall or tweet any more. *I'm cut off from the whole world, so why stay?* one guy's last note read.

The story said that particular suicider was all of nineteen years old. The reporter quoted John Donne's *No man is an island, entire to himself*, and went on to talk about how, in the aftermath of the supervolcano eruption, we were all cast back on our individual resources in ways we couldn't have imagined before first Yellowstone and then the whole country fell in on themselves.

Actually, before the supervolcano went off, Marshall Ferguson wouldn't have been caught dead reading a newspaper. That
was something else he left to his father and other antiques. If he
needed news or anything else, he got it off the Net with his laptop or his smartphone.

He'd got a lot of his fun in the virtual world, too. He hadn't
spent *all* his free time playing World of Warcraft with buddies
scattered cross the world, but he had spent quite a bit of it in
front of a monitor.

Now those choices were mostly closed off. Even when he
had power, the WoW servers often didn't. He had the game on
his hard drive, of course, but playing solo was to the massively
multipersonal variant very much as masturbation was to sex.
Better than nothing, yeah, but nowhere near so good as the real
thing.

When the Net was up, seeing yesterday's story in tomorrow's
Times just reminded you how pathetic a paper was. But it was
yesterday's story only if you'd found out about it yesterday. When
you read it for the first time as it ran in the newspaper, it seemed
new to you. Sports broadcasters doing the Olympics had called
some of their shows plausibly live. The *Times*, these days, was
plausibly live, and seemed authentically live because its competi-
tors, which should have been really live, were in fact too often
dead.

And damned if Marshall didn't find a substitute—well, a substitute of sorts—for his MMRPG. One of his friends' dads dug a
beat-up maroon box out of the back of a closet and presented it
to Lucas. The game was called Diplomacy. The board was a map
of Europe with funky boundaries: the way things had looked before World War I rearranged political geography.

Fighting World War I was the point of the game. You could
negotiate before you moved. You had to write down your orders.
No fancy graphics or anything, but it turned out to be a pretty

good way for a bunch of guys to kill a Saturday afternoon ... and evening. They finished up by candlelight.

"Gotta hand it to my old man," Lucas said after Austria-Hungary's red pieces had conquered a majority of the supply centers on the board and therefore won. "That's not half bad."

"Pretty good, in fact," Marshall agreed, thinking his own father would probably get off on it, too. Another question occurred to him: "How long has your dad had this, anyway? I mean, dig it—the pieces are *wood*, man. When was the last time you saw that?"

"Dad told me he played it when he was in high school," Lucas answered. That put it back in medieval times, or maybe further: Lucas' father was paunchy and bald and graying. He might not actually have more miles on his odometer than Marshall's father did, but he sure looked older.

"It's a hella good game," Marshall said, and all the players gathered around the board nodded. Judiciously, Marshall went on, "About the only thing wrong with it I can see is, how often can we get seven people together and, like, blow off a whole day?"

More nods from his comrades in skulduggery (you didn't have to tell the truth while you were negotiating—only your final written orders counted). A guy named Tim, with whom Marshall had gone to high school and who didn't seem to have done much since, eyed the board and the other players.

"When you wargame online, there's lots of other people all the time," he observed. "Or there used to be, when the power worked all the time. Here, it's just us, y'know?"

People nodded yet again, with more or less patience depending on their own personalities. Tim was fun to hang out with, but he'd never be the brightest LED in the flashlight. He was the kind of guy who ordered pie à la mode with ice cream on it. He had no clue that he'd just said the same thing Marshall came out with a little while before. Tim had no clue about quite a few things, but he'd done a better than decent job of playing Italy in the game. Winning with Italy wasn't impossible, but Marshall could see it wouldn't be easy, either.

Lucas said, "It may not be as tough as you guys are making it out to be. I mean, we aren't all stuck in nine-to-fives." His mouth twisted. "No matter how much we wish we were."

He was living with his dad, the same way Marshall was living at his old family house. Three of the others shared an apartment that would have been about right for one of them. Tim had lived out of his car for a while, till gas got too scarce and too expensive to make that practical. Now he was just kind of around. Maybe he crashed on one girlfriend or another, or on one girlfriend and another. Marshall didn't know the details. These days, with so many people from sea to shining sea scuffling, asking a whole bunch of questions was the worst kind of bad form.

"We'll try," Marshall said. "What else can we do?"

Louise Ferguson fidgeted while she waited for the bus. It was—surprise!—late again. When cities had trouble getting enough fuel for public transit and police cars, you knew the world was going to hell in a handbasket. It wouldn't be going to hell in anything requiring gasoline, that was for sure.

Like most cars, hers sat in the garage under her condo almost all the time, a monument to the way things had been before the supervolcano erupted. She hoped Mr. Nobashi would understand. He still drove in to the ramen works two or three times a week. But then, he was a fancy executive, not an administrative assistant. And he got his pay straight from the home office in Hiroshima. With the way the dollar had nosedived against the yen since the eruption, that made his salary go a lot further, too.

Here came the bus at last. It left a black plume of diesel fumes behind it as it rumbled north on Sword Beach. It wasn't supposed to do that. It was supposed to be clean, and not stinky. God only knew the last time anyone'd serviced that overworked engine.

Before the eruption, even people who didn't think of themselves as green would have had conniptions about that smoke-belching bus. Not today, Josephine! Anything that dumped CO_2 into the air and helped fight the supervolcano's big chill was wonderful, even if it smelled nasty.

The bus stopped. Louise handed the driver a buck and a half. Like a lot of SoCal towns, San Atanasio had stopped using computerized bus passes. When the computers didn't run all the time, you couldn't rely on them the way people had for so long. You had to make do with simpler things.

Mr. Nobashi, for instance, had brought an abacus into the ramen works. It wasn't just for show, either. The way his fingers flicked the beads was a sight to behold; Patty from the Farm Belt called it a caution. He was about as fast and accurate with the abacus as Louise was with a calculator. Next thing you knew, he'd dredge up a slide rule from somewhere.

Only a few cars shared Sword Beach with the bus. Most of the traffic was bicycles, with occasional full-sized trikes and skateboards. From what the papers said, random street crime (except for bike thefts) was way down. Getting away was harder than it had been, and people were more willing to chase you. The world was less impersonal, less withdrawn, then it had been when the automobile was king.

The bus stopped at Sword Beach and Braxton Bragg Boulevard. Louise got out there, because it turned the wrong way on Braxton Bragg. Back in the day, she would've grumbled at walking a couple of blocks from the bus stop to her workplace. When everybody did it, it was no big deal.

No big deal when it wasn't raining, anyhow. Right this minute, it wasn't. The spring sun, the sun that the supervolcano eruption had turned pale and watery, was shining as brightly as it ever did these days. Louise had stuck an umbrella in her purse just the same. No guarantee it wouldn't be raining when she came out this afternoon. And wasn't that a hell of a thing? If you couldn't trust SoCal weather, what could you trust?

Nothing. Nothing and nobody. Louise's mouth thinned to a bloodless line. She made herself relax, because otherwise she'd screw up the lipstick she'd so carefully applied before she left. But if having James Henry hadn't taught her that lesson once and for all, she couldn't imagine what would do the trick.

Here was Ramen Central. The sliding security gate was open: the only connection between the property and the outside world. Steel fencing topped by razor wire protected the rest of the perimeter (for that matter, razor wire topped the gate, too). Despite fence and wire, they'd still had stuff disappear from parked cars. That was why they had a full-time armed security guard.

He touched the brim of his drill-sergeant hat in what was almost but not quite a salute. "Mornin', Mrs. Ferguson," he said.

"Good morning, Steve," she said. She'd given up trying to get the big Hispanic guy to call her Louise. He'd served a long hitch in the Army, he'd fought in Afghanistan, and he had a strong sense of rank and hierarchy. Sometimes all you could do was roll with things.

She remembered having that thought before she went into the building. The power was on, which made everything seem almost the way it was before the supervolcano threw things for a loop. Almost, but, as with Steve's touch of the hat brim, not quite. Before the supervolcano, she wouldn't have heard anybody here burst into tears.

Which she did, right as the door closed behind her. It wasn't just anybody, either. It was Patty, who'd been here since dirt and who, as far as Louise could tell, had a soul machined from the kind of steel that went into armor plate for tanks. These weren't little sniffly tears, either. She was weeping and wailing as if she'd just found out her oldest son had been eaten by bears.

Hoping Patty hadn't found out something too much like that, Louise rushed toward the older woman's office. She almost ran into Mr. Nobashi, who was coming out. The salaryman looked upset, too: not only because Patty was crying but also, Louise judged, on account of what had made her cry. Whatever it was, he must have told it to Patty, and the telling must have set her off.

"Oh. Mrs. Ferguson," he said. He wasn't terrific with English. What he did to her name usually made her want to snicker. Not this morning. And what he did next scared the crap out of her: he bowed low, the bow of inferior to superior, and went on, "So sorry. I am so sorry."

"So sorry for what? What happened?" Louise managed. Patty'd told gruesome stories about the manager from Japan who'd worked here before Mr. Nobashi. The guy'd thought the rules here were the same as they were on the other side of the Pacific. He'd gone home in a hurry, and the company got hit with a big, juicy sexual-harassment suit.

Mr. Nobashi had to know about that. In all the time Louise had worked here, she'd never heard that he'd fallen off the path of virtue. And if he chose now to do it, would he come on to Patty? She was about as sexy as a snapping turtle, and had the same kind of wattle under her chin. Wouldn't Mr. Nobashi decide to try and butter his biscuits with somebody younger and cuter?

But Louise turned out to be wasting her time worrying about that particular misfortune. "Hiroshima call me just now," Mr. Nobashi said. "Oh, Jeeesus Christ! How I can tell you? Home office say, with times so hard, we not profitable enough in America. They close this office. They send me home. You people . . ." He gave that humiliated bow—that had to be the kind it was—again. "So sorry!"

"Close . . . this office?" The words sounded as strange, as wrong, coming from Louise's lips as they had when she heard them from her boss. The ramen company's corporate headquarters in the USA had been here on Braxton Bragg Boulevard since the 1970s. Wouldn't closing it deprive college students yet unborn of the chance to harden their arteries with cheap shrimp, chicken, beef, and Oriental noodles?

More to the point, wouldn't closing it pound one more nail into the coffin of San Atanasio's economy? Most to the point, wouldn't closing it cost one Louise Ferguson her job at a time when people swarmed like so many starving locusts on any work that appeared? Too often, that was about what they were.

"*Hai*. Please believe me, I do everything I know how to do to stop this," Mr. Nobashi said miserably. He spread his hands, palms up. "I fail."

Patty came out of her office. Her face looked like the Mask of Tragedy with runny mascara streaks. "I been here twenty-six years," she said, maybe to Mr. Nobashi, maybe to Louise, maybe only to herself. "Twenty-six years," she repeated. "What am I gonna do without this place?"

Mr. Nobashi bowed to her the same way he'd bowed to Louise, or it might have been even deeper. "Please excuse me," he said. "I am so sorry. Oh, Jeeesus Christ, I am so goddamn sorry." For the first time, Louise heard him spice up his English the way he did his Japanese. He went on, "Like I tell you before, I do all I can to keep this location open. I think company make big mistake to close it. But I cannot stop them."

It's not my fault. That was what he was trying to say. No doubt it was the truth, the whole truth, and nothing but the truth. It cut no ice with Patty. "You're closing this place," she said in *J'accuse!* tones that made it sound as if Mr. Nobashi would be out front in person, nailing boards across the doorway. "What am I supposed to do for work now?"

It was a good question—a hell of a good question, in fact. It was the good question uppermost in Louise's mind, too. Mr. Nobashi had the grace to look distressed. And well he might. They were sending him back to Hiroshima. They weren't firing him, laying him off, downsizing him, shit-canning him. Call it whatever you pleased, but they weren't doing it to him. Whereas the ramen works' American employees . . .

"Before I leave this country, I write you most excellent letter of recommendation," Mr. Nobashi said. "And you also, Mrs. Ferguson." Before either woman could interrupt to tear him a new asshole, he rushed on: "I know this is not enough. Please understand, I know very goddamn well. But it is the only thing I can do now."

He sounded like somebody throwing old clothes in a trash bag to give to the Red Cross after an earthquake—or after a supervolcano eruption. Yes, he was doing what he could. That wasn't anywhere near enough, though, not if you had the misfortune to be on the receiving end.

"My husband's outa work now, too," Patty said, and started crying again. "How're we s'posed to make the mortgage payments if we're both collecting unemployment, huh? We're neither one of us spring chickens any more. Gettin' somethin' new wouldn't be easy even if times was good. When times're this shitty, we're screwed."

That was the word, all right. Louise had enough trouble making payments as things were. She had no one to fall back on now. Two unemployment checks were bound to be better than one.

Her cell phone chose that moment to go off in her purse. She reached in to kill it. She'd get the voice mail later on— unless the power died again, which wouldn't affect her phone but would affect the network's ability to reach it and be reached. With power failures so frequent, the you-must-take-care-of-it-right-this-second-if-not-sooner fixation of the years before the eruption was fading. Later would do, because later often had to do.

"What about Steve and the other guards?" she asked. She was thinking *What about me?* but Patty'd already taken care of that.

"It is most unfortunate situation for all concerned," Mr. Nobashi said, which meant the security guards were screwed along with everybody else.

Well, almost everybody else. "*You've* still got a job, Mr. Nobashi," Patty said bluntly. "You may have to go back to Japan to do it now, but you've still got it."

"Please excuse me." Mr. Nobashi got out of there at top speed, perhaps to spread the good news to the rest of the building.

"That rotten, no-good pissant." Patty usually talked loud. Now she had no reason on God's green earth to care if Mr. Nobashi heard her. "I oughta pinch his little head off."

"Tell me about it!" Louise said.

"I gave this lousy company the best years of my life," Patty went on, as if she hadn't spoken.

"Tell me about it!" Louise said again. Patty sounded the way she had herself when she talked about leaving Colin, substituting only *company* for *man.* It had been true for Louise, it was just as true for Patty, and it did neither of them one single, solitary goddamn bit of good.

"I oughta burn this stinking place down." Patty shook her head. "Nah. If I do, the fucking noodle people'd collect insurance. They'd laugh. . . . Well, fuck 'em all." She went back into the office that had been hers and soon would belong to nobody.

Fuck 'em all. The fired person's motto all through history— and that did no one any good, either. Alone there in the hallway, Louise fished out her phone. Might as well see what the message was.

It was from Colin. Louise ground her teeth loud enough to

make any dentist who heard her sure he'd be sending his kids to Harvard. Just what she needed right now! She almost deleted it without listening to it. Almost, but not quite. Shaking her head, she held the phone to her ear.

"Hello, Louise," the familiar, once-loved voice said. "Wanted to let you know we found out for sure: Kelly's pregnant. Sorry, but I'm afraid that means I won't be able to keep sending you little bits and pieces for your kid any more. Way things are, and the way our bills will shoot through the roof, we're gonna have to hang on to every nickel we've got. The ramen place doesn't pay too bad, I bet, so you'll be fine as long as you kinda watch it. Well, take care. 'Bye."

"You son of a bitch!" Louise snarled. "You *fucking* son of a bitch!" That was what Colin was, all right. With a few quick, savage pokes, she did scrub the message. But she couldn't get it out of her head so easily. *You'll be fine as long as you kinda watch it.* Watch what? She had exactly nothing to watch now, here or from her ex-husband.

How long could she make nothing last? How much severance would she get? How soon could she start collecting unemployment? How much would it be? She had no idea. She'd have to find out, though, and in a hurry. She didn't even know where the closest unemployment office was.

Well, as long as this crappy joint had power, she could Google that and find out. What would Mr. Nobashi do if he caught her? Fire her? Laughing a wild laugh, she hustled back to her computer.

XIII

Kelly broke a couple of eggs into a measuring cup. They were going to go into a meatloaf; the store had had ground beef for the first time in quite a while.

They sat there side by side in the bottom of the Pyrex cup. To Kelly, it looked as if they were two big, baleful eyes staring up at her. She gulped. Then she did more than gulp. She ran for the bathroom. She made it in the nick of time.

Scope got rid of some of the revolting taste—some, but not enough. The horrible stuff had gone up her nose. That meant she would keep tasting it all night. They called it morning sickness, but they lied. They did for her, at least. She could toss her cookies any old time. She'd found out more about vomiting these past few weeks than she'd ever known before.

Colin walked in just as she was lying down on the couch. "Don't kiss me!" she warned. All the Scope in the world wouldn't be enough to make him happy if he did.

"What happened?" he asked. Not *What's the matter?*—he didn't need to be a cop to figure out what was up with that.

She pointed feebly toward the kitchen. "The eggs. They were looking at me. You want dinner, *you* make it."

"Okay," he said, and did. The meatloaf came out ever so slightly scorched on the bottom and blander than she would have fixed it, but it was plenty edible. Colin cooked well enough. He'd never be great; neither his skills nor his repertoire reached far enough for that.

At the moment, Kelly wouldn't fuss. She was just glad the meat loaf seemed inclined to stay down. Maybe the blandness even helped.

"Better now?" Colin asked.

"Uh-huh." She nodded. "Thanks. You never can tell when it'll get me. I sure can't, anyway."

She washed the dishes. After Colin had cooked supper, that seemed only fair. Marshall was out doing something with his friends. What and with whom, she didn't know. Marshall was an adult, and she didn't pry. Whatever it was, she hoped it didn't involve too much money. Colin's ex had fired her son right after ramen headquarters shuttered. If she had to stay home herself, she saw no point in paying him. Which made sense, but making sense didn't mean it did Marshall any good.

Colin was not happy to have his younger son out of work. Kelly tried to soften it: "Times are tough everywhere. It's not like he's the only one."

"I know," Colin growled, "but he's the only one here."

"He's still writing," Kelly said.

"He sure isn't selling much," Colin answered, which was also true. Kelly had learned to recognize the SASEs Marshall included with his manuscripts when they came back. Every time her stepson picked one up, he looked disgusted. But he kept sending his stories out over and over, by snailmail and e-mail. If anything would let him escape from his current dead end, they were it.

But would anything? Marshall didn't want anyone but editors looking at what he wrote. Again, Kelly didn't pry. She wouldn't have wanted anyone prying into what she was up to if she were in Marshall's Nikes, either—*do unto others* and all that good stuff.

"He's gonna need to get himself a real job now, a job job." Colin paused, then tempered that ever so slightly: "Or at least find another kid who needs babysitting."

"But—" Kelly left it right there, because she didn't know where else she could go with it. It wasn't that there were no real jobs; some work still got done in spite of everything that had happened to the country. Damn few new ones turned up, though, and next to none of the ones that did were for kids just out of college with a degree in creative writing.

As for babysitting, the only reason Marshall had done so much of that was that James Henry Ferguson was his half-brother. Sure, Louise would give him a good reference, but so what? Rug rat minder wasn't his chosen career path.

Which wasn't the only complication. If Colin felt like locking horns with his son, Kelly didn't know what she should do. Play peacemaker? Stand clear and let them go at it? Whatever she did or didn't do, she saw ways to wind up in trouble with the greatest of ease. That was one part of marrying somebody with grown kids she hadn't thought about enough.

Colin chuckled. It wasn't a cheerful chuckle: more the sort he might have given after spotting the driver's license that dumbass bank robber left behind. "If he doesn't find anything in the next few months, he can start making money taking care of his legitimate half-sib."

"That's true." Kelly knew she sounded surprised. She hadn't looked so far ahead. She would have bet Marshall hadn't, either. She added, "Don't rub his nose in it right now, please. It's not what he wants to do."

"I know," Colin said. "But you do what you've got to do, not what you want to do. A lot of people haven't figured that one out yet, even with the supervolcano yelling in their faces. They still try and do whatever they want, and then they get mad when it doesn't work the way it used to."

"Yup." Kelly nodded. "I wonder what I'd be doing if my chairman didn't know the head of the geology department at Dominguez."

"You'd've made it," Colin said with great certainty. "You're the kind who does. You wouldn't've stuck it out for your thesis and your degree and everything if you weren't the kind of person who tended to business. You wouldn't've been out there in the cold with your darn seismograph for me to make a jerk of myself over if you didn't take care of business." This time, his chuckle was self-conscious—not the kind of noise he usually made.

"Best chilly morning in Yellowstone I ever had," Kelly answered. That made him smile. He needed reassurance he was okay with women in general and with her in particular. Having Louise dump him that way left him more deeply scarred than he showed anybody but her. Chances were it left him more deeply scarred than he wanted to show himself.

Reading by candlelight was possible, but it left a lot to be desired. They went up to bed before too long. Marshall hadn't come in yet. Kelly figured he eventually would, and she was right. She had to get up to pee in the middle of the night. The power'd come back on, too. She saw light around the edges of Marshall's door and heard him clicking away at the Mac.

Even if it cost her a reliable babysitter, she hoped he made it as a writer. Yes, you did what you had to do. Colin was dead right about that. But if what you had to do could also be what you wanted to do, you were looking at something as close to happiness as you were likely to find in this old world.

She went back to bed. She fell asleep again as soon as her head hit the pillow. That was one more thing the baby was doing to her. She would have liked it better if she didn't have so much trouble getting started in the morning. Coffee tasted so horrible she couldn't stomach it. That was Junior's fault, too. She would have been grumpier if she'd stayed awake longer.

Bryce Miller had got his share of rejection slips for things he'd written. He was resigned to that. When you wrote poems modeled after ancient Greek efforts from poets long dead by the time of Christ, you needed to get used to rejection.

But he was getting different rejections these days. He kept sending out poems. And he also kept sending out applications to every college and university that had a job opening even faintly related to the kinds of things he could do. Some of them just ignored him. Others cared enough to tell him they wanted nothing to do with him. It was a compliment . . . of sorts. He would have liked a compliment of the sort that came with paychecks attached.

It wasn't that he hated what he was doing at Junipero High. He could still have been back at the DWP, for instance—now, *that* had been a crazy-making job, at least for him. He felt all throttled back, though. He was teaching so many classes and so many kids that he had no time or energy for anything that looked like scholarship. He also got tired of teaching nothing but the basics of what he knew. Sure, that was what high school was all about. He understood the problem. He got tired just the same.

So he cast his curriculum vitae upon the waters and waited to see what he would find after God knew how many days. The institutions of higher learning that did deign to answer—a bit more than half—were politely apologetic. No, they were politely hopeless. They had no openings. They were contracting, not expanding. They'd been contracting even before the supervolcano made classics and history seem even less relevant than they had back in the good times.

"At least I can do most of this by e-mail when the power's on," he told Susan. "It doesn't cost me as much in postage as it would have thirty years ago." He grinned crookedly. "And the ones who do answer tell me no a fuck of a lot faster than they could've in the old days."

"Funny, Bryce. Har-dee-har-har. See? I'm laughing." She was just finishing her own dissertation. She knew everything there was to know about Frederick II, the Holy Roman Emperor who was called *Stupor Mundi*: the stunner of the world. The world, unfortunately, had a new stunner now. Her chances for landing an academic job might have been better than Bryce's, but that sure didn't make them good.

"Hey, you'll do it, whether I manage or not. I can be your kept man," Bryce said.

"Right. Whatever you're smoking, let me have some, too," she answered. "I wonder if your high school needs two Latin teachers who can do world history, too." Before he could say anything, she quickly added, "Yes, I'm kidding. You're lucky Junipero needs one person in that slot."

"Lucky. Uh-huh." But Bryce didn't push it. As things went these days, he *was* lucky. He had work. As long as he stayed careful and lucky, it let him pay the rent, eat, and put aside a widow's mite for the day after tomorrow. If Susan added even a little something to the pot after they got married, they'd . . . kinda get along.

Maybe things would come back to normal by the time they hit middle age. Geologists and climatologists were still hashing that out. Bryce got distant, possibly distorted echoes of the argument from Colin: Kelly was one of the people doing the arguing. Right now the answer seemed to be *Nobody knows for sure, but it doesn't look so good.* Or *so hot,* if your taste ran to old-fashioned slang and bad puns.

"It's not fair!" Susan burst out.

Bryce nodded. "Nope. It's not. But I don't know what to do about it, hon. Fair or not, we're stuck with it."

"Shit," she said. "When Rome fell, it fell an inch at a time, and the Romans kicked and bit and clawed as hard as they could. Mother Nature didn't whack 'em upside the head with a shillelagh."

"And you're not even Irish," he said. She made as if to whack him upside the head. Luckily, she wasn't carrying a concealed shillelagh.

Two days later, Bryce looked forward to getting back to his apartment and pouring down a beer. Trying to explain the ablative absolute was as foredoomed as the charge of the Light Brigade. High school kids just didn't get a language that used cases, not prepositions and word order, for its special effects—and the ablative absolute was some of Latin's Pixar splendor.

He'd explained till he was blue in the face, but they didn't see it. Well, Olga Smyslovsky—Sasha's younger sister—did, but she spoke a language with more cases than Latin when she went home from school. Like Sasha, she had trouble with Latin vocabulary, but the grammar was a piece of cake for her. Nice to know it was for somebody.

Bryce wondered why he bothered opening his mailbox. He didn't expect any bills. Junk mail was way down since the eruption. Paper was scarce and expensive, and so was everything else. Businesses hunkered down, the same as the people who mostly didn't patronize them.

"What's this?" he wondered out loud, plucking an envelope from the box. It was from Wayne State. Wayne State, he read on the printed return address, was in Wayne, Nebraska. *One more "Screw you very much for your interest" letter,* Bryce thought.

He was damned if he remembered sending any kind of application to Wayne State. Maybe it was a preventive rejection—don't you dare try to land a job with us! Were there such things? He wouldn't have been surprised, not even a little bit.

He took it upstairs. He wouldn't even be bummed when he got one more *Are you kidding us?*—he was hardened to those by now. Nobody else would be there to pay any attention to him, anyhow.

Another gaudy sunset poured carnival-glass light into his living room when he opened the curtain. He hardly noticed it, which only went to show you could get used to anything. The first thing he did after opening the curtain was to try a lamp. It lit. He nodded to himself—he'd be able to nuke some leftovers tonight. Power had been on when he left Junipero, but that didn't mean it was bound to stay on.

He turned off the lamp. The red-gold sunset was enough to read by for the moment, so he'd use it. The power company made up for being out of action half the time by jacking up the rates when it actually worked. That endeared it to everybody, as if it cared.

"The envelope . . ." Bryce said, as if he were in a tux handing out Academy Awards. Yeah, as if! He opened it. Out came a sheet of—surprise!—Wayne State letterhead. He unfolded it and read the laser-printed missive inside.

Dear Dr. Miller, the letter said, *We would be most interested in considering you for the assistant professorship position opening this coming fall. As you may be aware, Professor Smetana, who had held this position, recently passed away due to lung disease caused by the supervolcano eruption. We do have state-mandated funding for the position, and are anxious to fill it as quickly as possible. I look forward to your prompt response. Sincerely*—and the department chair's signature.

"Fuck me," Bryce said softly. Why had the lightning struck

him? That was sure what it felt like. Two answers sprang to mind. Either or both might be true. If they didn't fill the slot in a hurry, their state-mandated funding was liable to dry up and blow away. And they probably figured he'd work cheap. They were probably right, too.

His eye went back to the middle of the paragraph. *Professor Smetana . . . recently passed away due to lung disease caused by the supervolcano eruption.* Wayne State. Nebraska. Uh-huh. How far was Wayne from the Ashfall State Historical Park? A long-ago supervolcano blast had buried rhinos in ash; he'd seen some of their remains in Lincoln after barely surviving this latest explosion. Paleontologists had shown that they'd suffered from ash-induced lung troubles, too. Those were back, bigtime: Marie's disease, otherwise known to broadcasters as HPO, the acronym for a cumbersome medical term. Poor Professor Smetana had a lot of company.

Bryce went into the bedroom and turned on his computer. He'd send an e-mail right away and follow it up with a snailmail letter in case it didn't get through. He wrote the e-mail to the address under the signature. Then he Googled Wayne State's Web site. He clicked on the link.

That server is temporarily unavailable. He swore at the error message and tried again. He got it again. Then he realized that, while he had power, Wayne State might not.

Where the hell *was* Wayne, Nebraska? A little more Googling showed him it was about a hundred miles from Omaha, north and a bit west. Wayne State had about 5,000 students. The town of Wayne—named after Revolutionary general Mad Anthony, Wikipedia explained—had 6,000 more.

Do I really want to move there? Bryce wondered. L.A. made every other place in the world except maybe New York City, London, and Paris seem like the boonies by comparison. Wayne *was* the boonies: the terminal boonies, if you wanted to get technical. You'd have to make your own fun. Boy, would you ever!

And what were winters there like? L.A. had got snow every winter since the eruption. Quite a few places, these days, were getting snow in summertime. Midwestern winters hadn't been fun before the supervolcano went off, not if you were a California kid, they hadn't. Did Wayne do its best impression of pre-eruption Winnipeg nowadays?

How he'd handle winter wasn't the only thing he needed to worry about. What would Susan think? Would Wayne State have a job for her, too? It didn't seem likely. How would she feel about that?

After thinking about Susan—quite a bit after thinking about her—Bryce remembered his mother. Barbara Miller hadn't been thrilled when he moved up to the Valley. What would she say if he went two thousand miles away?

I want you to be happy. That's what she would say, sure as God made Greek irregular verbs. And she'd be lying through her teeth. That was what the math guys called intuitively obvious.

"One thing at a time," Bryce muttered, fishing his phone out of his pocket. First step was finding out what Susan thought.

His stomach rumbled, loud enough to startle his cat if only he'd had one. He stuck the phone back where he'd got it. No, first step was dealing with those leftovers. Whatever Susan thought wouldn't change a hell of a lot in the next half hour. Yes, people were animals. Better not to be a hungry animal. He headed for the kitchen.

If there was a drearier place in the world than the Torrance office of the California Employment Development Department, Louise Ferguson couldn't imagine what it might be. The way things looked to her, Satan would have had a tough time devising a drearier place in hell.

She sat on a hard, uncomfortable plastic chair of dispirited grayish blue in the waiting area. Water ran from her umbrella and puddled on the dispirited grayish brown linoleum under her feet. She'd had to walk several blocks from the bus stop to the EDD office. Three people on the bus were sneezing their heads off. She hoped she wouldn't come down sick.

Somebody a couple of rows behind her in the waiting area coughed as if he'd smoked four packs a day for the past thirty years. The chill and the rain made people get sick more easily than Southern Californians were used to doing. When they weren't sneezing and hacking, they bitched about it.

Louise wished San Atanasio had an EDD office. But Torrance was the biggest South Bay city, so such things aggregated here. She had to make the long bus trip instead of a short one. If she did catch something because of that, would the EDD care? It was to laugh.

The waiting area was packed. She counted herself lucky to have a chair. Whites, African-Americans, Hispanics, East Asians, South Asians, Samoans . . . The crowd was as diverse as L.A. County. People chattered in English, Spanish, Japanese, Korean, something guttural that might have been Arabic or Farsi or Armenian for all of her, and in a language or two she couldn't come even that close to identifying. She smelled stale sweat, stale booze, tobacco smoke clinging to clothes (you got in big trouble for trying to smoke in here), and assorted colognes and hair goops.

A middle-aged woman with a long, lined face and pulled-back hair who looked like an escapee from a 1920s elementary schoolteachers' lounge stood up and used a bullhorn to cut through the buzz of talk: "Nine-thirty appointments! Take your places in the lines, nine-thirty appointments!"

People stood up and hustled to get into the lines that eventually put you face-to-face with an EDD clerk. A baby who'd been sound—and soundlessly—asleep while Mommy sat started screaming when Mommy got up. Mommy tried to comfort the kid, but didn't have much luck.

Louise sat tight. She was a ten o'clock appointment. She'd got here early because that was how the bus schedule worked. Trying to jump the lines was an even worse sin than lighting a cigarette. You got an Official Black Mark on your record. A couple of those would cost you a week's benefits.

Men and women who'd been standing took the chairs of those who'd risen to get in line. The waiting area didn't empty out; new people kept coming in all the time. The SoCal economy sucked. The whole country's economy sucked. Jesus H. Christ, so did the whole world's. But the USA was screwed worse than everybody else.

If the government didn't keep printing dollars and handing them out, no one would have any. If the government did keep printing them and handing them out, pretty soon they wouldn't be worth anything. That was well on the way to happening. The prices these days! But Washington seemed to have decided that inflation at least put a Band-Aid on disaster.

Even though Louise had major doubts that that was wise, she grabbed everything the law said she was entitled to. If she lost the condo . . . She had no idea what she'd do if she lost the condo. Live in her car with James Henry? Beg money or a room in the old house from Colin? If it were just her, she would sooner have jumped off a high building and ended things in a hurry. But you couldn't do that when you had a little guy to worry about. She couldn't, anyhow.

The refugee from whacking kids on the knuckles with a ruler raised the bullhorn to her mouth again. "Ten o'clock appointments!" she blared. "Take your places in the lines, ten o'clock appointments!"

Louise jumped up. All the lines were long, but one she particularly wanted to avoid. A chunky woman named Maria—

Anglo, not Hispanic—proved that the EDD didn't discriminate in hiring on the basis of race, gender, religion, national origin, sexual orientation, or competence. She always took twice as long to accomplish half as much as any of the other clerks. Some of the rest were better, some worse, but only fools and newbies got into the line that led to Maria. It was the shortest of them all—and with good reason.

Only a couple of minutes before ten now. So said the clock on the wall. It worked whether the power was on or not (it was this morning), which meant it ran on batteries. You got to try for your appointment at the scheduled time. You got it . . . when you got it.

Slowly, she moved toward the window. The EDD wasn't so heavily fortified as the post office on Reynoso Drive, but the windows were barred like the ones in an old-fashioned bank. The twenty-something guy in front of her wore a stingy-brim fedora that would have been ridiculously out of date when he was born but had turned hip again with the passage of the years. He also had on a loud houndstooth jacket; as far as Louise was concerned, that went beyond hip to tacky. From one of the jacket's inside pockets he pulled out an airline-drink-sized bottle of vodka. He drained it in a quick gulp, then stuck it back in there again.

That was one way to make time in line go by. Bringing booze into the EDD office was Against the Rules, too, but Louise wouldn't say anything unless the man in front of her got loud and rowdy. He didn't seem likely to. He just wanted to numb the world a little. How could you blame him?

She'd got to within three people of the front of the line when the Asian woman at the window turned out not to have some bit of paper she needed. She didn't savvy much English. The clerk, a prim white man with a neat gray mustache, knew not word one of whatever language she spoke.

The hipster in front of Louise performed a theatrical half turn. "Give me a fucking break!" he said, and then, faintly embarrassed, "Sorry about that."

"Don't worry about it," she answered. "We could all use one."

He grinned at her. "Yeah!"

After what seemed like much too long, the clerk got a rush of brains to the head and asked if any of his fellow civil servants could communicate with the Asian woman. The EDD personnel were as diverse as the people whose employment they were supposed to be developing. Sure as hell, somebody proved able to talk with her. Then they had to figure out what to do about the paper she didn't have. Louise didn't know what they decided; they still weren't speaking English. But the woman left the window. By the unhappy look on her face, Louise guessed she'd have to come back when she found whatever the hell it was. With a loud sigh of relief, the blocky Hispanic guy behind her stepped up.

"He better have *his* shit together," the man with the stingy-brim muttered darkly. Louise found herself nodding.

Evidently, the Hispanic fellow did. He stepped away from the window folding his check and sticking it in the right front pocket of his jeans. *You'd better have your shit together, too,* Louise thought as the hipster took his place. He must have, because he collected his check and got out of there in jig time.

"Name and Social," the clerk with the gray mustache intoned as Louise took Mr. Stingy-brim's place.

"Louise Ferguson." She gave him her Social Security number, too.

He entered them on his computer keyboard. Next to it sat a mechanical gadget that let him issue checks even when the power went out. It had to date from the seventies, maybe earlier. It must have gone into a box as soon as the EDD computerized. That nobody'd thrown away the box, and that someone had known where to find it again, impressed and horrified Louise at the same time.

"All right, Ms. Ferguson, now I need to see the evidence that you've been actively seeking employment during the past fortnightly period," the clerk said. Could anyone who didn't work for the EDD bring out things like *actively seeking employment* or *fortnightly period* as if they actually belonged to the English language? Louise wouldn't have bet six inches of used dental floss on it.

None of which had anything to do with the price of beer (high, like the price of everything else). Louise pulled out application letters from her purse and shoved them at the clerk. They were genuine, all right. She would have done anything short of turning tricks to escape the EDD's clutches. Christ on a crutch, who wouldn't? The only trouble was, nobody wanted to hire her . . . or, by appearances, anyone else.

He shuffled through them and noted them in her computer file. Then he did the same thing on her file card (more boxes that must have been exhumed from storage). Grudgingly, he said, "This appears satisfactory."

"Good," answered Louise, who would have hit the ceiling in seventeen different places if he'd tried telling her anything else.

He poked one more key. The printer on a shelf by his monitor hummed and spat out a check that would let her eat—not well, but eat—and pay some of what she owed on the condo. Some of what she owed would come out of what she'd saved while she worked at Ramen Central. Sooner or later, her savings would run dry. What she'd do then—she didn't want to think about now.

She put her applications and the check into the purse. Then she got out of there as fast as she could. Who hung around the EDD one second longer than they had to? Nobody, that was who.

It was still raining. It was raining harder than it had when she got there, in fact. Up went the umbrella. She splashed toward the bus stop. It was nothing but a bench—no roof or anything. Not many SoCal bus stops boasted roofs. How often did you need to keep off the rain here?

Often . . . now. The Retarded Transit District needed to improve the stops like this one. And where would the money for that come from? Local government agencies needed to do a million other things even more. They didn't have the money for those, either. Back in the day, they might have got it from Sacramento or Washington. But Sacramento had been broke before the eruption, and Washington was even broker than Sacramento. If that wasn't a measure of how screwed Washington was, nothing ever could be.

A Hispanic woman came up to stand beside Louise. She had an umbrella, too. Pretty soon, they'd both be soaking wet from midthigh down. Bumbershoots helped only so much. "I wonder how late the goddamn bus is gonna be," the Hispanic gal said.

"Late." Louise heard the doleful certainty in her own voice. If some modern Mussolini promised to make the buses run on time, he'd get elected in a landslide. And then he'd break his promise, sure as hell. Money was scarce. Fuel was scarcer. Spare parts were damn near extinct, and nobody seemed to be making or buying more.

"You got that right." The other woman took a pack of cigarettes out of her purse, extracted a cigarette from the pack, and lit it, all without getting wetter than she was already. Louise admired the dexterity as much as she wished she weren't getting the secondhand smoke.

The cigarette did do one thing, though: it made the bus come. The Hispanic woman had to drop it, only half done, on the sidewalk to board. Serious fines backed up the rules against smoking on public transportation.

Far more bicycles than cars used the streets. Some pedalers wore raincoats that reached down to their ankles. Some—the dumb ones, as far as Louise was concerned—tried to manage umbrellas. Some just said the devil with it and got wet. The bus had to go slowly to keep from mashing them.

Every so often, the driver honked his horn to remind the people on bikes that he was there—and to make them clear out in front of him. He didn't have much luck with that. The pedalers not only didn't clear out; they slowed down to piss him off. Some of them flipped the bus the bird.

If Louise had sat behind the big steering wheel, she knew she would have wanted to run over two or three of them to encourage the others to get some sense. The driver clutched the wheel tight enough to make his knuckles whiten, so maybe he was fighting the same temptation.

People got on. People got off. Before the eruption, only the poor rode the bus in L.A. If you could afford a car, you drove one. Who could afford a car now? Hardly anyone, which meant the bus attracted a higher class of passenger than it had once upon a time. *I'm on it, for instance,* Louise thought, quite without irony.

She got off at the stop closest to her condo. The walk back got her wetter and did nothing to improve her temper. She checked her mailbox. The mail wasn't there yet. She'd have to come down through the rain again to get it. And what would it be? Bills and ads. What else came these days?

"Mommy!" James Henry squealed when she walked through the door. He ran to her. She was the best thing that had ever happened to him: that was what that run said.

"Was he good?" she asked Marshall.

"Good enough," James Henry's half-brother answered. "Listen, Mom, I've got to go now that you're finally back."

"Not my fault the trip took so long," Louise said. "The bus

was impossible. And those selfish idiots on bikes only made things worse."

Marshall's eyes glinted. He'd ridden his bike over here to babysit. Was he one of the people who diddled buses for the fun of it? If he was, Louise didn't want to hear about it. He did say, "It'll cost you an extra twenty bucks." His voice was almost as hard and flat as Colin's.

"Twenty!" Louise spluttered indignantly.

"You're late. Late, late, late. And you're lucky I'm not saying fifty."

Sharper than a serpent's tooth . . . ran through Louise's head. But she paid him. Somebody who wasn't related to her by blood *would* have squeezed an extra fifty out of her. She couldn't afford it, but she didn't want to take James Henry to the unemployment office in the rain, either. You couldn't win. You couldn't even come close.

That twenty, of course, came on top of what she'd to pay him to watch James Henry for as long as she'd thought she would be gone. She'd just spent a fair part of her unemployment check. Did Marshall care? Yeah, right!

Out the door and into the rain he went. Louise sighed. She knew she'd call him the next time she had to go to the EDD office. If she could call him. If her phone had power. If the cell towers had powers. Sometimes, these days, even old-fashioned landlines didn't work, not that she had one.

"Mommy!" James Henry said again. *We're together again at last,* he meant.

"Hi, kid," Louise answered. Her own voice sounded hard and flat in her ears, too.

XIV

Colin sat in an interrogation room with Gabe Sanchez, waiting to grill an armed-robbery suspect named Cedric Curtis. "I was here when the uniformed guys brought him in," Gabe said. "We got him out of his regular clothes and into the jail suit, y'know?"

"Oh, sure," Colin answered. Inmates in the San Atanasio City Jail wore orange jumpsuits that made them look like animated carrots.

Sanchez wrinkled his nose. "Dude had the stinkiest feet in the world, man, that's what. We made him put his shoes back on."

A uniformed cop brought in Cedric Curtis. He was twenty-two now, and looked as if he might have been a linebacker in high school. His head was shaved. He wore a goatee, and had a nasty scar on one cheek. He hadn't bothered with a mask when he knocked over the Circle K, which was a big reason he was here now.

"We are filming this interview." Colin pointed up to a surveillance camera in one corner of the interrogation room. "Do you understand that, Mr. Curtis?"

"I hear ya," the suspect answered indifferently.

"Do you understand?" Gabe growled. He was playing bad cop today. "You gotta answer yes or no. Not like you don't know that. Not like you've never been here before. So, do you?"

Curtis looked as if he was thinking about a smartass comeback. Whatever he saw in Gabe's face, and in Colin's, made him change his mind. "I understand," he admitted in grudging tones.

"Okay. Now we're getting somewhere." Colin went through the Miranda warnings against self-incrimination. He could have been shaken awake at three in the morning and delivered them perfectly, the way a priest treated so rudely would have come out with a flawless Hail Mary and Our Father. "Do you understand that, too?"

Cedric Curtis nodded. "Yeah."

"Okay," Colin said. "Do you want to talk with us? Do you want an attorney present before you do?"

"I'll talk with you. Why not? Fuck, you got me, don't you?" Curtis said.

Maybe it'll be easy for a change. That'd be nice, Colin thought. Aloud, he said, "Are you confessing you robbed the convenience store and threatened Mr. Leghari with a pistol?"

"The raghead guy in there? Yeah, I done that." Curtis nodded. "Weren't no bullets in the gun, though."

Maybe that was true and maybe it wasn't. If it was, the kid had a few loose screws, or more than a few. An awful lot of convenience-store clerks packed heat of their own, commonly in a drawer under the register. Either Cedric had got the drop on Ahmed Leghari or he was one lucky fellow. Well, either way this did look like an easy one. "Would you care to tell us why you knocked over the Circle K, Mr. Curtis?" Colin asked.

By the way Curtis looked at him, *he* was the dummy. "On account of I didn't have no money," he said.

Thank you, Willie Sutton ran through Colin's mind. He didn't bring it out. Cedric Curtis wouldn't know Willie Sutton from a hole in the ground. He did say, "Plenty of ways to get money where you don't end up talking with us."

"Like what?" Curtis was openly scornful.

"They call them jobs," Gabe Sanchez said dryly. Colin shot him a warning glance. Even that might be skating close to the edge. You never could tell what a gung-ho defense attorney could build from a crack like that. *Look at the racist cop disrespecting my client!* he'd thunder.

But Curtis wasn't offended. He threw back his head and guffawed. "Jobs? For me? You gotta be jivin', man. Ain't no jobs for me. Ain't no jobs for nobody like me. Weren't no jobs for nobody like me even before that fuckin' thing blew up. Only got worse since. So I can deal rock—an' you'll bust me. Or I can do this shit—an' you'll bust me."

"You don't look like you've missed a lot of meals," Gabe said, which was true enough.

"I got two kids to feed. I got an old lady, too," Curtis replied. Whether she was his children's mother, he didn't say. "Like I told you, gotta get Benjamins some kinda way, law or no law."

A gung-ho lawyer could make something out of that, too, especially with things the way they were nowadays. Plenty of potential jurors might be out of work themselves. Even ones who weren't would have cousins or brothers-in-law who were. In tough times, they might not want to come down hard on a guy who stuck a gun—an unloaded gun, the lawyer would insist—in a scared clerk's face so he could feed his little children.

Well, that wasn't Colin's worry, or not very much of it. He had the arrest. Now he had a confession to go with it. The DA would carry the ball from here.

In the meantime, he nailed things down as tight as he could. He asked Cedric Curtis to describe the crime. Curtis did, with almost as much detail as the Circle K surveillance camera showed.

Whatever a defense lawyer did, he wouldn't be able to claim his client hadn't done it.

When Curtis finished, Gabe said, "Odds are you'll do some time. That'll keep you fed, anyway, even if prison rations aren't anything to write home about."

"I know about jail food," Curtis said. "There's enough of it, no matter how shitty it is." No, he hadn't worried about getting caught.

"Okay," Gabe said. "So you'll have three squares and a cot for a while. But what about your kids? What about your girlfriend? Who's gonna take care of them while you're in the pokey?"

Cedric Curtis looked astonished, as if that had never occurred to him. *Probably never did,* Colin thought sadly. It wasn't as if he hadn't seen reactions like that way too many times before. One of the things that made criminals what they were was an inability to look ahead. Everything that happened after they did what they did came as a complete surprise to them. Even after they got busted, did time, got out, and pulled another one, they were amazed all over again when they quickly turned into two-time losers.

"Aw, fuck," Curtis said softly. Maybe he could learn after all. But what lesson would he draw from this? *Don't knock over convenience stores?* Or *Don't get caught after you knock over a convenience store?* Colin couldn't be sure. He knew what how he'd guess, and didn't like it.

Well, Cedric wouldn't be his problem for a while. The uniformed cop came back and took the robber away. "Nothing left of this one but the paperwork," Gabe said.

"Yeah." Colin wished he sounded—and were—happier.

"Lighten up," Gabe told him. "He *will* do time. If he'd lifted canned goods, unh-unh. But no jury's gonna buy that he stuck a gun in a guy's face just so he could buy groceries for his brats. I mean, juries are dumb, but not that dumb."

"You hope. We hope," Colin said.

"Honest to God, they aren't," Gabe insisted. "Me, I'm going outside to celebrate with a cigarette." He grinned wryly. "Way to party down, huh?"

"If you say so." Colin went back to his desk. He stolidly started working on Cedric Curtis' file. The more you did now, the less you had to do later. But he hadn't got far when his phone rang. He picked it up. "Ferguson . . . Say what? . . . Are you sure? . . . Aw—fudge . . . Okay, what's the address? . . . Right. I'll get there soon as I can. 'Bye." He slammed the phone down.

Gabe Sanchez was just coming back from his nicotine fix when Colin stood up. His face must have been all over thunderclouds, because Gabe blurted, "Jesus! What hit the fan now? Your family okay?"

"Huh? Yeah, they're fine," Colin answered. "But there's a little old lady dead over on 139th Street, and the cop who found her says it sure looks like the Strangler got her. I'm on my way there now. Wanna ride along?"

"Shit, I'm dying to," Gabe answered. But he walked out to the parking lot with Colin. Colin had known he would. They wasted a couple of minutes filling out the required forms for getting a car: like a lot of Southern California towns, San Atanasio had really tightened up as gas got scarce and expensive. But no one would say boo to this trip, not when Colin scribbled *South Bay Strangler* on the line labeled *Reason for utilization of automotive vehicle.*

The sun shone as brightly as it ever did since the eruption. The sky tried to be blue, but didn't quite seem to remember how. It was somewhere in the high sixties. Seattle summer? It could have been worse. It had been last week, and no doubt it would be again before too long.

North on Hesperus to Braxton Bragg. East on Braxton Bragg to Sword Beach. Left onto Sword Beach, then a right at the next light and onto 139th. The corner there had a liquor store and a seafood restaurant that charged too much for some of the most mediocre dinners Colin had ever regretted ordering.

Once you turned the corner and headed up 139th, you fell back in time. Most of the houses on the little street had gone up not long after the war to give the kids of the Baby Boom bedrooms of their own. Some were even older: they looked like adobe even if they were stucco, and had roofs of Spanish (well, Spanish-style) tiles. They'd been moved here when the Harbor Freeway pushed through to San Pedro at the start of the Sixties.

Back then, San Atanasio had been white and Japanese. Oh, a few Mexican-Americans, but from families that had been in the States for generations. (Colin's secretary, Josie Linares, came from a family like that.) Now there were whites and blacks and Mexicans and Salvadorans (the Cubans in San Atanasio mostly lived farther south and east) and Koreans and Vietnamese (the Japanese had moved south to Torrance and Palos Verdes when the blacks started coming in) and . . . everything under the sun.

What there wasn't was a lot of money. Not in this part of town. The cars that sat in driveways and on the street—and, here and there, on lawns—looked as if they'd been sitting a long time even before the supervolcano did its number on gas prices. A couple of them were up on blocks. The rust they showed argued they'd been on blocks quite a while, too.

A black-and-white with its light bar flashing was parked in front of 1214 West 139th. A heavyset black woman and a skinnier Hispanic woman, both getting close to middle age, descended on Colin as he got out. "Did that lousy son of a bitch do for old Mrs. Mandelbaum?" the black woman demanded fiercely.

"I don't know yet, ma'am," Colin said. "I got here from the station as fast as I could when the call came in. That was ten minutes ago, fifteen tops."

250 I HARRY TURTLEDOVE

"They ever catch that bastard, they oughta hang him up by the nuts," the Hispanic woman said.

Privately, Colin agreed with her. He wouldn't say so publicly. Gabe Sanchez would: "That sounds goddamn good to me."

"How come you ain't caught him?" the African-American woman asked. "You shoulda done it a long time ago, you wanna know what I think."

Colin agreed with her there, too. All he could say, though, was "We're doing our best, believe me. And now I need to see what we've got here."

He started up the driveway to the house. The lawn was green. That meant less than it would have before the supervolcano blew. No more brown, neglected lawns in L.A. these days, not with all the rain that came down. But it was also neatly mowed and edged. Well kept-up: that was the phrase.

Just about all the South Bay Strangler's victims who lived in houses had kept them up well. For a split second, Colin wondered if that meant anything. Then he saw a guy in a blue sweatshirt—a Filipino, was his first guess—standing on the front porch, and forgot about that. "Who are you? What are you doing there?" he barked.

"My name is Oscar Flores, sir." Filipino, sure enough: name, looks, and accent all told the same story. "I had not seen Mrs. Mandelbaum for several days, so I flagged down the police car when it came by. The officers, they had to break down the front door"—which stood open behind him—"and they told me not to go in after them. But I am afraid there is no good news inside the house."

Colin was afraid of the same thing. The sick-sweet odor welling out through the door might have been stronger, but there was no mistaking it. Something in there had died a while ago, and he could make a good guess about what it was.

"Maybe it's natural causes." Gabe Sanchez grabbed for whatever straws he could find.

"Nah." Grimly, Colin shook his head. "They wouldn't've called for us if it was natural. They just would've sent for the meat wagon, and that would've been that." Gabe's heavy-featured face fell. Colin had got one step ahead of him.

Into the house, with another warning to Mr. Flores not to follow. Colin didn't know what he expected. Overstuffed Victorian furniture, probably. That was the kind of stuff you figured a little old lady would have.

What he saw instead was Fifties or Sixties modern: almost as outdated, but in a very different way. Sharp angles. Plastic. A low chair that looked as if no little old lady who wasn't also a gymnast would ever be able to escape it. An abstract clock on the wall.

"Meet George Jetson," Gabe muttered, which wasn't far wrong. Colin was reminded of the spidery building in the middle of LAX that had been planned as the control tower but ended up as a restaurant that didn't do much business because it was so hard to get to. That pieces of concrete started falling off it a few years before the eruption didn't help, either.

One of the uniformed cops came back into the living room. She looked green around the gills. Who would blame her? That smell was stronger in here. And she'd just been with what caused it. She managed a nod. "Lieutenant. Sergeant. She's . . . back here." A gulp punctuated the short sentence.

"Thanks, Jodie," Colin said, as gently as he could.

The hallway between the living room and the bedroom had dozens of pictures on the wall: Mrs. Mandelbaum and her children and grandchildren and maybe great-grandchildren. There were even a couple of old black-and-whites showing somebody who'd likely been Mr. Mandelbaum.

In the bedroom lay the old woman's earthly remains. Near them stood the other officer from the black-and-white, a strapping ex-Marine named Albert. Strapping ex-Marine or not, he looked greener than Jodie had. He managed the pale ghost of a smile, almost as if he were the sun outside. "Sorry to bring you out for another one, Lieutenant. If it is, I mean."

"Oh, it is," Colin said. "Or else it's a copycat, which would be about as bad—or a little worse, depending on how you look at things." His hands folded into fists. "Maybe he slipped up this time. Maybe we catch a break."

How often had he said something like that? As often as the Strangler murdered someone in San Atanasio, plus a few more times when he was talking about dead old ladies in other South Bay towns. How many times had he been right? The next would be the first.

Out in the living room, Jodie started talking to somebody. Colin spun on his heel and hurried up that icon-filled hallway. If Oscar Flores had got snoopy, tearing him a new asshole would make Colin feel a little better. It was the one thing he could think of that might.

Only it wasn't the neighbor who'd worried about poor Mrs. Mandelbaum. It was Dr. Ishikawa and Mike Pitcavage, with a DNA technician trailing the coroner. Nodding towards Ishikawa, Pitcavage said, "I hitched a ride on the ambulance. When I heard it might be another Strangler case, I wanted to see it for myself as soon as I could."

"Okay," Colin said: more an acknowledgment than anything resembling thanks. That the police chief rode in the ambulance and not in his own car spoke unhappy volumes about what the supervolcano eruption had done to fuel supplies and San Atanasio's sorry economy.

Pointing back to the hallway, Jodie said, "This woman had a lot of family. They'll be screaming when they find out."

Chief Pitcavage's mouth twisted. "Why didn't they call her and notice she didn't call back, then? How much do they care?"

"We'll find out when we get in touch with them," Colin said. "Chances are, we'll find out in stereo." Notifying next of kin might have been the part of the job he disliked most.

"Let's have a look at the body and see if we can determine whether it is a Strangler case," Dr. Ishikawa said. "The media will be most interested in learning about that. Of course, Lucy is the one who will make absolutely certain."

Lucy Chen, the DNA tech, reminded Colin of a Chinese version of his wife. They were about the same age, and they both had the same air of unhurried competence. But Lucy was an expert on the double helix, not on the behavior and misbehavior of magma.

"Happy day," Colin said. Lucy's presence, and Jodie's, kept him from adding some stronger opinions. As far as he was concerned, the one good thing about the eternal-seeming power and gas shortages was that the blow-dried dimbulbs with the expensive clothes took longer to get to a crime scene. If they wouldn't have shown up at all, that would have pleased him even more. Some things, though, were too much to hope for.

"It'll be back here, I bet. I'll follow my nose," Mike Pitcavage said. He found Mrs. Mandelbaum's bedroom with no trouble at all. He was younger than Colin, but he'd been a cop even longer because he hadn't gone into the service before putting on the blue uniform. How many tract homes had he walked through? Enough so, dozens of different floor plans seemed as familiar as the house he lived in, no doubt.

The coroner squatted by the corpse. His nose wrinkled; the smell in the bedroom was pretty bad, all right. "What do you think?" Colin asked, keeping his voice as neutral as he could. He knew what *he* thought, but that wasn't what he was trying to find out.

"If the DNA does not show this to be a Strangler case, I will be very much surprised," Ishikawa replied. Lucy Chen nodded. After a pause for breath (and after his face announced how much he wished he didn't need to breathe in there), the coroner added, "Most of the victims are discovered in a less advanced state of putrefaction."

"You got that right, Doc," Pitcavage said. "I just hope the stink comes out of my suit." Colin hadn't worried about that. Like most people, he wore more wool than he had before the eruption. It was warmer than the synthetics. But the chief, also in wool, remembered that it also trapped odors better.

Albert stuck his head into the bedroom. "Sorry to bother you, sir," he said, addressing his words to Chief Pitcavage, "but the first news truck just pulled up."

Oh, well. The vultures hadn't taken *much* longer than usual to start spiraling down to a story. Colin wasn't sorry the chief had come. Otherwise, *he* would have had the dubious privilege of enlightening the men and women of the Fourth Estate.

Then Pitcavage said, "I think I'll duck out the back door. Colin, you can handle the ghouls today." Colin's face might have been something—all the cops, Lucy, and even the staid Dr. Ishikawa started laughing. The chief thumped him on the shoulder. "I'm kidding. I really am."

"You'd better be." By the way Colin said it, everybody else thought the joke was a hell of a lot funnier than he did. He said it that way because that was how he felt.

"I am. I'm here. I'm stuck with it. I'll deal with them." Pitcavage walked out to face the reporters. Christians might have gone to face lions with that same exalted determination. But dealing with the media was more like getting trampled by a herd with mad cow disease. Colin thought so, anyhow. Suddenly, calling the next of kin didn't seem half bad.

———

Oklahoma City reminded Vanessa Ferguson of Schrödinger's cat. Even the locals seemed unsure about whether their town was dead or alive.

Denver, now, Denver was definitively deceased. Same with Salt Lake City. But both those places were only a few hundred miles from what had been Yellowstone National Park in happier times and was currently the world's biggest red-hot hole in the ground.

There were something like 1,200 miles between the supervolcano caldera and Oklahoma City. That didn't mean ashfall hadn't reached the city. Oh, no. Oklahoma City, in fact, had taken a bigger hit than places like Los Angeles, if not so bad as the towns and farms up in Kansas where Vanessa had been excavating. As with the Kansas prairies, prevailing winds had dumped lots of ash and dust on Oklahoma City's head.

The eruption had been a while ago. To Vanessa's way of thinking, Oklahoma City should have picked itself up, dusted itself off—literally and metaphorically—and got on with its life. Maybe it should have, but it hadn't. Little by little, she started to see why. The countryside was in worse shape than the town.

None of that was her worry, though. She'd made it to Oklahoma City. She'd escaped from the grave-robbing crew that was picking through the mortal remains of Kansas. She's had as much of that as she could take, and more besides. She wasn't supposed to be in Oklahoma City right now. She was supposed to be back with the crew. Had she been in the Army, they would have called it going AWOL. She wasn't in the Army, no matter how hard they tried to make her feel as if she were. As far as she was concerned, she'd informally resigned.

She had cash in the pockets of her jeans, too. Some of it came from what they'd paid her to make like a ghoul. That was a startling wad, at least by pre-eruption standards. It wasn't as if she'd had anything to spend it on while she was scavenging. Too damn bad the galloping inflation made it worth so much less than it would have been before things hit the fan.

The same sadly held true for the greenbacks she'd come by in unofficial ways. She felt guilty about that private grave-robbing, but not very guilty. It wasn't as if she were the only one. Oh, no—not even close. Some of the card games the scavengers got into . . . That much cash wouldn't have paid off the national debt, but it sure would have made some Vegas blackjack dealers raise an eyebrow.

So here she was. She could eat for a while. She could stay at a Super 8 motel that seemed pathetically eager to get her business. And she could shop for a clunker at used-car lots whose salesmen made the Super 8 desk clerks seemed stoic by comparison.

"Yes, ma'am, I would be dee-lighted to sell you a vee-hick-le," said one fellow whose plaid jacket was plainly made from the skin of a particularly gaudy 1970s sofa. And he explained why he would be so dee-lighted, too: "Business ain't been what you'd call brisk lately."

"I believe *that*." Vanessa tried to sound as cutting as she could—which was saying a good deal. She assumed any and all used-car salesmen were there to shaft her. She waved at the lot. "Your cars are sitting there gathering dust."

That was the exact truth. Red cars, blue cars, green cars, black cars, white cars? No—they were all grayish brown cars. Some of them showed hints of their original color. None showed more than hints.

"You know how it is, ma'am." The salesman spread his hands in resigned embarrassment. "We clean 'em off, an' then we get more wind outa the north or the west. Still an awful lot of that horrible dust."

He wasn't wrong. Having spent so long closer to the eruption site than this, Vanessa knew as much. She was damned if she'd admit it, though. Give a salesman an inch and he'd take your wallet. Her mouth twisted into a sneer. "Chances are you don't clean them because this way you can hide a lot of what's wrong with them."

He clasped both hands over his heart, as if he'd just taken a mortal wound. "Now, ma'am, that just ain't fair. Not even slightly, it ain't. Let me show you this here Ford. Honest to Pete, it's as good as the day it was made, or even better."

"How many recalls has that model been through?" Vanessa retorted, and the salesman looked wounded again.

He tried for a comeback: "That particular vee-hick-le, I happen to know, has been supervolcano-ized."

Vanessa had never quite made up her mind whether she hated the language of hucksterism worse than the language of bureaucracy or the other way round. She withered the man in the bad jacket with a glance. "Oh, cut the crap, why don't you? If it's got a heavy-duty air filter, just say so, for Christ's sake."

"I don't speak of our Lord and Savior that way," he said stiffly.

"I told you to cut the crap," Vanessa said. "You need me worse than I need you, but you won't get me." She walked off that lot.

Two days later, she found a Toyota a few years newer than the one that had perished in her escape from Denver. The salesman there didn't speak of Jesus at all. He wore a corduroy coat that hadn't been stylish for a long time but wasn't aggressively ugly. The Toyota was more expensive than she liked, but not impossibly so.

"I think we've got a deal," he said at last. "I'll need to see some ID before we finish the formalities."

"Here you go." She showed him her license from Colorado.

He looked at it. "Miz Ferguson, this expired three months ago."

"Well, so what?" Vanessa said. "If you expect me to go back

to Denver and renew it, you're out of luck." She didn't say *shit out of luck*, and patted herself on the back for her restraint.

He sighed. He might have been showing restraint, too. "I can't sell a car to anybody with an expired license. The second you drive it onto the street, you're in violation of the law." He spread his hands. "You see my problem?"

"I see it, all right. What the hell am I supposed to do about it?" Vanessa's tone took on a certain edge. She'd traded favors for favors before. She hated herself every time she did it—how could you not? But she wanted wheels. She *needed* wheels. If she had to do it one more time, maybe she could turn off her mind and not think about it while it was going on. She'd sure tried to do that with Micah Husak. Afterwards? She could worry about that, well, afterwards.

Instead of pulling down the Venetian blinds in his miserable little office, the salesman said, "You wait right here. I've got to go talk to my manager."

Vanessa sat there and fumed. *If he thinks I'll take care of them both, he's got another think coming,* she told herself. *No way I do gang bangs, God damn men and their horny souls to hell.*

But the salesman's manager turned out to be a woman. She was about fifty. She didn't try to hide it. She was short-haired and looked tough. Her pinched mouth said she was used to beating men in their own ballpark. It also said she didn't especially enjoy winning—or anything else.

"Carl tells me you don't have a current license," she said.

"That's right," Vanessa answered. "I got to Camp Constitution with the clothes on my back. I've been there or in a scavenging detail since right after the eruption. I wasn't really worried about renewing the damn thing, you know? There's got to be some kind of way you can sell me a car. It's not like this outfit doesn't need my money."

By the way Carl's eyebrows lifted, she'd nailed that one. The manager's face never changed. Vanessa wouldn't have wanted to play poker against her, even for nickels. "You *could* get a license from the Oklahoma Department of Motor Vehicles," the gal said. "You might be able to, anyhow. It would take some time. I don't know if they'd want to issue you one with only that to show for ID."

"Or?" Vanessa said. "C'mon. There's got to be an *or*. It's not like I don't have this year's license because I'm a fuckup. I don't have this year's license 'cause there's nothing left of Colorado."

"I understand that. It's not like we don't know about the supervolcano here, either." The manager clicked a fingernail against the arm of her chair, considering. "How would this be? We'll charge you an additional out-of-state identity-confirmation fee of, say, a thousand dollars. In exchange for that, we will overlook your lack of documentation and we will try to contact Colorado authorities to make sure you are the person your expired license says you are."

Chances were those Colorado authorities were dead, dead and buried under volcanic ash. The knowing gleam in the woman's hard gray eyes said she knew as much. *She's making this up,* Vanessa realized. *It's an excuse to screw an extra grand out of me,* that's all. Even with inflation making the dollar leak value the way a blown-out tire leaked air, a grand was still a fair chunk of change.

"How about making your fee five hundred?" Vanessa said.

The manager smiled. No one would ever accuse her of owning a sweet smile. No, it was more like a piranha's. "A thousand," she said flatly. Vanessa realized something else: this wasn't the first time she'd played this game. More like the eleventy-first, or the hundred and eleventy-first. Sure as hell, the woman went on, "You can take it down the street if you want to. You won't get off cheaper anywhere else, and you'll end up with a crappier car than that Toyota."

"At least fill the gas tank all the way to the top," Vanessa said, throwing in the sponge.

"I think we can do that much," Carl said. The manager sent him a flinty stare: Vanessa'd won back something over ten percent of the bribe, anyhow. She got the strong, strong feeling not many people did so well against this gal. Would the cost of the fill-up all come from Carl's share? Vanessa wouldn't have been a bit surprised.

That was Carl's problem, though, not hers. The mountain of forms you had to fill out to buy a car in Oklahoma was every bit as tall as the one California made you climb. Vanessa signed on a great many dotted lines. Carl drove the Toyota off the lot and came back a few minutes later with a pained expression and, presumably, a full tank.

Vanessa laid out the cash, including the thousand-dollar fee (nowhere, she'd noticed, was it mentioned in all that paperwork: one more surprise—not!). She got into the car and headed south. She hadn't been behind a wheel for years, but she still knew how. And she was on her way at last!

XV

If you went barefoot in the park in Guilford, Maine, you'd get frostbite, and in a hurry, too. Rob Ferguson didn't much care. He had rubber overshoes on over his New Balances. He wore a fur cap with earflaps and a red star. It was ratty, but he didn't care—it kept his ears warm. All of him was warm enough, in fact, except his nose. He didn't think his nose would ever be warm again. As long as it didn't turn black and fall off, he'd have to be content.

Kids slid down toward the river on sleds. Kids on ice skates spun on the frozen Piscataquis. The river had a deep, stone-hard crust even though it was past the alleged first day of spring and well on its way to Tax Day. Rob'd tried ice skates a few times. He was convinced the Devil had invented them to punish sinners' ankles. They sure punished his. If you weren't ice-skating by the time you were two, you'd never get the hang of it. That was his theory, and he was sticking to it.

He refused to abandon it even though both Biff and Charlie could propel themselves pretty well on skates with blades. They were no threat for Olympic gold. They'd never hoist the Stanley

Cup. But they could get from hither to yon without going ass over teakettle. And neither one had ever strapped on skates before coming to Guilford. It didn't seem fair.

A snowball flew past Rob, not quite close enough to make him duck. Everybody from age four on up threw them all the time. One angry town meeting had resulted in an ordinance against using a rock core. A good many people had wanted an ordinance banning any and all snowball-flinging. That failed— too many folks enjoyed it. The failure helped make the meeting angry.

Rob enjoyed snowballs. There went Jim Farrell, with his charcoal-gray fedora—the most recognizable one, perhaps, since Fiorello La Guardia's—just aching to be knocked off. To scoop up snow in mittened fingers took only a few seconds. To let fly seemed to take no time at all.

The snowball flew straight and true. It *paffed* into the side of Farrell's hat. There it exploded. The hat ended up at Farrell's feet. His own hair wasn't much lighter than the snow through which he walked.

He stooped to retrieve the fedora, carefully brushing what was left of the snowball from it before setting it back on his head at the proper jaunty angle. Only then did he look around to see which miscreant might have assailed him.

He looked no farther than Rob. "Oh. You." He might have found half of Rob in his apple. "Why am I not surprised?"

"Why, Professor Farrell, sir, whatever could you be talking about?" Rob exuded innocence the way an EPA toxic-waste site exuded dioxin.

"So you deny it, do you?" Farrell rumbled. He stooped again. When he came up, he came up firing. The snowball caught Rob dead center. The retired history professor beamed. "That'll teach you, you rapscallion! I couldn't have done better with a catapult."

Instead of reretaliating, Rob clapped his hands in muffled admiration. "I've been called a lot of things, but never one of those before. Sounds like a hip-hop onion, you know?"

Farrell made a face, more at the music than at the pun. "Loud obscenity never appealed to me, even with a heavy bass line."

"Well, not to me, either," Rob admitted. "If you're white and you aren't Eminem, you've got no business rapping."

"No one has any business rapping," Farrell said firmly. He sighed. Vapor gushed from his mouth and nose. "I have always taken it as an article of faith that the Founders knew what they were doing when they added the First Amendment to the Constitution, but some of what's passed for music the past twenty years does make me wonder."

Rob bowed, which made him need to grab his cap to keep it from falling off. "At your service, Professor."

Farrell shook his head. "I wasn't referring to you and your fellow demented Darwinian amphibians. I truly wasn't. You're amusing, even clever—not something I say lightly."

"I know. Thanks." Rob bowed again, more sincerely than he'd expected. A compliment from Farrell was praise indeed, not least because the old man didn't give forth with them very often.

"And you don't seem to feel obligated to blow out every eardrum within a furlong," Farrell added.

"That depends," Rob said judiciously. "Since we got to Guilford, the power hasn't been on much around here. Hard to knock crows out of the sky with acoustic guitars."

"You would if you could, you're telling me." Jim Farrell sighed again. "At my advanced age and state of decrepitude, I didn't think I could be so easily despoiled of one of my few remaining illusions."

"Yeah, right. Now tell me another one." Rob couldn't match Farrell's syntax or vocabulary, and sensibly didn't try.

"We're going to come through this winter with the greatest

of ease." The de facto boss of Maine north and west of the Interstate threw back his head, almost far enough to make that trademark fedora fall off again. He laughed to show he was telling another one. He put enough vinegar in the laugh to show he didn't expect to be taken seriously.

"Yeah, right," Rob repeated. He hadn't come through this winter with the greatest of ease himself, not with that bullet grazing his leg he hadn't. But that wasn't what the professor was talking about, and they both knew it.

Farrell adjusted the hat. His extravagant eyebrows twitched. "This past winter was colder than the one before it. Fool that I am, I hadn't dreamt it could be. Those who are alleged to know about such things claim the one ahead will be harder yet."

One of the people alleged to know about such things was the stepmother Rob still hadn't met. He wondered, not for the first time, if this wasn't the right moment to make tracks for the opposite corner of the country. Things in SoCal weren't . . . so bad. What came out of his mouth, though, was "As long as we've got firewood and meese and MREs, we'll get by."

"Why anyone would want Reagan's attorney general . . ." Farrell held up a gloved finger. "He was a fat fellow—I give you that. Tubbier than I am, which isn't easy. Render him down for oil, and he could likely keep the lamps burning quite a while."

Rob hadn't been talking about the Meese called Ed, and knew Farrell knew as much. The professor enjoyed, even reveled in, being difficult. Rob eyed him. "You've dropped a good bit of weight since I first met you," he said truthfully.

"So have you. So has everybody in these parts," Farrell replied. What twisted his mouth wasn't a smile, even if it tried to be. "We're eating less and working harder. Once upon a time, large parts of the world had so very much that even poor people could become obese, and commonly did. As recently as a hundred years ago, that would have been unimaginable. My Greeks and Romans would never have believed it."

"Huh," Rob said. Farrell was good at teasing, or sometimes startling, thoughtful noises out of people. "Hadn't looked at it that way, but you're not wrong." When the illegal immigrants who mowed lawns in L.A. sported double chins and potbellies—and a lot of them had—the traditional meaning of *poor* needed revising.

Well, the supervolcano had gone and revised it, all right. It sure as hell had.

"'Once upon a time,' I said." Farrell sounded as academically mournful as if he were discussing the fall of Rome. "No more, not around here. They say we may be able to plant the Midwest again in a few years. But if the weather keeps getting worse, how much will grow even if we can? We are still working through our pre-eruption surplus, and sooner or later—sooner, now, I fear—we'll come to the bottom of that."

"We've got the mooses." Rob tossed out another possible plural. The word wasn't so bad as *mongoose*, but it came close.

"We've barely had enough to feed us this time till warmer weather comes again." Farrell gestured with that index finger once more. "Nota bene: I do not say *warm weather*. This benighted part of the world won't see warm weather till long after I'm dead and buried—or perhaps I should be cremated, if I ever aim to warm up in this world. But I digress."

"You do? I'm shocked, Professor. Shocked, I tell you!" Rob hadn't seen *Casablanca* for nothing.

"If digression was good enough for Herodotus, it's good enough for me," Farrell said. And he digressed some more: "There are two kinds of modern historians of the ancient world, you know."

"Now that you mention it," Rob said, "I didn't."

He slowed Jim Farrell down not a jot. "There are those who like Herodotus, and there are those who like Thucydides. They're easy to tell apart. The ones who like Thucydides are the ones with the tight assholes."

Rob didn't know what he'd thought Farrell would come out with. Whatever it was, that wasn't it. He barked surprised laughter. Then he said, "I thought we were talking about moose." Maybe doing it right would keep the professor on track.

"No, we were talking about the absence of moose," Farrell said with relentless precision. Maybe doing it right wouldn't, too. "And more and more of them are absent, too. Unless I'm very much mistaken, we're hunting them far faster than they can breed. We're having to go farther and farther afield for firewood, too."

That, Rob knew. Maine had abundant second-growth woods. Not many people had farmed its stony soil in the second half of the twentieth century, or in the twenty-first, and trees reclaimed fields by the multiple square mile. An awful lot of those trees, though, had gone up in smoke the past few winters. Many more would burn when the weather worsened again.

Sooner or later, the woods would get logged out. Sooner or later, the ground would be bare and smooth as a baby's backside—only much colder. Or maybe all the people would give up and move away before that happened.

From what Rob had seen of Mainers, he doubted that. They would hang in there till a glacier grinding down out of the north drove them away. Even then, they'd dynamite the leading edge of the ice as long as they could.

The wind picked up. Farrell stuck his hands into the pockets of his overcoat. After a moment, Rob followed suit. That glacier didn't feel very far away at all.

On my way home! The words chimed inside Vanessa. They should have had four exclamation points, to say nothing of a heavenly choir singing hosannas. "California, here I come!" she caroled, not exactly in tune but with great sincerity.

Every mile she drove took her farther south, farther from Oklahoma City, farther from the supervolcano. Those miles didn't take her all the way out of the ashfall zone, though. She'd have to go way the hell down into Mexico to manage that. She would sooner have gone to hell for real. Not that she had anything enormous against Mexico, but she was all done with detours.

She hoped so, anyhow. The Toyota didn't sound as smooth as it had when she drove it off the lot, and she wasn't even out of Oklahoma yet. Would it keep running all the way to L.A.? "You fucker, you'll keep running if I have to push you across Texas," she told the machine.

It kept running. She supposed—she hoped—that meant it got the message. Southern Oklahoma didn't look too bad. It mostly wasn't coated in volcanic dust and ash. If it had been right after the eruption, rain and wind had got rid of the bulk of the shit. People were trying to grow crops here, which would have been unimaginable up in Kansas.

But what you could see wasn't always what you got. It wasn't all of what you got, either. How much invisible crud still fouled the breeze? How much was getting sucked into her air filter? Jesus Christ on a pogo stick, how much was getting sucked through the air filter and into her engine's innards?

If she got into trouble, what was she supposed to do? Get a tow back to Oklahoma City and complain to Carl and the tough broad who told him what to do? That was pretty goddamn funny, wasn't it? She had no AAA. What point to keeping it up in Camp Constitution or while she was playing vulture in Kansas?

She didn't have plastic, either—just the cash in her billfold. She'd cut up her Wells Fargo Visa when she moved to Denver. Wells Fargo was wounded. All the big banks were, with the new mortgage shock that screwed whole states. But Wells Fargo kept breathing, wounded or not, which was a damn sight more than she could say for her Colorado credit union.

Down I-35 she rolled. Somewhere near Fort Worth, she'd get on I-20, which would take her southwest to I-10. I-10 she knew, or at least the part of it that ran through Los Angeles. There, it went by the Santa Monica Freeway or the San Bernardino, depending on whether you were west or east of downtown. Yes, it ran all the way across the country, but she'd rarely needed to worry about the 3,000 miles or so that weren't in her own back yard.

Driving on I-35 could have been driving on the Interstate any place out in the boonies. The landscape was flat and boring, but she wasn't there to sightsee. She just wanted to make miles. When she remembered she was driving on an expired license, she slowed down a little. A ticket was the last thing she wanted. When she forgot, she put the pedal to the metal again.

She had to slow down not long after she got into Texas, because she met up with a hellacious rainstorm. Even though she cranked the wipers up to high, she couldn't see farther than six inches past the end of her hood. That didn't worry everybody. Several cars roared past her. She'd long been convinced that most people were assholes. Here they were, proving the point for her one more time.

Then *everybody* slowed down, even the assholes. Vanessa feared she knew what that meant: somewhere up ahead was a fender-bender or worse. She hit the SEEK button on her radio again and again, trying to find a station that gave traffic reports.

In L.A., it would have been easy. (In L.A., she would have known where on the dial to look, but she didn't think of that.) Here, she went through a shitkicker station, someone explaining how the supervolcano was connected to the Blood of the Lamb, somebody singing mournfully in Spanish to the accompaniment of accordions and electric guitars, an earnest woman talking about post-eruption agricultural issues, and several other things she had less than no interest in listening to. She swore at the radio. That didn't help her get the traffic news, but it made her feel a little better, anyhow.

The rain drummed down on the Toyota's roof. She wondered if it would leak. She remembered her old man talking about a car he'd had that was as wet inside as it was outside. The Toyota stayed dry, at least in the passenger compartment. That was one technology they'd managed to improve.

She crawled along. At last, through the curtains of rain, she saw cops—or were they Texas Rangers?—in slickers doing something with a truck and trailer on this side of the road that closed it down to a single, very cramped, lane. A little farther on, a VW Beetle—a new, postmodern one, not an ancient, funky beater— lay on its back, looking too much like an oversized dead bug. The roof was partly smashed. She couldn't see who, if anyone, was still inside. That might have been just as well.

Because of the downpour and the wreck, she didn't make it to the I-10 the first day, the way she'd hoped she would. She pulled off the Interstate in Cisco, still on the Fort Worth side of Abilene. There she discovered the Texas institution called the access road: the street full of motels and restaurants and gas stations paralleling the highway, with ramps leading on and off. They didn't have those in L.A. or Denver. She found a place about on the level of the Super 8 she'd had in Oklahoma City and pushed greenbacks at the desk clerk.

As she paid, she asked, "Do they know when the storm's supposed to stop?"

"Tomorrow? The day after?" the black woman answered. "Whenever it does. It's in the Lord's hands, honey."

"Terrific," Vanessa muttered. She'd hoped the Lord might keep her from getting soaked when she walked across the parking lot to the Applebee's next door, but He didn't seem cooperative.

And He wasn't. Umbrella or no umbrella, she got good and wet by the time she reached the restaurant. She ordered a double gin and tonic to improve her attitude. The waitress carded her. From a guy, that might have been flattering. Here, it just pissed her off. Showing the deceased Colorado license alarmed her, too.

But the waitress cared only about the birthdate. She went away. She came back with booze. What more could you want? Vanessa chose chicken fajitas from the menu. "If I never see another MRE as long as I live, that'll still be too soon," she told the gal.

"You were in one of them camps?" the waitress asked. By her drawl, she'd never gone farther than a long piss from this miserable little hole in the ground.

"Afraid so," Vanessa said.

"Lotsa folks are stuck in 'em, and they ain't supposed to be real nice," the waitress said. "You're lucky you got out."

"Tell me about it," Vanessa said with feeling. What did they call luck? The residue of design, that was what. It sounded impressive, and as if it ought to mean something. Odds were it was nothing but bullshit, the way most impressive-sounding slogans were. Her luck was the residue of not being too fussy about whom she blew, and she'd tried her best not to think about it since she did it.

"Well, I'll take your order to the kitchen." The waitress hustled away. She was perky and built. A guy probably would have watched her ass. Vanessa concentrated on the level of gin in the glass. To her, that was a hell of a lot more interesting.

If you expected grand cuisine, Applebee's was the wrong place for you. Better than MREs, it definitely was. Vanessa got outside of the fajitas faster than she'd imagined she could. She got outside of another double gin and tonic, too. She lurched when she went back to the motel. She got wetter than she had on the way over to the restaurant, but she cared less.

Next morning, the motel had donuts and granola bars and coffee in the lobby. The spread wasn't exciting, but it was free. It was also fast. Vanessa wanted to get on the Interstate and make more miles. She hurried to the car. It was still raining hard. At least it wasn't snowing. She hadn't had enough practice with the white stuff to feel easy about driving in it.

I-20 was full of eighteen-wheelers. Every time one of them growled past her, it threw more water onto her windshield than her wipers could handle. For a few scary seconds, she'd go next to blind. Then the wipers would catch up. She'd be able to see . . . till the next honking big truck came along.

She wondered why a no-account stretch of Interstate through the middle of Texas was as truck-packed as the Long Beach Freeway coming up from the harbor. And then, all of a sudden, she quit wondering. These swarms of diesel monsters were heading for Los Angeles, just like her. Without them, L.A. would starve, to say nothing of running out of everything it needed besides food.

Somewhere a little farther along in west Texas, this highway would join I-10, and I-10 would take her home. Till she moved to Denver to be with Hagop, she'd spent her whole life in San Atanasio. If—no, when—she made it home, she vowed she wouldn't live outside the city limits ever again, either.

Miles. More miles. Still more miles. She couldn't go as fast as she wanted to, because of the rain and because of the accidents people who went as fast as they pleased to in spite of the rain got into. She snarled at those blockheads as she crawled past the smashed vehicles they'd infested. Some of the blockheads stood glumly on the asphalt, staring at the havoc they'd wreaked.

When she finally inched past one horrendous pileup, she saw her snarls there were wasted. Some of the people who'd caused that wreck would never cause another one. She wasn't sorry the rain kept her from getting a good look at the bodies. She had no trouble imagining what they'd look like. They'd look like the photos in her dad's cop books, the ones Rob had used to gross her out when she was little. He'd got his butt warmed for that, which didn't do squat to stop her nightmares.

And then, just when she started getting close to the I-10, things slowed down again. Vanessa said something that should have turned all the rain pouring down on the whole state to superheated steam. That improved her attitude, but not the traffic.

In due—no, in overdue—course, she discovered this slowdown didn't spring from an accident. Instead, an electric signboard sat on the shoulder. It said I-10 CHECKPOINT AHEAD. PREPARE TO STOP. Then it blinked out. And then it said the same thing again. Blink. Message. Blink. Message . . .

Vanessa lost track of how many times she read it before she rolled past the signboard at last. What she said about stopping for a checkpoint—what she said about *preparing* to stop for a checkpoint—made what she'd said about the earlier wrecks seem an endearment by comparison.

Then she said some things about the idea of checkpoints, too. What did they need them for, whoever *they* were? Wasn't this the United States? Wasn't it a free country? If it was, what business did it have checking on who drove to California? You couldn't hijack a state and fly it into a skyscraper or a government building.

She got her answer to that when she came up to the checkpoint. STATUS EVALUATION CONTROL—SUPERVOLCANO EMERGENCY AUTHORIZATION ACT, the sign there announced. As far as she knew, the supervolcano was unauthorized. The act authorized things like Camp Constitution and its many unpleasant siblings, the scavenger programs in the Midwest, and maybe this status evaluation control thingy, too. *An unnatural act, is what it is,* she thought.

Trucks breezed through. Their reasons for heading west were obvious enough even for government functionaries to grasp. People in cars, though . . . People in cars got the same friendly greetings Taliban terrorists toting AK-47s would have earned going through airport security.

A fellow in a uniform Vanessa didn't recognize scowled at her expired Colorado license: not because it was expired but because it was from Colorado. "Why are you going to Los Angeles?" he demanded.

"Because I lived there my whole life till I went to Denver," she answered, which was nothing but the truth.

Truth or not, it didn't impress him. "Have you got any family there? Can they vouch for you?"

What if I say no? Vanessa was tempted to. Her attitude towards authority's pushes had always been to push back as hard as she could. She was able to learn from experience, though. She didn't always, but she could. This guy's humorless face said any answer he didn't like would keep her off the I-10.

And so, feigning meekness she didn't feel, she answered, "My father is a police lieutenant in San Atanasio." He'd never heard of her old stomping grounds; amazing how a face all slabs and angles could show such eloquent disbelief. Quickly, she explained, "It's not far from LAX—a little south and a little east."

"That's what you say, anyhow," he answered, his voice as stony as his eyes. He pulled out a cell phone. "I don't suppose you've got a number where I can contact this individual?"

Vanessa could have taken the cop shop's number off her own phone. She could have, but she didn't need to. Dad's work number had been ingrained in her head since she was a kid. She needed to add an area code to it now, and she did as she rattled it off. At the uniformed man's annoyed glower, she repeated it more slowly.

He punched the number into his phone, turning his back and

stepping away so she couldn't follow his conversation. He didn't look so sour—or rather, he looked sour in a different way—as he stuck the phone in his pocket and swung toward her again. "You appear to have been telling the truth," he said, sounding quite humanly surprised.

"Of course I was!" Vanessa yipped. She was surprised herself, and furious, that he should doubt her. She prided herself on her honesty. She said what she meant even when keeping her mouth shut would do more good.

"Hunh!" Her father couldn't have snorted better than this guy did. "You listen to the bullshit we hear here, you wouldn't go *of course*."

"You sound like a cop, all right," Vanessa said.

"Yeah, well, you'd know, wouldn't you?"

"Can I go on, then?" Vanessa itched to floor the gas pedal. If she drove fast enough, maybe she could get back to L.A. before this piece of junk crapped out on her. Maybe.

"I . . . suppose so," the uniformed man answered reluctantly. "If you haven't got a place to stay and a job to look forward to, though, you're a damn fool for heading that way."

"The last place I had to stay was Camp fucking Constitution," Vanessa said through clenched teeth. "Whatever I end up with in L.A.—even if I sleep under a goddamn freeway overpass and dumpster-dive for dinner—it can't be worse than that. NFW."

"Hunh!" the guy said again, even more dubiously than before. But he stepped back and jerked a thumb to the west. "Go ahead, then. You'll find out."

Vanessa didn't waste time thanking him. She mashed the accelerator with her foot. Smoke spurted from the Toyota's tailpipe. *So what?* she thought, and burst into more verses of song nobody but her could hear: "California, here I come! Right back where I started from!" Had anybody from Stephen Foster to Irving Berlin to John Lennon to Bob Dylan to Stephen Sondheim ever penned a finer lyric? She didn't believe it, not even for a minute. She sang it again, louder yet.

It wasn't as if Marshall had never seen a typewriter before. He had. Old people kept them around as souvenirs of bygone days. A few offices even had electric ones, for dealing with carbon-copy forms. But he'd never expected to discover one on his desk next to the iMac.

"Found it in a pawnshop on San Atanasio Boulevard," his father said, not without pride. "You've been bitching about how you have trouble writing when the power goes out. Well, now you can."

"Yippee skip," Marshall said. "Um—most places these days want you to submit your stuff in Word or RTF. How am I supposed to get those out of this—thing?" It was a Royal manual portable, what a college student might have used in a 1970s dorm room.

Dad exhaled through his nose, which meant he was bent out of shape—he must've thought Marshall would fall on the ancient machine with a glad cry. He sounded hyperpatient as he answered, "You can get words out of it, right?"

"Maybe." If Marshall seemed dubious, well, he was. He poked one of the keys. It went down partway, then stopped—he'd taken up the slack, or whatever. He poked again, quite a bit harder. *Clack!* The key hit the black rolling pin (he supposed it had a real name, but what that was he didn't know). The carriage advanced a space. For somebody used to effortless computer keyboards . . . "I dunno, Dad. It's got a monster touch."

"You'll get used to that," his father said, though how he knew it or whether he knew it Marshall couldn't have guessed. "And you *can* get words out of it. People got words out of them for more than a hundred years."

"Words, yeah, but not Microsuck Word."

Dad waved that aside. "Incompetent, irrelevant, and immaterial," he said, like a lawyer objecting in court. "So you send somebody a hard-copy manuscript. If he likes it and he's got power, he can scan it to OCR and get his own Word file. And if he doesn't have power, he won't be able to do anything with Word or RTF files any which way."

Marshall opened his mouth. Then he closed it again. He couldn't think of anything to say to that. After a moment, he tried, "Suppose I get something halfway done on the computer while we've got electricity, but I do the rest on this—thing?"

"Then *you* scan it and clean it up and do your twenty-first-century thing on it." Dad had all the answers. He also had all the reasons: "But you can't use 'The power's out again' for an excuse so you don't write. If you've got to, you can use legal tablets and a ballpoint."

"You're shitting me!" Marshall's experiments along those lines had not been happy ones. He'd tried, yeah, but he thought writing by hand was as primitive as branding. Some people thought branding was cool—one step past tats, they called it. He couldn't imagine anyone finding writing by hand cool.

But Dad just shook his head. "Nope. Pen and paper were good enough for Shakespeare and Abe Lincoln and dudes like that. I know they aren't in your league as a literary artist, but—"

"Oh, give me a fucking break!" Marshall knew when he was whupped. "Look, I'll try the tripewriter, okay? There! You happy now?"

"Dancing in the daisies." If Dad was, his face and his voice hadn't found out about it. He glanced east. He'd been doing that a lot lately; Marshall didn't think he realized how much. He did say why, though: "Your sister will be back in town in a few days."

"Yeah. How about that?" The last time Marshall'd seen Vanessa was when he'd helped load her U-Haul so she could move to Colorado to be with her rug merchant. Old Hagop hadn't worked out any better than Bryce Miller did before him. She'd been goddamn lucky—and goddamn quick, which went with it—to get out of Denver alive when the supervolcano blew, too. Hundreds of thousands of people hadn't.

Her father coughed. "God knows how long she'll need to land work. Not a lot of it around. She may have to stay here for a while."

"How about that?" Marshall repeated tonelessly. Vanessa would quarrel with Dad—they were too much alike not to. Marshall knew she'd quarrel with him, too. She always bossed him around, and he wasn't going to take it the way he had when he was a kid. He tried a question of his own: "How's Kelly like the idea?"

"She's not jumping up and down about it," Dad allowed. Marshall would have bet she wasn't. He didn't think his step-mom had ever actually met his sister. Vanessa would quarrel with her, too. Maybe Vanessa didn't quarrel with everybody, but she came pretty close. Sighing, Dad went on, "We don't always do what we want to do. Sometimes we do what we've got to do."

"Right." Marshall left it there. Since he had no steady work and was living here, he didn't see how he could claim having Vanessa do the same thing wouldn't fly. But he sure thought so.

"It will work out," his father insisted. If that wasn't the triumph of hope over experience, then Marshall didn't know what the hell it was. A ham sandwich, maybe. Dad lumbered out of his room, shaking his head like a bear bedeviled by bees.

For lack of anything better to do, Marshall fiddled with the typewriter. When he ran in a sheet of paper, it came up crooked. He messed with the little chromed levers till he found the one that loosened things and let him straighten it.

He started typing. Christ, the thing was noisy! *Clack, clack, clackety-clack!* And you had to punch every key *hard*. With his index fingers, he managed okay right away. His pinkies, though, should have done more barbell work. He had to make himself mash them down. When he goofed, he couldn't just run the cursor back and retype. He had to fix the mistake. Somewhere—maybe at the pawnshop where he'd found the typewriter—Dad had come up with a little bottle of correction fluid.

The stuff smelled as if it ought to get you high. The fine print on the label swore it was nonaddictive. With a stink like that, it was missing a hell of a chance if it was.

Marshall finished a page and then, to his surprise, another one. This antiquated gadget wasn't what he was used to, but it might not be *so* bad. It was kind of like Diplomacy compared to World of Warcraft. Bells and whistles? Fuhgeddaboutit. But you could manage without them. If you didn't already know about them, you wouldn't even miss them.

"Fuck me," Marshall said softly, and scribbled a note to himself. There might be a story in that—however he wound up writing it.

XVI

Las Cruces behind Vanessa. Snow on the mountains ahead of her. They weren't great big mountains—nothing like the Rockies when you saw them from Denver—and didn't look as if they ought to have snow so far down them. This was only a little north of the Mexican border, after all, and it was allegedly spring.

No matter what the season, they had snow halfway down them. On the other half, streaked and patchy now but still there, lay the gray-brown of volcanic ash, a color she knew much too well and hated much too much.

A red light on her dashboard flashed to life. Alarm flamed in her—flamed and then faded. This one was shaped like a gas pump, and warned her of nothing worse than that she was getting low. She already knew that. She'd been sending the fuel gauge baleful looks since well before she rolled through Las Cruces.

Here came an offramp, with a truck stop by it. Vanessa pulled off I-10. She'd get gas for the car. And she'd buy some lunch. With the kind of food you could find at places like this, she'd probably get gas for herself, too.

She'd never had anything to do with truck stops till she drove the U-Haul from L.A. to Denver. On the way there, she'd discovered they were less awful than she'd always thought. Not great, necessarily, but less awful. Nowadays, you took whatever you could get, because too goddamn often you couldn't get anything at all.

This truck stop looked quite a bit like that one in Nevada— or had she already got to Utah by then? Nowheresville, USA, any which way. A convenience store. A broad expanse of asphalt. Filling stations. A garage. Restaurants. Yup, a truck stop.

Oh, and trucks. Lots and lots of trucks. Mostly eighteen-wheelers, but plenty of smaller ones, too.

There was one difference here. A couple of Bradley fighting vehicles in desert camo trained their cannon on the stop. A soldier or National Guardsman or whatever strolling back toward them from the convenience store paused to light a cigarette. The Feds were big-time serious about not letting anything that even looked like trouble start on the lifeline to Los Angeles.

Vanessa pulled into a Chevron station. It had as many pumps for diesel as for gasoline. Prices were—well, what went a couple of steps past appalling? The country was fucked. Hell, the whole world was fucked. And who paid for it? The poor bastard who needed a fill-up and some stomach ballast, that was who. *Me, in other words,* Vanessa thought.

She drove over and parked near the Denny's. It wouldn't be great, but it wouldn't be terrible, either. She didn't feel like surprises right now. Most of the business they did would be with truckers—there weren't many ordinary cars here. She counted herself lucky that that officious asshole had finally deigned to let her travel the Interstate at all.

Men's eyes pawed her when she walked into the joint. Any woman between fifteen and forty who wasn't butt-ugly had to get used to that feeling. Vanessa wasn't—nowhere near—and she had. Which didn't mean she liked it. It always made her feel like a warm piece of meat with some convenient holes. And it was a lot stronger than usual here, because there were so many guys of the annoying age and so few other women to help defuse it.

A couple of soldiers were damn near salivating. She ignored them; to her, they were only horny puppies. They reminded her of Bryce, even though he was a year older than she was. He'd always be a puppy, no matter how old he got. Thank God she hadn't gone and married him!

She sat down at the counter. Fewer guys would be bold enough to bother her here, right in front of the scurrying waitresses and the cooks. She could hope so, anyhow.

"What'll it be, dear?" One of the waitresses paused in front of her, pad in hand. She was past fifty, wrinkled and tired-looking even if her eyes were friendly. Men wouldn't bug her—not too often, anyhow.

"Cheeseburger and coffee, please."

"Fries or coleslaw with your burger?"

"Uh, coleslaw."

"You got it. I'll bring the coffee right away. The other stuff is made from scratch, so it'll take a few minutes."

"Sure," Vanessa said. The explanation had to be for people who'd never gone to anything fancier than a Burger King in their whole lives, people for whom Denny's was a major step up. Were there really people like that? By the way the waitress delivered the warning, there were plenty of them. And what did that say? It said the country'd been fucked, or at least fucked up, long before the supervolcano blew.

When the food came, the patty in the cheeseburger looked like a patty. The bun . . . The bun looked more like a hockey puck cut in half horizontally than anything else Vanessa could think of. She pointed at it. "What went into that?" she asked, distaste clotting her voice.

She didn't faze the waitress a bit. "Rye flour, oat flour, a little bit of wheat flour so it rises some, anyhow. What we could get," the middle-aged woman answered. "Try it, sweetie. It's better'n it looks."

"How could it miss?" But Vanessa did try it. She'd had worse. It was tastier than an MRE, no doubt of that. Talk about praising with faint damn! The coleslaw was nothing to write home about, either.

She was resignedly working through the meal when a man sat down beside her. She glared at him—it wasn't as if there weren't plenty of other seats at the long counter. Christ, she hated testosterone and the way it made half the species stupid.

But the guy didn't bother her. He was about forty, maybe a year or two past it. He had a long, pale face; he looked a little like Nicolas Cage, only rougher. Just how much he looked like the actor Vanessa couldn't be sure—he wore the thickest beard she'd ever seen on a man. It might have been a pelt. Like his hair, it was black as shoe polish, only it had a few white threads on either side of his chin.

"Hallo, Yvonne," he said to the waitress. "How are you today?" He had some kind of accent, not at all thick but noticeable.

"Hey, Bron. I'm okay. How're you?" she said, so he was some kind of regular.

"I'll do." He shrugged. He had wide shoulders and a narrow waist. He wore jeans and a T-shirt, which in this weather was an invitation to pneumonia. Muscles slid smoothly under the skin of his arms. They were nearly as hairy as his cheeks, except for a big, pink, nasty-looking scar—a burn?—on his left forearm. On the back of his right hand, where the hair was thinner, he had a tattoo: a cross, with a C above and below the right bar and a backwards C above and below the left bar.

"What'll it be?" the waitress—Yvonne—asked.

He pointed to Vanessa's plate. "Give me what she's having. It doesn't look . . . too bad."

"Hey! This is a high-class joint!" the waitress said, for all the world as if she were really and truly affronted.

"Yes? And they let you work here even so?" Bron returned. That would have pissed Vanessa off, but the waitress just cackled. Bron paid attention to Vanessa for the first time: "How bad is it?"

"Could be worse," she said—a line from a book she'd liked when she was a very small kid. You were supposed to sound like a little old man when you said it (that was how Dad had always read it, anyway), but she didn't go that far.

He shrugged again. "I wouldn't be surprised if it could be better, too." He had a distinct odor. Vanessa hadn't been used to noticing that before the eruption, except for slobs and the occasional unfortunates who couldn't help it. Since . . . Hot water was harder to come by now, especially in places like Camp Constitution. She'd inured herself to stinky people. But he wasn't stinky, or not exactly. He smelled like . . . himself, she supposed. To her surprise, she rather liked it.

That might have been what made her answer him instead of going back to pretending the seat beside her was still empty. "Everything could be better these days, you know?" she said.

"True." He rolled the *r* when he said it. After a moment, he went on, "We could be in Minnesota or Maine or some other place where it gets really cold. This—this is nothing much."

Not with that fur you've got to keep you warm. But Vanessa swallowed the crack, even if he practically invited it by coming in here with nothing over that T-shirt. She chose another tack: "I've got a brother up in Maine. I think he's still up there, anyhow. I haven't heard from him in quite a while."

"If he is in such a place, he may not have power for his phone. Up there, many areas have had no power at all for a long time."

In such a place. The phrase stuck in Vanessa's ear as the waitress set a plate in front of Bron. Few English-speakers would say anything like that. You might write it, but you wouldn't say it.

Bron fell to. He ate with wolfish directness. His teeth were very white, or that black, black beard and mustache made them seem so. He paused halfway through the burger to remark, "Yes, could be worse or better. In the middle."

"Uh-huh." What came out of Vanessa's mouth next amazed her: "I like your beard."

That got his complete attention. He looked her up and down. For once, it didn't feel like a groping; she knew she'd invited it. His eyes were a lighter brown than she'd thought at first. *A sniper's eyes* went through her mind—they had that careful but aggressive directness to them. He held back half a beat before answering, "I like your you."

The little pause seemed to give the handful of ordinary words extra weight. *Careful,* something in Vanessa's mind warned. But she didn't feel like being careful. She'd been careful since the eruption, not that she'd come across anybody she gave a rat's ass about since then. And how much trouble could you get into at a Denny's Formica counter?

"Thanks," she said. "I'm Vanessa—Vanessa Ferguson."

"Hallo, Vanessa Ferguson," he said gravely. "I am Bronislav Nedic." Those watchful eyes flicked to find Yvonne. She was over by the register, talking with another, younger, waitress. Even so, he lowered his voice a little before going on, "People who have trouble pronouncing Bronislav call me Bron."

"I can say Bronislav." Vanessa had a good ear. Even so, she could tell her *o* wasn't just like his. And she had as much trouble with his *r* as he did with an American one.

He smiled just the same. "You can," he agreed. "Good for you. I am glad."

"Where are you going?" she asked him. She assumed he had

to be going somewhere. Not even lunatics would stay at this miserable truck stop. Only soldiers who had to follow orders got stuck doing that.

"I have outside a truck full of chicken legs," Bronislav answered. "I take them to a freezing—no, a frozen—warehouse in Los Angeles." He raised an eyebrow. His were dark and thick, like all of his hair. They didn't quite meet above his long, sharp nose, but they came close. "And you?"

"I'm heading for L.A., too." Vanessa surprised herself with how glad she was to hear he was westbound. If he'd been going the other way, they would have been passing ships. Now ... Well, who the hell knew about now? "I was born there. I lived there till a little before the eruption, so I'm heading home."

"Born in Los Angeles." He shook his head in slow wonder.

"People are, you know," Vanessa said with a touch of irritation. Outsiders often assumed anyone who lived in California came from somewhere else. It never failed to annoy the genuine natives.

"I am sure it must be so," Bronislav Nedic said, shaking his head again. "It still seems very strange to me."

Experimentally, Vanessa gave a light touch to the tattoo on the back of his hand. His flesh seemed half a degree hotter than hers. That was a good sign. She didn't know where attraction came from, or why. She recognized it when it did, though. To cover what she was thinking, what she was feeling, she asked, "Does this mean something, or is it just a design?"

She got more than she'd bargained for. "That is the Ocilima, the four Ss with the cross," Bronislav answered, his voice as solemn as if he were intoning prayers in church. "They look like Cs to you, I know, but the Serb alphabet is like the Russian—its C is S in yours. They stand for *Samo sloga Srbina spasava*: only unity will save the Serbs." His mouth twisted into a sour, wistful smile, which made him look more like Nicolas Cage than ever. Since

Vanessa liked Nicolas Cage, that wasn't so bad. He added, "I was not born in Los Angeles, you will figure out. I was born in Yugoslavia, a country that is not a country any more."

"Oh," Vanessa said, and not another word. She supposed she could have found Yugoslavia on a map—back in the days when Yugoslavia *was* on the map—but that was as much as she knew or cared about it.

Bronislav didn't notice her indifference. His eyes were far away from the New Mexico Denny's. He was seeing other mountains than the ones here, other times. "I fought for the Serbs against the terrorist Bosnians and the Nazi Croats. I fought, but we did not win. And so . . . I sit at this counter here, next to you, and my country is broken all in pieces."

"Is that where you, uh, hurt your arm?" Vanessa didn't want to touch the scar the way she'd touched the tat.

He nodded mournfully. "It is. And I was lucky, if you want to call it luck. The RPG caught the fellow standing beside me square. They never found enough of poor Vlade to bury."

"Oh," Vanessa said again, on a different note this time. Being her father's daughter made her know from a very early age that human beings could do horrible things to one another. She'd seen more since the eruption. But . . . "You were in a war." That, she hadn't seen.

"I was in a war, yes. And now I have that truck full of chicken pieces to take to California. Life does strange things." Bronislav set money on the counter. Then he said, "If you have a number where I can call you when I am in Los Angeles . . . Maybe we see what strange things life does to us."

Or maybe I decide this was just a way to waste time in a nowhere Denny's. But Vanessa gave him her cell number instead of making one up. He entered it in his own phone. And he gave her that number, which she took in turn—mating rituals of the twenty-first century.

She paid for her own lunch. Bronislav tipped better than she did. But then, chances were he would stop here again. She wouldn't, not unless God had an even more twisted sense of humor than He'd already shown. Vanessa slid into her car. She half expected it to crap out right there, just to show her what kind of sense of humor God had. It started okay, though.

Back onto the Interstate. Into the fast lane. Past the trucks. Arizona ahead, then California. Home! Who woulda thunk it?

And if Bronislav called—no, when, because he would—she'd figure out what she wanted to do. Maybe she'd have other things that needed taking care of: shampooing her tortoise, or something. Maybe she wouldn't, too. She hadn't wanted anybody, even a little bit, for a long time. It made her feel more alive. She drove on toward L.A., happier than she remembered being since the eruption.

Louise Ferguson glumly studied her bank statement and her three credit-card bills, all of which had chosen the same day to arrive. If that didn't prove misery loved company, she was damned if she knew what would.

She'd been robbing Peter to pay Paul ever since the ramen works let her go, and robbing James to pay Peter, and robbing Mark to pay James, and robbing Luke to pay Mark, too. She was running low on saints and apostles. Even more to the point, she was running low on money.

"Shit," she said softly: the perfect one-word summary of the situation.

It wasn't as if she hadn't been looking for work since she got laid off. The California Employment Development Department had no possible complaints on that score. She sent out applications online whenever the condo had power. When it didn't, she rode the bus all over the South Bay. She talked to personnel officers, cooks, pet-store owners . . . anybody who'd listen to her and pay her more than unemployment doled out.

No one wanted to hire her. She was on the wrong side of fifty—not far on the wrong side, but she was. Only a few movie stars managed to stay hot-looking at her age. She wasn't bad—she knew as much—but not bad didn't cut it. She had some office skills, but she wasn't a computer whiz, either.

And even if she were hot *and* a computer whiz, chances were it wouldn't have mattered. Nobody was hiring anybody much. When a job did open up, it was guaranteed to have a zillion people clamoring for it. Somebody in that zillion would always be better qualified or cuter or younger or more male or whatever than Louise. Which meant . . .

"Shit," she muttered again.

She looked back over her shoulder at James Henry. Little pitchers had big ears. Big mouths, too. Whatever they heard, they came out with. But he was busy with Duplos and toy cars.

And so she fished her phone out of her purse. She wondered if she'd have to give it up. Landlines were cheaper. With power so spotty, they might even be more reliable, regardless of whether they were less convenient. For now, though, she called Colin's cell.

She hoped she wouldn't get his voice mail. That would be a pain. He *would* call her back. He was nothing if not reliable. Reliable to a fault, she'd thought back in the day. Even so, returning her call would give him one more edge. As if he didn't have enough already. Yeah, as if!

But he answered after the second ring. "Hello, Louise. What's up?" As usual, he didn't waste time beating around the bush.

"Colin, I need to borrow five hundred dollars." She wasn't normally so direct herself. Desperation did terrible things to people.

A long pause on the other end of the line. Then he said, "You need me to give you five hundred dollars, you mean."

Louise felt the blood mount to her cheeks and ears. It wasn't quite so bad as a hot flash, but it came close. "I'll pay you back as soon as I can," she said, hating to beg and knowing she had no choice. "As soon as I get work." That sounded better.

"This isn't the first time," he said heavily.

"I know. Believe me, I wouldn't be doing it unless I had to," Louise answered. "As long as I had a job, I didn't."

"Yeah." In her mind, she saw him grudge a nod, admitting she was right about that much. But then he said, "It's not so easy for me right now, either."

"I know Kelly's going to have the baby." Louise didn't quite gloat over the word. He wouldn't have to work so hard playing dad to the little brat as she had being single mom with James Henry, but he was no youngster himself. He'd feel it. Oh, would he ever!

"It's not just that," Colin said. "Vanessa's back in town—"

"Yes, I know," Louise broke in. "She called me. We're going to get together for lunch in a couple of days." God only knew when she'd see Vanessa again after that. They'd got along spikily even before she divorced Colin. There weren't too many people Vanessa didn't get along with spikily.

"Let me finish," Colin said in his I'm-holding-on-to-my-patience voice. "She's staying here right now, till she finds her own place—and till she finds some way to pay for a place of her own."

"Oh? How's that working out?" Louise asked with more interest than she'd expected to show. It had so many . . . intriguing possibilities.

"Well . . ." Another longish pause from her ex. At last, he said, "I haven't told her to take her show on the road, anyhow. Not yet, I haven't."

"How's she doing with Kelly?"

"I haven't told her to take her show on the road yet," Colin repeated. "Louise, I'll write you the darn check, okay?" The line went dead.

She put the phone back in her purse. Yes, that *was* interesting, wasn't it? He'd rather give her money and quit talking to her than tell her how things with Vanessa and his new wife were going. Louise nodded thoughtfully. She could paint her own pictures. She could, and she did. Having painted them, she slowly smiled. What she wouldn't have given to be a fly on the wall at the old house!

James Henry chose that exact moment to look up from his own mayhem. The Duplos and cars had turned into something very much like a demolition-derby course. "Mommy?" he said.

"What is it, dear?"

"How come you were talking to Uncle Colin?" That was what James Henry called him. It wasn't accurate, but there was no accurate name for what Colin was to James Henry: nothing shorter than *father of my half-brothers and half-sister*, anyhow.

"How do you know I was?" Louise answered one question with another.

" 'Cause you were talking about money."

"Oh." That was more a sound of pain than a word. He was big enough to notice what was going on around him, all right.

Too many questions there, and all of them too pointed. Louise had always believed in being straight with children. She did her best now: "He's going to loan me some money. Do you know what *loan* means?"

"You have to give it back?" Her son sounded doubtful.

Louise nodded. "That's right. When I get some more of my own and I can afford to, I'll pay it back." She believed it when she said it. No, this wasn't the first time she'd had to hit Colin up. She didn't like to think about paying it all back . . . and so, most of the time, she didn't.

James Henry found another question with sharp teeth: "How come Marshall doesn't come around and watch me any more? He's silly!"

"He is silly," Louise agreed. "He doesn't watch you so much any more because he did that while I went to my job. I haven't been able to do that for a while now."

"Why?" James Henry asked—the little kid's favorite comeback.

"Because the company I worked for wasn't making as much money as it wanted to, and so it didn't need as many people as it had before. And I was one of the ones it let go."

"Why?" he asked again.

"I don't know," Louise answered, which was the Lord's truth. How much of all this he understood was liable to be a different question altogether. Talking about money with a preschooler was much too much like getting up on a stump in Peru and spouting Estonian.

Sure as hell, he just looked at her—looked at her with Teo's dark eyes. She was his mother. She was *Mommy*. Of course she knew everything. That was a law of nature, same as the sun coming up every morning and going down every evening. It was a law of nature if you hadn't started kindergarten yet, anyhow.

Tears stung Louise's eyes. If only the world really worked that way! Mm-hmm, if only. When you looked at it from the far side of fifty, you wondered if you truly understood even one single goddamn thing. And the older you got, the less likely it seemed. She'd been sure about Colin. Then she'd been sure about Teo. Then . . . At least then she'd had a job, for Christ's sake.

Now . . . Now she wasn't sure of anything, and she didn't have a job or much else. "Shit." Her lips shaped the word again—silently, she thought. James Henry giggled, anyhow. Either she hadn't been silent enough or he could read lips. Both possibilities made her want to go *Shit* one more time, but she didn't. She fixed herself a drink instead.

Kelly'd got past the worst part of the pregnancy. She didn't fall asleep if you looked at her sideways. She didn't work at random times any more, either. They called it morning sickness, but what did they know? It had got her whenever it felt like getting her, as when those egg yolks started staring up at her so malevolently.

She wasn't quite out to there yet, either, out to where she just wanted to have the kid and get it over with. It was going to be a girl. She and Colin were going to name it Deborah. You couldn't go far wrong with a name from the Bible—well, not unless you picked something like Jezebel or Habakkuk. So thought Kelly, who didn't have that kind of name, and Colin hadn't argued with her. They didn't argue much, which Kelly took as one more good sign.

She should have been happy, in other words. And she had been happy, right up till that dusty Toyota pulled up in front of the house and Vanessa got out.

She won't stay for long, Kelly told herself. She kept telling herself, over and over. *She won't stay for long*. Vanessa prided herself on making her own way. She couldn't make her own way out of here soon enough to suit Kelly.

She didn't know what the trouble was between the two of them. She believed that the first time it crossed her mind, anyhow. The first time, yes. Not the second. By then, she'd worked out what was going on—not what to do about it, but what it was.

She was a dog and Vanessa was a cat. It was about that simple. Kelly liked cats. But when you weren't one and when you ran into somebody who was . . . Life got more interesting than you really wanted it to.

Vanessa was younger than she was, prettier than she was, more graceful than she was. She'd been on the road for a while. She was grubby and looked tired as she walked up to the door. Kelly opened it. Vanessa looked at her and said, "Oh. You must be Kelly."

In another tone of voice, or without that flat *Oh*, it would have been fine. As things were, Kelly's hackles rose. She still didn't know what they were, but, whatever they were, up they went, all right. "Uh-huh," she said, her own voice colder than post-eruption winter at the South Pole. "Come in." She had to make herself get out of the way so Vanessa could.

Once past the front foyer, Vanessa looked around. "It's . . . different," she said, as if that should have been a hanging offense on the off chance it wasn't.

"Yes. It is." Kelly hadn't known she could sound any chillier. She surprised herself, because she had no trouble at all. The decor everywhere but in Colin's study had still been Louise's when she started hanging out with him. The front room didn't look like a rummage sale in a Russian Orthodox monastery any more.

"Well . . ." Vanessa had said, and then, "It's better than Camp Constitution, anyhow." By the way she said it, it wasn't one hell of a lot better than the enormous refugee camp.

"Thanks," Kelly'd answered. "If it doesn't suit you, I'm sure you can find a motel." She knew that was a mistake as soon as the words were out of her mouth. Too late then, of course. Things would have been bad enough even without a formal declaration of hostilities. Now? Now they'd be worse than bad enough.

"Where will you put me?" Vanessa had asked. It wasn't *No fucking way I'm going to a motel, lady*, but it might as well have been.

"One of the upstairs bedrooms. Colin says it used to be yours a long time ago." Stressing the last four words, Kelly'd hit back.

"Oh, boy. Back to high school," Vanessa had muttered.

If they hadn't already got on bad terms, Kelly would have forgiven her that one. Having to move back into your parents' house was every grown American child's nightmare. As things were, Kelly wasn't in a slack-cutting mood. "Come on up, why don't you?" she'd asked tonelessly.

Marshall was clacking away down the hall, behind a closed door. Eyeing the yellow tape on the door—POLICE LINE! DO NOT CROSS!—Vanessa'd curled her lip. "My God, hasn't he changed at all?" she'd said.

"You'd know better than I would." Kelly had knocked on Marshall's door.

The clacking stopped. "What?" Marshall had sounded irritable, or as irritable as he ever sounded. He didn't like getting interrupted while he was writing.

This was a special occasion, though, or Kelly thought it was. "Your sister's home," she'd answered.

After a few seconds, Marshall had said, "Cool." He'd started typing again. Kelly wondered if he was ripped. She didn't smell weed in the hallway. As far as she knew, he didn't smoke much while he was working. He saved it for other times.

Vanessa'd looked ready to detonate. Again, even not liking her much, Kelly'd had trouble blaming her for that. But after a sentence—two at the most—the typing had stopped once more.

Out came Marshall. He'd nodded to Kelly, then (and only then) to Vanessa. "Hey," he said to his sister.

"Hello, you big lunk. It *is* good to see you," Vanessa answered. "So you finally graduated, did you?"

" 'Fraid so," Marshall admitted ruefully. He'd staved off the evil day as long as he could, till UC Santa Barbara requirements and Colin's unwillingness to write any more tuition checks at last conspired to cast him forth into the real world.

"And?" Vanessa'd asked. Kelly was impressed at how much snark she could pack into a single word.

By the way Marshall's eyebrow had twitched, so was he, and not favorably, either. "And so I'm back in San Atanasio instead of up at UCSB," he'd replied. With a certain snarkiness of his own, he'd added, "You're here, too."

"Only till I find somewhere else," Vanessa declared.

"Job market's a little tough around here right now," Marshall said. "Ask Mom if you don't believe me."

"Half the time, Mom doesn't know enough to grab her ass with both hands," Vanessa said scornfully.

Marshall lobbed a grenade: "Didn't see her moving to Denver."

Vanessa reddened. Kelly remembered wondering if she ought to run for a bomb shelter, and where she might find one. She sure wouldn't have wanted that look aimed her way. But all Vanessa said was "Listen, do you use that stupid, noisy typewriter in the middle of the night? My room's right on the other wide of the wall, you know."

"I use it whenever I feel like it," Marshall had answered. If the lights were on at night, there would be power for his iMac, too. He still preferred the computer, and it was a lot quieter. By the gleam in his eye, though, the Royal portable from the pawnshop was liable to get some workouts in the wee smalls.

"Excuse me," Kelly said. "I'm going downstairs to check on the rabbits." The kitchen wasn't a bomb shelter, but it might do for one in a pinch.

"Is that what I smell?" Marshall said. "Where'd they come from?"

"Your dad traded some brandy to another cop for them," she said. "I think that guy raises them."

"Bunny's not bad." Marshall sounded surprised that that was so.

"Better than MREs. Anything's better than MREs." Vanessa spoke with great conviction.

Kelly had been basting the rabbits when Colin came in. "Is that Vanessa's car out front?" he'd asked after he kissed her.

"Yup," Kelly said, and not one word more.

"How's she doing?" he inquired.

"She's here." Again, Kelly kept things as concise as she could.

Colin grunted. He chuckled, not in any enormously cheerful way. "Yeah, we're all here. One big, happy family, right?"

"If you say so," Kelly'd replied.

"I just did. 'Course, because I say it, that doesn't make it true." Colin sighed. "Be an awful lot simpler if it did, y'know?" Kelly didn't say anything at all that time. But she did nod.

XVII

The Frozen Tundra. That was what Packer fans called Lambeau Field in December and January even before the supervolcano erupted. Teams from warmer climes, teams that played in air-conditioned domes on ground-up tires dyed green, often turned up their toes when they had to play in cold and snow on dead grass (also sometimes dyed green).

They still stubbornly, defiantly, played outdoor football in midwinter in Green Bay. Bryce Miller remembered hearing that one fan froze to death in a playoff game the year before, no matter how much antifreeze he'd poured down. The big squawk wasn't about his untimely passing—it was about who would inherit his season tickets.

Green Bay lay some distance east of Wayne, Nebraska, but less than a hundred miles farther north. Bryce had discovered more about frozen tundra than he'd ever wanted to know. It was barely autumn, but much of the campus already answered to that description. All you had to do was cross the street from the student union building and there you were, out in the middle of icy whiteness waiting for Jack London to mush past in a sled pulled by White Fang and Buck.

Frozen tundra. Oh, yeah. The soccer pitch was frozen tundra with nets. The baseball field was frozen tundra surrounded by fences, with dugouts and bleachers on the sides. The softball field was a smaller version of the same thing. Out beyond them was a walking path that skirted a golf course—still more tundra, with skeletal trees sticking up out of the snow and making it drift against their trunks.

Past the golf course, past the campus, gently rolling Nebraska farm country stretched as far as the eye could see. Before the eruption, it had yielded bumper crops of wheat and corn and soybeans. Cattle had grazed on green grass and fattened in feed lots.

Again, Bryce remembered the exhibit at the University of Nebraska museum in Lincoln. Ashfall State Park lay west of Wayne. He didn't need to think of all the rhinos done in 12,000,000 years ago by that earlier supervolcano blast. Most of the livestock and an awful lot of the people across the modern Midwest had already died of HPO, just like those poor, extinct rhinoceroses.

Except for the small town of Wayne and the anything but enormous Wayne State campus, there was nothing but frozen tundra for miles and miles in every direction. Bryce's breath smoked as if he were a three-pack-a-day guy. In spite of long johns, jeans, and a heavy coat that came down to his knees, he felt sure he was freezing his balls off.

For this you left Junipero High? For this you left SoCal? he asked himself, not for the first time. Since he unquestionably had, he asked himself a couple of more questions. *Why? Were you out of your ever-loving mind?*

He shook his head. In spite of everything, he didn't think so. He'd spent a lot of time and a lot of effort making himself as

much at home in the Hellenistic world as anyone could who happened to be born 2,300 years too late to see it in person.

That thought made him laugh, so his breath smoked even
more. Vanessa's brother's band had that song called "Came Along
Too Late," about not being able to watch Alexander conquer the
Persian Empire. Squirt Frog and the Evolving Tadpoles did all
kinds of strange things. That one hit Bryce where he lived.

A crow cawed harshly. There it was, on the crust of the snow,
a lump of coal with wings. Not even post-eruption winter was
enough to drive away the crows. A couple of others walked along
purposefully, a good bit farther away. Mice, maybe. The cold
wasn't enough to do in the mice, either. They found this and that
under the snow, and dug tunnels through it. Every so often, one
would pop out for a look around—and some lucky crow would
cash in a meal ticket.

Bryce wondered if he ought to cash in a meal ticket himself,
back at the cafeteria in the student union. He was going to teach
his class on ancient Greece in an hour. He sometimes thought the
cafeteria specialized in ancient grease itself.

More crows flew up, calling in alarm, as he walked back toward the student union building. They ate what students threw
away. But they were also more wary than they had been. In these
hard times, eating crow wasn't always just a figure of speech.

Some of what the crows, and the people who fed them, got to
eat . . . Potatoes. Lots of potatoes. Potatoes grew in cold climates.
Turnips and parsnips grew even better. In SoCal before the eruption, Bryce had sometimes eaten sweet-potato fries instead of
regular spuds. The cafeteria in Wayne often served turnip and
parsnip fries. The parsnip fries turned out to be pretty decent.
Bryce didn't think you could do anything to a turnip that would
make it exciting. If french-frying didn't turn the trick, what
would?

He went inside. It was warmer in there than outside—all

the way up into the low fifties. Everybody around here should have been cold all the time. In the clothes Bryce had on, though, the feeble heating felt tropical. A guy walked by in a T-shirt: Midwest bravado. He did have a sweatshirt and a jacket on his arm. Go outside in a T-shirt and you were asking the coroner to call.

"Thank you," the gal in charge of such things said when he handed her his faculty meal ticket. She looked like every other oldish woman he'd seen in school cafeterias since kindergarten. There was probably a factory in Elbonia or somewhere that manufactured them preaged.

Bryce grabbed a tray and approached the food. The rule was that you could take what you wanted but you got only one pass; the powers that be decreed that that cut down on waste.

Potatoes. Turnips. Parsnips. Rye and oat flour. Beets. Coleslaw—cabbage and carrots didn't need long growing seasons. Sauerkraut. Kimchi (well, Nebraska kimchi, anyhow, though Bryce didn't think it would have been anywhere near potent enough for real Koreans).

He got some chow. They had what they called pizza. The crust was dark enough to show it was mostly rye. The cheese was thinly spread; with so many cows dead, people had stopped taking milk for granted. They'd had to. The sausage . . . There wasn't much of it, either. And it looked funny.

Pointing to a round of it, Bryce asked the student dishing stuff out, "Do I want to know what goes into that?"

"It's meat," she answered. "What else do you need to know?"

"Nothing," he said after a barely perceptible pause for thought. "Let me have a slice, please."

"You got it." She put it on a plastic plate and handed it to him.

He found a place, sat down, and ate. The coleslaw was actually pretty good. The french fries had been sitting under a heat lamp too long, but that could happen at a real fast-food joint, too. As for the pizza, well, he'd had worse. He didn't think he'd ever had stranger, though. If Finns had invented the stuff instead of Italians, it might have come out like this.

The sausage was definitely mystery meat. As the girl had suggested, some mysteries were better left unsolved. Bryce had read *Shogun*—he'd raced through it in three or four days, in fact. Because he'd liked it so much, he'd got *Tai-Pan* and *King Rat*, too. *Tai-Pan* was pretty good: not so good as *Shogun*, but still pretty good. *King Rat* was nothing like the other two, but also pretty good. Right this minute, remembering what the POWs in *King Rat* had chowed down on, Bryce wished he'd never found it no matter how good it was.

He dumped his trash and stowed his tray, dishes, and flatware on the rotating shelves that delivered them to the dishwashers. Then he put his knit cap back on, pulled it down so it covered his ears, and headed out into the cold again to go teach his class. The Peloponnesian War today, or the start of it. He'd done big chunks of Thucydides in the original. Now it paid off.

What the kids at Wayne State thought of things like the Melian Dialogue, he wasn't sure. Some of them got it, and saw that that kind of thing applied to any situation where people tried to govern themselves responsibly. More, he feared, didn't—which was the kind of problem people who tried to govern themselves responsibly had to deal with.

Or to duck. Washington these days reminded him of a broken-backed man's brain. It still sent out frantic messages— orders, even—but not all of them got through. He finished the lecture and headed for the bus stop.

Wayne and Wayne State were better off than a lot of places. The power here stayed on better than it did in Los Angeles. Natural gas got through. There wasn't a lot of gasoline, and what there was was hideously expensive, but that was worse in SoCal, too. Things here didn't depend on the port and on one long highway connecting the coast to the rest of the country.

Then again, this was Wayne, Nebraska. The Frozen Tundra, as he'd thought before. Along with fast food, it had a Chinese place and a pizza place that also did spaghetti. No takeout Thai. No Peruvian. No pupusas from El Salvador. No sushi. No Korean barbecue. No Persian. No Israeli. No Moroccan. No . . . no nothin', except for Chinese and sortakinda Italian.

Here came the bus. It had studded snow tires, and chains over them, too. That struck Bryce as suspenders and belt, but what did he know? About snow and coping with it, not much. He knew he wouldn't have wanted to walk or bike back to his place in town, not in weather like this. And he knew he wasn't rich enough to keep driving back and forth, even for short hauls.

Body heat warmed the inside of the bus some—enough to prove that some of the bodies warming it hadn't been washed for a while. One more constant of the new era. You did what you could, and you did what you could afford, and you said the hell with the rest.

Not much traffic on the road back to town. Bryce guessed there'd never been a whole lot. There just weren't enough people in these parts to create much traffic. To someone who'd squandered countless irreplaceable hours crawling along the 405 because of a wreck five miles ahead, that was a prodigy.

Bryce got out near the center of Wayne. Nothing was more than three or four stories high. A lot of the buildings were of red or brown brick. To someone from a state where quakes were an everyday worry, that was a prodigy, too, but not such a good one.

The main drags were plowed. That was how the bus had come this far. Bryce walked a block in the street. He had to watch for oncoming cars—not too big a worry, with gas so scarce and so expensive—and he had to be careful not to slip and fall on his ass. Then he had to climb up onto the drifts to go the rest of the way to the apartment he and Susan shared.

Even this recently after the end of summer, it had been cold enough long enough for the snow to have a good solid crust. The drifts bore his weight. Most of the time, anyhow. Falling through into the snow and then struggling to pull himself out again wasn't the most enjoyable thing he'd ever done. And he didn't want a repeat performance, so he watched where he put his feet. Once had been an experiment; twice would definitely be perversion.

He made it back to the building without going into the deep freeze. The little rectangular mailbox—just the kind you'd also see in SoCal apartment buildings—was empty when he turned the key in its lock. Either Susan had already got whatever there was or the mailman (or mailwoman, if you needed a word with a built-in oxymoron) hadn't managed to mush through the snow. The USPS took its adaptation of Herodotus' version of the pledge of the Persian Empire's couriers less seriously than it had once upon a time.

He clumped up the stairs. A second-floor unit was better than one down below. You didn't have herds of shoes migrating over your head. The neighbors on either side of the place weren't too noisy, either. All that could have been worse, as he knew from experience.

Susan was tapping away on a laptop at the kitchen table when he came in. It wasn't warm inside, any more than it had been in the student union or his classroom or the bus. But it was warmer, so it felt warm. And the hug she gave him raised his temp several more degrees—or it sure seemed to, anyhow.

"How's it going?" he asked.

"I'm getting there," she answered. "Long-distance thesis writing ... This way, I get snarky e-mails—sometimes even snarky letters I can barely read when the power in L.A. goes for a while—instead of face-to-face snark. I'm glad stuff stays on most of the time here. I couldn't finish without the Net. The Wayne State Library tries, it really does, but it doesn't have most of what I need."

Bryce nodded. "I know that song." The classical holdings here were severely limited, too.

"Sure." She smiled at him. "If you didn't know what I was going through, I'd drive you totally up the wall instead of just three-quarters of the way."

"Yeah, right," he answered. "Like I'm not already up—or off—the wall any which way." Susan thought that was funny. Bryce wished he could have said it without dredging up uncomfortable memories. Vanessa had had no idea how crazy he'd get when he was studying for his orals. How could she have? She'd never done anything like that. She'd bailed out of college before she graduated and started working instead. That had hassles of its own—Bryce discovered some of them later—but they weren't the same hassles. The differences had only made for more friction between them.

He wondered how Vanessa was doing. He'd have to ask Colin next time he talked to him or e-mailed him. He hadn't done that as often as he should have since he moved to Nebraska. Hell, he hadn't done it as often as he should have after he moved up to the Valley and couldn't get over to the Ferguson place so easily any more.

Susan had said something. She stood there, waiting expectantly for him to answer. Woolgathering about your ex was not a good thing to do, not when it made you zone out on your current squeeze. "Sorry." Bryce spread his hands in what he hoped would be apology enough. "Brain fuzz."

"A likely story," Susan answered darkly. "I *said*, how do you want me to make the potatoes tonight?"

"I dunno. Cooking them ought to be good," Bryce replied. She rolled her eyes. So did he, for different reasons. You could do only so much with potatoes. Whatever you did, they were still potatoes when you got through with them. He supposed he should have been glad they had enough potatoes, and didn't need to worry about going hungry.

He should have been, and in a way he was. But he remembered better times. So did his whole generation. If the climate didn't improve by the time they died off, they'd bore the living shit out of the cadre rising behind them by going on and on about the good old days. Well, yeah, every generation did that, so why should his be any different? The difference was, for them the good old days really would have been good.

There was a joint on Hesperus, a little north of the police station, with a name Colin Ferguson had loved for years. HEINRICH'S HOFBRAU AND SUSHI BAR, the sign over the door declared. It had always drawn a fair number of cops at lunch and dinnertime. The way things were these days, it was crawling with blue uniforms and off-the-rack suits. You could walk there from the station. You could, and the policemen and -women did.

As a waiter led Colin and Gabe Sanchez to a table, Colin remarked, "I always wished this joint served pizza, too."

"Oh, yeah?" Gabe said. "How come?"

" 'Cause then you'd have the whole Axis, all in one place."

That got the kind of disgusted snort he'd hoped for. They sat down. The waiter set menus on the table in front of them and went away. The menus had two sides—not Column A and Column B but German and Japanese. "More soba noodles than ever," Gabe said, eyeing the Japanese side.

"Soba's buckwheat," Colin answered. "Kasha, if you're Jewish."

"Sure, man. Hell of a lot of Hebes named Sanchez."

"Mm, right." Colin had to remind himself what he was talking about. "Buckwheat's one of those grains that grow quick, so you can raise it in the kind of crappy weather we've got nowadays."

"Oh. Is that where you were going with that? I gotcha," Gabe said. When the waiter came back, he ordered some of the soba noodles. Colin went Teutonic, with sauerkraut, potatoes, and pork.

The dish proved heavy on the spuds and kraut, light on the pork. You could raise pigs anywhere, on almost anything. What meat there was these days was mostly pork. Some chicken remained, though the corn that had fattened hens was mostly a memory.

Beef? Lamb? Rare and even more expensive than everything else. Good fish was scarce, too, which didn't do the sushi part of this operation any good. Squid, though . . . There was lots of squid. By all the signs, squid were oceanic cockroaches. If you dropped an H-bomb on the Marianas Trench, somehow the squid would survive.

"And when you've been squid, you've been did," Colin murmured.

"What's that?" Gabe cupped a hand behind his ear.

"Nothing," Colin said. "Believe me, nothing. My brains are dribbling out my ears, that's all."

"And I'm supposed to notice this on account of . . . ?" Gabe asked.

"Who said you were supposed to notice it?" Colin returned.

Gabe let out another snort. Then he found a question Colin had been asking himself a good deal lately, too: "What's it like having your daughter home again?"

"It's—interesting, anyway." Colin wished he'd ordered a beer with lunch, even if department regs frowned on such things and even if barley shortages made beer almost as expensive as gasoline. He almost left the answer short and unresponsive. But Gabe had been his buddy as long as they'd both been on the San Atanasio PD. If he could vent to anybody, Gabe was the guy. Sighing, he went on, "I wish to Christ Vanessa and Kelly'd hit it off better."

"That's not good," Gabe said.

Colin clapped silently, applauding the understatement without making everybody in the place stare at him. "It wouldn't be good even if Kelly wasn't expecting. Since she is, it's doubleplus ungood."

"It's what?" But then Gabe's heavy features cleared. "Oh. From that book. *1984*." He chuckled self-consciously. "Dunno if I've even looked at it since 1984. Sometime in high school—I'm pretty sure of that."

Colin had read it more recently—quite a bit more. The politics were out of date. Nobody could deny that. The politics had been out of date well before the Cold War went bye-bye. But the thoughts on the way corrupt and narrow politics produced a corrupt and narrow language seemed more important than ever in this age of pious bullshit. They did to him, at any rate. Most people, by all appearances, didn't give a rat's ass.

If he was going to vent, he was going to vent. Not much point to doing things halfway, was there? With another sigh, he said, "And she's got herself a new boyfriend."

"A punk? A gangbanger?" Gabe's older daughter was in high school. Those were the kinds of boyfriends that gave him nightmares.

But Colin shook his head. "Well, no."

"Oh," Gabe said again. As he had with *1984*, he remembered slowly, but remember he did. "Please, Jesus, not another guy older than you are."

"Not that, either," Colin admitted. "This one's, I dunno, maybe forty."

"Not too bad, not for the age she is now," Gabe said. Colin nodded this time; that was true. Gabe asked the next logical question: "So what don't you like about him?"

"It's not even that I don't like him," Colin said, which was also true . . . to a point.

"Huh," Gabe said, as if a perp gave him an unexpected reply in the interrogation room. "He got a record?"

"Not any place I can find," Colin answered. He wasn't surprised Gabe would assume he'd checked. He had, as soon as he'd got Bronislav Nedic's name. Did that mean he didn't trust his darling daughter's taste in men? Now that you mentioned it, yes.

"Huh," Gabe said again. "What is it, then?"

"You wanna know what? I'll tell you what—he scares the crap out of me, that's what." There. Colin had said it. He sure hadn't said it to Vanessa, or even to Kelly. That was one he'd kept bottled up ever since he'd met Bronislav. He hoped like hell the big Serb hadn't noticed it, too.

He succeeded in surprising Gabe, anyhow. Sanchez's graying eyebrows leaped toward his hairline. "*Scares* you?" By the way Gabe repeated it, he could hardly believe his own ears. "How come?"

"I did my hitch in the Navy—you know that." Colin waited for his friend to nod before continuing, "I never saw combat. But I knew some guys—Navy and Marines—who'd been nasty places and done nasty things. Heap big nasty things, if you know what I mean."

"Uh-huh." Gabe nodded again. "This dude is like that?"

"In spades, doubled and redoubled." Colin tried to put what he felt into words: "Those guys, whatever they were up to, they were doing it 'cause they had orders to do it, whatever *it* was. And maybe things got hairy, but they got hairy because that kind of stuff was what they did. You with me so far?"

"Yeah. Or I think so."

"Okay. This fella, he did that kinda stuff, too. He's got an ugly old scar to prove it, but you don't need the scar to know. You just need to see the eyes. Only I don't think he did whatever he did because those were his orders. He did it 'cause he went looking for it and he found it."

After another pause for thought, Gabe said, "Not a German shepherd. Not a police dog. A wolf."

"Bingo!" Colin exclaimed. "That's better than I worked out for myself—a lot better, matter of fact."

"You scared he'll take it out on Vanessa, whatever it is?"

"It wasn't that kind of vibe, or I don't think it was," Colin said after some thought of his own. "But I don't think she's got a clue about what she's hanging out with, either. I don't want her getting hurt."

Gabe laughed a singularly mirthless laugh. "You fall for somebody, man, that's the chance you take. Me and my ex . . ." He shuddered; he had more than his share of godawful memories to go with the good ones. "You and yours, too. And it's not like this is Vanessa's first race around the track, right?"

"Right. Right, right, right." Colin still wished Vanessa could have stayed together with Bryce Miller. But she damn well hadn't, any more than Louise had stayed together with *him* or Gabe's then-wife with him. If Vanessa hadn't gone to Denver to stay with that gray-haired rug seller . . . That hadn't lasted even as long as Bryce had. This one, now? "Everything you say makes good sense, but I'm worried just the same."

"Well, then, you don't need to worry about lunch." Gabe put money on the table. "Come on. Let's get back to work."

"Why not?—and thanks. Maybe it'll take my mind off things."

"Hope so. But that's not why I said it. I want my cancer fix, and I'll get it on the way back to the station." Gabe gave forth with a theatrical sigh. "Hard times for a smoker these days. If you're in a building that's not your own house, they'll bust you for lighting up. I tell you, man, it's almost easier to smoke dope."

Colin kept his mouth shut tight. Every one of his children

used weed—Vanessa less than her brothers, but she did, too. The only good thing about it, he thought as he and Gabe tramped along Hesperus toward the station, was that the smoke smelled better than tobacco. Gabe wouldn't even have agreed with him about that.

Some people set out to be writers from the time they were small. Marshall wasn't any of them. He'd chosen creative writing as a major at UCSB because it would let him stay in school an extra quarter or two. He'd submitted for the first time because that prof made him do it.

And he'd got accepted because . . . Maybe God knew why. Marshall had no idea.

He'd sold several more stories after the first one, too. He was good enough to be a professional writer. That much seemed plain. What also seemed plain, unfortunately, was that he wasn't good enough, or maybe productive enough, or maybe just lucky enough, to make a living at it.

That was how come he'd wasted so much time babysitting his tiny half-brother, a kid whose very existence weirded him out. His father gruffly insisted that time you got paid for wasn't time wasted. Marshall wasn't convinced. Dad didn't care. The next time Dad cared about Marshall's opinions would be the first.

Now, though, Mom was out of work herself. That meant she had much less need for babysitting services. It also meant Marshall's income tanked.

Dad did not approve. Marshall had to care about Dad's opinions, because the house belonged to Dad. His old man was willing—not eager, but willing—to feed him and let him keep sleeping there as long as he looked for work. And, with a cop's relentless thoroughness, Dad checked up on him to make sure he did.

Some of the interrogations were almost as sharp as if he were under suspicion of knocking over a McDonald's. He complained about it once: "The state unemployment office isn't as tough as you are!"

His father just looked at him. Somehow, Dad could make his blunt features do an amazing impression of a snapping turtle. "The unemployment office doesn't have you sleeping under its roof," he said tonelessly. "I darn well do. If you aren't happy about the situation, you're welcome to pack your bags and go somewhere else."

Marshall shut up. Without money, where was he supposed to go? He could sleep in his car. . . . Yeah, right, the car he couldn't afford to gas up. Or he could apartment-surf among his friends. Only most of them were in the same boat. They were crashing on one another, or back with their folks, or seeing what sleeping in their cars was like.

Everybody was in that same boat. Trouble was, it was the *Titanic*. No—what was the name of that other liner, the one that got torpedoed? To Marshall's amazement, he dredged it up from the depths of U.S. history boredom. The *Lusitania*, that was it. When the supervolcano blew up, it torpedoed the whole goddamn economy.

Marshall pointed that out, with profane embellishments. Dad went right on looking as if he were paddling along in the Mississippi, waiting for a fish to swim by so he could bite it in half. "I know it's hard to find anything," he said when Marshall ran down. "But you've got to try. Vanessa's trying."

"She sure is," Marshall agreed. Having his big sister home again had not proved an unmixed blessing.

Dad stopped doing reptile impersonations and looked quite humanly pained at the pun. "She's looking for work," he said, so there could be no possible misunderstanding. "She's looking hard, too. The least you can do is try as hard as she does."

"She's not writing," Marshall said.

"Look, son, it's great that you've sold some things. I'm proud of you for that. I'm bust-my-buttons proud," his father said. "But you aren't exactly James Michener yet."

"I hope not! Isn't he dead?" Marshall said.

"You're not George Carlin, either, and he's dead, too," Dad said. There he surprised his son—Marshall would have bet he'd name Bill Cosby. Even dead, even after a long, successful career alive, Carlin seemed too edgy, too freaky, to appeal to a cop. You never could tell, could you? Dad went on, "Neither one of them died broke, though, and neither one of them needed to scuffle for an outside job. Till you don't need to, you're gonna scuffle."

So Marshall scuffled. Every once in a while, he got a day's work moving stuff off a truck and into a warehouse or out of the back of a store and into a truck. That didn't happen very often, though. Most of the guys who got those jobs were browner than he was and spoke Spanish. The people who did the hiring figured those guys were less likely to piss and moan about doing hard work, wouldn't complain about their shitty wages, and wouldn't start yelling about workers' compensation if they screwed up their backs.

They were right, too. They knew it. So did Marshall. And so did the brown, Spanish-speaking guys who got hired instead of him. Their part of the deal was to do as they were told and shut up about it.

He tried to get a job that would let him write. By now, he had enough sales to put together a decent résumé. No large American corporation seemed to be looking for anybody who could turn out a respectable short story, though. No small American business seemed to be looking for anyone with that skill set, either.

Jesus H. Christ, no escaped lunatics seemed to be looking for somebody who could crank out a respectable short story. Well, no: a few lunatics remained on the loose. They ran the e-publications and print magazines that occasionally—much too occasionally, as far as Marshall was concerned—bought the stories he did write.

He kept sending stuff to *Playboy* and *The New Yorker*. You sold something to a market like that, it paid no-shit eating money. Of course, all the writers in the world who used English knew as much (so did some who had to get their stuff translated from Japanese or Russian or Hebrew). The top mags could pick and choose. They could, and they did. Marshall got rejected over and over again.

He hated getting rejected. He never would have submitted the first story that sold if Professor Bolger hadn't required it. In high school, he hadn't dated much because he hated it when girls turned him down. This was the same kind of thing, and the noes hurt just about as much.

He had dated. Eventually, he got too horny not to. When a girl let him get lucky, the reward made up for all the failures that came before it. Now he felt the same way when an editor let him get lucky.

Here, for once, he'd gone someplace Vanessa wouldn't follow—or wouldn't push ahead of him. Vanessa could get into a revolving door behind you and come out in front. But she said, "I couldn't stand people telling me no all the goddamn time."

"They don't tell you no all the time," Marshall said. "Sometimes they tell you yes. That's the payoff."

She shook her head. "Too much of one, not enough of the other."

He didn't want to argue with her, so he let it alone. Arguing was her thing, not his. She'd argue at the drop of a hat, and she'd drop the hat herself if she needed to. But deliberately put herself in a spot where she might get rejected? That, no.

Of course, when she dated she was the one getting the attention, not the one giving it. She wasn't used to coming on to somebody and getting shot down in flames. Maybe that had something to do with how she felt. *Or maybe I'm full of crap,* Marshall thought. It wouldn't be for the first time if he was.

He was a writer. He called himself one, anyhow. The world believed him, to the extent that it was willing to give him money for what he wrote. It didn't give him as much as he wanted or needed, but it gave him some, so it did believe him. And he had no idea what went on inside his sister's head, even if she was somebody he'd known his whole life. *No* idea. Hell, half the time he had no idea what went on inside his own head. More than half the time, it often seemed.

Did other writers, real writers, writers who honest to God made a living slapping words on paper, feel the same way? If they didn't, how could they know? If they did, how could they write so well? Questions came easy. He wished he knew where God, or Whoever, stashed the answers.

XVIII

Winter in Maine. Back before the supervolcano erupted, back before Squirt Frog and the Evolving Tadpoles found themselves stuck in Guilford with the Greenville blues again, that would have meant Norman Rockwell paintings, or more likely Currier and Ives prints, to Rob. He would have thought of Christmas trees (or, being the cynical sort he was, of pine-scented air freshener).

These days, winter in Maine brought two things to his mind. *No, three things,* he told himself, starting his own mental Python routine. They were, in no particular order, not freezing to death, not starving to death, and marrying Lindsey.

He knew the third one was coming. He had a date and everything. He'd asked Lindsey, and she'd said yes, fool that she was. He would have been a lousy marriage bet in ordinary times. But then, in ordinary times he never would have wound up stuck in Guilford and got to know her to begin with. Jim Farrell had already agreed—or threatened, depending on which way the wind was blowing—to perform the ceremony. Life would go on.

It would if he, to say nothing of the whole region, could manage not to freeze and not to starve. A hell of a lot of second-growth pines had already gone up in smoke so the stubborn souls who wanted to keep living north and west of the Interstate wouldn't freeze to death. These days, people had to cut down trees a lot farther away from the little towns that dotted the countryside. Then they had to bring them back to the towns to go up in smoke. They mostly had to do it without help of the internal-combustion variety. Life got interesting sometimes. Not warm, but interesting.

Life got hungry, too. Just as there weren't so many trees running around nearby these days, there also weren't so many moose on the loose. Rob had eaten some things he never would have imagined downing in pre-eruption Los Angeles. Squirrels, for instance, weren't just for cats any more. They were surprisingly tasty, though there wasn't much meat on a squirrel carcass. The same went for robins, though the weather had got so nasty that not many robins came this far north any more.

Rob wore snowshoes on his feet. He had a rifle in his hands. A DayGlo orange vest told the world—and, more particularly, the numskulls also prowling this part of it with rifles—that he wasn't a moose, a squirrel, or any other refugee from *The Rocky and Bullwinkle Show*. He'd been wearing that vest when he got shot. Did wearing it some more make him an optimist or a fool? Was there any difference?

Moving on snowshoes was like riding a horse. For a while, your thigh muscles had to do things they weren't used to doing. They pissed and moaned about it, sometimes loudly. Then they did it often enough to decide you weren't trying to torture them after all.

So he glumped along between the Piscataquis and Manhanock Pond. The river was frozen. So was the pond—which, being several miles long, would have done for a major lake in SoCal. Here, it was just one more souvenir of the retreating glaciers.

Like Minnesota, Maine was littered with lakes and ponds and puddles. To an L.A. guy, so much fresh water sitting around doing nothing seemed perverse.

At the moment, most of Manhanock Pond was a king-sized ice cube sitting around doing nothing. If the weather was any indication, the glaciers had just stepped around the corner for lunch, and they'd be back any minute. Scientists loudly insisted the eruption wouldn't trigger a new Ice Age. They couldn't have proved it by Rob.

A crow flew by, or maybe it was a raven. Rob watched it go without moving the rifle. Even if he could have hit a crow on the wing with a rifle, a .30-06 round would have turned it into no more than an explosion of black feathers against the sky. Birds were for shotguns. With his piece, he had to go after bigger game.

Except for the faint crunch of his snowshoes over the drifts, it was eerily quiet. Winters up here were like that. Get away from town and it was as if you were the only living thing as far as your eye and your ear could reach. No, not as if. Very often, you were.

Rob was now. No cars on the roads, that was for sure. Route 6 to the north and Route 23 to the east (to say nothing of Route 150 to the west, which was exactly what Route 150 deserved to have said of it) were covered with as much snow as the rest of the landscape. If you had to travel these days, you went by snowshoes or skis or horse-drawn sleigh—or, in a desperate emergency, by snowmobile. Those beasts murdered the silence for miles around.

Off in the distance, coming up from the southeast, something moved. Rob was immediately alert. It might be a moose. He didn't think that was likely: there were more towns, with more hunters, down in the direction of I-95. Moose had been scarcer in those parts before the eruption, too. But, while it was unlikely, it wasn't impossible.

He stood very still. Moose didn't see in color, so if this was one it wouldn't be able to tell how hideous his DayGlo vest was. It might mistake him for a Christmas tree or something, even if he wasn't loaded down with tinsel and tacky ornaments.

He needed no more than a few seconds to realize that whatever was coming his way wasn't a moose. He needed a little more time, but not a lot, to figure out what it was: a dogsled, straight out of the Yukon. A slow grin spread across his face. That was another way to get around in this frozen part of the world, at least if you had enough moose meat or kibbles or whatever the hell to keep your huskies happy.

Right behind the first sled came another one. Rob could pick out the exact moment when the passengers saw him—the dogs of the lead sled swerved in his direction. More slowly than he might have, he realized he didn't have to keep standing there as if frozen by the weather. He waved, feeling stupid.

The people in the dogsleds waved back. As the sleds neared, Rob decided he was glad he had the rifle. The huskies seemed no more than a step removed from wolves, and a small step at that. If they hadn't been hitched to the sleds, they might have decided to hunt him.

When the sleds stopped, one of the passengers pushed back the hood of his—no, her—furry, Eskimo-style parka. To Rob's amazement, styled blond hair cascaded out. "Hi," she said. "I'm Marie Fabianski, from CNN. Can we interview you?"

She spoke slowly, with spaces between her words. She might have been going into a foreign country where the natives couldn't be expected to speak or understand English very well. A cameraman in the second sled aimed his weapon at Rob's bearded, none-too-clean face.

"Um, okay," Rob mumbled. He wasn't usually thrown for such a loss, but he'd been away from anything wider than small-town gossip since not long after the supervolcano blew.

"Terrific!" Marie Fabianski smiled a multikilowatt smile. She had dazzlingly perfect teeth, whether on her own or thanks to a talented dentist Rob couldn't even begin to guess. "We're here to do a feature to show the rest of the country—to show the rest of the whole wide world—how the people in these parts are getting along. Isn't that exciting?"

Sure as hell, she was treating him like a native, and a dim-witted native at that. "What if we'd rather be left alone?" Rob said. There wasn't much point to staying on the wrong side of the Interstate if you wouldn't rather be left alone.

So it seemed to Rob, anyhow. Marie Fabianski's smile never wavered. "The public has the right to be informed!" she said in ringing tones. "It wants to know what's going on in these forgotten corners of the country."

"Oh, horseshit," Rob said. With luck, that would spoil some of the footage the cameraman was getting, though they might just bleep over it. He went on, "The American public doesn't give a rat's ass about us up here. It's proved that ever since the supervolcano went off. And you know what else? We have the right to remain silent."

He might as well have saved his breath. She sure kept on with her spiel as if he hadn't spoken: "Do you know, uh . . . ?" Then she did pause. She had to look down for a second to check her notes. Nodding to herself, she started over: "Do you know Professor James Farrell, former unsuccessful Republican candidate for the House?"

"Yeah, I know Jim," Rob answered.

"He is virtually the tsar of this new Siberia, isn't he?" Marie Fabianski rolled on. She had all her preconceptions neatly lined up in a row. If only they were ducks!

"Now that you mention it," Rob said, "no."

"Do you know where in this frozen wilderness Professor Farrell is currently residing?" she asked him. "We'd like to get to the bottom of his extraconstitutional authority."

When everybody with Constitutional authority forgets we exist, what are we supposed to do? But Rob didn't come out with it. What was the use? What was the point? Marie Fabianski wouldn't listen to him. Chances were she didn't intend to listen to Jim Farrell, either. CNN wouldn't have come up here to listen. It was coming up here to talk. Of course, she'd never met Jim. If she had to make sure she got his name right, she didn't know much about him. The confrontation might prove interesting, in the matter-antimatter sense of the word. And . . .

"As a matter of fact, he's right over there in Guilford." Rob pointed in the direction from which he'd set out. "If you give me a lift back to town, I'll introduce you."

"That would be wonderful!" Marie Fabianski exclaimed, which definitely proved she didn't know what she was getting into.

Rob rode with the cameraman and the writer. God forbid he should pollute the talent with his touch, though both Marie and he wore enough layers of clothing to make any contact between them strictly a rumor. He'd never been in a dogsled before. The running huskies pulled it along at an amazing clip. They leaned into their harness for all they were worth. Dogs got off on working. *No wonder I like cats better,* Rob thought.

When they stopped in front of the Trebor Mansion Inn, the huskies stood there panting, pink tongues lolling out of their mouths. They were ready—hell, they were eager—to run some more.

Dick Barber came out, wearing a Navy peacoat and watch cap. One corner of his mouth turned up slightly as he said, "You brought me some summer people, Rob? Way to go!"

Guilford hadn't seen much in the way of summer people (or, for that matter, summer) since the supervolcano erupted. Rob snickered. To a Californian, the whole idea of summer people had always seemed bizarre to begin with. The CNN crew looked blank. One of the prerequisites for working in TV had to be a vaccination against irony.

"Who, ah, *are* your friends?" Barber asked.

"We're from CNN," Marie Fabianski said brightly. "We understand that James Farrell is staying here. We'd like to interview him and learn more about current conditions in this part of the country."

A Maine Coon cat studied the huskies from a safe distance. The dogs saw it and barked furiously. The cat, perhaps a coward but for sure not a fool, decided somewhere else was a good place to be and departed thither at high speed. Dick Barber seemed as bemused by it as he was by the descent of the media. "You would?" he said. "Are you sure?"

"Would we have come all this way if we weren't?" she returned. *All this way* was a couple of hours' drive up from Portland in good weather. Not much of that since the eruption, and Guilford was indeed a long way from the rest of the world.

"Who knows?" Barber said. "But if he wants to talk to you, I won't try to stop him. Just remember, you brought it on yourselves. Why don't you come into my parlor? I'm not even a spider." He didn't say anything about whether Marie Fabianski was a fly.

A fire burned in the fireplace there. That meant it wasn't frigid: it was just cold. And just cold, in the middle of a post-eruption winter, felt wonderful to Rob.

While the cameraman photographed the room and set up his tripod and some battery-powered lights across from the couch, Barber whispered, "You went out after moose."

"Yeah, well, this is what I found," Rob said defensively. "Or I mean, they found me."

Jim Farrell swept into the parlor. He was elegant in his trademark fedora and a dark gray topcoat that remained dapper even if it showed it hadn't been new for a while. Not much clothing north and west of the Interstate had been new any time lately.

"An invasion by the Fourth Estate!" he boomed in his resonant baritone. "How quaint! How outdated!"

He didn't faze Marie Fabianski. She must have got a double dose of the antisarcasm serum. Before long, they sat side by side on the couch. The lights went on. So did the little red LED on the camera. "I'm CNN correspondent Marie Fabianski, speaking to you from the Trebor Mansion Inn in Guilford, Maine. With me is retired Professor James Farrell, who some call the de facto dictator of half the state of Maine."

"*Whom*, dear. *Whom* some call the de facto dictator," Farrell said genially.

"I didn't think you were an English professor," she retorted.

"I wasn't. But I do prize accuracy—which is more than a lot of people and organizations can claim these days." Farrell named no names. He didn't even name any initials. The jab went home even so.

Standing quietly beside Rob, out of the shot, Dick Barber grinned. That mention of the Trebor Mansion Inn would have been worth a lot to him back when there were summer people. Now it was no more than a might-have-been.

"I've heard it said that you are the big boss in this part of the country," Marie Fabianski tried again. "Is that true or isn't it?"

Rob expected Farrell to come back with something like *I've heard it said that CNN hires lady reporters because of how pretty they are. Is that true or isn't it?* Instead, the old man complained, "A minute ago, you said I was a dictator. Now I'm only a big boss? Make up your mind, please!"

"Well, *are* you a dictator?" She sounded flustered. Things weren't going the way she'd expected. She'd never tried dealing with Jim Farrell before, which had to explain a good deal.

He beamed at her like your kindly grandfather, if your kindly grandfather happened to be a retired history prof and a political gadfly. "Do I look like a dictator?"

"Dictators can look like—"

He overrode her: "Do I sound like a dictator? More to the point, do I act like a dictator? If I am a dictator, where's my army? Where's my harem? Most important of all, where are my tax collectors? Hard to be a dictator without what I believe the heathens term a revenue stream."

"If you're not a dictator, what would you call yourself?" Out of her depth, Marie Fabianski did her best to swim. She was game, anyhow.

"Someone who knows a little something about how to live without the so-called modern conveniences," Farrell answered. "Someone who didn't go to Washington and hole up there, unlike a certain Congresscritter I could mention. Someone the people around here trust. And I'm entertaining. We mostly can't watch CNN and the other comedy channels any more. The poor, benighted citizenry has to content itself with me."

She gaped. She gestured to the cameraman. He killed the bright lights and the video camera. Sighing, she said, "I don't think we've got much of a story here."

"I don't think you want your network to look like a pack of fools," Dick Barber said.

"Of course she doesn't, Dick," Farrell said. "They're trying to get by as best they can, just like us. We don't want to get to the point where we start eating each other, and they don't want to lose ratings. No matter where you are in the world, it's not easy. It never was, even before the eruption."

Before the eruption. Rob wondered how many times he'd said that and thought that in the days since. He was starting to take the new, harder, life for granted, but he still remembered the old one. He remembered the difference. He knew how big it was. Things wouldn't be the same again, probably not till long after he was dead.

If they ever were. That they looked bigger every day.

324 | HARRY TURTLEDOVE

A Hawthorne cop had got killed in a shootout with a bank robber. The robber was also deceased, which didn't surprise Colin Ferguson a bit. The police tended not to take prisoners in those situations.

When the coroner finally released the robber's corpse, a few grieving relatives and friends might lay him to rest. Funerals for officers slain in the line of duty were much bigger affairs. Cops and politicians from all the surrounding towns came to pay their respects. Fallen soldiers often didn't get such a fancy sendoff.

Colin hadn't known the dead policeman. He was here at Chief Pitcavage's behest, as the official representative of the San Atanasio PD. He hadn't worn his uniform for a while. It felt scratchy. The navy blue cap with the shiny brim was an unfamiliar weight on his head.

The casket was closed, so he didn't have to go through the macabre ritual of filing past the body. From what he'd heard, the poor bastard in there had stopped a charge of double-aught buck with his face. The undertakers couldn't make him look even halfway presentable.

And so Colin sat on the uncomfortable wooden pew while the minister told the audience and the TV cameras from several local stations what a fine fellow the late Office McClintock had been. McClintock left behind a wife and two boys who were too little to understand what was going on. Their mother did; she sobbed quietly through the eulogy.

Of course the minister did his best to dance around the question of why God had let Officer McClintock stop a shotgun blast with his face if he was such a fine fellow. What could you do but dance around that question? It had no answer, or none Colin could see.

But if it had no answer, what was the point of the church?

Maybe the ceremony made the widow feel a little better. Maybe it just made her remember more and hurt worse. He had no answers to that one, either.

He listened to the pious phrases and kept his trap shut. More often than not, that was the best thing you could do. He wasn't here to argue religious questions. He was here to show the San Atanasio Police Department's flag, or he would have been if only the San Atanasio PD had a flag.

After the eulogy ended, he did have to go up and murmur words of condolence to Mrs. McClintock. "I'm sorry," he said. "I'm sorrier than I know how to tell you."

She nodded jerkily. Behind a black veil, her face was paper-white. "Thank you for coming," she whispered. Her boys stared up at her. The older one might have been three. He knew something wasn't right. What it was hadn't sunk in yet.

Not for him it hadn't, anyway. He didn't know how lucky he was to be so little.

The cops milled around, talking to people they knew in other departments. It was a bad scene. They all knew they might have drawn the short straw the same way. Police work wasn't soldiering, but it came as close as anything inside the USA.

A lean LAPD sergeant came up to Colin and said, "You're that Ferguson guy, right? From San Atanasio?"

Colin nodded. "Guilty. Um, do I know you?" The other guy's face didn't look familiar.

But the sergeant answered, "Oh, we've met, all right. You bet your sweet ass we have." He did lower his voice to make sure the widow couldn't hear that.

"Tell me where?" Colin said. He was usually good at placing people. This time, though, he drew a blank.

With a sour chuckle, the guy from LAPD said, "At the Braxton Bragg offramp to the 110. You were gonna have your troops machine-gun me if I didn't get the fuck out of the way."

"Oh." Colin chuckled, too, in mild—but only mild—embarrassment. "We really needed that oil."

"I guess!" the LAPD sergeant exclaimed. "I promised myself I'd punch you in the nose if I ever ran into you again."

"Well, you can try." Colin unobtrusively shifted his weight. He hadn't been in a fistfight since his patrol-car days, but if this guy wanted to work out his grudge . . .

He didn't, or not enough to start something here. "Nah," he said. "You were doing what you thought you had to do. I'll tell you, though—it rubbed me the wrong way when you made me back down."

"You're LAPD. You're used to telling the little departments what to do," Colin said. "Gotta feel funny when the shoe's on your foot and not the other fellow's."

"It'd look that way to you, wouldn't it?" the LAPD sergeant said. "I'm not talking about how the San Atanasio PD made my department back down. I don't want to slug the San Atanasio PD. *You* made *me* back down. But hell, you were just doing your job, same as poor damn McClintock was doing his. Sometimes you're the windshield, sometimes you're the bug, that's all."

"Mm." Colin would rather it were department to department, not man to man. "I don't know your name," he said. Knowing it—and remembering it—might prove worthwhile.

"I'm Jack Winters."

"Good to meet you, Jack. For whatever it's worth to you, it wasn't personal." Colin held out his hand. After a moment, Winters took it. He squeezed with brief, controlled strength, then let go. Colin decided he might have been lucky the LAPD man didn't feel like brawling.

"Take care," Winters said, and walked away. Before long, he was lost in the throng of dark blue uniforms.

His duty and the department's done, Colin drove back to the station. He had to go slowly, because bicyclists made up almost all of the traffic. They gave him curious looks as he went past them—not, he judged, because he was in uniform in an unmarked car, but because he had a working automobile. He saw only a couple of others on the twenty-minute trip. There were many more people on skateboards on the sidewalk than drivers.

Nobody was buying new cars, either. Not only was nobody buying them; hardly anyone was making them. GM had declared bankruptcy again. Ford had tossed in the sponge. Toyota and Hyundai were shuttering American plants. The massive layoffs in the auto business after the eruption only planted another lily on the economy's chest.

When Colin got back, he walked into Mike Pitcavage's office. "How was it?" the chief asked.

"About as gruesome as you'd expect," Colin answered. Both men grimaced, almost identically. Colin went on, "The widow's . . . stunned. That's the only word that fits. Never gonna be the same for her and those kids."

"They nailed the son of a bitch who shot McClintock, anyhow," Pitcavage said. "That's over. She won't have to wait for them to try him and convict him and then wait another twenty years till they stick a needle in his arm." He made a disgusted noise, down deep in his throat.

"Yeah." Colin nodded. He felt the same way. Any cop would—justice deferred was justice denied. An awful lot of justice was being denied in California these days. He didn't want to dwell on that, so he told the chief about his encounter with Jack Winters.

"Heh," Pitcavage said. "He should've swung on you. That would've given everybody something to talk about besides the sermon."

"It wasn't worth talking about," Colin replied. "And the gossip would've been about my busted snoot."

Pitcavage waved that aside. Sure—why wouldn't he? It

wouldn't have been his ox getting gored or his nose getting punched. And his department would have scored the publicity. LAPD would have got egg on its face. If Colin had got blood on his . . .

When you were a chief, maybe you didn't worry about such minor details.

You had to look at the whole picture, right? That was what it took to run a department, even a small one like San Atanasio's, right? Mike Pitcavage sure seemed convinced it was. Colin? Colin had one more reason to count his blessings for not winning the chair Mike was sitting in now.

Whenever Bronislav drove into the L.A. area, he stayed down in San Pedro. That was partly because he hoped to pick up more hauling work at the port, partly because a good-sized Serbian community had settled there. He could hear his own language, and speak it. He could eat familiar food. He could drink familiar booze. It wasn't the old country, but it was as reasonable a facsimile as he was likely to find on the shores of the Pacific.

He could introduce Vanessa to all those things, too, and show her off to his friends. She rode the bus down there every chance she got. When she landed a job, she told herself, she would drive. In the meantime, she had better things than gasoline to spend her money on.

She'd fallen in love with a guy she knew in high school—in love enough for him to pop her cherry, anyhow. She'd been living with him when she met Bryce. And then, in short order, she'd fallen in love with Bryce and was living with him. She really had thought that would last. For a while, she had. For a while, it had, too. She remembered telling him *If I can't make it with you, I can't make it with anybody*.

But she couldn't make it with him. How on earth could you get excited about, or even interested in, poetry written a million years ago in a dead language? When he did make brief forays into the real world, all he wanted to do was screw. He didn't want to go out to dinner, he didn't want to go shopping at the mall, he didn't care about movies, he didn't dance.

He did go to the occasional baseball game. He approached baseball the same way he approached his ancient poetry: as an archaeological problem. Vanessa's interest in sports was almost as great as her interest in spiders.

So—Hagop. She hadn't fallen in love with him, no matter how much she'd tried to tell herself she had. He was a lifeline when she got sick of boring Bryce. If only she hadn't followed him to Denver . . .

Well, now she was starting to think even that might have been worthwhile. If she hadn't gone to Denver, she wouldn't have been coming back to L.A. from the east and stopped in at that Denny's outside Las Cruces. She never would have met Bronislav Nedic.

And that, obviously, would have been the biggest tragedy since Shakespeare hung up his quill pen. Bronislav made her happy in ways she hadn't even imagined before they met. She wasn't used to being happy. She still complained, but her heart wasn't always in it.

In self-defense, she'd learned bits and pieces about Hellenistic poetry. She'd learned bits and pieces about the rug business, too—mostly about how everybody who had anything to do with it was the biggest robber not currently residing in San Quentin.

And she learned from Bronislav, too. They were walking along a street not far from the harbor when she saw a restaurant with way too many consonants in the name. Nobody from the former Yugoslavia seemed to have heard of Vanna White. "Is that place any good?" she asked, pointing.

His expressive eyebrows came down and pushed together in

the center. "I don't know," he said. Plainly, he didn't care for the question.

Vanessa couldn't see why he didn't like it. "Shall we find out, then?" she said.

"No." Bronislav picked up his pace to hurry past the restaurant.

Vanessa had to almost trot to catch up with him; his legs were longer than hers. "Why not?" she demanded when they were level again.

He stopped short—so short that she took an extra step and a half past him and had to turn back, feeling foolish. He was angry. No, he was furious. She needed a couple of seconds to realize how furious he was. Unlike hers, his rage burned cold. "The people who run that place, they are not Serbs. They are Croats," he said.

By the way the last three words came out, they might as well have been *They are baby-butchering, carrion-eating filth*. Vanessa didn't get it. "So?" she said. She knew just enough about the old, deceased Yugoslavia to recall that almost everybody in it had spoken a language called Serbo-Croatian. If both groups had used it—and they must have, or they wouldn't have given it their names—how different could they be?

She proceeded to ask Bronislav that very question. He stared at her for close to half a minute with those disconcertingly sharp eyes. At last, he said, "You are an American." He spoke softly and with great care, as if reminding himself. Vanessa got the feeling that that was just what he was doing.

It pissed her off, because the way he said it meant *You don't know jack shit*. "You are, too," she reminded him—he'd already told her, more than once, that he was a U.S. citizen, and that he was proud of it. "What's so awful about Croats?"

He patted his left arm with his right hand. "They gave me this." Then he stretched out his right arm so his cross-and-four-

C's tattoo came all the way out from under his sleeve. "If I go in there and they see this"—he tapped the tat with his left forefinger— "maybe we just fight. Or maybe they kill me, or I kill them."

He spoke as matter-of-factly as if he were talking about the chances of rain tomorrow. That made what he was saying more scary, not less. "Why?" Vanessa asked. She wasn't used to feeling out of her depth, but she sure did now.

Bronislav gave her *why*, in great detail. He hated Croats with the bitter passion someone could only feel for a close relative. She tried to imagine hating her little half-brother that way, tried and felt herself failing.

Bronislav had no trouble at all. He hated the Croats because he was Orthodox and they were Catholic. He hated them because they used the Roman alphabet and he used the Cyrillic. He hated them because he used hard vowels while they used soft ones.

"Say what?" Vanessa asked—that one meant nothing to her, not as a reason to hate and not at all. Nothing. Zilch.

"For *milk*, they say *mleeyehko*." Bronislav said the word very slowly, and looked as if he wanted to wash his mouth out with soap while he did it. "We say *mlehko*. You see the difference? You hear, I mean?"

"Yes, but—"

He talked through her answer: "*Mleeyehko*. Peh!" He spat on the sidewalk in disgust. "It is how fairies talk."

That was even less PC than her old man. Then Bronislav talked about how, during the war, the Croats had jumped into bed with Hitler with open legs. They'd tried to murder everybody they could reach who wasn't a Croat, and they'd done a damn good job of it. If you listened to Bronislav, the Croat irregulars, the Ustasha, had been vicious enough to horrify the Gestapo.

"And the Croats, they still have Ustasha today," Bronislav said. "They are as bad as their grandfathers were, too. I fight—

fought—them in Eastern Slavonia. It is part of the Serb home-land that the Croats stole when they ran out of Yugoslavia. They always steal everything they can grab, Croats."

"What would they say about Serbs?" Vanessa asked, perhaps incautiously.

With great dignity, Bronislav replied, "I do not know. I do not care. Whatever it is, it would be a lie."

They didn't eat at the Croat-run restaurant. Where there was one, though, there were bound to be more. Vanessa wondered if she'd already seen some and assumed they belonged to Serbs. Did all the Serbs and Croats in San Pedro feel about each other the way Bronislav felt about the people from the other side of the tracks or the border or whatever you wanted to call it?

She didn't ask him. She didn't think she wanted to know badly enough to put up with another frozen explosion. And he'd intimidated her. She didn't realize that till she was riding home on the bus the next morning. Even after she did realize it, she didn't want to admit it to herself. But it was true.

XIX

Even these days, sometimes you really wanted a car if you could possibly get hold of one. Colin didn't care to think about taking Kelly to San Atanasio Memorial on his bike when she went into labor. Bringing the baby back that way didn't seem any too practical, either. The bus also wasn't the best bet. Talk about jumping on the kid's immune system with both feet!

And so he made damn sure the Taurus was in decent working order well before the due date. As it had when he went to Officer McClintock's funeral, the mere act of driving felt funny. It wasn't that he'd forgotten how or anything; he hadn't. But it wasn't part of his routine any more.

"I don't take it for granted the way I did once upon a time," he told Kelly when he pulled into the driveway after taking the car to Jiffy Lube for a tuneup. Then he nodded to himself. That was a big part of the change he'd noticed, all right.

Kelly nodded with him. She knew what he was talking about; it wasn't as if she'd driven to CSUDH every day before she went on maternity leave. "I bet they were glad to see you when you rolled in," she remarked.

"Oh, boy, were they ever," Colin said. "They sure don't do the kind of business they used to. We thought gas was expensive before the eruption? Lord! What did we know?"

"Who can afford it now, except for something special?" Kelly agreed. She set one hand on the shelf of her belly. She had quite a shelf to set it on. It wouldn't be much longer.

"I was shooting the breeze with the manager while they were working on the car," Colin said. "Probably lucky I went in when I did. Their parent company is talking about filing for bankruptcy."

"How many more people will that throw out of work?" she asked.

"I don't know. Manager wasn't happy about it, I'll tell you that. I guess he'd be one of them."

San Atanasio Memorial, by contrast, was part of one of the few industries the supervolcano hadn't ruined. People got sick and broke bones and had babies after the eruption, just as they had before. If anything, they got sick more often than they had before, thanks to extra lung problems and more hunger and colder weather coupled with less heat.

Unlike most of America, the hospital had power all the time. It was heated to sixty-five degrees, which felt tropical to Colin. Such extravagance cost, of course. He thanked heaven for the good medical plan that went along with his line of work. Without it . . . Without it, he might have been filing for bankruptcy along with Jiffy Lube.

He'd stayed with Louise when all three of their children were born. Now he tried to coach Kelly through the breathing exercises she'd practiced getting ready for the day. He hadn't told her that they'd done Louise no good he could see. Everybody was different. They were supposed to help some women have an easier time.

It wasn't fun for her. He hadn't figured it would be. They

called it labor for a reason. Louise had been younger than Kelly was now when Marshall was born. Then again, she'd had James Henry, too, and she was quite a bit older then. It could be done.

Done it was, after nine tough hours. In the process, Kelly called Colin some things he hadn't suspected she knew how to say. As things turned serious, she also yelled, "I'm shitting a goddamn bowling ball!" That one cracked up the maternity-ward nurses, who evidently hadn't heard everything after all.

The bowling ball turned out to weigh eight pounds one ounce and measure twenty-one and a half inches. Colin cut the umbilical cord after the doctor tied it off. He'd done that with his older children, too. The feel of the surgical scissors slicing through that finger-thick cord was like nothing else he'd ever known. He'd always thought that that cut ought to hurt the mother or the baby or maybe both of them, but it never seemed to.

Deborah Michelle Ferguson rooted at Kelly's breast when the nurse set her there after she went on the scale. "How are you, babe?" Colin asked.

"Hammered," she answered. Even though it wasn't warm in the delivery room, greasy sweat made her face shine under the fluorescent lights and matted her hair. "I want to sleep for a month." Her mouth twisted into a wry, weary grin. "I know—good luck."

"Well, I wasn't gonna say that," Colin told her.

"No, but you were thinking it." Kelly's gaze traveled down to the little pink critter in the crook of her left elbow. "I've got milk! How about that? Me and Elsie the Borden Cow."

"Elsie's got milk," a nurse said. "For the next couple of days, you've got colostrum. That's what the baby needs right now."

"Uh-huh," Kelly said. "The supervolcano probably took care of Elsie, anyway. Didn't quite get me."

"Elsie's still around. She'll last as long as she moves milk and cheese and glue and whatever," Colin said. "After that, she's short ribs."

"Short ribs! Oh, my God! I just realized how hungry I am! That's hard work to do on an empty stomach!" Kelly's eyes swung toward the nurse in appeal. "What can I eat? When can I eat it?"

"We'll bring you a tray after we take you back to your room. Dinner tonight is sliced chicken breast, boiled potatoes and gravy, and stewed carrots and raisins. Jell-O for dessert," the nurse answered.

Colin thought that sounded much too much like hospital food. Kelly exclaimed, "Wow! It sounds wonderful!" She was ready to eat a horse and chase the guy who'd been riding it.

"I'm gonna call Marshall and Vanessa and your folks," Colin said. He leaned down and kissed Kelly on the forehead. She tasted sweaty, too. He also kissed his new daughter, who paid no attention to him whatsoever.

"Mazel tov!" Stan Birnbaum said when he heard the news. Kelly's father relayed it to her mother. Colin could hear Miriam Birnbaum burst into tears before she got on the line.

"Awesome!" was Marshall's comment, which would do for an English rendering of mazel tov. "Tell Kelly I'll spoil the little brat rotten. Woohoo!"

Vanessa sounded more restrained than her brother: "Congratulations, Dad. They're both all right?"

"They sure are," he answered proudly. "And the old father isn't doing too bad right now, either."

"Okay," she said. If he was on Cloud Nine, she was on Cloud Three—Three and a Half, tops. She got off the phone fast enough to annoy him. What was she doing? Waiting for an important call instead? To her right now, the Serbian hit man or whatever the hell he was would probably qualify.

Sighing, Colin called Gabe Sanchez. "You're a lucky bastard, you know that?" Gabe said as soon as he heard that mother and daughter were doing well.

"Thought had crossed my mind," Colin admitted.

"I'm jealous, is what I am." Gabe was bound to be kidding on the square. His own love life hadn't been nearly so fortunate as Colin's since his divorce. And the divorce itself was nastier than the one Colin went through. *They said it couldn't be done,* Colin thought, *but what the hell did they know?* Gabe went on, "I'll let the rest of the troops know."

"Thanks, buddy," Colin told him.

He went back to the room Kelly was sharing with a gal who was about to have twin boys. The mere idea was plenty to make him cringe. He pulled the curtain around Kelly's bed to give them the illusion of privacy. No sooner had he got there than an Asian gal from the kitchen carried in a tray.

"Food!" Kelly cried, like stout Cortez or Balboa or whoever it really was discovering the Pacific. Only the conquistador didn't make the ocean disappear. The way Kelly inhaled the hospital dinner was a sight to behold. She gulped the apple juice that went with it, too. Then she delivered her verdict: "That was the best lousy meal I've ever had."

Colin actually knew what she meant. He didn't tell her so, for fear she wouldn't believe him. But hard work and crappy chow in his Navy days made him understand.

A nurse brought in the baby, wrapped in a pink blanket. "You can have it sleep by you tonight if you want," she said. "Or we can just bring it in when it needs feeding."

"Do that, please," Kelly said. She'd been all for keeping the kid by her side through the night till Colin talked her out of it with tales of how frazzled Louise had been after doing that with Rob.

"Okeydoke," the nurse said now. "Might as well get what sleep you can, dear."

"Right," Kelly said. After the nurse went away, she muttered, "If I get any sleep at all on this miserable hospital mattress." She punctuated that with a yawn. "If I can't sleep on it tonight, I never will."

"Hope you do," Colin said.

"Tonight. Tomorrow night. Then I go home, and the fun really starts," Kelly said.

"We'll manage," Colin told her.

"You already know what you're doing. You've done it before. For me, it'll all be on-the-job training." Kelly rolled her eyes. "Christ, Marshall knows more about taking care of babies than I do. He's sure had more practice."

"We'll manage," Colin said again. "And you'll do great." He believed that right down to his toes. Kelly wasn't as aggressively organized in everything she took on as he was. But whatever she tried, she did a good job at it. He couldn't imagine motherhood being any different.

Louise Ferguson and James Henry walked into the Carrows on Reynoso Drive. "Hello," said the smiling young woman who seated people. "One and a high chair?"

"Two and a high chair," Louise answered, looking around. "We're meeting somebody, but I don't see her yet."

"Okay. Come this way, please." The young woman took her and James Henry to a table. "Is this all right?"

"Sure," Louise lied. She'd sat at this table when she told him she was pregnant with James Henry right after Teo skipped on her. She couldn't remember a less pleasant lunchtime, even if the BLT had been pretty good. But ingrained politeness kept her from asking to sit somewhere else. *Death before being difficult* might have appeared as the motto on her family crest.

She held her son on her lap till a Hispanic kid brought the high chair. She wondered if he was legal, and how closely Carrows checked. Just closely enough to keep from getting into hot water with Immigration, odds were. A waitress brought a menu for her and a children's menu for James Henry. She also doled out a couple of crayons so he could color on it.

"Thank you," he said gravely.

The waitress blinked, then grinned. "You're welcome! You're a *good* boy."

"He is," Louise agreed. It was true, no matter how much he'd complicated her life. Her own smile faded when she looked at the prices. She hadn't been here for a while—not since she lost her job at the ramen works. *It's just Carrows, for crying out loud, not Wolfgang Puck,* she thought. But when groceries were hideously expensive and energy even further through the roof, what could you expect?

Even if it brought back those bad memories, the BLT was one of the cheaper things she could get. Pork hadn't gone up as much as beef and lamb. Plenty, but not as much. On the kids' menu, chicken nuggets were also less outrageous than the cheeseburger. Outrageous, yeah, but less so.

Now—where had Vanessa got to? Louise hadn't seen her since she got back to Southern California. Vanessa had a habit of running late. Louise had had that habit, too, but Colin cured her of it. A cop had to stay on time, and he made her do the same thing. She hadn't slipped too badly since leaving him.

"Are you ready to order, ma'am?" the waitress asked.

"Not for me, not yet, but could you get him the nuggets and fries, and apple juice to go with 'em?"

"I'll do that." The waitress hurried away.

Louise wondered why. The place wasn't crowded. Were there any crowded restaurants left in the whole country? If what Carrows had to charge was any indication, there wouldn't be. Louise also wondered if she would even recognize Vanessa. She hadn't seen her daughter since before the eruption. She hadn't seen Rob in even longer, but neither had Colin, so that didn't count the same way.

The waitress delivered the nuggets and fries and juice. James Henry started slaughtering them. He wasn't neat—what little kid is?—but he wasn't fussy, either. All of Louise's other kids had been. Maybe this straightforward voracity came from Teo. It would be nice if something good did.

Here was Vanessa, across the grassy strip in front of the restaurant. She'd cut her hair short. It didn't fall past her shoulders, the way she'd always worn it before. Maybe that was what made her look harder, tougher, than Louise remembered.

When Vanessa walked into the Carrows, Louise waved. Her daughter waved back and came over to the table. Louise decided the haircut wasn't what made her look tougher after all. It was something in the line of her jaw and, even more, something in her eyes.

No matter what it was, Louise got up and hugged her. "Good to see you!" she said.

"Good to be seen," Vanessa answered. That was such a Colin thing to come out with, it cooled half of Louise's pleasure at the meeting. But then Vanessa added, "Hi, Mom," and you couldn't go very far wrong with that. She eyed James Henry. "So, this is the new kid, huh?"

"This is James Henry," Louise agreed. As Vanessa sat down, Louise went on, "James Henry, do you know who this is?"

"A lady," her son said, a fry twitching at the corner of his mouth the way a cigarette would have in Gabe Sanchez's.

"She's not just any lady. She's Vanessa, your big, big sister, the way Marshall is your big, big brother."

"Oh." James Henry digested that—and more of the french fry. "Is she gonna babysit me, too?"

"Well, I don't know. We'll have to wait and see," Louise answered.

"This is all too bizarre," Vanessa said. "I come back to SoCal and I've got a little brother and a tiny sister. I mean, bizarre."

"That's right. Kelly had her baby," Louise said. "How is she?"

"Kelly's okay," Vanessa answered. "The baby is noisy. Like a yowling cat, only more annoying."

So were you, dear. Before Louise could even think about saying it, the waitress came back. Louise did order the BLT, in memory of lost time. That was the name of a book, a book she hadn't read. She didn't suppose she was likely to start it now, either. Vanessa, unburdened by memories of sitting at this table before, chose the fried chicken.

In the end, Louise did ask, "And how are you getting along with Colin's new wife?"

"Okay, I guess." By the way Vanessa's mouth narrowed, it wasn't all that okay. She went on, "She's pretty boring, if you want to know what I think. I mean, unless you're talking about geology or something. And geology doesn't get my rocks off—not even close."

Louise needed a second to realize that was a pun. She sent Vanessa a reproachful look. The kids got that kind of bad joke from their father, too. Did that mean James Henry wouldn't do such horrible things when he got bigger? She could hope so, anyhow.

When the food came, she discovered that the BLT wasn't just like the one she'd had on that bad day with her ex. That one had been on wheat, before wheat got very scarce indeed. This one came on rye, and not the kind of rye they'd had before the eruption. It was more like chewy flatbread than slices off a proper loaf. It wasn't terrible, but it was definitely different.

"How's yours?" she asked Vanessa—the batter coating on the fried chicken wasn't the color it would have been in the good old days, either.

But her daughter answered, "Hey, it's fresh food. I'm not

gonna complain. After all the MREs I've eaten, I bet I've got more preservatives in me than the stuffed animals at the museum."

"Isn't that something?" Louise said, to cover her own surprise. In her experience, Vanessa could always complain about something or somebody. Maybe the time she'd spent in Camp Constitution had done her some good after all.

Louise knew better than to say anything like that. Vanessa would only indignantly deny it. Vanessa was always sure she was fine the way she was, thankyouverymuch.

So Louise tried, "Had any luck finding a job?" She confidently expected to hear a no; she sure hadn't had any luck herself. Then they could commiserate, and piss and moan about the miserable state of the world.

But Vanessa answered, "I think so. Looks as though Nick Gorczany wants me back at his widget works." She added something else, too low for Louise to catch.

"I'm sorry. What was that?" Louise cupped a hand behind her ear. Sure as hell, her hearing was starting to go. She hated that. It was one more sign she was getting old, and off God's warranty.

Vanessa's eyes flicked to James Henry. He'd scarfed down his lunch and was busy coloring some more. He couldn't have cared less. Vanessa repeated herself, a little louder this time: "I *said*, I didn't even have to screw him to get him to offer me the job."

"Oh." Vanessa sounded uncomfortable, and she was. Said one way, that would have been the kind of sour joke women made when they talked about the pains of living in a world with men in it. But Vanessa hadn't said it that way, or Louise didn't think she had. Hesitantly, Louise asked, "You're not kidding, are you?"

"Christ, I wish I were!" her daughter said. Vanessa stabbed at the chicken thigh on her plate as if she were imagining a bigger, sharper knife piercing a different flesh. She chewed savagely and gulped ice water. Just when Louise decided she didn't intend to go on, she did: "You do what you've gotta do, that's all. We didn't know how good we had it before the supervolcano erupted, and you can sing that in church, Mom. Life sucks now. Yeah, life sucks, and sometimes we've got to do the same goddamn thing." She looked away, her eyes full of rage.

"Do you . . . want to talk about it? To get in touch with your feelings?" Louise had always believed getting in touch with your feelings was the best thing you could possibly do. She sure hadn't been in touch with hers through most of her marriage to Colin. Once she was, she got away. She got free. She found brand-new love, brand-new delight.

She also found single parenthood in middle age. There sat James Henry, happily coloring away. Well, anything you did in this old world was liable to have consequences. And wasn't that the sad and sorry truth!

Vanessa shook her head, sharply enough to make Louise sure that gesture, like the way her daughter cut the chicken, was full of suppressed violence. "No, I don't want to talk about it," Vanessa answered. "And even if I did, you wouldn't want to hear about it. Trust me on that one. What I *want* is to forget it ever happened. But you can't always get what you want, can you?"

Louise thought of the Stones song. It was an oldie to her. To Vanessa, it would be from as deep in the past as "Stardust" or "Camptown Races." From before she was born. What could be deeper in the past than that?

"Well, what *do* you want to talk about?" Louise asked.

Her daughter's features softened a little. "I've got a new boy-friend," Vanessa said. "This may be the real deal."

"Tell me about him," Louise urged. Vanessa had been sure Hagop was the real deal, sure enough to go to Colorado to be with him. Before that, she'd been just as sure about Bryce (since

Bryce and Colin had stayed friends, Louise was anything but sure about him). And before Bryce, she'd gone on and on about how she was going to have her high school boyfriend's babies. What was his handle? Peter, that was it. Louise hadn't thought about him in years. Colin hadn't been able to stand him, which made Louise recall him more kindly now.

"His name is Bronislav—Bron, if you have trouble with it. He's been in the States for close to twenty years. He still has an accent, but his English is really good. He's got amazing eyes. Eyes like a saint's in a painting, all big and brown," Vanessa said.

"What does he do?" Louise asked. *St. Bronislav?* she wondered, but only to herself. Vanessa had never talked about any of the other men in her life in those terms—for sure she hadn't.

"He's a long-haul trucker here, but back in Yugoslavia he was a freedom fighter," her daughter said.

A freedom fighter is a terrorist we like. Louise could hear Colin's voice inside her head. He'd probably been talking back to some politician or other jerk on the TV when he said that. She didn't quote him to Vanessa. For one thing, she would rather have passed a kidney stone. For another, even if she had wanted to do any such thing, her daughter wouldn't have listened. She didn't need to be Henry Kissinger to understand that much about diplomacy.

"He really was," Vanessa said, as if Louise *had* spoken up. "The Croats over there, they were a bunch of filthy Fascist thugs. And the Bosnians were just like the Taliban."

Louise knew little about the woes of the ex-Yugoslavia, and cared less. She did wonder what the Whozits and the Waddaya-callems would have said about Bronislav's cause—but not enough to antagonize Vanessa by inquiring. Some questions were more trouble than the answers were worth.

"And you know what else?" Vanessa added.

"No. What?" Louise said.

Had Vanessa announced that her new squeeze had a neck-lace of human ears he'd brought from the old country, she wouldn't have been surprised. When Vanessa said, "He's a ter-rific cook, that's what," she was—surprised enough to burst into laughter.

Vanessa looked irate. "I'm sorry," Louise said. She meant it; good manners mattered to her. "But I wasn't expecting that."

"Well, he is," Vanessa insisted, as if Louise had tried to deny it. "He makes better stuff than the chefs at the Serb places down in San Pedro."

"If you say so." Louise hadn't known there were Serb places down there. She couldn't remember the last time she'd gone to Speedro. To shop at Ports of Call Village before the eruption, probably. Except for Ports of Call, what reason would she have had to go there? It wasn't one of L.A.'s better neighborhoods, which was putting things mildly.

"I do." Vanessa knew what she knew. What she knew wasn't always so, but she knew it anyway.

"Dear, I hope you're happy. I hope everything works out just the way you want it to." Louise did hope so. She'd hoped so every single time. Vanessa threw herself headlong into life, the way she threw herself headlong into all kinds of things. And she threw herself out of love as abruptly as she dove in. She wasn't made for halfway measures.

When the waitress brought the check, Vanessa grabbed it. Louise squawked. Her heart wasn't in it, but not even the com-mittee that handed out best-actress Oscar nominations would have realized as much. Vanessa didn't listen to her. That wasn't rare, but the effect this time came out nicer than usual.

"Don't worry about it, Mom," she said. "I've got work lined up for myself, and you're still looking. When you find something, you can take me out to celebrate."

"Well, thank you very much," Louise said. Vanessa'd even

let her down without costing her face. What was the world coming to?

"Thank you very much," James Henry agreed, looking up from his abstract expressionist masterpiece. Louise and Vanessa both laughed. Louise ruffled her little son's black hair. Even Vanessa's meeting with him had gone off better than she'd expected. A good day, all the way around.

Marshall Ferguson and his friends kept getting together to play Diplomacy. They all had a better idea of what they were doing now than they had when Lucas' father first brought the box out of the closet. Today, Austria-Hungary and Russia were ganging up on Turkey—if the Ottomans got loose, they had a way of metastasizing through the Mediterranean. Germany and France were trying to do the same number on England, which could be even more dangerous. But Marshall, who was playing perfidious Albion, talked Italy into stabbing France in the kidneys.

So he was doing all right for himself. Tim had Turkey this game. He found a way to save the sultan's bacon that wasn't in the rules. Just when things looked blackest, he pulled out a fat baggie of what looked like killer dope. Experiments immediately followed. It not only looked like killer dope, it *was* killer dope.

It was such killer dope, in fact, that everybody stopped caring about who wound up top dog in Europe. Marshall stopped caring about almost everything. Almost, but not quite. "Dude," he said languidly, "where'd you score such righteous shit?"

Tim giggled. Giggling was a hazard with what they'd just smoked, but Marshall wanted to know. It wasn't urgent—nothing was urgent, or would be for a while—but he did want to. When he asked again, Tim giggled some more.

"C'mon, man," Marshall said. "Dope like this is hard to come by these days." The supervolcano had done the same number on weed as it had on so many other cash crops. Climates that had been just right were suddenly too cold, and production in areas that went from too hot to just right hadn't ramped up yet. So good dope was indeed hard to come by.

But that turned out not to be why Tim was giggling—or not the only reason, anyhow. He also wasn't giggling just because he was stoned out of his tree, although he was. "You sure you want to know? You really, truly sure? Really-o, truly-o sure?"

"Talk, already." Marshall would have got mad if it didn't seem like too much trouble. "I don't want the trailer. I want the fuckin' movie."

He set everybody laughing, Tim included. "Okay, okay," Tim said. "Just remember, you asked for it. You wanna know where I got the shit? I got it from Darren Shitcabbage, man. How funny is *that*?"

Most of the erstwhile would-be masters of early twentieth-century Europe thought it was the funniest thing they'd heard in their entire lives, or at least since they got baked. Lucas damn near wet his pants, he thought it was so hysterical. "The chief's kid, dealing dope?" he said. "Oh, wow! That is too much, I mean way too much." He nudged Marshall. "How come you don't do that?"

Marshall smoked dope. Marshall bought dope. It wasn't as if he didn't support his local dealers. But he'd never had the slightest urge to move into the supply end of the business. You started getting into heavy shit when you did that, and dealing with some highly unpleasant people. From what he knew about Chief Pitcavage's son, Darren had himself a head start on that.

His old man wished he would have drawn his line closer to truth, justice, and the Drugs Are Wicked American Way. Marshall didn't draw it there, no matter what his father wished. But he did draw a line. Darren Pitcavage didn't seem to.

Marshall fired himself another fatty. If he got wasted enough, maybe he wouldn't remember any of this tomorrow. If he didn't remember it, he wouldn't have to figure out what to do about it, or whether to do anything at all about it.

He did remember. He'd known he would, no matter how much he smoked. You lost things for a while with weed—sometimes, anyway. But they mostly came back. He'd never been into drugs that bit chunks out of your life and swallowed them for good.

If he'd liked Darren Pitcavage better . . . If his father had liked Chief Pitcavage better . . . He still needed a couple more days to work up his nerve to go, "Dad?"

"What?" His father sounded distracted, and was—he was changing Deborah's diaper.

"Um—you know I went to Lucas' place over the weekend to play Diplomacy, right?"

"Yeah. How'd it go?" Dad had learned the game. He and Marshall sometimes played a cutthroat two-man version with a much newer copy of the game than the one Lucas' dad had resurrected. Each of them controlled three countries, with weak sister Italy vacant. No real diplomacy in that variant, but it was great for testing board maneuvers.

"We, mm, kind of got sidetracked after a while. Tim—" Marshall had to stop while Dad snorted and snickered. Dad never had been able to take Tim seriously, not even for a minute. Licking his lips, Marshall made himself go on, "Tim brought out some weed, some fine weed, and—"

"Now tell me something I didn't know," his father broke in. "Your clothes smelled like a hemp farm outside of Veracruz."

How Dad knew what a hemp farm outside of Veracruz smelled like . . . was a question for another day. And he hadn't even squeaked about the way Marshall's clothes smelled till Marshall raised the subject. *Discretion, from my old man?* Marshall wouldn't have believed it if he hadn't seen it with his own eyes. But there it was.

"Dad . . ." There was something in Shakespeare that Marshall couldn't quite recall about doing it quickly if you were gonna do it. He brought the words out in a rush: "Dad, he bought the shit off Darren Pitcavage."

Marshall's father held Deborah in the crook of his elbow. Even so, all at once it wasn't Dad standing there any more. It was Lieutenant Colin Ferguson, in full cop mode. "Tell me that again. I want to make sure I heard it straight." Most unhappily, Marshall repeated himself. His father took a few seconds to work things through, his face as expressionless as a computer monitor while the CPU crunched numbers on a big spreadsheet. Then he asked, "How much dope are we talking about here?"

"Tim had, like, I dunno, a few ounces," Marshall answered. "Like, enough to get us loaded but not enough to go into business for himself."

"Okay," his father said. To Marshall's amazement and relief, it did seem okay; Dad wasn't going to give him the sermon out of *Reefer Madness*. Instead, his father went on, "Did Tim say whether Darren Pitcavage was in business for himself? Or was this one friend selling some to another friend?"

Marshall had to think back. "Um, Tim didn't say one way or the other. But I know for a fact he's not tight with Darren or anything. He was, like, cracking up on account of he was buying dope from the police chief's kid."

"Uh-*huh*," his father said.

The grim finality in that almost-word made alarms blare in Marshall's head. "Dad," he said urgently, "for God's sake don't drop on him. If you do, he'll know I talked to you, and—" He didn't—he couldn't—go on.

For a wonder, he didn't have to draw his father a picture. "Nobody loves a snitch," Dad said. Marshall managed a nod. Dad continued, "But when somebody knows something important and he keeps quiet about it, a lot of the time that's worse." He waited.

Marshall nodded again—not with any great enthusiasm, but he did. Dad set a hand on his shoulder, and Dad was anything but a touchy-feely guy. "This may be that kind of important. I don't know for sure that it is, but I think I'd better find out."

"Try not to drag Tim's name into it," Marshall said again. "And—" He stopped short once more.

"Try not to drag yours in, too?" his father finished for him.

"Yeah." Marshall hated the dull embarrassment in his own voice.

"Darren Pitcavage is a nasty piece of work, no matter what his father does for a living," Dad said. "If it weren't for his father, I think we would've taken him off the streets a while ago. Well, maybe better late than never."

"If you say so." Marshall wasn't sure of that, or of anything else.

XX

Colin Ferguson contemplated ways and means of busting his boss' son without making it look like a coup d'état inside the San Atanasio Police Department. The more he contemplated, the gloomier he got. The case would have to be dead-bang, one hundred percent airtight. And it would have to get made without Mike Pitcavage's finding out it was even cooking.

Because if the chief did find out, something else would cook instead. Colin knew what, too: his own goose.

If, of course, there was a case. If Darren had sold Tim a few ounces and that was the only time he'd ever seen that side of the business, that was one thing. But if he'd sold a few ounces to a good many Tims, Dicks, and Harrys, that was something else again. That was a serious felony, was what it was.

If. Marshall didn't know for certain. Maybe Tim didn't know for certain. (Colin suspected Tim didn't know anything for certain, the alphabet very possibly included.) But the vibe was that Darren Pitcavage was doing some real dealing.

Do I want to put my neck on the block because of the vibe? Yes, that was the question, much more than *To be or not to be?*

Or Colin thought it was at first. Then he realized they were one and the same, only his version wasn't in iambic pentameter.

It was well before noon when he walked over to Gabe Sanchez's desk and said, "Let's go Code Seven."

Gabe blinked. "Early," he remarked, but then he patted his midsection. "Hey, I can always eat. Where you wanna go?"

"How about the Verona?" Colin suggested.

"Kind of a ways," Gabe said. And it was—the old-fashioned Italian place was closer to Colin's house than to the station. That was why he wanted to go there: he didn't want other cops overhearing him. He couldn't very well say that here. A clenched jaw and a raised eyebrow got some kind of message across—Gabe stood up with no more argument. "Well, I'm game. What's it doing outside?"

"We'll both find out."

It was chilly and cloudy, but not raining. Gabe lit a cigarette. They climbed onto their bicycles and pedaled off. Colin did a good deal of talking on the way. No one except Gabe could hear him then.

He finished just before they got to the Verona. "What do you think?" he asked.

"Holy shit," Gabe said.

Colin chuckled—not in any happy way. "Yeah, I figured that out for myself, matter of fact."

"I bet you did!" Gabe exclaimed. "You better watch who you talk to, too. Word gets back and you're walking around without your nuts."

"That also crossed my mind," Colin said. They went inside. The Verona was a refugee from the 1950s, with red-checked tablecloths, candles stuck in Chianti bottles (often useful now, not just for show), and posters of the Leaning Tower of Pisa and the Colosseum on the walls. They made spaghetti and meatballs, lasagna, ravioli—stuff like that. And they had a wood-fired pizza oven, so they stayed open even when the power went out.

Colin and Gabe decided to split a medium sausage pizza. The dough would be odd by pre-eruption standards. So would the cheese. The sausage would be pork or maybe chicken. By now, Colin made such adjustments almost automatically. Almost.

"I'll tell you who to go to," Gabe said when the pizza got there. "Talk to Rodney, man. He hates dealers with a passion, and he won't screw you."

"Even if it turns out to be nothing?" Colin said.

"Even then." Gabe took a bite from a slice of pizza. He chewed thoughtfully. "Could be worse. Could be better, too."

"Sure could," Colin agreed after a bite of his own. But he ate with more enthusiasm than he'd expected. The black detective had been on the mental list he was making, too—and, by the nature of things, that list wasn't very long.

He paid the tab. The cops unlocked their bikes from the little curbside trees to which they'd been chained. Gabe smoked another cigarette on the way back to the station. It started drizzling just as they got there. They hurried inside. Chief Pitcavage was gabbing with the uniformed officer at the front desk. He nodded amiably to Colin and Gabe. "Hey, guys. Wet outside?"

"Just a little, like it doesn't know whether to piss or get off the pot," Gabe answered. Colin was glad to let him do the talking. Dammit, he didn't have anything against Mike Pitcavage— except for raising a worthless kid and letting him decide he would get away with anything because his father was a bigwig in this town.

Pitcavage wouldn't think like that, of course. He'd think it was because he got the chief's badge and Colin didn't. Were things reversed between them, it would have been, too. Colin was positive of that.

He quietly checked which cases Rodney Ellis was working

on, then ambled over to his desk. "Want to talk with you about the witnesses to the robbery at that check-cashing place last Saturday," he said, as casually as he could.

"Well, okay," Rodney answered. That wasn't Colin's usual style, but it wasn't too far out of line, either. "Drag up a rock." He pointed to the beat-up chair by his desk.

"Let's do it in one of the interrogation rooms," Colin said. "Coupla things I want to bounce off you."

"However you want." Rodney got to his feet. He was solidly built, but moved as smoothly as the point guard he'd been in high school. They walked into one of the rooms. Colin closed the door behind them and glanced up at the camera near the ceiling to make sure the red light under the lens was off. He hadn't even sat down when the African-American detective asked, "What's really going on, man?"

"I've got a problem," Colin said. "Maybe you can give me a hand with it."

"I'm listening." Ellis showed no cards. Well, neither had Colin.

But he had to now. He had to if he was going to go anywhere with this, anyhow. He told Rodney what he'd heard from Marshall—what Marshall had heard from Tim, in other words. He named no names, though he was glumly aware Rodney would work out at least one of them without a hell of a lot of trouble.

When he finished, Rodney didn't say anything for close to a minute. Then, very softly, the other cop went, "Aw, shit, man."

Colin nodded. "Couldn't have put it better myself."

"It wasn't your kid who bought from Pitcavage Junior?" Sure as anything, Ellis could walk barefoot through the obvious.

"No, a friend of his. I've known, uh, him"—Colin almost said *Tim*—"since they were in high school. They kinda stopped handing out brains before the guy got to the front of the line, but

I'm pretty sure he wouldn't make up something like that for the fun of it. The way Marshall tells it, his buddy thought it was a big old joke."

"A joke. Uh-huh." Rodney didn't sound like somebody who was going to ROFL. "You believe this happened because your boy's friend says it did. You believe darling Darren's dealing." Those weren't questions, not the way he came out with them.

" 'Fraid so." Colin nodded again. He would rather have gone to Kelly's dentist father for a root canal without Novocaine, but he did. "Would I be talking about it with you if I didn't believe it?"

"Not fuckin' likely," Ellis answered, which was also the truth, the whole truth, and nothing but the truth. He eyed Colin. "What do you want to do about it?"

That was the $64,000 question, all right. Colin had been thinking of little else since his son gave him the unwelcome news. Sighing, he said, "Seems to me we've got to find out how deep Darren's in. If this was a onetime thing, if he scored more than he could use for a while and was selling some, then I guess we shine it on. But if he's *dealing* dealing, if you know what I mean . . ."

"Then we got to drop on him." Rodney didn't ask that, either—he said it. Colin made his head go up and down one more time. Rodney went on, "And whatever we do, we got to do it so Chief Mike doesn't know we're doin' it."

"Probably a good plan," Colin agreed, so dryly the other cop guffawed.

"I trot over to the chief's office now, man, you're fucked," the African-American detective said.

"Yeah, I know." Colin left it right there.

Ellis stared up at the acoustic tiles on the ceiling. He let out a sigh of his own. "And if I don't go to Pitcavage, if I start working this like it's a case, and he finds out, I'm fucked, too."

"I'm sorry. Shit, I'm sorry all kinds of ways," Colin said. "If you want to make like this entire conversation never happened, hey, I can see why you would. Long as you don't rat me out, I won't hold it against you."

"Wanna know something weird, Colin? I believe you," Rodney said. "Anybody else in the whole wide world'd be blowin' smoke up my ass. Pitcavage sure would, Lord knows. But you, I believe. Doesn't matter any which way, though, on account of I'm in. If Darren's dealing, he's got to pay the price, same as anybody else. Wasn't for his daddy, he woulda paid some prices a while ago by now. 'Bout time he finds out the rules don't have *except for you* in 'em anywhere."

"Looks that way to me, too," Colin said. He hadn't been so relieved since . . . since when? Since Kelly'd said she'd marry him—that was the only answer that crossed his mind. "Thanks, man," he added a moment later. He'd never been one for big shows of gratitude.

"It's cool, Colin." Yes, Rodney'd known him long enough to have a notion of how he ticked. "Anybody who deals, he ain't no friend of mine." He peered up at the ceiling again, as if trying to extract wisdom from the random patterns of holes in the tiles. "Talk about friends, though . . . We end up busting the chief's kid, this whole goddamn department'll go off like a grenade."

"That did occur to me, yeah," Colin said. "Be careful while you're working on it. Be careful who you pick to help you, too. You know the old line—three guys can keep a secret as long as two of 'em are dead."

"I didn't, but I like it." Thoughtfully, Ellis continued, "Not the only reason to be careful. Darren, he'll make a lot of cops. A couple of the brothers who haven't been here since dirt, maybe not. Let's hope he's one of the white guys who figure all black folks look alike."

"That's a bunch of bull, too," Colin said. "You don't look one damn bit like Halle Berry."

Rodney laughed. "Well, you got that right, anyway. Long as we're here, you wanna really talk about the robbery?"

"Sure. Let's do it," Colin said, so they did.

Deborah started to nurse. Kelly felt her milk let down. That was a sensation she'd never known—never even imagined—till she had the baby. Well, so was labor, but this was a lot more pleasant than that.

Deborah sucked and gulped, sucked and gulped. Then she tried to gulp when she should have been sucking or something, because she choked and swallowed wrong. The first time that happened, it had horrified Kelly. Now she got that it wouldn't kill her firstborn daughter. She pulled Deborah off the breast and hauled her up onto her own shoulder, patting her on the back till she could breathe easily again. It didn't take long. Then the baby went back to supper.

Kelly'd just switched her to the other side when her eyelids started to sag. Up on the shoulder she went once more. Kelly wanted to get a burp out of her before she crashed. She also checked the baby's diaper. Deborah was dry. That was good.

"Okay, kid, you can sack out now," Kelly said, rocking in the recliner. With luck, Deborah would stay sleep long enough for Kelly to make dinner, perhaps even long enough to let her eat it. That was bound to be against the babies' union regulations, but the local hadn't come down on Deborah yet.

The front door opened. Somebody was back from work: Colin or Vanessa. "Don't sl—" *Wham!* Too late. Deborah jerked and yelled. "Shit," Kelly muttered.

Vanessa sauntered into the front room from the foyer. "Aw, did I wake her?"

"Yeah, you did. Thanks a bunch." Kelly was too frazzled to stay cool; maybe that horseshit *Aw* had something to do with it. No, for sure it did. "I tried to tell you not to slam the goddamn door, but did you listen? Fat chance."

Vanessa blinked. Kelly'd done her best to play the easygoing stepmom—till now. "Well, excuse me, Ms. High-and-Mighty," Vanessa said. "Can I kiss your ring?"

"You can kiss my ass, Vanessa," Kelly said, meanwhile rocking to try to calm Deborah down again. "Now that somebody's been dumb enough to hire you, the sooner you get the hell out of here, the happier everybody else will be."

"Fuck you, too," Vanessa snarled. She stomped up the stairs and slammed the door to her bedroom, too.

Kelly's stomach churned. She didn't like fights. She didn't do them very well, or she didn't think she did. And she was damn glad she'd already nursed Deborah, because if she hadn't the baby would be chowing down on sour milk right this minute.

Deborah was just going back to sleep when Colin walked in. On the off chance that she might be, he closed the door quietly. When he walked into the front room, he stopped short. "Good God in the foothills!" he said. "I've seen guys we tased who didn't look so ready to bite holes in things. What did I do? Whatever it is, I'm sorry."

"*You* didn't do anything," Kelly said, and not another word.

"Uh-oh." Colin didn't need any fancy DNA analysis to work out what must have happened. "You and Vanessa fired away, huh?"

"Yeah, we did." Kelly sighed. She wasn't proud of it, not even slightly.

"What went on? Do I want to know?"

She told him. It didn't take long. She finished, "You go upstairs, you'll hear a different version, though, I bet."

"Uh-huh. Hearing a bunch of different stories comes with

being a cop. So does deciding which one you believe, or whether you believe any of them," Colin said, the corners of his mouth turning down. "I already have a notion about that, but I am gonna go upstairs." And he did, more slowly than Vanessa had. He knocked on her door. She said something. Kelly couldn't make out what, but Colin answered, "It's me," so she must have asked who was there. The door opened, then closed again.

Rocking Deborah, Kelly could hear Colin's voice and Vanessa's, but, once more, she couldn't follow what they were saying. By their tones, she counted herself lucky there. Then Vanessa was, in the classic Nixonian phrase, perfectly clear: "Get out of here! Everybody hates me!"

If she'd been thirteen, that kind of thing would have come with the territory. Kelly remembered screeching the same words in the same tone. But since Vanessa was more than twice thirteen . . .

The door to her room opened and closed again. Colin came down the stairs. His face held no expression at all. Kelly got to her own feet as fast as she could without bothering Deborah. The baby muttered, but her eyes stayed shut. "I'm sorry," Kelly said.

"Not your fault." Colin went into the kitchen. Kelly followed him. He got the Laphroaig bottle down from the top shelf of the pantry and poured himself three fingers' worth.

"I'm gonna put her in the crib. Fix me one, too, would you? Not quite that much," Kelly said.

He gave her a surprised look. "You don't drink this stuff."

"Tonight I do."

Deborah went into the crib with another mutter, but no more. Kelly hurried back to the kitchen. Colin handed her the dose of scotch. That was how she thought of it, all right. They clinked glasses. She drank. She still didn't see how he could enjoy the taste, but she wasn't drinking it for the taste. She was drinking it for the booze.

"How was the rest of your day?" she asked. "Better than this, I hope."

"Not so you'd notice," Colin answered. "Darren Pitcavage . . . deals everything this side of real estate and old Buicks. Setting up a buy is gonna be a piece of cake, looks like. Not just a felony bust—a big-time felony bust."

"I'm sorry." Kelly felt the inadequacy of words.

"Yeah, me, too." Colin's eyes slid toward the stairway. "But I'm not sorry Vanessa doesn't know thing one about this. Way she is right now, if she did she'd probably get hold of Darren and let him know we were looking at him."

"She wouldn't do that!" Kelly exclaimed.

"Oh, I think she might," Colin said.

"But that's illegal, isn't it?"

"Sure, if you get caught. Lots of things are illegal if you get caught."

"Mm," Kelly said. "Uh, does Marshall know not to talk with her about this?"

"Well, I haven't told him not to," Colin answered. "But I don't think he wants to talk about it with anybody. He wants to make like it never happened and he never had anything to do with it. And he doesn't talk to Vanessa any more than he has to, in case you didn't notice."

"I did," Kelly said. "I wondered if you had. Shows what I know, doesn't it?"

"She *will* get a place of her own pretty soon," Colin replied, which might or might not have been a non sequitur. "We'll all be happier once she does, too. She's okay in small doses—and she'll decide we're okay in small doses, too."

"I'm sorry," Kelly said once more.

He shrugged. "Nothing to be done about it. Yeah, she's prickly. But she's honest as the day is long. I don't have to worry that Mike's getting ready to come after her the way I'm going after Darren."

"That's so," Kelly said, which was as much praise as she felt like giving Vanessa just then. She changed the subject, or at any rate deflected it a little: "What will Mike do after you grab his son?"

"I'm not looking forward to that." By the way Colin set his jaw, he really wasn't looking forward to it. He went on, "When Darren got in trouble before, Mike always dickered it down to a misdemeanor. Five gets you ten he tries it again. But I don't care how hard he tries. Not a chance in church the DA will play along, not this time."

"Can he stay chief if his son gets arrested for something like this?" Kelly asked. Under that question lay another one, one she left unspoken. *If he does have to step down, will they offer you the job? Will you want it if they do?*

"I don't know. I don't think there's any rule that would *make* him quit, but it wouldn't be easy for him to go on like nothing was wrong." Colin also heard the underlying question, which surprised Kelly very little. He went on, "If he does resign, I wouldn't take the slot on a bet. No way, not after I went and knocked him off his perch. Besides, I don't want it any more."

He'd told Kelly the same thing before, and more than once. But when he'd told her before, he'd had about as much chance of being elected Pope as of being named Chief of the San Atanasio PD. If Mike Pitcavage did have to resign now, in offspring-induced disgrace, the city council and the DA and the other people who ran San Atanasio might well want to put him in charge of the department for a while so he could straighten it out and get it back on its feet.

And she could see how, with his strong sense of duty and responsibility, he'd be tempted to accept the job, at least as a caretaker. But his reasons for steering clear looked good to her. There was also one he hadn't mentioned: "If they did name you chief, you'd start telling them to piss up a rope in about three days. Or if you didn't, you'd want to so bad you'd explode like the super-volcano."

"I wouldn't tell 'em to do that in three days." Colin affected righteous indignation—brief righteous indignation. "I'd hold out for a week, easy. A week and a half, if everything went good."

Laughing and liking him very much in that moment, she gave him a hug. "Think so, do you?"

"Darn right I do." He laughed, too—again, though, not for long. "Mike, he can tell those people what they want to hear. What they need to hear, the way they need to hear it. That's an art. Honest to God, it is. I've watched him do it, and I've watched him get what he needs 'cause he can do it. When I realized he could and I can't—and you're dead right; I can't, not for beans—that was when I figured out I was barking up the wrong tree when I put in for chief to begin with."

"You're fine the way you are. Better than fine," Kelly said. "I'd rather have you than somebody who pats me on the back so he can feel where the best place to stick the knife is."

"Well, I'm glad you think so. Not everybody does—you don't believe me, all you've got to do is ask Louise." Colin let out another sharp, short chuckle. "And I make a pretty fair cop, if I do say so myself. But if you're gonna be chief, you have to know how to handle all the political stuff. I can't, and Mike Pitcavage can. If he's got to step down on account of his rotten kid, they'd better pick somebody a lot like him to take his place."

Kelly listened hard. She couldn't hear any rancor or bitterness. She thought she would have if they were there. Colin could hold things in, but only by keeping quiet about them. When he did talk, he meant what he said.

"I am sorry I had the row with Vanessa," Kelly said. Unlike

her husband, she wasn't altogether blind to the power of positive hypocrisy. "I wish it hadn't happened." That much was true. The rest? Maybe not quite.

"If she wants to give you a hard time, that's between her and you. Meeting my new wife and getting along with her, it can't be easy for a grown kid," Colin said.

"Marshall hasn't had any trouble I've seen," Kelly said tartly.

"Marshall's Marshall. He doesn't get himself in an uproar about stuff. Vanessa . . . does. She'll go to war over commas. Makes her a darn good editor. Makes her kind of a pain, too. And she's a woman, and so are you." Colin set a fond hand on the curve of her hip. But then he said, "That's not where I was going with this."

"Where were you going, then?" Kelly asked.

"If she gives you a hard time, that's her business, hers and yours," Colin said. "But if she gives a little tiny baby a hard time, that's a whole different ball game. That's being mean for the sake of being mean. She knew what she was doing when she slammed the front door, all right. I called her on it, too. She didn't like that very much."

He hadn't raised his voice. Kelly would have heard if he had. No, Vanessa was the one who'd started yelling. But Colin didn't need to make a lot of noise to get his message across. Kelly'd known that as long as she'd known him. Vanessa wouldn't have cared for his opinion, even delivered quietly.

"As long as it happens just the once, I'll forget about it," Kelly said.

"Sounds about right." There, Colin's agreement seemed reluctant. He went on, "Since she has landed a job, she will want a place of her own. She'll want one, and she'll get one." And if she had some not-so-discreet encouragement from her father to speed her on her way, that wouldn't bother Kelly a bit. *Not even half a bit,* Kelly thought as she started fixing dinner.

Dick Barber eyed Rob in mock reproach as they came up to the Episcopal church. Snow swirled through the air. It was one of the months with a vowel in it, so of course snow swirled. "The things some people will do to get out of climbing a ladder every time they want to go to bed," Barber said.

"Don't listen to him, Rob," Justin Nachman said. "Now that you're officially moving out of the tower, I'm gonna sublet it. I'll be rich, man. *Rich!* He chortled unwholesomely and rubbed his mittened hands together in gloating anticipation a ham Shylock would have envied.

"I wasn't listening to him. You don't need to worry about that," Rob answered. "Of course, I wasn't listening to you, either."

"Hey, there you go," Charlie Storer said. "Equal-opportunity discrimination."

Rob waited for the next smart-ass crack to come from Biff Thorvald. But Biff was less into them than his bandmates and the proprietor of the Trebor Mansion Inn. And he had more distractions. He was making sure his little son, Walter, didn't trip on the rough sidewalk. He was also shepherding Cindy along. His wife's belly bulged again. That made her balance less sure, but she at least knew enough to be careful. Walter wanted to go running all over creation. It wasn't as if he even walked very well, because he didn't. Toddlers always wanted to do more than they possibly could, though.

And this makes them different from other people how? Rob wondered.

Others going into the church waved to him and called congratulations. Some were people he knew in Guilford. Others—more—taught or worked at Piscataquis Community Secondary School with Lindsey.

"When was the last time you were in a church and it wasn't for a town meeting or something like that?" Barber asked.

"Oh, wow." Rob had to think about it. Like most of his family, he thought freedom of religion implied freedom from religion. Mom drifted from one New Age almost-faith to another, but Rob, like his father and sister and brother, pretty much did without. Then a memory came back. "My senior year in college, I went to a wedding at an old mission north of Santa Barbara. Don't jinx me—that one didn't last."

"This isn't a church wedding, anyway, even if it's in a church," Charlie said.

That was also true. They went into the church. Standing up at the front, instead of a minister in his clerical vestments, was Jim Farrell in his decidedly secular ones. The fedora and fur-trimmed topcoat set him apart from the crowd at least as well as a white dog collar would have.

The wedding was *the* event of the winter social season: from lack of competition, as Rob knew perfectly well. Lindsey's mother had come over from Dover-Foxcroft to attend. Her father had come down from Greenville—even farther—with his girlfriend. Said girlfriend was a smashing brunette, and was about Lindsey's age. Whether she'd caused the breakup between Lindsey's folk or come along afterwards, Rob didn't know. *Maybe I'll get the chance to ask later on,* he thought. For the moment, the atmosphere was what the diplomats called correct. With luck, it would stay that way.

Having winter guests in Guilford from such distant towns (Dover-Foxcroft was ten or fifteen miles away, Greenville about twenty-five) brought home to Rob how tightly his mental horizon had contracted since he came here. Guilford and its immediate environs were all that concerned him from day to day. News from other places north and west of the Interstate trickled in every so often. It was well out of date by the time it did. He cared no more than the people whose families had lived here for generations. When it did trickle in, it was news to him. What else mattered?

When most of the snow melted and the roads cleared during Maine's short stretch of alleged summer, news from the great big wide world came in along with canned goods, sacks of flour, gasoline, condoms, and other vital supplies. Once upon a time, Rob had been a news junkie. Now? Hey, it was a long way away and it had happened a while ago. He couldn't do anything about it. So why get excited?

For this performance, Dick Barber was playing the role of his father—nowhere near the worst casting in the world. Justin was his best man, Charlie and Biff his groomsmen. Lindsey's principal, who looked like a pit bull with gold-framed glasses but actually seemed pretty nice, did duty as the matron of honor. Her bridesmaids were a couple of teachers. She'd told Rob her dad's new arm candy had tried to volunteer for one of those slots, but was more or less politely discouraged.

Next thing Rob knew, he was standing in front of Farrell. He couldn't quite recall how he'd crossed the intervening space. Teleportation seemed unlikely, but he couldn't rule it out. Lindsey stood beside him, so everything else receded into the background. Her dress was white, if not exactly a wedding gown. He'd borrowed a blue blazer and tie from Dick Barber. Weddings, funerals, and gunpoint—yes, this was one of the happier reasons to don a tie.

Jim Farrell beamed at the two of them. "I have the honor to be standing in this place by virtue of authority invested in me as the law west of the Pecos—or at least west and north of I-95. If I say you're married, you're as married as you're ever going to be in these parts. Have you got that?"

Rob managed a nod. Next to him, Lindsey did, too. Her eyes sparkled. Rob doubted he would have got on with her so well if she didn't think Jim was one of the funnier critters on two legs.

"Along with marrying you, I'm supposed to stuff you with

good advice like force-fed geese," Farrell went on. "That's a hot one, isn't it? I never tied the knot myself, and I stopped caring about the amusement value of the fair sex a few years ago. So you're thinking, *Well, what the devil does he know?* We might as well be at a town meeting, hey?"

This time, Rob didn't nod, but he came close. Laughs and chuckles rippled through the pews.

"But I am an escaped—excuse me, a retired—historian, so I may possibly have learned a little something. Possibly," Jim Farrell said. "People do seem to get along better when they're willing to put up with each other's foibles. If you're convinced you have The One Right Answer"—Rob heard the capital letters thump into place—"good luck with the rest of the human race. If you think you're going to impose it on everybody else No Matter What"—more loud caps—"even good luck won't help."

"Amen," Dick Barber said quietly: pious agreement to a secular thought.

"Oh!" Farrell raised a gloved forefinger, as if at an afterthought he liked. "People have been screwing each other for as long as there've been people. You should probably do some of that, too."

More laughter came from the audience. Rob had all he could do not to snicker out loud. Lindsey *did* squeak.

"You can laugh, but you can't hide," Farrell said with mock severity. "Since you aren't even trying, you must want to go through with this. Rob, do you take Lindsey as your wife for richer and poorer, in sickness and in health, and for as long as you both shall live?" He might have been thinking *or until one of you reaches for a lawyer,* but he didn't say it.

"I do," Rob answered. Official it was, yes.

"Lindsey, do you likewise and likewise, respectively, and for just as long?"

"I do," she said. Yes, it was very official.

"Then I do, too—pronounce you man and wife, that is," Farrell said. "Mr. Ferguson, you may kiss Mrs. Ferguson."

Rob did. Lindsey still hadn't decided whether she'd take his last name or keep Kincaid. Rob wasn't about to commit litcrit, though. He'd got a ring on a trip of his own to Dover-Foxcroft. He slipped it onto Lindsey's finger. That was another way to make things official. And there was one more, but that would have to wait till after the reception.

Moose meat. Roast goose. Stewed squirrel. A home-smoked ham. Potatoes. Parsnips. Pickled mushrooms. Sauerkraut. Moonshine vodka and applejack. Store-bought whiskey somebody'd been saving for a snowy day.

Squirt Frog and the Evolving Tadpoles provided the dance music, with a local kid filling in for Rob. The kid wasn't terrible, but Rob didn't think he needed to worry about getting booted out of the band. On the dance floor, he was no threat to the ghosts of Michael Jackson and Fred Astaire. He didn't worry about that, either.

The reception was a success. Everyone had plenty to eat. Nobody punched anybody else. No one groped Lindsey's dad's hot girlfriend (or if anyone did, she didn't squawk about it). What more could you want?

Jim Farrell laid on his sleigh to take the newlyweds back to Lindsey's apartment. "How about that?" Rob said as she unlocked the door. "We're really married." He picked her up and carried her over the threshold.

"Darn right we are," she agreed. "And what do you propose to do about it, Mister?"

"I already proposed," he pointed out. "Why don't we go back to the bedroom, huh? I expect I'll think of something." They did, and he did.

XXI

Louise Ferguson hadn't heard from her eldest son more than a handful of times since the supervolcano erupted. He seemed content to stay up there in Maine. That struck her as somewhere along the range between masochism and madness, but it was his life.

The postcard she found in her mailbox today bore a picture of the business end of a mosquito silhouetted against the sun. Beneath it was the legend THE STATE BIRD OF MAINE. She grunted laughter. That was the kind of thing he'd send, all right. She would have recognized the style even if she hadn't recognized the spiky script on the back.

By the time you read this, I'll be a married man, he wrote. *Her name is Lindsey Kincaid. She teaches at the high school in town. So maybe one of these days you'll have grandkids running around under the snow here. Say hello to anyone you happen to run into.—Rob.*

From the postmark, the card had taken almost three weeks to cross the country. The USPS was one more outfit that had been in big trouble even before the supervolcano erupted. Trying to cope with all the insanity since the eruption hadn't made it run better, or more efficiently. What could you do? The postcard *had* eventually got here.

She wished some of her bills would come so slowly, and that the bastards who sent them out would take *the Post Office sucks* as an excuse when her own payments ran late. The longer she stayed out of work, the later some of them got, too.

She would have been out in the street with her worldly goods piled on the curb if so many other people didn't have the same problems for the same reasons. They weren't too big to fail—the classic phrase from the recession before the eruption (a recession that now looked like pretty goddamn good times). But they were too numerous to evict, even if they had failed. *Pay what you can when you can* was rapidly ousting *e pluribus unum* as the national motto. Louise expected she'd start seeing it on coins and bills any day now.

If she wanted to keep collecting her divorced single mom's mite from the California EDD, she had to keep looking for work. When she could, she did it on the Net and with her phone. When she couldn't, she gritted her teeth, forked over some of her unemployment check to Marshall, and climbed aboard the bus for new adventures in Jobseekersland.

She had no enormous hope. Hope was not one of Jobseekersland's natural resources—certainly not since Yellowstone blew up. But you had to go through the motions, and to be able to document that you were going through the motions, or your EDD checks would dry up. Going out to look for work was a pain in the ass. Losing the unemployment checks would be a supervolcano eruption in your own life.

And so, glumly, Louise walked into Van Slyke Pharmacy, at the corner of Van Slyke and Reynoso Drive. It was a mom-and-pop place, not part of a chain. Along with the usual patent medicines and shampoos and school supplies and whatnot, it sold brightly painted pottery artifacts that might be decorative if you were tasteless enough, stuffed animals that looked sort of but not quite like famous cartoon characters, and a bunch of secondhand books.

The pharmacist's bad haircut and funky glasses frames warned that he might actually enjoy the ceramic tumors he was trying to unload. The badge he wore on his pastel polyester shirt said his name was Jared. Louise wanted to giggle. To her, Jared was a singing smiley on her computer that butchered ballads in Spanish, complete with wretched guitar accompaniment.

"Help you?" he asked. His lenses made his eyes seem enormous.

"Well, I'm looking for work," she said resignedly. One more humiliation, then on to the next.

But instead of going *Sorry* or *Not today* or *We don't need anybody,* Jared said, "I was going to post on Craigslist when the power comes back on. If it ever does. What was your last job?"

"I was an administrative assistant at the ramen company's headquarters on Braxton Bragg," Louise answered in astonishment.

"Why did you leave?"

"I didn't have much choice. They closed down their American operation."

"That's right—they did. I remember hearing about that." The pharmacist nodded. "You can answer the phone? You can type? You can handle an inventory spreadsheet when there is power?"

Louise managed a dazed nod. "I can do all that. I'm not exactly an Excel whiz, but I can cope if it's not too complicated."

"I'll give you a try, then," Jared said briskly. "I had to let someone go last week. I feel bad about it, but she just couldn't do the work. If you can't, I won't keep you, either. But if you can, I'll be glad to have you. I can't do all that stuff and run the place, too, not if I want to sleep, I can't."

Louise could hardly believe her ears. "What kind of money are we talking about?"

He told her. It was less than the ramen works had paid, but it whaled the tar out of unemployment. "Medical after six months," he added. "It's not a terrific plan, but it's better than nothing."

"When do I start?" she asked. If she couldn't stand it, she'd start looking for something else, something better. The best time to look for work was when you already had some.

"Monday morning, ten o'clock sharp," he said. "I'll have paperwork for you to fill out then. Can't do anything without the paperwork."

"Better yours than the EDD's," Louise said from the bottom of her heart.

"That's a good way to look at things," Jared said. "Tell me your name, why don't you? Me, I'm Jared Watt."

"Pleased to meet you, Mr. Watt." Louise gave her own name. "You've got no idea how pleased I am to meet you."

"Oh, I just might, Mrs. Ferguson."

"It's Miz," Louise said.

"Okay. Ms. Ferguson." Jared Watt repeated it, perhaps to help himself remember. "Like I say, I just might. You aren't the only one who's had a tough time the past three, four years."

"I feel great now." Louise meant every word of it. An indifferent job in a business that didn't look to be thriving with a boss who definitely seemed peculiar? Hey, it was work! No wonder she meant every word. "If I never see that Torrance unemployment office again, it'll be too soon."

"Well, all right," the pharmacist said. "If I can't drive you loopy, I don't expect anyone can."

"I'm not even worried about it." Louise meant that, too. Whether she'd mean it by closing time a week from Friday might be another story altogether. *It'll be a week with a paycheck, anyhow,* she thought. *They don't make weeks any better than those.*

Colin Ferguson looked at his watch. It was only twenty-five past two. He would have bet it was four o'clock. *Time flies when you're having fun,* he thought, and then *Yeah, as if!* He hadn't been this nervous since, well, the last time he was this nervous. And that was . . . probably when he'd asked Kelly to marry him. A while ago, in other words.

He looked at his watch again. It was 2:26. He made himself *not* look at it, or at the clock on the cop-shop wall. The bust would go off the way it was supposed to. Or it wouldn't. Whichever, he'd pick up the pieces and go on. What else could you do?

At 2:39 by the clock on the wall, his cell phone rang. He hauled it out of his jacket pocket. "Ferguson."

"We have ourselves a bust, Lieutenant—best damn bust since Beyoncé." Rodney sounded happy as a sheep in clover. And well he might have; he went on, "Weed. Meth. Coke. H. Possession with intent to sell. Oh, and a .45 automatic, which he had sense enough *not* to pull when we dropped on him. We grabbed his laptop, too—see what kind of good shit he's got on the hard drive, and where that leads us."

"Okay. That all sounds good." Colin couldn't decide whether to be delighted or mournful. He went both ways at once, and felt torn to pieces on account of it. Tim had known what he was talking about after all. There was never any guarantee of that, not even when you asked him something as basic as his name. "Lucky for him he didn't go for the .45," Colin went on, bringing himself back to the matter directly at hand.

"Yeah, that would've been the *last* dumb thing he ever tried," Rodney agreed. "This way, he'll get some more chances whenever they finally decide to turn him loose. Wanted to let you know everything went smooth. We're gonna bring him in now."

"Good job, man. Thanks. 'Bye." Colin stowed the phone. Nobody involved in taking Darren Pitcavage down had put anything into the San Atanasio PD's computer system. Nobody'd said anything over the department's radio net. What Chief Pitcavage didn't see or hear, he couldn't warn his son about.

Well, they didn't have to worry about that any more. Mike Pitcavage would hear now. Colin couldn't imagine that that would do him—or Darren—any good, though. Would he try to bargain this bust down to a misdemeanor, too? *Good luck,* Colin thought. If the DA went along with a deal like that, he deserved to be out on the street and sleeping in a park five minutes later. For that matter, the chief would deserve to be out there sleeping alongside him if he had the gall to propose something like that, didn't he? So it seemed to Colin, anyway.

He had no trouble picking up just when people not in the know at the station found out what had happened. The buzz of conversation in the big open office suddenly picked up volume and changed tone. Yes, that was what amazement sounded like, sure as hell.

Gabe Sanchez also picked up on it right away. He, of course, wasn't a person not in the know. He caught Colin's eye and looked a question at him. Colin nodded back. Gabe grinned and gave him a thumbs-up.

The next interesting question was how long Mike Pitcavage would take to start blowing gaskets. In a way, there should have been a pool on that. Colin knew he would have put down some money. When he got into the Super Bowl pool every year, no way he could stay out of this one. But a pool would have turned people not in the know into people in the know too damn soon. Besides, the chief would've wanted to get into it, which would have been . . . awkward. Pitcavage always joined the Super Bowl pool, too.

By the clock on the wall, the chief left his exalted private office and burst into the big central one exactly four minutes and forty seconds after Rodney called. For once, Pitcavage's Armani suit flapped on him like an ordinary cop's threadbare threads from Sears or Men's Wearhouse. For once, he didn't look like the CEO of a successful medium-sized corporation. He looked like any poor bastard who'd just found out his one and only son was arrested on serious drug charges. He looked like hell, in other words.

His blindly staring eyes caught and held Colin's. "Ferguson!" he croaked. "I need to talk to you." How much did he know? How much did he suspect? Or was Colin just the first spar he saw and grabbed after his yacht ripped its belly out on the rocks?

Colin heaved himself to his feet. "What's up?" He wouldn't be able to hide knowing for very long. Nor did he intend to. But he didn't want to do a sack dance over Pitcavage's fallen frame, either.

The chief gestured: follow me. Colin did, out of the big office, up the hall, and outside. One glimpse of Mike Pitcavage's ravaged face was plenty to scare away a couple of curious smokers.

"They've arrested Darren," Pitcavage said. He had the dazed look of a man who'd just staggered free of a bad car crash and didn't quite realize yet he had only a few cuts and bruises himself. "Arrested. Drug possession. Drug dealing. Felony. Oh my God!"

"I'm sorry, Mike," Colin said. That had the advantage of being nothing but the truth.

Truth or not, he might as well have saved his breath. Locked in some personal hell, the chief went on as if he hadn't spoken: "A felony rap! Hard time! They'll take DNA samples! Jesus wept!"

He isn't running on all cylinders—nowhere near, Colin thought with rough sympathy. Hard time was, well, hard time. It wasn't designed to be fun for anybody. It might end up even harder for a police chief's kid, because they'd have to segregate him from most of the rest of the prisoners to keep him safe. But a swab on the inside of his cheek was the least, the absolute very least, of Darren Pitcavage's worries.

Mike Pitcavage seized Colin's arm and squeezed, hard. He might be stuck behind a desk, but he was still one hell of a strong man. "I've got to talk to the arresting officer, talk to the DA, get it down to something possible, something reasonable," Pitcavage said, squeezing, squeezing. If he kept that up, pretty soon Colin wouldn't have any circulation in his left hand. "Drug dealing? A felony? No way! I'll fix it up."

No, he didn't have all his oars in the pond. "Mike," Colin said, as gently as he could, "I don't think that will do you any good, or Darren, either. Think it through. You're liable to make things worse, not better. What if the reporters get hold of it? Can't you see the headlines, man? 'Chief scores cushy plea deal for his son! Film at eleven!' " He did his best to imitate a pompous TV talking head.

"He's my kid, Colin. I've got to try. DNA samples? My God, this will kill Caroline." Pitcavage might even have been right about that.

Whether he was or he wasn't, though, had nothing to do with the price of lemonade. "You won't help him, Mike," Colin said, doing his best to get through to the other man. "You'll make things worse. The DA won't listen to you. He can't. And if you piss him off, he'll probably find some new counts to throw at Darren."

"They can't charge him with a felony. They *can't*!" Pitcavage wouldn't listen.

In Colin's experience, saying what *they* could or couldn't do was usually a bad plan. Telling *them* to their faces that they couldn't do this, that, or the other thing was even worse. As soon as you told them, they'd go ahead and do it anyhow, just to show you a thing or three.

He tried his best to spell that out for the chief. "You're against me, too! I might have known!" Pitcavage yelled, loud enough to make the smokers spin toward him to see what was going on.

Chief Pitcavage stormed back into the station, shoulders hunched, head pushed forward, hands thrust into trouser pockets. Colin stared after him. He'd known it would be bad. He hadn't imagined it would be as bad as this.

"What's eating him?" one of the smokers asked the other, or Colin, or possibly God. He'd been out here polluting his lungs when the news broke. *One more reason not to smoke,* Colin thought, and didn't enlighten the guy. He'd find out soon enough. The whole department would know before the sun went down.

Vanessa surveyed her new apartment with something less than delight. It was a standard SoCal pattern for a small one-bedroom. Front room going back to dinette, with cramped kitchen to one side of the eating area. Bedroom through a door in the front-room wall opposite the couch. Bathroom behind the bedroom and next to the kitchen, so the builder could save money by running the pipes for both off the same main line.

The rug was one small step up from outdoor carpeting. The linoleum in the kitchen and the bathroom had seen better decades. The furniture was old and ratty. Coffee table, end table, dinette table, and nightstand and dresser in the bedroom all had identical tops of very fake wood. She didn't want to think about how many people had fucked on the mattress before she moved in.

Her own furniture was back in Denver. Scavengers wouldn't have got there yet. One of these years. By then, ash and rain probably would have made the roof cave in. Gone. Well, the whole Midwest was gone.

Her old room in her father's place had been more comfortable than this. Well, the physical arrangements had. But everybody there took everything she said the wrong way. And there was her new half-sister screeching at odd hours. That drove Vanessa straight up the wall. Did it ever! You couldn't ignore a crying baby, no matter how much you wanted to. Evolution had designed those noises to stab your head like an ice pick. You had to *do something* about them so the little monster would shut up.

Vanessa knew what she wanted to do. But punting an infant got you talked about in this effete age. Moving out seemed the better choice.

Or it would have, if she hadn't been all but run out by Kelly. She was Colin Ferguson's *daughter*, goddammit. Just because this chunky stranger was hauling her old man's ashes, did that give the bitch the right to put on airs and boss her around?

Kelly sure seemed to think so. So did Vanessa's dad. Marshall . . . Marshall shut himself in the room with the stupid police tape on the door and clattered away on that horrible antique of a typewriter. It was almost as annoying as Deborah. And he turned out silly, saccharine stories, full of erratic grammar and punctuation. She'd told him so when he asked her to read one. She hadn't seen any more after that.

Of course, his prose looked like Edward Gibbon's when you compared it to the subliterate garbage Nick Gorczany cranked out. Vanessa had forgotten how very delightful life at the widget works was before she headed for Colorado.

Maybe Gorczany had forgotten, too. When she set a memo on his desk heavily edited in red, he'd looked from it to her and back. "*So* good to have you on the job again, Vanessa," he'd murmured.

"*So* good to be back," she'd answered, and walked out of his office with her head held high. If he was going to get snide, she'd get snide right back. Yes, she needed work. But she needed her self-respect even more.

The one thing wrong with self-respect was, it wouldn't buy groceries or pay the rent. The job would . . . more or less. Nick

Gorczany hadn't got himself that big old house in Palos Verdes Estates by overpaying his employees. If you didn't like what he gave you, you could always go out and find yourself better-paying work.

"Ha," Vanessa said, chopping cabbage in the crowded kitchen of the small one-bedroom in San Atanasio: about as far from the boss' Palos Verdes Estates estate as you could get and still stay in the South Bay. "Ha, ha. Ha, ha, ha."

It didn't get any funnier, even if she made more laughy noises. Laughy? She nodded to herself. It bore the same relation to *laugh* as *truthy* did to *truth*. It wouldn't go into the OED any time soon, but it filled a need. It did for her, anyhow.

She counted herself lucky Nick Gorczany had remembered she knew what she was doing when it came to translating bureaucratic horseshit into English. Her father and Kelly might have given her the bum's rush even if she hadn't snagged a job.

"They have expelled you from what is yours by right," Bronislav said the first time he saw her apartment. His big hands folded into fists. "If it were not your father, I would make him pay for dispossessing you. We Serbs, we know too much about being wrongly dispossessed."

"Don't do anything like that! Don't, you hear me?" Vanessa exclaimed. Bronislav was ready to turn a family squabble into an international incident. Vanessa had started learning what she could about ex-Yugoslavia. She didn't want him to call her *American* any more, not the way he had in front of the Croat eatery in San Pedro. From everything she could see, Serbs did that kind of thing a lot. She was sure Gavrilo Princip would have agreed. So would Archduke Franz Ferdinand, these days the namesake of a band almost as quirky as the one her brother played in.

And Rob was married, up there in the glacial wilderness of Maine. He hadn't bothered to let Vanessa know, not firsthand, but he'd sent cards to Dad and Mom, who'd both told her. Vanessa had trouble imagining a woman rash enough to want to tie the knot with her big brother, but there you were.

Here she was, all right. "Don't!" she said one more time. She didn't want Bronislav turning Dad's car into an IED or anything like that. She wasn't sure he knew how to do such things, but he was liable to. He was liable to want to show off for her, too. That was how he would think of it, anyhow.

"All right," he said now. Did he sound sulky, like a kid deprived of his favorite toy? Damn straight he did.

So she found something else for him to do. And he did, with the same kind of enthusiasm he'd probably shown for guerrilla warfare while Yugoslavia was falling apart. But bedroom explosions had aftermaths much more enjoyable than those involving *plastique*.

Some of the things he did . . . "Where did you learn that?" she asked, her heart still thumping.

"I am a Serb. It is in my blood," Bronislav replied with dignity. And maybe that was true, and maybe he'd picked it up from a jowly hooker in Barstow or Phoenix or Las Cruces or one of the other towns on the route that fed Los Angeles. How could you know for sure?

Simple. You couldn't. But Vanessa chose to believe him. Choosing to believe was part of what love was all about. So was forgetting you even had a choice. Vanessa tried her best to do that, too.

When the phone rings at 3:25 a.m., it's never good news. If you've won the Nobel Prize or $150,000,000 in the lottery, they're always considerate enough to let you sleep in before they tell you. When the phone goes off in the wee smalls like a grenade on your nightstand, they're calling to let you know something is wrecked or somebody's hurt or somebody's dead—if you're really lucky, all of the above.

Colin knew it was 3:25 because the glowing hands on the windup clock by the phone told him so. When power started erratically going in and out, the San Atanasio PD issued one to every cop on the force. The bean counters hadn't squawked about that; you didn't want people (especially people who worked the evening and night shifts) not showing up because their electric clocks crapped out on them.

The power was out now. Without the glowing hands, it would have been absolutely dark in the bedroom, not just almost absolutely dark. Colin fumbled for the phone. He snagged it in the middle of the third ring—and in the middle of Kelly's groggy "What the fuck?"

"Ferguson," he said, sounding at least something like his ordinary self.

"Lieutenant, this is Neil Schneider at the station." All right: it was a police emergency, not a family disaster. That was better. Or maybe it was—the sergeant didn't sound even remotely ordinary. He might have been trying to get back up on his feet after taking a sucker punch in a bar fight. And what he said next explained why he sounded that way: "Chief Pitcavage is dead, Lieutenant."

"Oh, sweet Jesus!" Colin blurted. Ice and fire chased each other along his nerves. He wasn't sleepy any more. He both was and wasn't astonished. "What happened?" he managed after a moment.

He ate his gun was what he expected. Mike Pitcavage had definitely freaked at Darren's arrest. Colin had known that would be bad. He'd had no idea it would be as bad as it was.

"Caroline just found him—they've got separate bedrooms, you know," Sergeant Schneider said.

Like an idiot, Colin found himself nodding there in the dark, as if Schneider—or anyone else—could see him do it. He did know the chief and his wife slept apart. Mike was liable to get called out at odd hours, and he didn't want to bother Caroline any more than he had to.

The cop at the station went on, "She went in there with a flashlight. Dunno why. Maybe she thought she heard a noise and wanted to get him. Whatever. She found him on the bed with a bottle of pills next to him and a plastic bag over his head and fastened tight around his neck. He'd been gone for a while—he was getting cold."

"Jesus!" Colin said again. So Mike hadn't shot himself. Maybe he hadn't wanted to leave a mess behind for Caroline to have to clean up. Well, when you killed yourself you left a mess behind whether you wanted to or not. Colin found the next obvious question: "Was there a note?"

"If there was, I don't know anything about it. I don't *think* Caroline said anything about one, but I can't tell you for sure. I didn't catch the call," Sergeant Schneider replied.

"Okay," Colin said. It wasn't—nowhere close—but he was starting to see what the picture looked like.

"Uh, Lieutenant, is there any way you could come in for a while?" Schneider asked hesitantly. "I mean . . ." His voice trailed away.

"Be there fast as I can." The plea didn't surprise Colin, much as he wished it did. With Captain Miyoshi on the shelf after stomach-cancer surgery, he was the most senior man available. And people would know he'd orchestrated Darren Pitcavage's arrest. Without a note from Mike, they wouldn't be able to prove that was why he'd done himself in, but it sure looked like the way to bet.

"Thank you, Lieutenant," Neil Schneider said. "Thanks very much."

"Yeah." Colin hung up. He pulled the nightstand drawer open and groped for the flashlight that lived in there. He imagined Caroline doing the same thing a couple of miles away. No one could see his grimace, but he felt it.

"What happened?" Kelly asked just as his fingers closed around it. "Somebody committed suicide. Who? Why?"

"Mike Pitcavage. Don't know why yet, but it's gonna be a hell of a mess." Colin had already flicked on the light and was squinting against the beam when he realized he'd cussed in front of his wife. Well, too goddamn bad. This was already a mess. It called for cussing or praying, one. It probably called for both, but Colin had not even a nodding acquaintance with prayer.

"My God!" Kelly said. She jumped to the same conclusion people at the cop shop had to be reaching: "Is it because you busted his worthless kid?"

"Don't know," Colin repeated, as stolidly as he could. "If it is . . ." He didn't take that any further.

If the chief had killed himself because of Darren's arrest, Colin was anything but sure he could go on at the San Atanasio Police Department. How many people there would blame him for Mike's suicide? Enough to make him persona bigtime non grata? He had the bad feeling the answer to that one couldn't be anything but yes. He was a long way from sure he didn't blame himself, when you got right down to it.

"That would be awful, Colin!" Kelly exclaimed, so she could see it, too. Well, it wasn't anything complicated, worse luck.

By the flashlight's white glare, he put on jeans, a sweatshirt, and his beat-up old denim jacket. The middle of the night wasn't the time to worry about suit and tie. He looked a lot like the way he had when he first met Kelly at the late, ever so lamented Yellowstone. "I'll be back when I can," he told her, brushing his lips across hers. "Try and grab some more z's."

"Any other time, I'd tell you you were out of your mind," she said. "The way Deborah runs me ragged, I may have a chance of doing it."

He hurried downstairs. He started to roll his bike out of the foyer and onto the porch, but shook his head, went outside on foot, and got into the Taurus instead. Sometimes speed mattered. To his relief, the car started.

The streets were eerily empty. He drove past two people showing bike lights and one moron who wasn't. Crunching the fool would have been just what he needed now, but he swerved and missed. Having the guy appear out of nowhere in his headlights startled him so much he didn't even honk.

When he pulled into the lot, he had no trouble finding a space. Most of them went begging most of the time—who drove to work these days? He hurried inside. The lights were on: the station had its own generator, and for the moment the generator had fuel.

"Here he is!" somebody said as he came through the doors. That wasn't relief. It sounded more like a heads-up to alert people who hadn't seen him yet. The looks the cops and clerical staff gave him had that same feeling.

Neil Schneider came up to him. "Sorry to roust you, Lieutenant, but . . ." The droopy, graying blond mustache the sergeant wore gave him a mournful aspect even when he was happy. When he had something to be unhappy about, as now . . .

"I'm here, all right," Colin said. "Has anybody told Darren yet?"

By the way the rest of the cops looked at one another, he knew nobody had. "We thought you ought to be here," Schneider said. *We thought you ought to do it,* he meant.

Colin sighed. "Okay. Get him out of his cell. Bring him to interrogation room two. I'll handle it in there." If he was top dog for the moment, they could damn well follow his lead.

He didn't have to wait long in the interrogation room—the

jail was right next to the station. Two policemen led in Darren Pitcavage. He wore a bright blue jumpsuit with SAN ATANASIO CITY JAIL stenciled on the chest and back in white; his hands were cuffed behind him.

"What's going on?" he demanded when he saw Colin. He was bigger than his father, and looked a lot like him, but with little of the older man's polished hardness. Scowling, he went on, "My pop'll eat you without salt when he hears you hauled me outa my cell in the middle of the night for the third degree."

"We didn't bring you out for anything of the kind," Colin said wearily. He wished he were home in bed, or anywhere else at all but here. "And your father . . . Your father won't do anything like that, either, I'm afraid."

"Huh? The fuck he won't, man." Darren spoke with the certainty of someone who'd rarely heard *no* in his life. "You guys try and screw me over, you think Dad'll let you get away with that shit?"

Mike Pitcavage alive wouldn't have let them do anything to his son, not if he could help it. Colin wondered if he wasn't alive for no better reason than the humiliation he felt at not being able to help it. He took a deep, miserable breath. "Darren, your father won't do anything to stop us. Your father *can't* do anything to stop us."

"What are you talkin' about?" Darren said. "Of course he can. He's, y'know, the *chief*."

"No, he can't. No, he isn't," Colin said. "Your father is dead, Darren. He killed himself earlier tonight, or that's what it looks like. That's what we took you out of jail to tell you. I'm sorry, if it means anything to you."

Darren Pitcavage gaped at him. "No. No fuckin' way." He shook his head. "Dad'd never do anything like that. You're bullshitting me, trying to soften me up or something."

"I wish to God I were," Colin replied, which was the exact

and literal truth. "If you don't believe me, ask some of the other people here. It's not like you don't know most of 'em." He hadn't known all of them, or he wouldn't be wearing that jumpsuit now—and his father probably wouldn't be dead. Colin made himself go on: "I know you know Neil Schneider. Ask Neil. He's the one who phoned me with the news."

"I don't need to ask anybody. I know you assholes are all in it together." But Darren didn't sound so sure any more. He was starting to get that poleaxed look, the look anybody gets on hearing a loved one has unexpectedly died. He blinked a couple of times—blinked back tears, Colin guessed from the way his eyes brightened under the fluorescents. When he spoke again, the bluster had drained from his voice: "What—what happened, man?"

Briefly and baldly, Colin told him, finishing, "That's just the way I got it from Sergeant Schneider. Now you know as much as I do. I *am* sorry. I wish like anything I didn't have to give you news like this."

"Dad. Oh, my God. Dad." Darren believed him now, all right. Tears ran down his face. "What's Mom gonna do now? What am I gonna do now?"

Colin had no idea what Caroline Pitcavage would do. Darren Pitcavage would probably do seven to ten, with time off for good behavior and prison overcrowding. That, he didn't say. Darren would have to find out for himself.

XXII

When Bryce Miller waited at the campus bus stop for the ride back into the town of Wayne, it was twenty-one below zero. It *was* the late afternoon, to be fair. The day's high hadn't been anywhere near so frigid. It had only been eleven below then.

Not much snow was falling. The air couldn't hold much moisture when it got this cold. But every flake that touched his cheeks and nose—the only skin he showed—burned as if it were dipped in battery acid.

"Hope the bus comes," said a woman standing there with him. "Can't wait around real long in this. Gotta go inside and warm up." It wouldn't be hot inside, either. It would be above freezing, though. No matter how many layers you had on, you'd turn into an icicle pretty damn quick in this. Bryce had known it would be cold here when he left SoCal. He hadn't dreamt it could get *this* cold.

He was thinking hard about retreating to a building when the bus grumbled up. "Extra blankets on the seats," the driver said. She was using one. Bryce gratefully swaddled himself as the bus pulled away from the curb. It helped—a little. Nothing could help much, not in this, hellfire probably included.

He didn't want to unwrap and get out when the bus got to his stop in downtown Wayne, such as downtown Wayne was. Only a couple of blocks to his apartment. He counted himself lucky not to be devoured by a polar bear before he made it.

It was above freezing in the apartment. Not a lot, but it was. Susan wore almost as many clothes as he had on. "Brr!" he said. "That's just brutal out there." She hugged him and kissed him. When they both had on so many layers, the hug seemed hardly more than virtual. The kiss was fine, though.

Then Susan said, "Colin Ferguson still works for the San Atanasio Police Department, doesn't he?"

"Sure," Bryce said. "How come?" It wasn't as if Susan brought up Vanessa's dad very often—or at all, if she could help it.

"Because the chief of the San Atanasio PD just killed himself. It was on CNN. Michael Pit . . . Pitsomething. Something weird."

"Pitcavage," Bryce said, and Susan nodded. He went on, "That's awful! Did they say why? Colin didn't like him a whole bunch, but you wouldn't wish that on anybody."

"They said his son's in jail on drug-dealing charges, but they don't know if that's what made him do it or not. It sounds like they don't know. He didn't leave a note, they said."

"Holy crap," Bryce said, and then, "Do you mind if I call Colin?"

"After this? Of course not. It's not like you're calling to dish about Vanessa," Susan said. Bryce chuckled uneasily. She knew he wasn't a hundred percent over his ex. She knew he wouldn't be any time soon, either, too. As long as she also knew he had zero intention of doing anything about it (assuming Vanessa wasn't over him, which she totally was), that was . . . pretty much okay with her.

He got out his cell and pulled up Colin's number. On the second ring, the familiar voice said, "Hey, Bryce" in his ear. After a beat, Colin went on, "So you heard even back there, huh?"

" 'Fraid so," Bryce answered. "I'm sorry."

"Me, too. Everybody's saying that a lot today. Listen, let me call you back in five minutes, okay? I want to walk out into the parking lot."

"Sure. 'Bye," Bryce said. Colin wanted to talk without fifty people listening in on his end, but he didn't want to say so while they were listening in.

"What's going on?" Susan asked when he took the phone away from his ear. He explained. He'd just finished when the opening chords of "Came Along Too Late" came from the phone. Hey, how many Hellenistic ring tones could you find?

"I'm here," he said, raising it again.

"Yeah, and I'm here, which is more than Mike Pitcavage can tell you right now," Colin replied. "I always knew he cut his rotten kid too much slack. If Mike hadn't, Darren never would've turned into a dealer, and he damn well did. The evidence we've got, not even the dumbest jury in the world'll acquit him, and that's saying something. But Jesus H. Christ on a pogo stick, Bryce, I never dreamt Mike would go and do anything like *that*."

"I believe you," Bryce said. Colin sounded plaintive, almost pleading. Those were notes his voice almost never struck. The last time Bryce could remember hearing them was when Louise left him. Colin had never dreamt she would go and do anything like that, either.

Of course, Bryce wasn't sure how reliable his own memories of that time were. Vanessa had just traded him in on a new—no, actually on an older—model, so he also hadn't been at his own dynamic best.

"I know you do. It means a lot to me." Colin hesitated, then went on, "Means a lot to me right now that *anybody* believes me. Some of the people here, it's like they think I drove Mike to it on purpose when I set it up so we went after Darren and dropped on him."

"Oh, Lord!" Bryce hadn't thought of that. He realized he should have. "Talk about blaming the messenger!"

"Yeah, well, that's how it looks to me, too." Colin sighed. "But it sure doesn't look that way to everybody. Funeral'll be in three, four days—after the coroner's office finishes the autopsy and releases the body. All the crap you have to go through to make sure what looks like a suicide isn't a homicide. This one looks as cut-and-dried as they ever do, but you still have to connect the dots."

"Sure," Bryce said. The Hellenistic kingdoms had had their bureaucratic rituals, too.

Colin sighed again. "Not too long before you called, my landline rang, and it was Caroline Pitcavage. She uninvited me— disinvited me? whatever the hell—from the funeral. Said she was sorry and everything, but seeing me there would only remind her of what I'd done to their family."

"Ouch!" Bryce wished he could have found something more consoling than that, but it was the best he could do.

"*Ouch* is right." This time, Bryce judged, Colin's pause was for a nod. "I've known Caroline Pitcavage . . . gotta be twenty years now. Yeah, Mike beat me out for chief. Doesn't mean I want to see him dead. Doesn't mean I'd try to make him dead, either. She's known me twenty years, too. If she doesn't get that, she's never known me at all." *Plaintive* was the word, sure as the devil.

"She can't be thinking straight right this minute." Coming up with that made Bryce feel a little better. He hoped it helped Colin some, too. Whether it did or not, it was bound to be the truth.

"I know she can't. I understand it. In my head, I understand it," Colin said heavily. "In my gut . . . She might as well've kicked me in the gut when she said that. And she's not the only one who feels that way, either. I don't know what I can do about it. I don't know if I can do anything, this side of quitting the force."

"Don't!" Bryce exclaimed. "If you do, they win."

"I know. But if I don't, they're liable to win, anyway. Too damn many of 'em. Happy day, huh? Listen, good to talk to you and everything, but I've got to go back in there and make like I'm useful," Colin said. "Take care." Bryce started to answer, but found himself talking to a dead line.

A skeleton crew of uniformed cops patrolled the streets of San Atanasio. Some rode black-and-whites. More pedaled bicycles. There was talk of buying horses. The glut of rain in the L.A. basin had produced a glut of grass. Feeding them would be cheap. It would certainly be cheaper than buying gas for the police cars. But then, what wouldn't?

And another skeleton crew of cops and clerical personnel kept the station open. The rest of the San Atanasio PD, along with the city council and the mayor, had gone to pay Mike Pitcavage their final respects.

Colin Ferguson sat at his desk. He wished he were at the funeral, even if Caroline and most of the other cops on the force screamed abuse at him there. That, at least, would be out in the open. He could have stood there and taken it or he could have screamed back at them. What he really wanted to do was scream at Darren Pitcavage, who'd got out of his cell to attend the services.

Instead, he had to stay here by himself and be miserable. Well, almost by himself. His secretary was one of the handful of clerical people who'd stayed behind to catch phone calls and do whatever else needed doing. Josefina Linares practically radiated indignation. "It's not fair, Lieutenant, the way they treat you," she said. "It's not even close to fair."

"Thanks, Josie. I appreciate that." Colin meant every word of it. "But it's the way things are."

"Is it your fault Chief Mike had a kid who's a dope pusher? I don't think so!" Josie said. "Darren shoulda got in trouble a long time ago. He might've known not to be such a jerk then. But Chief Mike kept going to bat for him, so he decided he could get away with anything. I'm here to tell you, though, the world doesn't work that way."

"I don't think it does, either. You're right," Colin said. With some Hispanics, he might have made that last *Tienes razón.* He spoke Spanish—not well, and with a horrible Anglo accent, but he did. It would only have annoyed Josie, though. She was American American, as she would tell you at any excuse or none. She had less sympathy for illegal immigrants than Colin did, and was more likely to call them wetbacks.

"But when Chief Mike had to see what kind of little shit he raised, when he couldn't stick his head in the sand any more, he got too ashamed to live. That's what happened. It's not your fault." Josie sounded positive.

That was how it looked to Colin, too. That was how he hoped it was. But he was less sure than Josie seemed. Mike Pitcavage hadn't left behind any reason for killing himself. He'd just gone ahead and done it, damn him. That left plenty of room for people to blame Colin. And people, starting with Pitcavage's widow, *were* blaming him.

Josie didn't notice he hadn't answered. "It will blow over, Lieutenant. You wait and see. Have faith, that's all."

If his having faith was a prerequisite, it would never blow over. After working with Colin so long, Josie had to know as much. She said it anyway. *She* had faith. Maybe that would do.

When she saw Colin didn't feel like talking, she shrugged and walked away. He might sit there moping, her attitude declared, but she had work to do.

It was getting toward noon when Rodney Ellis came over to Colin's desk. "Want to go to Heinrich's for lunch?" the black detective asked. Caroline had also called to invite him to stay away from the funeral. He was getting the same kind of almost silent treatment Colin was, too. If anything, he was getting it worse. He'd run the Darren Pitcavage bust. And he *was* black, which sure didn't make his life any easier.

"Hey, why not? I'm accomplishing so much here." Colin grabbed his slicker. It had been raining when he pedaled in this morning. The minister would probably say the heavens were weeping for Mike Pitcavage. Ministers said that kind of stuff. Just because they said it didn't make it so.

It was still raining—drizzling, anyhow. Luckily, the Hofbrau and Sushi Bar was close. On the way, Rodney asked, "So how do you like being a nigger, man?"

"Say what?" Colin wondered if he'd heard that right.

"How do you like being a nigger?" Rodney repeated. He laughed harshly. "Yeah, I know—if you called me that, I'd clock you. But it's sure as hell how they're treating you since Mike decided to punch out for good. They leave you out of everything. They do their best to pretend you aren't around, even when you are. That's what being a nigger in a white man's world is all about, or part of what it's about, anyway. Welcome to the club, dude." He held out a hand.

Colin shook it. "Thanks. Thanks a bunch. If it wasn't for the honor of the thing, I'd rather walk."

If you had to be a restaurant these days, a Japanese-German restaurant was the right kind. You could still get raw fish, or squid and octopus if you couldn't. And German cuisine ran to the kinds of things people raised in a cold country. Potatoes. Turnips. Pork if you happened to have a pig. It might not be exciting food, but it was there.

They took a long lunch. When they got back, the station had filled up. The cops and clerks and secretaries had returned from the memorial park. "How was it?" Colin asked Gabe Sanchez— somehow, Caroline had left him off her we-don't-want-*his*-kind-here list.

"Not so good." Gabe hesitated, then went on, "Better you hear it from me than from somebody else, I guess. The preacher didn't quite come out and say you put the rubber band around Mike's neck to hold the bag in place. Not quite—but he might as well have."

"Christ! Just what I need!" Colin said. "Let me guess—a bunch of people bought it, starting with Caroline and Darren."

"Right the first time." Gabe nodded unhappily. "I'm sorry, man. I'm sorry as hell. No good deed goes unpunished, is what they say."

"Yeah, that's what they say, all right," Colin agreed. The conventional wisdom wasn't worth a pitcher of warm piss most of the time. This once, the multiheaded *they* monster had hit the nail right on the thumb.

Marshall Ferguson had told his father what he knew. Because he had, one man was in jail and another man was dead. When you were sort of on the edge of making your living as a writer, you thought you knew how powerful words could be. They could make people think. They could make people feel. And there you were at the strings, as if you had a violin or a guitar.

Words could make people die.

He'd never imagined that. If he hadn't talked to his dad, Mike Pitcavage would still be wearing fancy suits and getting expensive haircuts. It wasn't as if Marshall had had any great liking for the chief or his son. Getting Darren busted didn't break his heart. He wouldn't have been bummed if Mike had resigned in disgrace. He might even have been proud, though he never would have shown it.

But when Mike Pitcavage killed himself . . . Marshall wasn't proud of that. He'd always pretty much skated through life. The worst things that ever happened to him were grandparents passing away and his folks breaking up. He'd been little when his grandparents died one by one, and they hadn't been young. He'd grieved, yes, but not enormously. And, while the breakup hurt like hell, he knew more people with divorced parents than with fathers and mothers who'd stayed together.

He didn't know anybody else who'd driven someone to suicide. Vanessa might have wanted to, to show what a femme fatale she was. That was different, though. For one thing, it was bullshit. For another, even if it weren't, dying for unrequited love was a long way from dying because your son was looking at a felony rap.

No way could he talk to his friends about any of this. If they found out the chief's suicide had rocked him, they would also have to find out why. He didn't want them knowing he'd talked to his father.

He couldn't talk about it with Dad, either. If anything, Dad was hurting worse than he was. A lot of the cops seemed to have decided it was *his* fault Mike Pitcavage no longer occupied the big office with the window.

"This really sucks, you know?" Marshall said to Kelly. He could talk to her, after a fashion. But she was bound to be hearing it from his father, too. Getting it in stereo was the last thing she needed, especially when she was taking care of Deborah, too.

"It totally sucks," she agreed. "I'd like to go to the cop shop and bash their stupid heads together, you know?"

"Yeah." He nodded. "Like we expected Pitcavage to do that, or wanted him to. No way!" When he said *we*, he meant *I*.

For a wonder, she got that. "You did the right thing, Marshall. You—" Deborah chose that moment to wake up with a yowl. "One moment, please," Kelly said, like an old-time telephone operator.

She came back with the baby and started nursing her. For modesty's sake, she covered her breast with a blanket. It didn't bother her, but she'd discovered it did bother Marshall.

For a bigger wonder, she remembered what she'd been saying when she got interrupted, and picked up where she'd left off: "You did the right thing. You can't help it if Mike Pitcavage did a back flip into an empty pool on account of it. That's not your fault."

Marshall desperately wanted to believe it wasn't, but he couldn't help asking, "Whose fault is it, then?"

"His. Or Darren's, for dealing drugs to begin with. Or nobody's. Sometimes stuff just happens. The supervolcano wasn't anyone's fault. It just happened."

"People aren't like that, though. I don't think they are, anyhow." Marshall believed in free will. But if he was predestined to believe in it, how much good would that do him?

"Well, I don't, either," Kelly admitted. "Would turning it into a story make it any clearer in your own mind? Or I guess I mean, would that make it any better for you? I know you've got some of your story ideas by taking off from things you went through."

She paid enough attention to him to notice something like that! The only other person who did was his father, and Dad paid such close attention that half the time Marshall wished he wouldn't. Right now he felt like that about the whole thing with the Pitcavages.

Which didn't answer her question. Slowly, Marshall said, "When I do that, I, like, file the serial numbers off first, know what I mean? I don't see any way to do that with this one. And it doesn't look like the kind of story that's got a happy ending for anybody."

"No, it doesn't, does it?" Kelly nodded. "Stories don't have to, though."

"No, they don't. But the ones that don't are a lot harder to sell." Marshall wouldn't have thought of it in those terms if not for the lessons from his still-struggling career. He'd sent out a couple of pieces he'd been proud of, to have them come back over and over with rejections that said something on the order of *We'd like to see more from you, only not so gloomy next time.*

Kelly raised an eyebrow. "I hadn't looked at it like that. You don't see many tragedies on TV, either."

"Part of it, I guess, is that most people's lives are pretty miserable a lot of the time. They don't need stories to remind them about it—or editors sure don't think they do," Marshall said. "That's always been so, I bet, but it's got worse since the supervolcano blew."

"Everything's got worse since the supervolcano blew." After two or three seconds, Kelly corrected herself: "Almost everything. I'm married to your father now, and I wasn't before. And we've got this little portable air-raid siren here now, too." She grabbed one of Deborah's pajamaed feet. The baby hardly knew she had feet yet. Marshall remembered John Henry discovering his. Tiny people could be pretty goddamn funny. That was bound to be one of the things that kept their parents from booting them.

"You know what? I think she looks like you," Marshall said. Talking about his half-sister was one way not to dwell on the bigger problems of Life, the Universe, and Everything.

"Babies look like babies, is what babies look like." But Kelly went on, "You really think so?"

"I do," Marshall said. "Dad's face is kinda squarer than yours, and a kid with his nose would already have a bigger one than she's got. Take a look at Vanessa's baby pictures if you don't believe me. He takes after Dad more than Rob or me."

"Well . . ." Kelly, Rob realized belatedly, didn't want to look at Vanessa's baby photo. She slid Deborah out from under the light blanket and raised her to a shoulder. "I sort of thought the same thing, but I wasn't sure. I know my folks think she does, but they aren't exactly objective."

"No, huh?" Marshall said. They both laughed.

Kelly quickly sobered, though. "I hope this story has a happy ending. It's eating up your father, too."

So much for babies. So much for distraction. "Yeah, I know," Marshall said. "He'd be even worse if it wasn't for you."

"Thanks. That's one of the sweetest things anybody ever told me," Kelly said. "I just wish I could do more. I wish anybody could do more. . . ." Deborah burped lustily, then spat up. Babies could be distracting in all kinds of ways.

Colin Ferguson chained his bike to the rack outside the San Atanasio Police Station. Some people made a point of greeting him as he walked to his desk. More made a point of pretending he didn't exist. It had been like that ever since Caroline Pitcavage found her husband's body. He kept hoping things would loosen up—a hope looking more forlorn by the day.

"*Good* morning, Lieutenant!" his secretary said loudly. She left no doubt about whose side she was on.

"Hey, Josie," Colin answered, at a much lower volume. He wished there were no sides to be on. His wish seemed no more likely to be granted than his hope.

On his desk was a report about a home-invasion robbery

from two nights before, at an old tract house near Sword Beach and 135th Street. The bad guys hadn't shot anybody, but they'd had guns. Jesús Villarobles, the homeowner, was still at San Atanasio Memorial with a concussion from the pistol-whipping they'd given him.

He turned the page. Had they left fingerprints behind? Things would be easier if they had. Before he could find out, his phone rang. He picked it up. "Colin Ferguson, San Atanasio PD."

"Hello, Lieutenant. This is Lucy Chen, over in the lab. Could I see you for a few minutes, please?"

"Sure," Colin said, thinking *Nice anybody wants to.* "What's cooking?"

"I'd rather talk about it here than over the phone, if that's all right."

"O-kay. Be right over." Colin didn't scratch his head, but he wanted to. He felt eyeballs boring into his back as he got up and walked out of the big, communal office. He might have been doing nothing more dramatic than taking a leak. Those eyeballs skewered him anyway.

The lab was down the hall, a couple of doors past the men's room. The air inside it held a faint chemical odor. It wasn't unpleasant, but it was always there.

"What's going on?" Colin asked Lucy. Whatever it was, he felt sure it would be something he needed to know about and no one else did. The DNA tech didn't get excited without a good reason, or sometimes even with one—yet another reason she reminded Colin of his wife.

"This is a DNA analysis I ran last night," Lucy Chen said, handing him a printout. "Tell me what you make of it."

Colin wasn't a DNA expert. He wasn't a fingerprint expert, either, but he made a pretty fair amateur. He made a pretty fair amateur at DNA patterns, too, also because his line of work had turned him into one. And the pattern on the printout looked familiar. He'd seen it, or one much like it, way too many times. He whistled softly. "Lucy, if this isn't the South Bay Strangler's DNA, it's mighty darn close."

"It isn't." She took another printout off the countertop and gave it to him. "This one is from the Strangler."

He held one in each hand. Excitement tingled through him. They *were* close. A break! At last, a break! After so many years, a break! If you had a relative's DNA, you at least knew who the perp's relative was, which put you a hell of a lot closer to grabbing him, too. He hefted the printout that didn't come from the Strangler. "So, who does this belong to?"

She looked at it. She looked at him. "Darren Pitcavage," she answered.

"You're kidding," he said automatically. One look at her face told him she wasn't. He floundered: "But that's crazy. It's impossible. If that one's from Darren, who—?" He ran out of words, but waved the other printout.

"It may be crazy. It is not impossible. We did the autopsy on the chief just a few days ago, so I had easy access to a DNA sample from him." Lucy handed Colin one more printout. "This is from Darren's father."

He examined it. He examined the Strangler's pattern. No, he wasn't a DNA expert, but he was a pretty fair amateur. He was plenty good enough to understand what he was seeing. "They're the same," he said dully. "Mike Pitcavage's DNA and the South Bay Strangler's DNA are the same."

"That's right." Lucy Chen's mouth twisted as her head bobbed up and down. "I didn't want to believe it, either. I still don't want to believe it. But that's what the evidence shows. Unless the chief has an identical twin I don't know about . . ."

"He doesn't." Almost blindly, Colin reached for the countertop. He needed something to steady himself. Who wouldn't, with the underpinnings of his world knocked out from under him? Yes, cops went bad. That was why police departments needed internal-affairs units. But bad like this? "Jesus!" he choked out.

"Are you all right?" Lucy sounded genuinely alarmed. What did he look like? How gray had he gone? He wasn't just pale—he was sure of that.

And he wasn't all right, either—nowhere close—so he answered, "No." Before Lucy could ease him down into a chair or start CPR or do whatever else she thought he needed, he made haste to add, "But it's nothing you can do anything about. It's nothing anybody can do anything about, not any more."

"No, not any more," the DNA tech agreed.

Almost in spite of itself, Colin's mind started working again. Things that hadn't added up before suddenly made a lot more sense. "Well, now we know why he killed himself," he ground out.

"That also occurred to me," Lucy said. "No arrest. No trial. No jail cell. No waiting for them to stick the needle in his arm, if they ever get around to it. He took the easy way out."

"He sure did," Colin said grimly. "And now I understand why he always worked so hard to keep Darren from catching a felony rap. He wasn't just playing softhearted daddy. You get arrested for a felony, you have to give your DNA sample. And that would have pointed at him along with his worthless kid. No wonder he went off the deep end when Darren landed in trouble too deep for daddy to get him off. He totally flipped out—at me, mostly."

"I heard . . . something about that," Lucy said. Colin wasn't surprised. A police department was like any other small town. News got around fast. The cops smoking in the parking lot had heard Mike Pitcavage melt down. Their stories wouldn't have shrunk in the telling.

Once Colin's brain started grinding away, it didn't want to

stop. "Remember how, when we were at poor Mrs. Mandel-baum's house, he knew his way around like he'd been there be-fore? He, uh, darn well had."

"I *do* remember!" Lucy Chen exclaimed. "I didn't think much of it then, but I do. I just thought he'd been in a hundred places like it, so he'd kind of know where all the rooms were."

"Uh-huh. Exactly what I figured, too," Colin said. "He was a cop for a long time. Of course he'd seen places like that before. Right. He sure had."

"Hadn't he, though?" Lucy clicked her tongue between her teeth. "Where . . . Where do we go from here?"

Colin didn't answer directly, not right away. "Who else knows, besides you and me?"

"As soon as I was sure, I told Dr. Ishikawa and showed him the results," she said. "He told me to call you."

I owe the coroner one, Colin thought. Yes, Ishikawa would have told Lucy to call him because he'd been chasing the South Bay Strangler so long. But Colin judged that wasn't the only rea-son. Ishikawa would also know what was going on in the depart-ment. Nobody could blame Colin for the chief's sudden shuffling off this mortal coil now.

He made himself come back to the business immediately at hand. "Okay. Good, even," he said. "But this will have to get out. Not just to us—to all the other departments who've been after the Strangler." He let out a long, regretful sigh. "It'll have to get out to the TV and the papers, too. The suicide already has. San Atanasio's gonna be in the news for a while. So will I. And so will you, I'm afraid. Get used to it."

Lucy winced. "Can I go on vacation for about the next three years?"

"You wish!" Colin said. By her expression, Lucy did. You didn't go into her racket because you wanted your mug on TV. You didn't go into geology for the media exposure, either. Kelly'd survived it, back when the supervolcano was warming up for the big show. Colin was sure Lucy also would. He went on, "For now, though, give me enough time to get back to my desk, then call Neil Schneider and ask him to come in. I'm not gonna say boo. Let somebody else get the word out."

"Okay." She sent him a shrewd look. "He's one of the people who aren't real happy with you right now, isn't he?"

"Yup." Colin didn't waste time pretending he didn't know what she was talking about. "I don't even know whether he'd believe it hearing it from me. He will from you, though. He'd better."

"All right, Lieutenant. I'll do that, then." Lucy spread her hands. "This is gonna be pretty horrible, isn't it?"

"It won't be anywhere near that good," he answered. She laughed as if he were joking. They both knew too well he wasn't.

As soon as he came back into the central office, the dueling cones of overdone greetings and angry silence surrounded him again. He sat down at his desk and tried to do some useful work on the home-invasion robbery. The clock on the wall insisted he'd been in the lab less than twenty minutes. It only felt like years.

Sergeant Schneider's phone rang. He talked for a moment, then got up and headed for the door Colin had just used. Colin watched him out of the corner of his eye. As far as he could tell, he was the only one who did. When he himself moved around, everybody's gaze followed him. Maybe he could shed that, too.

For now, he waited. When Schneider came back in, he looked like someone who'd taken a left hook right on the button. He headed straight for Colin's desk. *That* made people stare at him, all right. Talking with the enemy, was he?

He was. He sat down on—sank down onto—the chair by the desk. Like a spooked horse's, his eyes showed white all around the iris. "My God!" he said.

"Yeah." Colin nodded. He saw no point in gloating. He didn't want to gloat. He wanted to cry, and he couldn't do that, either. He wondered if Caroline Pitcavage would be able to cry when she found out. That would be for later. *More collateral damage,* he thought miserably.

"Lieutenant, I've been kind of mad at you since . . . since . . . Well, you know since when," Schneider said. "I'm sorry. I'm sorry as hell. It wasn't your fault, not in any bad way." He held out a hesitant hand.

Colin took it. "Thanks, Neil. Don't worry about it. I know how you felt. Lord, I felt the same way myself half the time. I did." His voice hardened. "But I sure don't any more."

"I hope not! Neither do I. Neither will anybody, once I talk to a few people and they talk to some people, too. But I wanted to come to you first."

"Well, thanks. Some of them won't want to believe you, you know."

"Hey, I didn't want to believe Lucy, either. Who would? But there's the DNA."

"Uh-huh. There's the DNA. I still don't want to believe it. It all fits together too well not to, though," Colin said.

"It does, doesn't it?" With some effort, Schneider got to his feet. As he'd said he would, he started talking to people. Some of them did believe him. Some stormed off to the lab to see if he was making it up. Some who'd been angry at Colin came over to his desk to apologize—some, but not all. Well, in a world full of human beings, that was as much as you could hope for.

Not quite half an hour after Sergeant Schneider started spreading the word, Colin's phone rang. "Grab that for me, will you, Josie?" he called—he was talking with two cops and a secretary.

"Sure thing," she answered proudly. She'd been on the right side all along. A moment later, she said, "Lieutenant, it's a reporter from Channel Two. He wants to talk to you. Right away, he says." By her expression, she was trying to tell him it wasn't her fault.

Colin knew that—not that it would help. He sighed one more time. "Thanks, Josie. Put him through." Yes, it was beginning.